# The

# Liberators

Jerri Gibson McCloud

# The
# Liberators

## JERRI GIBSON MCCLOUD

Hourglass **Publishers**
Produced in the United States of America

This book is a work of Historical Fiction written by Jerri Gibson McCloud where the names, characters, and locations, are the product of the author's imagination, and any resemblance to actual persons living or dead, towns, business establishments, and events, is entirely coincidental. Please see the last pages for historical events covered in this novel.

Jerri's inspiration to write *The Liberators* is found on the last pages.

Visit her website at www.jerrigibsonmccloud.com

Library of Congress Cataloging-in-Publication Data:
        2012902693


ISBN-10: 0-9818155-3-7
ISBN-13: 978-0-9818155-3-4

Hourglass Publishers
Printed in the United States of America

# DEDICATION

To all the men and women of WWII who provided all of our yesterdays, todays and tomorrows...I thank you.

To E. W. Nunnery, WWII B-17 Bombardier, for taking me to a time and place I'd otherwise never have known. Without his interview for *The Gibson's of South Carolina* genealogy book, *The Liberators* would have never been written.
Thank you, E.W.

# ACKNOWLEDGMENTS

To my husband, the love of my life, for his support and encouragement, I send all my love and gratitude. Who, during my early writings, felt comfortable enough to tell me after reading one of my short stories, placed it on the coffee table and said, "This is crap. Everything is too easy, there's no suspense." After licking my wounds, I realized he was right on.

My gratitude and love goes to my Fact & Fiction Critique Group who are like family to me. Many thanks to Vic Kirkman, Loys Mundy, Liz Hatley, Elaine St. Anne, Marie McBride, Leon Coulter—a veteran, all of whom struggled through early critiques with great advice.

I would be negligent if I did not thank my Memoir Writing teacher, Margaret Bigger, who inspired me to heights unimaginable and set me on an incredible journey of writing. I thank her also for an early edit of *The Liberators*.

Judy Simpson, Queens University teacher/author, *Foundations of Fiction*, taught me that every story has a beginning, a middle, and an end, and who allowed me to work with her, editing, designing book covers, and putting together three anthologies for publication. I am indebted to her and am sorry she is no longer with us.

For the two years I spent with an international Yahoo Historical Fiction critique group who taught me what not to do when writing, I am indeed indebted.

Strange that it might seem to thank an agent who is *not* my agent, Donald Maass, for one sentence that helped me tremendously in my journey to the end of this novel.

My eternal gratitude goes to Mary Utting for her first edit—the most thorough person I have ever known. To her I am forever thankful.

When I ran into a blank wall, I e-mailed the Pentagon for answers and a kindly gentleman, a retired Naval Pilot, responded.

And lastly, to Patrick LoBrutto, my New York Editor, for all his invaluable insights and suggestions.

# Chapter One

*"The greatest man is he who chooses the right
with invincible resolution; who resists the sorest
temptations from within and without; who is
calmest in storms, and whose reliance on truth,
on virtue, on God, is the most unfaltering."
...William Ellery Channing*

"Bail out! Bail out!" Capt. Andrew Walters shouted through the intercom. Switching to radio communications, he called, "Come in Leader. Come in! This is *Alley Cat*. Mayday! Mayday!"

Ink-black smoke flooded the mortally wounded B-17G Flying Fortress which bounced helplessly out of control between antiaircraft bursts high above the *Initial Point*, Steyr, Austria. A 20mm blast burst through the starboard side of the plane. Acrid smoke poured from the control panel in front of copilot Tex. Andy gawked at the instruments for any sign of life—then at Tex. All controls...gone. This was it! The *Alley Cat*, fully loaded with 4,000 pounds of bombs, would crash short of her target.

Andy pushed the bell—no response. Nothing worked. "Bail out! Bail out!" he shouted again over the thunderous rush of air, roar of engines and exploding flak. Tex immediately exited the cockpit. Andy's quaking hands fumbled over a gap in his oxygen tank. He snatched a cord from the stationary tank and yanked another portable oxygen bottle mounted on the cockpit's sidewall. He slid from his seat down through the hatch to the fuselage below, crouched low, groped his way to the bombardier section. Bombardier, navigator, and engineer—gone. His breath came in terror-stricken gulps. *Oh, God. Only seconds to get the hell out of here. The Cat's going down!*

Ebony smoke seeped into his mask, absorbing precious oxygen. He dropped to his hands and knees, gasping for air. The crippled plane drifted in a wide spiral beyond the torturous flak zone. He wrestled back to his feet. The deafening buzz of Messerschmidts and Focke-Wulf 190 fighters surrounded the plane, closing in for the kill. Guns crackled, penetrating the plane, and the sputtering belches of the remaining fourth engine propelled him forward.

In search of his crew, he stumbled toward dark shadows scrambling to the rear exit. His chute's ripcord snagged. He jerked to a stop. The parachute burst open—inside the plane. Blood rushed from his head. He stood motionless. "Oh, Jesus!"

Cold sweat slid down his face—he smelled the scent of death. Numbness overtook his entire body as if he was already dead. He grappled with his chute, gathered it up cradling it in his arms. Adrenaline shot through his veins and pressed him forward. He lurched to the exit—parachute in arms. He jumped.

"May God have mercy on my soul!" he yelled. His life snapped in front of him like the pop of a rubber band.

### Christmas 1942 Fayetteville, North Carolina

"I'm quitting college and joining the Army Air Force." Andrew Walters announced at dinner on Christmas Day. He didn't have to wait long for the explosion.

"You're what?" His father half-choked on a piece of turkey.

*Of course. Why not? In all of my 22 years I never failed to disappoint my father.*

His mother, Jane, sat motionless, mouth partially opened. Her napkin fluttered to the floor. Andy watched as she tried to regain her composure. Words refused to surface.

The aroma of turkey-dressing, pecan pie, and stewed cinnamon apples lost their appeal in the tenant farmhouse. Hands on hips,

Andy refused to respond to his father's question eliminating a dreaded confrontation. He wandered over to the window and stared at the flat sandy fields surrounding three sides of the home where he and his father planted tobacco every spring.

Fourteen-year-old Betty Jane said in a singsong voice, "Andy's quitting school." He cut his eyes at her while she bounced in her chair; brown pigtails with red bows flapped up and down.

"What'll you do with all your girlfriends, Andy? You can't take them with you." Betty Jane reached for another serving of sweet potatoes dragging the sleeve of her red Christmas dress over the giblet gravy.

"Hush up, Betty Jane," their father said. "Look at your sleeve! You've got gravy all over your new dress." A low circle of gray hair bordered the bottom half of an otherwise hairless head. His eyes met Andy's. A deep furrow imbedded in his forehead; his speech, sharp and abrupt, cut the air. "Have you lost your mind, son? What do you know? You're still green behind the ears."

Andy glanced away and focused on family pictures decorating the kitchen wall over the cherry sideboard. A white crocheted runner festooned with a piece of carnival glass and a chipped blue and white plaster horse, reminiscent of a recent State Fair covered the top. He gathered his composure as he had always done—held his tongue. *Don't rush, don't rush.* He understood how his mom and dad felt and how the impact of a son and brother dropping out of college, leaving home and no one to help on the farm. But he was not about to back down from his own driving need to answer the call. *Why not? It was time.* He had his dad's attention now and faced him full on.

"Dad. Just listen to the radio! Look at the newspapers! The newsreels are full of it. Convoys fill the roads. The war's everywhere. I couldn't live with myself if I didn't do my part. You've heard President Roosevelt's call for help. My country needs me. I'm gonna be a pilot." Andy, hands on hips, stared into his father's flaming eyes.

"I didn't raise you to go get killed in a war, young man! You'll finish college and that's it! There's no way you're going to end up like me. If it wasn't for your scholarship, you wouldn't even be in college. Now, no more poppycock, ya hear?

"Dad, I…"

"I don't wanna hear it! You're not giving up a law career to fly…to fly a plane that'll probably get you killed!"

Andy didn't want to argue with his father. Clear in his mind were the years his dad pushed him beyond reason so he would excel at 'everything'… even to the point of frustration—a sense of failure if he didn't measure up. No matter what he did, it was never good enough for his dad. If he made a 'B' on his report card, his dad expected an 'A,' all 'As.' Only the best. The thought of letting him down was not an option. *This is the most serious decision of my life.*

He watched his father's huge hands, rough and calloused from years of work in the tobacco fields, pick up his pipe and struggle to hold the match steady. He lit it, pulled in several drags, and exhaled smoky wisps that curled up like genies belching streams of boiling anger above his head.

He looked at his mom as if he had never seen her before, knotted gray hair meticulously styled in a roll around her oval face. A matronly lady, with laugh wrinkles fanning from the corner of her eyes. When Andy hugged her, at five-foot four, she scarcely came up to his chin.

His father slammed his fist on the table. "I'm not believing this!" He rubbed his head and his hazel eyes became narrow slits.

"Dad. You're not listening! You've always said you didn't want me to be a sharecropper like you, and when I come back, *then* I'll pursue *my* dreams and become that lawyer! They'll hold the scholarship for me." Andy had watched financial struggles from crop losses and injury, and he was determined *not* to follow in his father's footsteps. *I'll be somebody the world will know.*

An awkward silence crept in until he said, "I signed up in October—didn't want to spoil Christmas."

"Andrew!" his mother said. "You've kept this from us for two months?" She pressed her lips together and smoothed her floral apron—the bib pinned at the top in each corner.

"Yes, Mom. You don't know how torn I've been. In two days I leave for basic training at Medford Air Field, Indiana."

"What?" Jane Walters sucked air as she slapped her right hand over her mouth. John shot a glance Andy's way. Betty Jane stopped smiling.

Andy noticed a stream of tears trickle down his mother's cheek. He pulled out his handkerchief, knelt down by her side, and wiped the tears away. He put his arms around her, looked into her deep blue eyes which mirrored his own and said, "Please don't be upset, Mom. I love you. I'll make you proud."

"I know, son, but …"

"Shussssh!" Andy said, putting his finger to her lips. It'll be okay. I promise." He brushed loose strands of hair from her face.

Betty Jane shoved her chair back, tears spilling from her blue eyes, and rushed over to Andy. She threw her arms around his neck before he could stand up. "I'm sorry, Andy. I didn't mean to make fun of you."

"Hey, Miss Betts. Don't worry. You just take care of Mom and Dad. You're a swell gal."

His father hooked each thumb around his pants' suspenders and then spoke, "I don't believe you did this without telling us. I'm angry enough to spit! What's gotten into you, boy?"

"Now, John. That's enough. Let's keep his last few days home pleasant as possible." She took a deep breath realizing what she had just said. She covered the lower part of her face with her hands.

"Dad, that's just it. I'm no longer a *boy*, and at some point you've *got* to realize that."

His dad licked his dry lips and quickly turned toward the window.

"Y'all do understand, don't you? I couldn't sit back and not join up." Andy searched each face for approval. A thousand different sensations flooded his body at the realization of the abrupt changes about to take control over his life and what it would do to his family.

The two days passed at a tornadic pace. An ever-increasing ache nibbled at Andy; the thought that his dad might not say goodbye to him. *Have I let him down so badly?*

At noon, the family piled in the 1939 green Plymouth sedan, Andy in the front passenger seat. The air inside was so cold, he feared his face would crack if he spoke, much like the last two days at home when his dad was around.

They arrived at the train depot in downtown Fayetteville. The infinite sky appeared motionless with the absence of clouds. Gray-white smoke lay heavy around the train hissing steam and penetrating the air of an otherwise crisp winter day. Andy reached in his pocket for his ticket and turned to Betty Jane. "Miss Betts, you'll be a young lady when I return. Hey! Don't forget to practice your music."

"Bet your bottom dollar. I'll miss you." Betty Jane hugged Andy and stepped back bleary-eyed.

He reached for his dad, "I love you. Take care of Mom. And don't work too hard. I'll be home before you know it."

His dad embraced him in silence, and then pushed back, looked into his eyes, made an attempt to speak, but swallowed the words.

Andy saw the hurt in his eyes—a look that would stay with him forever.

"I'm sorry, Dad." Andy grabbed him again for one last embrace before moving toward his mom.

He wrapped his arms around and squeezed her tight "Mom, now don't you go bawling. I don't want the fellas on the train to see *me* blubber. All right?" She was his best friend, someone he confided in. No matter what the hour, she was there for him.

"Andy, I love you so." Through her tears, she forced a smile and added, "Oh. Don't forget to wear clean underwear." She slipped something into his pocket.

"Yes, Mom." He gave her another hug and headed to the train.

He climbed the metal steps, turned and waved before entering the train. His chest tightened while he worked his way down the aisle of the passenger car. He lifted his Samsonite suitcase, held together with a belt strap, high onto the metal rack, and sat down next to the window.

Andy swallowed hard and wiped the grimy window with his sleeve. He waved to his mom and she shook a hankie at him. Betty Jane blew kisses but his dad lowered his head and walked away. The final "all aboard" sounded and moments later the train inched forward. The tracks curved to the right and Andy kept his eyes locked on his family until they became tiny black specks. *They'll be all right.* A dull, empty ache gnawed at his soul. *Hey, I'm allowed this today. Tomorrow, things will be great.*

The train hugged the rails, gliding along with a staccato click rising from beneath. A cloud of smoke from the black coal-fed engine left a streaming trail.

He swiped the window again with his other sleeve, removing the fog buildup from musty air in the passenger car. Something caught his eye. *What's that? A hawk! He must be looking for road kill. Hey, buddy; this is a train not a car. Do hawks eat road kill? Ummm...they eat the animals that eat the road kill. Yep. Looks like he's standing still. Wonder what my life's gonna be like in three months—a year? Where'll I be? I wanna be part of the action. Oops! He's gone. Where did he go?* Andy searched the sky for the hawk. Gone. The train rocked and Andy turned a deaf ear to the chatter surrounding him.

"Tickets, please. Got your tickets?" The conductor shouted as he came through the passenger car.

Andy reached in his pocket for his ticket and touched something unfamiliar. He pulled it out—a buckeye—a polished dark brown nut thought by generations to be a good luck piece.

*Thank you, Mom.* He slipped the buckeye back into his pocket, removed his ticket, and handed it to the conductor.

"Thanks, butch." The conductor added one more ticket to the stack.

Dusk pressed the daylight into a fine peephole in the sky. The evening clouds rolled in and he gazed out the window for one last glimpse before darkness set in. *There he is again. Can't be the same*

7

*hawk. I'm gonna soar through the air, smooth—just like him. Yeah, I'm gonna fly...fly....*

# Chapter Two

## McMillan Air Base, Texas Northwestern Tip

Andy, along with two new friends, Thomas "Bulldog" Murphy, and Mitch Connelly, completed basic training and traveled by troop train to the next post on snowplowed roads. Spirals of smoke from every home. Colorless. Freezing; McMillian Air Base in the Texas Panhandle.

Late one afternoon as the sun slipped into extinction, Andy received an order from Colonel Brawley to report to his office. *What is it? Does he have my assignment?*

"Where you goin', buddy boy?" Bulldog jumped in front of Andy. "You think you can get past me?"

"You big hunk of lard. Move it! I got orders." Andy attempted to get around Bulldog's 6'3" brawny body, but Mitch joined in.

"Can't let you out of here, Lieutenant. Why you going out in this snow?" Mitch grabbed Andy in a headlock.

"Cut it out, fellas. Move it, Mitch, or I'll mess up that handsome face and once your curly blonde locks grow out, I'll scalp you and sell it to a wig maker. If that's not enough, I'm gonna send a letter to that pretty wife of yours and tell her 'bout those babes you eyed the other night."

"You dirty rat. Trouble's your middle name." Mitch sent him a lop-sided smile.

Before Andy reached the barracks' door, he glanced at Brad Graham who pretended not to see what was going on. *One of these days I'll figure out why this fella hates everyone—mostly me.*

Daily, his stomach turned summersaults with the uncertainty of the next assignment. *I gotta make pilot's training and show Dad I'm not wasting my time—I gotta make him proud.*

The shadows from tall, graceful, dancing trees were like ballerinas performing behind a curtain. Andy scurried on.

He arrived as Colonel Brawley walked out of his office.

"By Gawd, Walters, you're the best enlisted man we've ever had." The colonel put his hand on Andy's shoulder. "I'm proud of you, son. Come into my office."

Andy's head swelled like an oversized watermelon. "Thank you, sir."

"I'm going to recommend that you be sent to Ludlow Air Field in Colorado for B-17 pilot training. That's where you belong."

"Thank you, sir." Andy's voice cracked and his veins tingled.

"We need the best there is for these bombers. That's why we're pushing you up the line. You'll do fine, Walters."

"I don't know what to say, sir, except, 'Thank you.'"

"Son, you owe me only your best and I've seen a lot of that already."

Andy's jaw hung low as he gave a weak salute to the colonel.

"Now close your mouth, son, and go get those Germans for me."

Andy felt the colonel's eyes on him as he turned and rushed from the building. Once out of the colonel's sight, he stretched his arms into the depths of darkness as far as he could reach. He jumped up, pumped his right arm, and let out a tremendous yell.

"Whoooooooeeeeeee!" The sound echoed throughout the camp, interrupting the hush of the evening.

His feet scarcely skimmed the ground as he rushed to the barracks. He felt light as a feather, and for a moment, he was a kid again.

He slowed his pace as he approached his home for the past few weeks. When he entered the barracks, the men lounged around reading books, listening to the radio, playing cards, writing letters—anything to pass the time. Cigarette smoke hovered around the light bulbs dangling on cords from the ceiling. Rows of bunks lined the barracks with footlockers at the end of each bunk.

Andy picked up a pad and pencil from his footlocker, sat down on his bunk, and started writing when Bulldog and Mitch rushed him.

"Ain't ya gonna tell us where they're sending ya?" Bulldog snatched the pencil out of his hand.

"I gotta go see the man tomorrow. Where ya going?" Mitch's eyes danced with excitement.

Andy jumped up and shouted, "Y'all sittin' down? Col. Brawly is sending me to Ludlow Air Field in Colorado for B-17 pilot training." His voice grew higher with each word.

"You old fart. You wasn't gonna tell us. You are one lucky son-of-a-gun!" Bulldog grabbed Andy again and pinned him to the wall.

Mitch rescued him. "Gosh, Andy. I hope I'm as lucky. I'd have some good news to tell Julie. Can't wait to see her. Did Col. Brawley say you would have a few days leave before reporting to Colorado?"

"Naw. They are so short of pilots, nobody gets a day off. Say, aren't you gonna be a daddy soon?"

"Yup. The baby's due any day now." Mitch's eyes had a distant gaze as he headed towards his bunk.

Andy stretched out on his bunk staring at the ceiling beams. His childhood dreams were about to come true. *I'm gonna fly. Fly like a hawk. You'll see, Dad.* A warm glow of self-satisfaction engulfed him, coupled with the nagging uneasiness of 'what ifs'. He pulled up the khaki wool blanket over his head closing out the day. *Tomorrow I'll throw my dreams into space to dance with the stars, and who knows what it'll bring. A new friend, a new love, or a new journey.*

The next day Mitch sprinted into the mess hall, his face so red Andy thought it might explode.

"I'm going to be a pilot. And lookie here." Mitch shook a letter in his hand. "Listen up, fellows. I'm a brand new 'Papa.' Mitchell James Connelly, Jr. was born a week ago. Seven pounds eight ounces and 21 inches long." He held out a photo. "Look at that kid. A chip off the ole block."

Andy jumped up from his food and grabbed Mitch. "Double congratulations, old man. I knew you'd make a damn good pilot— Papa, too. Fellow, you've got it all now. What more could you want?"

The redness disappeared and a frown arched itself on Mitch's forehead. "To see Julie and my kid. That's all I want right now but they won't let me go home."

"Yeah, that's got to be tough." Andy forced his movie star grin and slapped Mitch on his back. "We both are gonna fly all over Europe. Just wait and see."

All the fellows from Andy's barracks crowded around joining the celebration—all except Brad.

Brad didn't move from his table. *No matter how hard I try, it's never enough. I can't beat Andy at anything—not even pilot school. Good God Almighty! Now Mitch. Why the hell didn't I make it? Just a shitty bombardier. What crap! Everyone will know soon enough. Jeeze!*

He flung his arms around, leaped up, grabbed his tray, stumbled in front of the group, and stormed out of the mess hall after dumping his tray. *Look at them. They all hate me. Why?*

Twenty-four hours later as Mitch and Andy packed their duffle bags ready to leave for pilot's training, a corporal burst through the barracks' door." Lt. Connelly? A message for you."

Mitch's hand shook as he reached for the paper. The corporal saluted and rushed out of the barracks.

Slowly Mitch opened the paper. 'You are wanted at the base entrance.' He cut a glance at Andy.

"Mitch. What's wrong?"

"I don't know. I've got to go to the base entrance. Don't know what's up. Back in a while." He shoved the message into his pant's pocket, grabbed his officer's cap and jacket, and raced from the barracks.

Outside, he flagged a jeep. "Corporal. Got a few minutes?" He didn't wait for an answer. "Take me to the base gate."

"Aye, sir." He swung the wheel around and shoved the gas pedal to the floor.

Moments later they reached the gate. Mitch jumped out and walked to the guard station when from the corner of his eye he saw a car door at the entrance swing open. He stopped in his tracks and stared. His heart skipped a beat.

"Julie. Oh my God! Julie." He dashed through the gate and raced towards Julie—arms wide open. She held a baby blanket in her arms. He wrapped his arms around them. It was like magic. Like he'd never left for the Army Air Force. She was in his arms now and he'd never let her go again.

"Oh Mitch. I couldn't let you leave without seeing your baby." She pulled back the cover from the sleeping baby's face.

"Julie, he's…he's beautiful. I mean handsome."

"That's all right. You can say beautiful. He's just a baby now. Later we'll call him handsome." She took her finger and tapped the baby's cheek, rubbed the side of his face, and tickled his neck until he opened his almost black eyes.

"I don't believe it—is that red hair? Can I hold him?"

"Of course." Julie placed the baby in Mitch's arms.

Mitch pulled the blanket back to examine his son. "Look! His shoulders are broader than his head." Tears filled his eyes. "We did good, didn't we?"

"Yes we did, darling. The doctor said you should be proud. Most boys take a long time growing before their shoulders are wider than their heads. Says he's going to be a strapping boy."

He held his finger out and the baby grasped it. "You don't know how this feels, Julie. I'm so proud of him I could burst. And you, look at you. Even with that heavy coat on, you don't look like you

13

just had a baby. You're more beautiful than I remember." He leaned over and kissed her. "By the way, how did you get here?"

"Mom and Dad paid the airplane fair for me. Otherwise, you know I couldn't be here. You know they love you almost as much as I do."

"Wow! Please send them my thanks. I've got to get back. We're packing to leave for Ludlow, Colorado in a couple hours. I wish I could spend a few hours with you and the baby. It kills me to leave you now." He exhaled noisily before hugging the baby and handing him over to Julie. His felt like something squeezed his heart.

He searched Julie's eyes for a sign that all would be fine no matter what the future held. "I'll miss you more than you can imagine—little Mitch, too. How can I bear not seeing our boy learn to sit up, take his first step, and speak his first words? It's so unfair and I know how hard it is on you, my sweet Julie." He held his arm around the two of them and helped them into the waiting car.

"I love you, Mitch. I miss you. I sing our song every day, "All I Do Is Dream Of You"; and now I'll have to sing it for little Mitch as well."

He reached over and kissed her, and kissed the baby on his forehead. He choked back the sorrow at their departure. "Remember me." He eased the door shut. *Why did I say that? Of course they'll remember me.*

### Fayetteville, North Carolina – May 1943

"John. John. Here's a letter from Andy." Jane Walters scurried out to the tobacco barn waving a letter and holding up her skirt as bushes danced around her ankles.

John glanced up for a moment but went straight back to blade sharpening.

"John. Don't you want to read the letter?" She waited. "Well, don't read it. I'll tell you what it says. He's going to pilot training school. Oh, John, you know how much he wanted that. He hoped to get home, but they need all the men as quick as possible. Says you'd be proud of him." She stopped and read.

14

*Dad,*

*You wouldn't believe how hard I worked. You remember how sometime I'd skip a few tobacco plants in each row while hoeing. Guess you might say I've grown up a bit. I didn't skip one plant. I did everything they asked. You always said, 'Good work gets good rewards.' Well, today was my reward.*

*I get a little homesick sometimes, but then something happens to jolt me back to reality like the newsreels at the base theater. I can't wait to get over there and give our boys some help. All of us are eager to go but it'll be a couple more months of training.*

She continued to read until the end.

*Get this, Mom. There's this fellow, Brad, who wanted to be a pilot He's latched on to us—can't shake him, but he never actually joins in. It's nuts. He acts angry at me and now since I made pilot, it's worse.*

*Well, it's almost lights out. Oh yes, Mom, I'm wearing clean underwear every day.*

*Love,*

*Andy*

Jane shook the letter in the air as she watched John enter the barn. "What is wrong with you, John Andrew Walters? He's your son and he's trying so hard to make you proud. Least you could do is read his letters." Exasperated, she shouted loud enough for him to hear. "Well, I swan. I hope one day you won't regret your stubbornness and pushing. He can never please you!"

# Chapter Three

## Ludlow Air Field, Colorado

That's it. Set her down nice and easy," the flight instructor guided Andy. The enormous steel tank, the B-17G Flying Fortress, touched down bobbing a tad on two front wheels, the tail wheel gently eased down connecting to the asphalt and breezed toward the end of the runway. Andy turned the mighty Fortress, taxied to the hardstand, and flanked with other B-17s. His heartbeat calmed when the roar of the four Wright Cyclone engines settled into an idle. He didn't want to move. This was where he belonged. The drone of the engines continued ringing in his ears.

"Good job, Lieutenant. You're a natural. Keep her nose straight on the runway, and you'll do fine." The instructor, though a chunky man, easily climbed out of the co-pilot's seat and dropped down and out through the small hatch under the bombardier section. Andy followed.

"Thank you, sir." Andy reached for his instructor's hand and smiled into his deep-set eyes. Burned fuel from the four engines surrounded them.

"Crew assignments in a few days." The instructor shook his hand before leaving.

"Can't wait!" Andy shouted over his shoulder to the instructor.

He zipped up his jacket as early May forgot to warm up Colorado.

A few days later, a late season snow covered the ground, and the sun shimmered reflecting its brightness. Andy finished his coffee and stared at the coffee grounds in the empty cup. Ten grounds he counted. One for each crewmember. *Who will fly with me—Bulldog, I hope. But please dear Lord, no Brad.*

He checked his watch. *Oops! Time to go.* Andy hustled over to the Squadron Building for crew assignments. No more waiting. Finally, a crew of his own.

The wooden floor creaked when Andy passed through the door. All eyes followed him as he sat down among the men. He had earned recognition for his piloting and leadership skills.

After a brief welcome and explanation of the importance of crews working together, the CO (commanding officer) began with each crew assignment.

Lt. Mitch Connelly was the first name called, followed by nine crewmembers. Mitch stood up. Brad's name followed the co-pilot. Andy sighed with relief—no Brad in *his* crew.

Several crew assignments followed Mitch's group.

Next came Andy. "Lt. Andrew Walters." Then, his crew. Nine names called. The little boy inside him wanted desperately to come out, but he restrained him in spite of an overwhelming urge to stand up and shout for joy.

The CO completed all crew assignments with some men smiling broadly, others expressionless, and a few showing disappointment with their group.

Bulldog flashed a full-faced grin and rushed over to Andy. "How 'bout that, Andy. I'm your bombardier. Ain't you lucky? You couldn't do no better."

"Yeah, yeah, yeah, Bulldog. How did I get so lucky. I tell you one thing, I'll ride your back 'til you do everything perfect, ya hear?" Andy returned Bulldog's grin.

"I'll do you proud." Bulldog did not stop shaking Andy's hand until Andy pried it free.

He pushed Bulldog back. "I'm gonna need that hand, fella."

"Okay, fellas, gather 'round." Andy motioned to his new crewmembers. "Let's get to know each other." Andy got up, walked to the back of the room, and moved chairs around facing each other. Ten chairs.

They all sat down. Andy read from his note pad, "Let's start with you, Hitchcock."

A meticulous, sandy haired, tall muscular man with intelligent eyes, who scarcely appeared old enough to shave, spoke with a deep Western drawl. "My name is Bill Hitchcock. Call me Tex 'cause I'm from Texas." He stood and clicked the heels of his cowboy boots. "I'll be your co-pilot and I can't wait to fly with you men." Mostly he spoke with a sense of confidence. However, once in a while he slipped showing his youthfulness. When he finished, he glanced to his right.

"I'm Thomas Murphy. Bulldog to you. Don't mess with me or my buddy, Andy," Bulldog quipped, raising his enormous hands to smooth out a dark crop of short black  hair. "Guess we're the only ones that know each other." I'm your bombardier. He flashed a grin as big as a slice of watermelon. Bushy eyebrows shaded two brown eyes spaced far apart with a slightly flat nose and square jaw. Andy, at once, recognized how he got his nickname. Bulldog nudged the man sitting next to him.

"Bill O'Connor, but you can call me Pops. I'm the oldest fellow in this crew." He was on the wrong side of thirty, a fatherly type, squat of a man, with full jowls and a happy smile. He had a calmness and self-assurance that only comes with age. His balding head reflected the ceiling light. "Hell, I was down at the filling station pumping gas before you boys were out of diapers. There's not one of you over twenty-two, right? You need a navigator and that's me. No need to worry, you won't get lost as long as I'm with you."

Applause broke out with each man whooping it up in the already boisterous room.

"I'm your tail gunner, Anthony Campo." He sat with his chin resting on the high part of the chair. "You can call me Tony. Treat me right and I'll watch your back." His dark eyes were heavily circled and a thin mustache gave him the look of Clark Gable, though the resemblance stopped with his thin black hair. He spoke boisterously, cocked his head in an arrogant manor, and beat himself Tarzan style before turning to the next fellow.

"Yeah, and I'll bloody call in your kills, Tony, ole chap, once you quit the chest beating rubbish! Oh. My name is Paul Weathersby and, as you can tell, I come from England. Now, don't get excited. I've been an American for ten years. Bet I know more U.S. history than you'll ever know. I have proper diction. Can't you tell? I'm your radio operator. If we get to England, I'll take all of you up north to a grand 'ole pub for black pudding and later a pint of bitter." He swung around, "your turn mate."

"All right, Paulie," the next man said, instantly assigning a nickname to the radioman. I'm Sully… John Sullivan here. Your flight engineer." His brawny body dwarfed his chair and his feet appeared larger than a shoe on a Clydesdale horse. He shoved both hands in his pockets, threw his head back exposing a full face of freckles beneath short red hair.

"Guess I'm next. I'm William Wallace. They call me Billy," he said casting dark sunken eyes down at his feet. He reached up brushing his thin fingers through his miniature pompadour, and then glanced at his hand as if he didn't know what to do with it. "I know some of you men already. I'm your ball turret gunner." He managed a skeletal grin.

Out of character, Billy jumped up assuming the position of a boxer in front of Bulldog. "I'll take you on any day. I'll whip your tail!"

Bulldog scooted his chair over in front of Billy, and without standing tapped him on the ear. "You just wanna show up a big fella, eh? Okay with me. I can control you sitting down, ole buddy. You gonna need me one of these days but until then, you better watch yourself." He gave him a soft blow to the jaw that rocked Billy on his feet.

Billy shook his head. "You'll be safe when we're flying 'cause I need you to pull me out of the bubble if I get stuck. After that you'd better watch out."

Bulldog stood and placed his enormous hand on Billy's head while Billy danced around like a professional fighter. "That's my boy."

The crew roared!

Andy could not believe this introverted fella could possibly be brave enough for a ball turret gunner. He realized Billy's short thin stature would prove valuable when fitting into the turret bubble.

"Okay. I…I'm Charles Black and d…don't ask why they call me 'Whitie.' That's right, Whitie. I'm you're f…f…first waist gunner." Tall and thin, he bore a scar across his cheek from an injury years ago, he explained. After squirming in his seat and rubbing his hands together, he jumped up as if making way for the next fellow.

Everyone turned to the last chair pulled slightly away from the group. "I'm Nealy Gibson, second waist gunner." A bony man with large muscles and brown hair parted in the middle never made eye contact.

Andy stood, faced the group of men, feeling confident on the outside, while inside praying he wouldn't screw up. *I can do this Dad.* He propped one foot on the chair and calculated every word before speaking until a perfect fit for the occasion.

"Some of us are total strangers—ten strangers meeting for the first time. I see you looking around sizing up each man, wondering what the other fellow is thinking. Apprehensive, nervous, anxious. Eventually, we'll be like brothers; work as a team. Occasionally, we might not get along, but we need each other. Depend on one another. If you have a problem, I expect you to come to me. No negative thoughts are allowed while flying in my plane. This crew has now become our central focus—our miniature world. There is nothing, nothing more important than this crew. We'll train together, fly together, and fight together. It's important that we believe in each other and ourselves. We lookout for the crew—our brothers…."

The group discussion continued for quite a while with questions, answers, and a lot of joshing and joking.

"Looks like a good match, fellows. Now let's go celebrate and have some fun," Andy ended. He smiled broadly.

# Chapter Four

## High Wycombe, Northwestern
## Outskirts of London, England - August 1943

"Sir, I am your nurse, not your nanny! And I thank you to keep your hands to yourself." Nurse Rose Martin, fearing she might cut loose, allowing her temper to spill over onto her patient, spun around and hustled away from the injured British pilot.

"Blimey, ma'am, don't get your knickers in a twit. It was just a love pat."

Rose pretended to ignore him and moved on to the next patient calling her.

Two hours later, she grabbed her cape and traipsed the half mile from the hospital to the Nissen hut she called home. She longed for her bed in her family home. *What am I doing way over here? Mom, Dad, I miss you so.*

A cool mist trickled down her face while she scurried along in the evening darkness. Up ahead loomed her quarters, where a USAAF medical officer stood under the entrance light. She realized it was Lt. Col. Lawing, her superior officer, a surgeon assigned to the Provisional Medical Field Service School.

"Thought I'd catch you here," the colonel said. "Let's grab a drink at the Officer's Club?"

"Maybe that's what I need. This was a chaotic day with the less-injured men feeling their oats and anxious to be back in the sky."

He eased his arm around her shoulders sending a comfortable sensation throughout her weary body, and led her to a jeep whose driver sped to the club in what seemed like less than a minute to Rose.

Inside the club, a large Nissen hut, smoke curled to the ceiling, glasses clinked, and laughter abounded. Several couples danced and swayed to the music of "Two Sleepy People."

The colonel picked up two Cokes and brought them to the table.

"What? No beer for you?" Rose snickered. "'Fraid I might take advantage of you?"

"No…" His face flushed and he sat down harder than expected in the chair next to her.

"Now, now, Colonel. You needn't be afraid of me. How can a hundred and fifteen pound girl possibly entice you to do something you'd rather not." Rose turned her head to the side and gave him a teasing giggle over her shoulder.

"I…"

"There you go again. Swallowing your words." She touched his hand.

"Okay, okay. I'm hooked. What have I done to deserve you?" His hazel eyes penetrated hers. "You'll be sorry you're leading me on."

"Leading you on? Why sir," Rose said, putting on a sophisticated air like a British Queen, "I wanted only to show you I mean you no harm." Her repartee attempted to disarm him.

"Well, missy. You win. You have totally captivated me." He reached for her hand.

She snatched it away, placed it in her lap, and felt the fire race to her cheeks.

"Seriously, I have to be available when the RAF (Royal Air Force) returns from another midnight raid or if some of our critically wounded are flown here for serious surgery." He reached again.

Realizing she may have carried her jesting too far, she said, "Sir, I'm here as a friend. That's all. You, sir, are an excellent surgeon. One of the best and I'm proud to work with you. Don't go spoiling our friendship."

His brow creased. "Whoa! Nothing meant." He raised his hand high. "Let's talk about you. What does your father do for a living?"

"He owns a large tobacco farm in Fayetteville, North Carolina." She swallowed a sip of her Coke.

"An ole country hick, a what? What brought you out of the sticks?"

"You already know why I'm here, you jerk." She laughed at the thought of calling her superior a 'jerk.' "How do you get off calling me a country hick, city slicker?"

"Uh…like you called me a 'jerk.' And now 'city slicker.' You sure are bright eyed and bushy tailed to be so tired. Must be the Coke. " He struggled to change the subject.

"Now, back to reality. Your father must have lots of help on the tobacco farm."

She shrugged. "Just the Walters family. I went to school with their son. Nice family, great son. Where are you from?"

"My family owns a vineyard in California." His eyes twinkled.

"Oh. So that's what happened to you. You got wasted young." She giggled.

"Not so fast young lady. I'll have you know that I am a connoisseur of fine wines."

Rose grew serious. "My stars, why did you leave the winery to become a doctor and then serve your country?"

He propped his chin on his clasped hands. "I joined up when my wife left me—took our baby daughter and haven't seen either since."

Rose caught his hand. "I'm sorry. I'd never have guessed. Just shows how first impressions are not always correct."

"Thanks. May I call you Rose?"

"Isn't that strange for a superior officer, sir?"

"Well, you called me 'jerk.'"

She sent him a knowing glance and goaded him on. "I haven't figured out what to call you, so I just won't call you."

"You can start by calling me Rick."

"Nope. Can't. During surgery with all the other nurses around, I'm going to say, 'Here Rick' when I hand you an instrument. Don't think so." She couldn't contain her laughter any longer.

He leaned back while an arrogant smile crept over his face. "What's so funny?"

Her laughter was infectious—like a nervous release of tension.

He tilted his chair close to Rose, pulled her next to him and pressed his lips full on hers.

At first she struggled to be free but the sensuality of the moment overwhelmed her and she returned the kiss. After a moment or so, she pushed him away.

"Look, Colonel. I love the company and the flattery, but I'm not getting serious about anybody—not until this war is over. I value your friendship." She gazed over at the couples dancing close and for a fleeting moment wished she could feel that way about someone special.

"Okay, okay. You sure play it straight." He sat forward as if sizing her up. "Would you like to dance, young lady?" He stood and reached for her hand.

"I'd love to." She tilted her head back and sauntered to the dance floor with the colonel while "When the Lights Go On Again, All Over the World" played on. He held her close mimicking the other couples.

"Swishing that blonde wavy hair the way you do is lovely, my dear. And those dazzling blue marbles. I can't help but stare."

In his arms, comfortable and secure, she rested her head on his shoulder. Cigarette smoke filled the air and the aroma of beer pervaded the hut. The wooden floor creaked under their feet. *Feels good to be held close. Why can't I fall in love with this man? He's tried hard enough. Been kind to me. Older, but seems to really care for me.*

He lifted her chin and said, "I have some news for…"

"You're sending me back to the States." she interrupted with a taunt.

"You wish. No, our unit is transferring north to Snetterton Airfield in a couple of days. Surgeons are in great demand, and with all those airfields, they are desperate. The Brits can take care of their own and a few of ours down here."

She pressed back, shaken out of the moment. "Attacks by the Germans are still going on up there, aren't they? Just how bad is it?" A foreboding queasiness engulfed her body.

"I'll not lie to you. Actually we'll be safe compared to Coventry or Birmingham. They continue to sustain an occasional attack but nothing like the Blitz. You know I'll take care of you. Count on it." He leaned down and kissed her on the cheek.

For a few moments Rose tuned him out while she escaped to a safe place—home…spring, with the redbud trees blooming, and cherry blossoms blowing gently in the breeze…where she and her father walked the freshly planted tobacco fields to the Walters' home for a cold glass of tea…where peace resided and the horrors of war were far away…where…

"Rose." He waited. "Rose. What are you thinking?"

"I'm sorry. Let's finish our Cokes. I need to go."

"Sure thing."

Ten minutes later, the colonel escorted her from the jeep to the Nissen hut entrance.

"Sorry I cut it short. Thanks for a nice evening." She retreated and reached for the door.

He moved toward her, spun her around, cradled her in his arms, and passionately kissed her—another slow arousing kiss.

Her mind reveled in its warmth. She went into a tailspin—refusing to feel anything, yet she felt the electricity of his touch. *What am I doing?* She fought the battle of restraint and forced her release. With a springy bounce, she darted inside the hut.

Behind the closed door Ginny Corso said in her strong Brooklyn accent, "Hey, you. I'm dyin' over here and someone sent you in with your face matching your lipstick. What's got it blushing like that?" She dumped the laundry rescued from a clothes line in the back of the hut on her bunk.

"Oh, Ginny. What's wrong with me? Col. Lawing is a terrific fellow and why can't I fall for him? He's safe. As a surgeon, he'll probably make it through this war. Am I stupid?" Rose flipped around, arms up in the air, and crashed onto her bunk.

"You betcha. Don't be an idiot. You better latch on to this doc. If he cares, that's more than most relationships in this war. Nothin' you can't fix. I been workin' on one for a long time and am 'bout to capture him. It'll be sweet when 'he' realizes it." She returned to folding clothes.

"Yeah, but I don't love this one." Rose rolled over on her stomach.

"It's goin' to be slim pickin's after every mission. At least this beau is an officer. Dang! Wish I coulda been so lucky." Ginny shook a skirt and placed it in another pile.

"All that stuff is good because if something happens to him, then it won't hurt so much, right?" By then Rose sat straight up. The inside of the hut matched Rose's mood—dark and dreary—clothes hanging to dry obscured the view of other nurses trying to sleep before their next assignments.

"Yep. That figures. You're in a sulk. Gotta quit thinking 'bout a future and concentrate on today, I keep telling ya." She lifted the top of her footlocker and placed her undies inside.

"How, Ginny? How does a person live like that?

"It's war."

# Chapter Five

## July 15, 1943 – Prestwick, Scotland

One year after the United States Army Air Force (USAAF) officially arrived in Prestwick, Scotland, Andy's crew touched ground on the concrete runway at the newly named Royal Air Force's (RAF) St. Mawgan Air Field for an overnight stay. The entire 96th Bombardment Group (BG) traveled by train the next day to Bovingdon, located near Watford, north of London. The mid-summer day soaked the countryside mixing gray mist and steady rain; the fresh wetness saturated the air.

The next day the sun broke free of the morning clouds. A few veteran pilots who had a number of missions under their belts volunteered to fly the new crews over the destruction caused by German raids over Birmingham, Coventry, Amersham and Liverpool. Andy recoiled in horror after seeing it firsthand.

"These are the Luftwaffe's (German Air Force) favorite target—the midlands with heavy engineering and steel production. To the left is the huge Spitfire factory at Castle Bromwich on the outskirts of Birmingham. Look to your right. Those are 'shadow factories' set up by the British for aircraft production," the pilot explained. "The Brits converted existing automobile factories into aircraft, parts, and supply manufacturing plants. Makes sense with skilled labor already in the regions."

He continued, "We're now over Coventry. More shadow factories. Take a gander at the devastation the Luftwaffe unleashed on her."

Building after building—leveled—some still smoldering, roads obliterated, homes demolished, destruction everywhere. Debris scattered throughout the countryside—worse than anything Andy had ever seen.

Silence prevailed. Billy reached for a barf bag—his face ghostly white. A wave of nausea hit Andy. He turned away pretending to find another view. *Can't show weakness.*

This sparked the first awareness of the possibility of death to Andy and his men. No longer simply training. This was war. How war looked—how war smelled—how war changed people's lives forever. *Why do I want part of this, for God's sake?* He shook his head, *Okay, Okay! I want to help stop this horror. To end it.* He remembered how well his crew was trained and sat a little taller in his seat.

Andy encouraged his men daily while they worked through their insecurities, unaware of his. Though his eyes smiled, he knew these same eyes could narrow, turning steely black, much to the discomfort of the recipient. His easy Southern grace served him well when dealing with his men—tough but demanding respect—confident and steady—on the outside. He lived the part of a professional military man.

After disembarking from the plane, Andy observed that his men shared his feelings about defeating Hitler and winning the war. But then…

"Why the hell do you want to go through this." Tony had stopped and addressed the men. He rubbed his face over his sleeve.

"What would you rather do, big guy? Go home and let our country fall into the hands of Hitler?" Bulldog got into Tony's face.

"Hell yes! Why do I wanna get killed for this jerk, Hitler. What's gonna happen to us when we go on a mission with no fighter plans to go the distance and protect us to our IP (initial point) and back? This is crap!"

"Whatcha got under that uniform? A petticoat?" Bulldog shoved Tony back.

"Whoa, fellas. Cut the crap out. We just saw horrific sights and we must stand strong. It's the difference between men and boys. We have a choice—either grow up or fold up.

"But…"

Andy interrupted Tony. "Let it go! Take it easy. Both of you. I call the shots around here. Got it?" He paused for a moment forcing himself to cool down.

"Perhaps I should remind both of you, I am your commanding officer and I'll not have any of this with my crew." He signaled the crew members, who remained during the foray, to gather around.

"I realize all of you witnessed total devastation today—it was deplorable. I understand, but our hatred of the man who created all of it wells up inside each of us. Use that anger against him and not your fellow man. Now let's go get him! Dismissed."

Andy breathed a sigh of relief when he observed Tony toddle over to the crew members after Bulldog shook his hand.

That evening Andy sat on his own bunk too keyed up to go back to sleep. He pulled out a note pad and propped on his pillow.

*July 23, 1943*

*Dear Dad, Mom, and Betty Jane,*
*A week or so ago, we flew over the bombed out towns of Birmingham, Coventry, and Amersham. A devastating sight! I feel like we're marking time sitting here practicing combat fighting, instead of going after the Luftwaffe. We could be saving so many lives. What a waste, but I guess the general knows what he's doing.*

*Some of the men who have a number of missions under their belts are telling horrible war stories. I try to close my ears and think of anything but this hideous war. So many innocent people dying. Hitler is an unbelievable dictator. One day I'd like to face him. Bet he'd run. Think so?*

*The countryside is beautiful even though the rain persists day after day. The green checkerboard farms are a remarkable sight with massive planting and growing going on over here. Wish I could fly over Fayetteville and see what it looks like from the air.*

*More problems with Brad; he can't get along with a soul. He cheated Tex out of twenty bucks. I had to break up yet another fight. He hates me for it. Somehow I'm going to win this fella over, but so far, I haven't a clue just how to do it. You know I don't give up easily. He obviously has some internal problems and yet I see he has extremely good capabilities at other times. He excelled all during basic until something grabbed hold of him and wouldn't let him go. We need good men and he could be a good one if he could control his anger.*

*I miss you all. Dad, hope you're not working too hard. I know you. I'll be home one day and I'll be able to help.*

*Your loving son,*
*Andy*

*P.S. I got promoted to Captain few days ago.*

Andy folded the letter, slipped it in an envelope, and then stretched out on his bunk. *Why doesn't Dad write? Not one word. There's nothing I can do to please him. Even now. I don't give up easily. He'll see.*

One more day. *Wonder what's gonna happen tomorrow. No telling.*

\* \* \*

Two weeks later, August 1st, the 96th Bombardment Group transferred to Snetterton, England for combat duty.

Andy felt fortunate to keep his crew intact. They became brothers—that's the way he promised it would be. He asked no more or no less of his men.

Snetterton's accommodations resembled Bovingdon. Nissen huts mixed with a few wooden and stucco buildings.

Andy's finest day arrived when his superior officer announced the assignment of a spanking new B-17G Flying Fortress— *bulletproof? Well, maybe. They say she's a tank. Time will tell.*

Quickly he called his crew to meet him at the hardstand and his grin told the story.

"Okay, fellas. Here she is. This model is just off the assembly line. She's tougher, holds more fuel, and surpasses the other 17s." He made a theatrical gesture toward the Flying Fortress.

One by one, the crew climbed aboard examining every inch. It smelled like a new car. Andy and Tex settled into their seats with hands on the control wheels. After giving it the once-over, they climbed out of the plane as giddy as kids on Christmas morning. It was as if they had a brand new toy.

"Well? What'll we name her?" Andy asked as he stroked the silver exterior like a pet dog. It glistened in the unusual England sunlight and blue sky.

"*The Bitch* would be good," Sully suggested.

"Naw. We like her. How about '*Alley Cat*'?" Andy said.

Tony flashed a superior grin. "What a dumb name."

"Hey, what's wrong with that? An *Alley Cat* is a real combat animal. She'll scratch your eyes out." Tex dusted off his cowboy hat and a cloud of dust arose.

"She's a rootin' tootin' gal all right," Billy chimed in.

"How 'bout gettin' one of those artist dudes to paint a *Cat* face on a naked broad's body with a long curving tail?" Bulldog added as he shaded his eyes and gazed up at the bombardier section.

"Damn straight. That'd be swell!" Sully slapped his leg.

The others heartily agreed, except Tony who shook his head 'no.'

"Get on the stick, Bulldog, and find us an artist," Tex said.

"Do we need a vote?" Andy asked. All heads signaled "no" except Tony. A sense of pride and joy rushed over Andy. He spit in his hands and rubbed them together.

"All right! She's the *Alley Cat*, that is, unless you have a better suggestion, Tony," Andy announced. "We'll do a practice run at 1400. Be here."

Tony refused to look up. "It's a great hunk of metal."

Everyone scattered with an extra bounce in their walk, chattering endlessly with each other.

Andy knew the test would come soon and they'd all know if she was the tank they were promised. Would they live or die?

# Chapter Six

## Snetterton Airfield, England - August 17, 1943

Silence. Dreaded silence. Silence that sliced the air and riveted the soul of Capt. Andrew Walters. Red yarn stretched across the map from Snetterton Airfield to a target deep in the heart of Germany—a city the entire United States Army Air Force (USAAF) knew all too well. A dangerous double mission.

Andy forced himself to listen intently. His men depended on him, needed his leadership, followed his example. The responsibility gnawed at his stomach. *I can do this, Dad. I'll make you proud.* He lowered his head. *But what if I let them down, fail them, what if...* The shroud of death hung over him. Queasiness spread throughout his body as he studied the operations officer's swagger stick tapping on the target—the mission, Schweinfurt, Germany. Destroy the ball-bearing plants. Andy could have been in any building, any room, surrounded by anyone. The setting didn't register—like it didn't exist. Only the mission—his assignment—his men. *God help me be a strong leader.*

The gray-haired, gold-tooth operations officer continued in an upbeat tone while delivering every minute detail. He pointed to locations on the map to expect Luftwaffe (German Air Force) fire and flak—always near the IP (Initial Point).

"We'll have the entire armada in the air by 0900, barring weather conditions at the IP. Every enemy plane made, every antiaircraft shell fired, every searchlight that shines on our planes, uses these ball bearings. When we knock out the three ball bearing plants, we can slow those blasted Krauts down to a crawl, men. German planes have attacked our infantry something fierce and pushed them back. Your mission? Stop them! You men will put down a barrage of firepower like they've never experienced before!"

Yeah! Yeah!" The men jumped up shouting and shaking their fists in the air.

"Three hundred and seventy-six B-17s and B-24s are flying this mission. One hundred and forty-six will split off to Regensburg, and 230 will go to Schweinfurt, both smack dab in the middle of the Bavaria region. Group Mitchell, Freeman, Walters," he spit out numerous groups, "you will go to Schweinfurt; the balance to Regensburg. A number of P-47s will escort each group until their fuel is half spent, leaving you on your own."

Andy and the men sat on rock-hard benches in a jam-packed, smoke-filled, oversized Nissen hut and took note as the raspy-voiced major rattled on, stressing the gravity of the operation. The officer's voice soared like the volume control on a radio. "Good luck, men. Now, get the job done."

The briefing ended at 0700. After the major left the hut, Andy jumped up and pumped his arm. "Let's go get 'em, fellas!"

He watched his friend and bombardier, Bulldog—a cigarette dangled from his pinched lips. He popped up and followed Andy's lead and belted into song with a strong baritone voice:

*"Off we go into the wild blue yonder,*
*climbing high into the sun*
*Here they come, zooming to meet our thunder,*
*at 'em boys, give 'er the gun!"*

Andy joined in while Bulldog raced to the front of the room, grabbed the swagger stick, climbed up on a bench standing every bit of six-foot-three—two-hundred and fifty pounds, and looped the stick like a professional conductor. He flashed his huge watermelon smile between verses.

Brad dashed up to Bulldog and shouted, "What the hell are you so happy about? Don't you know you're gonna get killed? You're an idiot." He turned to walk away when Bulldog hopped down from his perch and seized him.

"Ole buddy, I've just about had enough of you and your mouth. Is it a crime to be happy once in a while? Huh? Huh?"

Brad spun around and threw a punch that glanced off Bulldog's jaw.

"Oh? You really want to mess with me, huh?" Bulldog lunged into Brad.

"Knock it off, fellas." Andy reached in to pull Bulldog off Brad. A fist met Andy's ear. At that moment Brad rolled on top of Bulldog. "Damn it! Cut it out!"

Andy wrapped his arms around Brad's chest and slung him to the floor. "Beat it. I don't need this crap from you."

Brad wiped a bloody lip. "Yes sir, Captain. Next time it'll be you, big shot."

"Threaten me? Man you are asking for it." Andy stood between each man gripping the front of their shirts. "Listen up, both of you. There is no place under my command for this rage to fester up. No place. Do you hear me?"

Brad turned away and Andy twisted his grip on his shirt pulling his face close to his. "Do...you...hear...me?"

"Yes sir, Captain. Showing your authority, eh?" He snarled.

Bulldog reached across Andy and grabbed Brad's shoulder. Andy knocked his arm away from Brad and barred his teeth at Bulldog. "You, big guy, are to leave this jerk alone. This mission is the toughest we'll experience so far, and you will act as your country expects. Now get out of my face."

Mitch marched up and caught Brad by the shoulder. "What's eatin' you, fella? You want to get busted—lose your rank?" He shoved Brad toward the exit. "Get out of here." Mitch shook his head at Andy.

Andy shrugged his shoulders and turned to Bulldog. "Listen, buster, one more fight and you'll be on your own. Yeah, he started it but you didn't have to continue it."

Bulldog picked up his hat and dusted it off. "He's going to get it one of these days. You'll see."

"You better worry about whether you're ready for a real battle, a battle your life depends on. Not a stupid scrap with a nut case. What were you thinking? I will *not* tolerate this behavior under my command."

Angst spread throughout Andy's body. *Good God. What did I just do to my friend? What will he think of me. Is Dad right?*

Bulldog hoisted his flight equipment and stormed out of the building.

Armed with their flight equipment, Andy and Tex followed Bulldog. Pops, the navigator, and the other crewmen waited beyond the briefing building. Tony, the tail gunner, sat on the ground doodling in the dirt. No one spoke. Andy strode toward the hardstand (concrete parking), and noticed his crew's eyes, dull as the fog they pressed through. They fell in behind Andy's group.

"What's the weather at the IP?" Pops asked Andy.

"Got a strong undercover (low clouds below the plane) obscuring the target area. Expected to clear later in the day. Fog and clouds here due to burn off before 0900."

A truck, canvas flapping, whipped off the road's edge, zigzagged through squishy mud deep enough to reach the tire rims, stopped to pick up Andy and his crew and haul them to their plane.

Bulldog jumped in the back and wedged his hind end beside Andy. "What'd I tell you 'bout them real eggs? I knew it. When we didn't get powdered eggs at breakfast, I knew this weren't no milk run, Andy."

"For God's sake, quit your worrying and focus on the job ahead!" Andy folded his arms across his chest, leaned against the hard steel wall of the truck, and realized that Bulldog didn't hold a grudge. *Thank you.* Relieved, he closed his eyes and ears to contemplate the mission before them. All the dark hours spent imagining what it was like, now lay behind him. *Dad, no need to push any longer. I'll make you proud. You'll see. Maybe I'll finally become the son you always wanted.*

Bulldog cleared his throat without missing a beat. "You see Brad go back to the barracks?"

The truck spun its wheels, kicking mud into the truck's bed and spattering the men sitting in the back until the wheels made contact with firm road surface.

"Nope. He's Mitch's bombardier and his problem now."

"That fella stays in trouble. From basic training on, military ain't changed him none." Fire brimmed from Bulldog's otherwise mischievous eyes.

Andy rubbed the two-day-old stubble on his chin. "You're right on. But we got a larger devil to defeat, and I aim to do my part in this war." His voice rose with each sentence, and his eyes flashed. "Look at the men around us—look at the bravery. Forget about Brad. He's a piece of shit, a piece of the devil, a piece of an unraveling human being full of hate. But now we've a job to do. Concentrate!"

Silence overtook the truck—each man appeared to Andy engrossed in thought. The only sounds came from tires splashing through water, and the roar of trucks and equipment racing toward different destinations. He noticed the anxiety that filled their faces as they looked to him for leadership. Though the crew's tenth mission, this was their first mission far into Germany. The truck stopped at the *Alley Cat.* Andy turned to face his men. "Got your flight bags, flak vests, parachute packs, and heated flight suits? Mae Wests (life vests) over your jackets…" *Damn, I feel like Mom.*

Billy, the ball turret gunner, interrupted, "Do we need these heavy sheepskin jackets? I'm sweating like a horse at the end of a race!" He reached up and brushed his fingers through his miniature pompadour and spat on the ground.

"Quit-ya-bitchin'," Tex said. "Once we get up to 25,000 feet with minus 30 degrees, something on you is gonna freeze. Let's hope it's just a hand."

Chuckles echoed from the crewmen.

The day felt strange to Andy. Different. *Is this the day our luck runs out? Real eggs for breakfast. Hmm....*

After each previous mission, Andy had counted the planes as they landed, ahead of and behind him. It became a part of him. One, two, three, etc., until the last plane landed. Yesterday, ten B-17 crews flew a heavy mission. Two planes did not return. Twenty names erased from the roster board. Smiles entered the front door, grief left the back door. Quietness engulfed the entire base last evening as reality of war set in. Nobody commented—best not to discuss it. Andy surmised his crew knew all too well what was at stake. They had a job to do, and nothing could stop them—nothing short of death. No one told them not to be terrified.

Andy's uncertainty of his leadership ability plagued his thoughts, but he forced a sense of calmness which reflected in his demeanor and transferred to the men.

On the hardstand, a warm, damp breeze lifted and ruffled his hair. He reached up, slipped his leather flight helmet on, and slid the goggles to the top. The earphones fell into place as he snapped the chin strap.

Andy stopped short and stared at the *Alley Cat*—there she sat, proud, cocky, with her nose pointed skyward through the mantle of fog, condensation dribbling down her gleaming silver body, ready for one more mission. His chest swelled. He climbed the ladder toward the bombardier nose, rubbed the *Cat's* name with his flight jacket sleeve, and patted the butt of the voluptuous nude painting of a female with a cat head crawling up the side of the plane. After climbing down, he sucked in occasional wisps of fresh air and whiffs of oil intermingled with pungent smoke from engine tests that hung close and overpowered the scent from unsullied growing fields adjacent to the airstrip. He gazed at the bustling ground crews as they scurried around, checking engines, loading and securing the bombs—one bomb had the name "Schweinfurt" painted on the nose with an American flag on each side. He smiled and sent a salute to the unknown patriot who painted it, then walked a little taller to the nose hatch.

He thought back to a month ago when she sat on the tarmac—a spanking new B-17G Flying Fortress hot off the assembly line. He had felt like a boy again on Christmas morning. *Will I dust her name another day? Will she survive this new battle?* He forced himself back to the reality of the day.

His insides twisted in knots as the responsibility soaked in. He reached in his pocket, touched the buckeye his mom had slipped in his pocket at the train station, rubbed it for luck, and forced his best movie-star smile that could outshine a sunny day. But inward, he knew the truth. *These are just boys. Scarcely unleashed from their mother's apron strings. God help me! I'm only twenty-two and as their leader, I feel ancient. We've yet to experience the fear others have—maybe today? Will I be the leader they need?*

"Okay, Captain. We're ready," Pops said. His tranquil attitude and happy smile comforted Andy during stressful times.

Andy addressed his crew. "Listen up, fellas. You guessed it. This is not our usual milk run, but look about you. We're only one of 376 Flying Fortresses and B-24s. I've no idea where all of those planes came from, but we'll lock up with them in the wild blue yonder."

He tapped Pops on the arm. "Here ya go," and handed him additional maps delivered to Andy at the plane for security reasons. "Study hard."

"What's with the long faces, fellas? This is our first real challenge. Come on, y'all. We're ready! A great team! Brothers. We will *not* perish." Andy walked over to each man and stared into his eyes. "Now let's hit it." He turned to his co-pilot.

"Let's go!" Tex drawled, as he headed for the starboard door carrying his cowboy hat and Texas boots. The others, except for Bulldog, followed his lead to weave their way to their stations.

Andy, standing under the nose hatch focused his attention on Bulldog with a nudge. "You know what a blivit is? It's you, fella. Ten pounds of shit crammed into a five-pound bag. Bet you can't get your bag off the ground!" Andy chuckled and added, "I'm watching you."

"Keep watching, my Captain." Bulldog caught the edge of the nose hatch and swung up and inside in one swift move. "Now that's the way to do it," he shouted down.

He stood inside the nose hatch peering down as Andy refused to be out done by his friend. "Look at Mr. Hot Stuff," he taunted loud enough for Andy to hear. "He thinks he's a young buck. Get a load of this, fellows."

Andy stuck his head in the nose hatch where Bulldog reached for his hand. "Nope. Don't need help." He popped up through the hatch to the cheers of Tex, Sully, Pops and Paulie. Andy took a bow after which Bulldog gave him a suffocating bear hug.

Bulldog shook his head, stepped into the bombardier's station, and crammed all of his brawny body onto his seat. He wore his flak jacket, but wrestled to position the lower flak apron. "Gotta protect my 'manhood' from shrapnel."

Andy hee-hawed at Bulldog's struggle.

"What y'all laughing at? Flak jackets save a bunch of lives, you punk," Bulldog shot back at them. "Someday I might wanna have kids."

Billy, the ball turret gunner, shouted, "You're lucky, Bulldog, you get to stretch out. I can't even wear my chute in this ball. It'll take me a whole minute to get out of the ball turret and get my chute on even if you was to help me. By then, I'd be just a splat on the ground."

"Quit your bitchin', shrimp. You don't gotta get down in that hole until we cross the North Sea," Bulldog said.

Andy pictured Billy's small thin frame and bony face which resembled a skeleton when he smiled.

Bulldog shouted, "Billy, I ain't gonna bail out on you. No way. What kinda jerk do you think I am?"

Sully, flight engineer and top turret gunner, chimed in. "I feel like a butterball with all this clothing on. Can't move."

Paulie shouted up to Sully, "I say, ole chap, do you know what a string of paper dolls looks like? That's you with your arms sticking way out from your body waddling to the plane."

"The Jolly Green Giant with red hair," drawled Tex.

"Settle down, men. This is a serious mission. We depend on each other. Don't need a weak link—not on this mission." In spite of all the joshing, Andy knew he could depend on his crew to do their job, no matter what fate lay before them.

Oil fumes drifted into the cockpit. Andy glanced back to the navigator's section below and to the right of Bulldog where Pops shuffled his charts, drift meter, and maps over a wooden table filled with tack holes engraved like a woodpecker's design on trees. Each item spread within Pops' reach.

Co-pilot Tex pulled out the required Cockpit Checklist and in a clear loud voice drawled out each item lest they forget something critical. Andy responded to each with "checked!"

"Gear switch?"

Andy placed his hand on the landing gear switch, checked that it was in the neutral position, "Gear switch neutral."

One by one the B-17s rolled down the airstrip. All except the *Alley Cat*. Working in unison, Andy and Tex started three of the four engines, but an obstinate starboard engine balked refusing to catch. The turbo in number four engine whined, coughed, belched clouds of black smoke, eventually caught with all four propellers fanning the air. Andy sighed, gave the mechanics on the ground a thumbs-up, and pushed the throttles forward.

Through his side window, Andy watched the edge of the tarmac as he taxied the *Alley Cat* into position for a run-up. He locked the brakes, revved the engines up to 1,500 rpm, checked the magnetos, and waggled the rudder to signal the tower that he was ready for takeoff. Receiving the green light, Andy turned to Tex and gave a thumb's up.

Holding at the beginning of the mile-and-a-half runway, he and Tex finalized the takeoff check and locked the tail wheel to keep the B-17 straight during the run.

Andy released the brakes, opened the throttles, and the plane accelerated forward. The *Cat* lumbered down the runway, stirring the remaining fog, speed increased, and controls became more responsive.

Andy pushed the wheel forward to raise the tail off the ground. When the airspeed reached 100 miles per hour, he eased the wheel back. The huge hunk of metal skipped on the runway a couple of times and lifted into the air. From the corner of his eye, something caught Andy's attention. *There he is! By God, the same hawk that followed my train from Fayetteville. He's racing us!* The hawk dipped his wing as the *Alley Cat* ascended. Andy gripped the wheel. Sweat clouded his eyes. He knew takeoff was the most dangerous time. After what seemed like forever, the *Cat*, packed to the hilt with bombs and fuel, accelerated its climb. At roughly 1,200 feet above ground, Andy said, "Landing gear up." He felt a satisfying clump as the gear seated itself just aft of the engines. Reaching airspeed of 150 mph, Andy throttled back, reducing the rmp from 2,500 to 2,300.

The *Cat* continued to climb at the rate of 200 feet per minute. He pressed the intercom button below his neck, "Put your oxygen masks on, fellas, we're approaching 10,000 feet."

Tex sounded a routine check with the crewmen to make certain their masks functioned properly when hooked up to the plane's oxygen supply. He checked for extra portable canisters—twelve.

After barreling through cloud cover, a burst of sunlight and infinite blue sky lifted the gloom, unlike the white fog Andy inhaled earlier and grew to expect of England's climate. Ahead of the *Alley Cat* loomed the 8th Air Force and the 96th Bombardment Group. Andy began the risky maneuver of easing into the assigned formation slot—the number two position—second lead squadron. They swung wide to enter the slot.

"Whoa! What's happening up there?" Bulldog shouted into the intercom. The plane bounced all over the sky—right, left, up, down.

"Turbulence in front of us!" Andy gripped the wheel and struggled to maintain control of the *Alley Cat.*

A jolt shook the plane like a giant hand and forced the *Cat* into a left bank and then a dive.

"Holy shit!" Tex shouted.

Andy reduced power and yelled, "Tex, hold it! Pull up, pull up!" With clamped teeth, he struggled to gain control of the plane.

"We're going down!" Tex shouted. "Nineteen thousand, eighteen, seventeen, sixteen, fifteen! Lost seven thousand feet!" Veins bulged in Tex's neck; hands grasped and yanked forcefully on the control wheel. "I can't pull any harder!" Back through the clouds the *Cat* dove.

Andy braced himself, straining with all his being to pull the wheel back. Every bone in his body quaked. He stuck to the back of the seat unable to move. *Gotta get out of here!* The ground rushed toward them.

He glanced at the "bail out" bell. Billy's face flashed in front of him—outside the bubble—waiting to slip inside. No parachute.

# Chapter Seven

## Schweinfurt Battle

"Hang on!" *Oh, God. Nobody can move. The Alley Cat can't survive this turbulence—the dive! It's gonna break apart!* Andy's guts wrenched. His feet braced against the floor. His arm muscles strained driven beyond their capacity.

"Pull, Tex, pull! Come on, baby! Come on!" Andy yelled through gritted teeth. His stomach rose to his mouth like the downside of a roller coaster racing to the bottom. Burning sweat dribbled into his eyes

Gradually, the wheel moved back, and the Fortress leveled off. Andy pushed the throttles forward and once again climbed toward the formation above.

"Whoowee! Good job, Tex!" The sweat from Andy's temples pooled in his chin pocket. He pressed the intercom, "You fellas all right back there?"

Eight answers responded in unison with jubilation in their voices like the lift of a death sentence. The smell of burning fuel filled every crevice of the plane.

"Hey fellas. We are a lucky son-of-a-gun crew!" Andy turned off his intercom and glared at Tex. "What the hell happened? Felt like we got tapped by one of our high squadron planes. Remember the turbulence that bounced us just before? Maybe they hit the same instability. All I know is that our props got out of phase."

"Yeah, is that what threw us into the dive?"

"Might be. When we get back to base, they'll check it out."

"Let's hope it's not a permanent malfunction."

"That could mean disaster. I'm gonna start testing soon as we catch up to the squadron. Hold your breath when we attempt to slip into formation again," Andy added. Meanwhile, he checked the gauges and made sure all the needles centered in the green.

Unable to complete his reckoning, Andy squeezed the intercom. "I knew we weren't going to crash, men. My life didn't flash in front of me." Andy lied, faked humor, and chuckled. "Didn't even think about a dame."

"G'wan, Andy." Bulldog mopped his forehead.

"By God, y'all did it, Andy. Y'all did it," Tony, the tail gunner, shouted. He hung tight to his .50 caliber gun.

"Yep!" Andy said. Tony's Southern speak sounded ridiculous for his jet-black hair, tanned complexion, and Italian heritage. "How was the tail ride going down?" Andy kidded.

"Felt like a stick of dynamite ready to explode." Tony messed with the trigger of his .50 caliber. "Lordy me, calm, sir, calm. Glad to ride the bottom side back up. Bet Bulldog pissed in his britches."

"What wuz you trying to do, scare the fool out of us?" Sully quipped. He fumbled around trying to round up his engineering tools. He slipped off his helmet and rubbed his hand over his hair. "Hell, Bulldog weren't the only one. I almost wet myself. Thanks a lot, ole buddy!"

"Just wanted to make sure y'all are awake," Andy said over the intercom. "Lucky no planes were in our path."

Billy drummed his fingers. "I thought for a moment I was in the bubble and prayed for Bulldog to come drag my butt out." He had slid off his parachute and attempted to center himself back on it.

"Lads, you don't know anything. You should eavesdrop on the ragging we're getting from the other pilots," Paulie, the British-American radio operator, said from his station, his foot propped against the plywood door to keep bitter air from seeping in from the bomb bay area. He rearranged his earphones. One side had peeled away from his ear. "The good ole boys are calling us 'show-offs.' Can you believe that? After we almost drank the North Sea!"

"It was a test to see how y'all react under pressure, men!" Andy gave way to a hearty laugh and eased the plane into its formation slot.

"Over the North Sea now. Test your guns," Andy ordered over the intercom.

The test firing of the previously loaded .50 caliber guns rocked the *Alley Cat* with each round and blasted a deafening sound.

Things hummed along peacefully for Andy and his crew and they all settled into a routine. The Fortress was fully loaded with fourteen 250-pound GP (General Purpose bombs with TNT) bombs and several M-17s. The inside temperature of the *Alley Cat* was –25 Celsius or –13 degrees Fahrenheit at 19,000 feet. Climbing to 25,000 feet with no fuselage heat, the temperature plunged to an unbearable –30 degrees.

"Hope y'all wore your heat suits," Andy said to his crew and pointed to Tex.

"I did, sir." Tex squeezed his intercom, "Pops, you keeping an accurate track of our position on that 'GEE' box thing?" Tex asked.

"What makes you think I got any information to feed that 'GEE' box thingy?" Pops replied. "After a dive like that, everything went a-flying. We'll be sitting ducks before long." He clicked off his intercom and tried to wipe the grin off his face.

Tex, eyebrows raised higher than the top of his helmet and his eyes stretched wider than saucers, turned to Andy, "Did you hear what the ole man said? We gotta get information from the other planes…and in a hurry!"

Andy had closed off the section below, but envisioned Pops stretching out his dividers on the navigation table. "Now Tex. You know better than to let Pops shake you up like that. He's got the maps tacked down sound as a nail. Besides, you better not let him hear you call him 'old man.' He could bust your chops. Think we've had enough excitement for one day."

Andy focused back on the job and after an hour in the air, ordered, "Remove the arming pins from all eighteen bombs." He checked the IAS (Indicated Airspeed Speed) reading of 150 mph calculating in his head to 206 mph because the IAS register declined with increased altitude.

For three hours they flew without incident. *How long could it last?* Andy knew it couldn't. He sensed something about to erupt. They flew in regular formation until the signal from the lead plane ordered them to tighten into combat box formation.

Maj. Sheldon ordered, "Group Walters. Move into Group Bennett's high squadron spot."

"Roger, lead plane."

The *Alley Cat* powered up to the high squadron starboard side of the formation. Several planes behind acted as their buffer. Andy never forgot the last section, 'Purple Heart Corner,' or 'Tail End Charlie,' who acquired their names when Luftwaffe fighters attacked from the rear with deadly accuracy. It was the weakest point in the formation—fewer planes to help the B-17s defend themselves.

Andy glanced up at the P-47 fighter escort planes, little friends, flying above the armada.

The formation reached the German border, and the P-47 fighter escort planes turned back—half their fuel spent. One by one, they abandoned the B-17s. Andy knew the Germans waited patiently.

They hid, ready to pounce on their prey the minute the little friends swung wide and headed home. He scanned the sky for bogies.

"Here they come, right out of the sun, straight at us!" Sully shouted over the intercom. He swung his twin 50s forward. One after another FW 109 German fighter closed at 500 mph. Sully spewed a round of bullets at the fighter flying within 300 feet.

"Yeeiiiii!" Sully ducked as the bandit exploded square in front of his face sending a rain of metal into his Plexiglas bubble, puncturing one corner.

"Sully. You okay?" Andy asked over the intercom.

"Yes sir."

"Bandits, 12 o'clock, heading straight for us! Sully? Bulldog?" The sound of panic erupted from Tex's throat.

Shouts came over the intercom from every defensive position of the plane, the tail gunner, the top turret, left and right waists, ball turret and bombardier: "Bandits, 3 o'clock, 6, 10, 12, 6 again." The intercom droned on…no let up.

Bandits polluted the air. The sky overflowed with German fighters, obvious to Andy, determined to protect their country—to die for their county—whatever it took. They kept coming, peppering the *Alley Cat* with rounds from their 50mm guns.

A B-17 exploded in the air after a 20mm cannon ripped through it from a Focke-Wulf. Parts plunged to the ground wiping out another B-17 in its path. No parachutes sighted.

Andy fought to keep the ship in the air and in tight formation. A strange feeling crept over him—like he wasn't piloting the plane—as if he watched from above. This wasn't happening to him or his crew. They stood outside with him cheering the *Alley Cat* on. *What's happening here? No time to wonder.*

Instantly he was back in the plane—petrified—like his crew. He tightened his grip on the control wheel to stop his trembling. "Two o'clock," he shouted through the intercom above the roar of the four engines and vibrations of the machine guns with their deafening sounds, shells flying everywhere.

"Watch our back, Tony." Andy stiffened.

"Gotcha, Captain," Tony replied.

Sully scanned the sky. "Bogies at 4 o'clock. Moving in fast." His voice shook as he powered his twin 50s at a ME-109.

Before Sully could swivel around on the metal floor plate, another bandit flew head on to the *Alley Cat*.

"FW 190 coming in at 12 o'clock," Tex shouted, his breath came in short bursts. "Shit!"

Bulldog pulled the trigger. BOOM! The fighter exploded, spreading metal as the Fortress flew through the ball of fire. "A split second later, we'd be shredded," he shouted. "That was in our face!" Bulldog watched the debris narrowly missing the top of the *Alley Cat*.

"Look out," Sully shouted, arms quivering. "He's yours, Whitie! Four o'clock!"

"Seven o'clock," Tony shouted, pulling his trigger finger, unloading a stream of .50 caliber gun power at the 109. "I missed the bastard!" He thrust his head to the left. "Nealy, 10 o'clock. Get him!"

Before Nealy could get off a shot, Sully fired, but missed the bandit. It exploded 300 feet in front of him, shot down by another B-17.

"By Gawd, did you see that?" Nealy shouted, reeling with astonishment, resting his finger on the trigger. "It looked like a Christmas wreath 'round that plane only there was no plane." He jumped back as blood spattered on his window. He gagged.

"Another B-17's going down," Whitie shouted through the intercom. "Oh, no. It's Dick's plane. Count the parachutes!"

Andy squinted at the black dotted carpet laid before them by antiaircraft fire from below. The Luftwaffe fighters peeled off, pulling back to avoid their own 88mm antiaircraft guns.

A radio call from the lead plane, Maj. Sheldon, interrupted Andy's concentration. "Black flak from antiaircraft fire peppering the sky. Heaviest yet. Hold your path."

"Yes sir," Andy replied. He had a visual. The flak mimicked dark holes in the scant lower ground cover.

"Okay, Bulldog. Stay alert. Cut your chatter, fellas," Andy ordered as they approached their IP. The plane shuddered unsteadily, bouncing and vibrating from the exploding antiaircraft artillery. Black puffs, flak you could lay down on, the most terrifying of all—flak that could take them out in a heartbeat.

The order came from the lead plane. Over the pinging of flak and vibration of the .50s, Andy felt the bomb bay doors opened by Bulldog and knew he dropped tinsel to throw off the enemy radar. Andy's eyes followed it down watching it sparkle from the reflection of the sun. It slipped in and out of the clouds and finally disappeared from sight. He hoped it would do the job.

Bulldog said, "Approaching."

"Button your lips, fellas," Andy said. "Keep your eyes sharp. Ready to lay eggs. We'll give those Krauts exactly what they deserve."

The *Cat* shot skyward from an explosion directly beneath. Andy heard throaty shrieks from the plane's cavity. He stared in numbed horror as two B-17s plunged earthward. Flak severed the tailpiece of a B-17 in the middle squadron, sending it spiraling in a southeasterly route into a second B-17 in the lower squadron. Two Fortresses taken out with one burst of 88mm antiaircraft flak. He swallowed hard.

Andy glanced at Tex whose facial muscles twitched uncontrollably. He reached over and punched Tex on the shoulder. No words were necessary. A sickening wave of terror welled up in Andy's belly. He swallowed again.

"Bulldog? Ready?" Andy asked, fearful of his bombardier's steadiness. His friend had the best seat in the house—he saw it all. The horror was too much for anyone.

"Yes sir." Bulldog uttered a weak response and immediately began the preparation of his equipment. Bomb bay doors remained open. The IP lay directly in front of them. Bombsight stabilizer— level. Prop back selector switches—on. Drift and dropping angle— preset.

Andy watched their leader send up the flare. "Signal, Bulldog?"
"Yes sir," Bulldog replied. The lead plane started its drop, and the others followed.

One, two, three and on up to fourteen, the bombs dropped in succession. The *Alley Cat* sprang skyward as the load lightened. Andy struggled to control the bounce.

"Hey, Cap'. That's like dropping a bomb in a pickle barrel from 25,000 feet," Bulldog joshed. He sounded calm from a good drop.

"Radioman? All bombs cleared?" Andy asked.

Paulie checked to see that all bombs had released and none jammed in the bomb bay. "All clear to close bomb bay doors."

"Any injuries or serious plane damage?" Andy asked each crewman for a visual report.

No major injuries reported by the crew. The Fortress suffered numerous holes throughout her fuselage but nothing to hinder her flight home.

"Good job, men," Andy said, as the plane picked up speed from its lighter weight now flying at speeds up to 160 mph. "Now let's head for the RP (Rally Point)." Andy knew that the point was chosen in an area out of range of enemy flak for re-forming into defensive combat wing formation, that he could not stay out of formation for too long, and a lone plane became a vulnerable target for the Jerries (German fighters).

"Taking evasive action now," Andy advised, although the *Alley Cat* continued its rough washboard flight as he made a wide swing heading for the RP and the 8th Air Force formation.

"Jumpin' gee hosifat!" Bulldog said. "Bandit coming in at 10 o'clock."

"I got 'em, I got 'em," Billy said. He swung both .50s around. Despite the obvious stress, Billy rarely missed nailing his target. "He dove under me!"

"Nine o'clock, Nealy," was heard by all as the Focke-Wulf 190 disintegrated before his eyes. "Whew boy! Mitch's plane took out that one."

"Watch it," Bulldog shouted as a 109 flew past. "Gotcha!" He fired his guns, but missed. "That son-of-a-bitch was smiling."
"Jumpin' gee hosifat!" Bulldog let go of his .50's as he watched the B-17 ahead.

In front a B-17's two port engines burst into flames, a hole in its starboard side. The crew bailed out. *Come on guys. Get outta there!* Andy counted the men. Only eight. Then he realized, "Damn! That's Mitch's plane."
Abruptly, it shuddered violently and exploded. "My God! Did they get out? Where are the other two?" Tex shouted.
"Watch it! Silver projectile…" Andy expelled his breath loudly. "Just missed a B-17's right wing. Oh, God! That's… that's Mitch's starboard door!" His body shuddered.
"Must not had a right waist gunner. Side was wide open for attack," Tex said.
"Gotta get back into formation. Not safe out here. Let's go!" Andy said. He searched the sky for his group.
Not far in front of the *Alley Cat*, the lead plane had dropped back and headed for the rendezvous point. With no warning, three cannon-firing 190 fighters came out of nowhere.
The lead plane fought with everything she had. One enemy fighter finally went down in flames. The second poured black smoke and headed straight for the lead plane—determined to take it out.

"Oh hell," Andy and Tex said in unison. Both planes exploded in midair.

"They never had a chance, Tex. Get going."

A man without a parachute passed directly in front of the cockpit. Andy read the sheer terror written on his face. He screamed—screams that fell on deaf ears. Andy gasped, swallowing air to hide his own guttural sounds.

BOOM! A gigantic jolt hit the belly of the *Cat*. "What was that?" Andy checked his instruments for any sign of damage.

"Took a hit near the starboard tire," Billy said over the intercom. From the ball turret, he searched every visible inch of the plane's belly. "Looks like it struck the landing gear."

"Best test it before landing," Andy said. "Anything else, Billy?"

"Appears all right."

"Keep your eyes peeled, Billy."

"Yes sir."

"Formation ahead." Andy sighed in relief at the sight looming in front—their own planes flying in and out of puffy white clouds.

"Four of our planes on our tail. Look at them bandits. They're going back after stragglers," Tony said. "My arms ain't stopped shaking yet. Feels like they're still pumping shells from the 50s. I already got my share of bandits today."

"There you go again, Tony. Quit bragging," Bulldog said. "Does this guy never shut up?"

The *Alley Cat* caught up with the 96th BG (Bombardment Group), and Andy slipped into her formation slot and winged her toward home.

Evening set in as they flew across the North Sea on course to Snetterton. The entire area socked in solid with fog. Andy searched silently. *Where are the lights? I can scarcely see the plane in front of me. No red lights. Follow him.*

"Tex. See anything? Fog's thick as cake batter. Hanging close to Ralph's plane."

"Don't see nothing."

"Well, we're going down, regardless. It's like flying blind. Whoa! There they are. Lights! *Glimmering and vast, my England, my England.* Never thought I'd say that! We can finally relax. What a helluva-day."

Tex stared at Andy.

The lights from the airstrip came into view, and one by one, the planes began their descent to the runway. First, planes displaying red lights indicating injured crewmen. Next, damaged planes. Radio signals were sent ahead of the landings. MPs, ambulances, and fire tender crews scrambled to the field. After damaged planes landed and ground crews cleared the tarmac, squadron bombers flying at the lowest altitude landed first at twenty-second intervals.

Andy glimpsed at Tex swabbing his face. He reached over and jabbed Tex's arm. "Had a good day. Dumped our entire load, came back with fuel to spare, and got another mission under our belts."

Tex nodded.

Andy lowered the landing gear. "What's it look like, ball turret?"

"Both wheels down. Can't tell if there's damage to the wheel itself."

"We'll find out soon enough. Crew, secure everything around you and strap yourselves down. Ball turret, get outta there."

While waiting for landing instructions, Andy's thoughts drifted back to Mitch's plane. *Disintegrated. Gone. Did Mitch bail out? Did they make it safely to the ground, or did a bandit pick them off as they glided helplessly through the air? How many more missions can the Alley Cat make before biting the dust?*

He fought forgetting-wanted to. At thirty-five missions, he knew he would be sent home—twenty-four to go. Flyby thoughts crammed his head while he eased into landing position. *Today was a lucky day. Will tomorrow be our day?* An echo of silent tension pressed against the *Alley Cat's* cavity like the weightless heat of sun against a windowpane.

After warning the base of a possible problem, the *Alley Cat* received clearance to land.

The ground raced to meet the *Cat* as Andy fought to keep her steady. The airstrip whizzed along under the Fortress' wingspan swirling the fog patches below as the wheels searched for contact. The port tire kissed the tarmac. She bounced hard, and the crew waited for the second touch-down. The second wheel…"Boom!"

"Oh my God!"

# Chapter Eight

Oh Jesus!" Andy labored to keep the *Alley Cat's* nose centered on the runway. The starboard tire exploded. The right landing gear collapsed under the weight of the plane.

"Holy shit!" Tex shouted.

Andy struggled to bring the plane to a halt. He sucked in his breath and held it.

The *Alley Cat* balanced on one wheel for a few short moments, then spun uncontrollably to the right. Her wing dipped and scraped on the tarmac, shooting sparks that threatened at any moment to ignite fuel in the wing tanks.

Andy bit his tongue hard and tried to swallow. His throat scratched like sandpaper.

"Get ready for a fast exit," he ordered through the intercom. Smoke poured from the starboard wing.

He braced for a sudden stop. It never came—the plane gradually slowed. The right wing dug across the paved runway plowing a deep furrow, gouging into the rain-saturated grass.

Fire tender crews raced toward the *Alley Cat* and medical trucks chased behind.

Engine four blazed with flames. Andy shut down the engines and ordered, "Out! Out!" He attempted to stand up, but his ankle gave way. Tex had rushed to the back of the plane to make sure the crew got out. Andy fell back into his seat as smoke filled the cockpit. He scooted down to the bombardier section, crawled on his knees to open the nose hatch. Jammed. He crept on all fours toward the back, feeling his way across the 8 ½-inch-wide crosswalk. He gasped for air. His lungs strained.

"Andy! Andy!" a faint call came from the rear of the plane. The sound of Bulldog's voice grew louder through the smoke-filled fuselage. Andy glimpsed a humongous bare hand fumbling around his head. Bulldog caught Andy's sheepskin collar, dragged him over the balance of the crosswalk, hoisted him up, and made haste to the starboard exit. Black smoke squeezed the oxygen from their lungs.

Tex met them before they reached the exit.

"Go! Go!" Andy yelled, fearful of an explosion. "Get outta here!"

Once outside, Bulldog eased Andy down onto the ground away from the plane.

"Thanks, Bulldog. Must be other damage to cause that much smoke," Andy said.

The fire tender crew smothered the Fortress with acid-soda snuffing out the flames on the wing, and black smoke seeped through the holes from fighter damage in the *Alley Cat*.

"Looks like black cat tails twirling upward from them holes. What a load of holes to repair." Bulldog unsnapped his helmet and pushed up his goggles exposing a forehead streaked with soot.

Billy spat on the ground and said to Bulldog, "Is that your war paint? Who you gonna attack now?"

"Be glad it ain't you, punk. Didn't you come through that gal darn smoke?"

Billy pinched his lips together and hovered over Andy after the medics placed Andy on a stretcher. "Wow, Andy. We thought you was a goner."

"Hey. Can't get rid of me that easily. Everyone all right?"

Andy glanced over at Nealy, his left waist gunner. He had knelt down on his knees and appeared to be praying.

Andy turned to the medic and pointed to Nealy. "Sergeant, take me to that man."

"Right away, sir."

The attendants lowered the stretcher to Nealy's level. "You all right?"

No response from Nealy—eyes closed.

"Nealy! Look at me!" Andy reached over and caught his arm.

"Look, fella. Every one of us experience fear in some form or another. Being afraid is no reason to feel ashamed. We made it! You don't need to be alone now. We're your brothers. Come on. You got a gal waiting for you back home?"

Nealy raked his sleeve across his eyes, peeked over at Andy, and stood. "Yes sir, sure do."

Andy grasped the back of Nealy's arm and urged him forward. "Go have fun tonight and when you get back to the barracks, write her a letter—let her know you thought of her during this mission and how it got you through it."

"I'll try, sir." Nealy gazed down at the ground as he walked along side Andy toward the medical truck where the crew watched and waited.

Andy responded, anticipating their questions. "Nealy's gonna join in the celebration. Take care of him for me tonight, ya hear?" He grimaced in pain when he tried to move his ankle. "Let's go." He circled his hand in the air.

Tex joined Andy. "Crew's okay. What happened?"

"Don't quite know. Must have jammed my ankle when we spun around."

"Hey, Cap'. What we gonna do for a plane?" Bulldog removed his flight helmet and ran his hand through a tussle of unkempt black hair.

"They'll have the *Cat* ready to go in no time. Don't you worry none, Bulldog. We'll be back in the air before the cows come home."

"Hurry back, sir."

Andy propped on his elbow and observed the crew standing at attention. *They're wondering what they're gonna do for a plane— and for a pilot.* His chest swelled with pride. *No one wants to fly without me...they depend on me...they feel safe...they know I'll take care of them. I am one lucky son-of-a-gun.*

"I'll be back tomorrow. You'll see. Finish debriefing and go have fun tonight. Y'all deserve it." Andy pumped his arm at his men.

"We'll have you fixed up in a jiffy, flyboy," the medical attendant said. The other attendant closed the doors and jumped into the driver's seat.

Fog rolled in waves across the airfield while the truck sped to the emergency field hospital. Andy's thoughts drifted back to Schweinfurt. The image of Mitch's plane exploding seared into his memory. *Only eight chutes sighted. No, Mitch!* He covered his face with his hands. This was not what he planned, not what he worked for, not the set-back he expected. *Now where do I stand with you Dad? Another failure? Crap!*

The attendant spoke. "You were lucky, Captain. The crews of many planes with landing problems don't walk away. Some don't get carried away either." He leaned over to examine Andy's ankle.

"Guess you don't know why these planes were given the name 'Flying Fortress'? The *Alley Cat's* a real tank! She got us home. She must have a hundred holes in her from this mission alone." Andy smiled at the reflection of the overhead light on the attendant's bald head.

"Yes, sir. They're tough machines. I've seen many a man come back alive in a plane that wasn't much more than a flying pile of rubble. At least it got them back home." The attendant squeezed Andy's ankle.

"Yeow! Go easy, fella."

"Sorry, sir. Just doing my job."

Andy, rested his head back, arm across his forehead, and waited for the bumpy ride sending shooting pain up his leg to end, and for whatever would come next.

They pulled in front of the field hospital, another vast Nissen hut, where the attendants gently lifted him from the truck, carried him inside, and slid him onto the examination table. By then Andy's ankle had ballooned.

"Well, we don't see any blood, Captain," the doctor said. He applied pressure here and there while rotating Andy's ankle.

Andy raised both hands to the side of his head, refusing to yell out from the pain. "Hey, Doc. You done yet?" he asked through gritted teeth.

"Just about. Don't think you have any broken bones. But you're going to have one helluva sore ankle. We'll get it wrapped, and tomorrow you'll be out of here."

"That's it?"

"Yep. Soon as a nurse is free, we'll send her in to bind it. You'll need to stay off it for a day or two. We'll send a pair of crutches with you."

"Thanks, Doc."

He studied the white anemic room with rows of tightly spaced beds, nearly all occupied. An antiseptic smell saturated the area. Thankful for a less serious injury, he wondered how many were critically injured, and how many had died in the Schweinfurt mission.

It had been a full day—too many close calls. He glanced at his watch, 2200. Wake up call had come at 0500. He poked at a tray of food—hunger never entered his mind.

Andy pressed his hands over his eyes as if to shut out the day, but he could not stop his mind from whirling. *When will the dying stop? I pray to God they end this war.* He couldn't flush Mitch out of his mind. *What a great friend! Oh, God. What will his wife and baby do without him?* Andy raised his good leg and kicked down into the cot. The jolt sent his injured ankle into spasms. His body was drained. Spent. Tomorrow would be better.

He pulled up the blanket and placed the pillow over his head to muffle moans coming from the back room, and soon drifted off into a troubled sleep.

The next day after breakfast, the doctor checked Andy's ankle and said, "So long. You're out of here."

"Thanks, Doc."

"Stay off it for a few days, and before long you'll be good as new."

"Will do."

Early as it was, Andy stepped outside into the blinding warm sun—unusual for England. It had rained during the night and left the air muggy as a steam shower. A jeep pulled up beside him.

"Capt. Walters?"

"Yes."

"I'm here to take you to your quarters."

Andy hobbled on wooden crutches over to the jeep, which, after a short ride, deposited him at his barracks. The small Nissen hut, which housed two sets of crew officers, resembled a metallic half-moon stretched straight back, anchored to the ground, a door in front with a window on each side of the door. Relief and dread accompanied Andy to the door. Reality became who was not inside. He lingered for a moment with his hand on the doorknob before entering.

Bulldog stomped out his cigarette and made a beeline to Andy. "Welcome back, Captain! You look swell. Hey, look y'all. Here's my buddy." He caught Andy around the shoulders and helped him along.

"Good to have you back, boss," Pops jested. He scratched the bald spot on the crown of his head.

Tex flipped over on the bunk knocking off the cowboy hat which had covered his face. "Howdy, Captain."

"Thanks, fellas." Andy stole a quick glance at the back of the hut. Empty. Empty except for one man—Brad. *How'd he make it back here? Was he in Mitch's plane? I don't believe this. Why did such a jerk get so lucky when Mitch's plane crashed over Germany? Why?* Andy searched Bulldog's face for answers.

Bulldog shook his head and took the lead. "Know whacha thinking. He dodged the bullet…went to sick bay."

"What? Don't joke." Andy felt his face light up like a red chili pepper.

"Naw. We done cut him loose. He ain't worth it. Don't have nothing to do with him."

Andy spun around and replaced the twinkle in his eyes with slits of steel. *Did Brad cause the loss of Mitch and his crew? Did an inexperienced bombardier replace him? Were there only nine crewmen on that mission?*

Andy squinted at Brad and could see no remorse from him. He tottered over to Brad and sat on one of the three empty bunks. After he took a deep breath and swallowed hard, he calmly said, "Any news from the eight that bailed out?"

"Nope." Brad replied, refusing to look at Andy. "Did eight bail out?"

Andy pressed his lips striving to maintain control. "That's what we counted. How many were on the…"

Brad interrupted. "Look, Walters. Don't blame me. I got sick! I'm sure they found another bombardier."

Andy's tone revved up a few notches. "My crew says you were fine when they came back. All it takes is one missing link to mess up an entire crew. You and Mitch had a complete understanding—he had confidence in you. What the hell were you thinking?"

"What the *hell* are you saying? You think I'm responsible for Mitch's plane going down? Huh?" Brad jumped to his feet, threw his cigarette to the floor, and stomped it out. His quivering lips and flushed face loomed over Andy.

Andy sprang up on one crutch and met Brad head on. "Buddy boy, I want to know whether or not I can count on you…that is, if you ever fly with me." His eyes blazed with fire.

"Hell could freeze over before I'd fly with you, buster. Now, get the hell out of my end of the barracks. You think you're Mr. Big, a hotshot captain. Who'd you know to get there so fast?"

"Oh, so that's what this is all about—me becoming captain? Don't think so. You're angry because you washed out of pilot school!" Andy shoved Brad out of his face. Before he hobbled away, he added, "You yellow bastard! You just answered my question. I don't need to know any more. The CO informed me that a new crew is moving in tomorrow. Their bombardier and tail gunner both died over Schweinfurt." Andy glanced back over his shoulder.

Brad spun around, rammed his right fist into his left, and threw himself onto his bunk.

Andy limped over to a wooden peg holding Mitch's uniforms and searched through them until he came to his dress uniform. A front shirt pocket bulged slightly. Andy reached in and pulled out a letter to Mitch's wife, unsealed:

*My dearest Julie,*

*I've put this letter in my best uniform just in case I don't come back. I love you and little Mitch so much. Through all the hell over here, I need to only think of you—your eyes, your smile, your cute little nose, your laughter—right away I feel better. I remember taking walks with you, holding your hand, stealing a kiss. Julie, that was heaven to me. How lucky for me that you agreed to be my wife. It seems impossible when I think of the joy and happiness we've shared.*

*Thank you for bringing our baby to camp before I shipped out. Next to marrying you, that was the happiest day of my life.*

*I hate thinking of the time when I might not be in your life. The thought of not being able to watch little Mitch grow up—pitching baseballs to him —college— marriage—grandchildren. I want to believe that I will always be there for him, but should something happen and I don't come back, I will take the picture of you and little Mitch to my grave. Julie, I know you will be the best mother ever. Just don't let him forget about me.*

*Now, I don't want you to be sad or mourn for me. Remember our love and what it meant to both of us. Now that you've opened this letter, please know I didn't die in vain. I died for you, Julie, and for my country. I died for a worthy cause—freedom for all the people in this world, an end to this horrible war, and an end to hatred. Freedom comes with a price. Hold your head high, and though I am not there physically, I'll always love you and little Mitch.*

*Mitch*

Andy slipped the neatly folded paper into its original creases and placed it back into Mitch's uniform. His eyes blurred. *Mitch, you were the greatest.*

He waited until he composed himself and then shuffled back to his bunk. After thinking about the letter *he* had to write, mulling it over in his mind, he reached for his pad and pencil. His thoughts drifted back home after announcing he had joined the USAAF. Fresh in his mind was his father's furrowed brow when he slammed his fist on the dinner table and bellowed, "I didn't raise you to quit college and go off to fight a war you'll probably die in. No sir! You are going to finish college, boy, and that's that!" He thought of his family standing at the Fayetteville, North Carolina's depot—on the wooden platform amid gray-white smoke and hissing steam pouring from the train. He saw the hurt in his dad's eyes—a look that would stay with him forever. His mother had slipped something into his pocket and said, "Don't forget to wear clean underwear." And Betty Jane, his fourteen-year-old sister waving a handkerchief had shouted, "Who's going to take care of your girlfriends while you're gone?" Her light brown pigtails bounced up and down.

With an ache in his heart and a knot in his stomach, Andy put the pen and pad down. He slid onto his pillow, closed his eyes, and shut out all home memories, allowing the last battle to roll over and over in his head. *Did I do enough? Could we have helped Mitch in any way? We lost 60 planes—60 out of 376. Over 600 men—600 grieving families. Families torn apart. Fatherless children. And for the living, yesterday was a gift, today is still a mystery; what will tomorrow bring?*

Several days passed, and Andy's ankle injury healed quickly. Lucky for the *Alley Cat* crew, the missions were uneventful milk runs. None of the crew had to transfer to other planes. The *Alley Cat* spent seven days in repair. Andy and each crew member never missed a day checking on her progress. The *Cat* was in their blood. Andy didn't know how to explain it, but the entire crew couldn't wait to get her back in the air. To do their jobs. To help their country.

*Look at them,* Andy smiled, observing his crew day after day overseeing the plane's repair progress. *They care as much as I do. We are truly working as a team.* He choked with pride.

One evening Andy, Bulldog, Tex, and Pops entered a softly lit USO Club. "You'll Never Know" reverberated from the jukebox. Andy pushed his way between couples dancing cheek to cheek on the scuffed wooden floor. Girls danced with girls, awaiting invitations from uniformed men.

Fresh popped popcorn launched a tantalizing scent as Andy wove his way in and out of rustic wooden tables and chairs to an empty table with no mugs. Bulldog trailed.

"Hey Andy, get a load of those gorgeous gams! I'm gonna find me a broad and have some fun. Get a load of that dish over yonder!" Bulldog scurried to the dance floor.

"Catch ya in a minute." Andy had picked up a pint of bitter (ale) on his way to a table and passed Brad.

"Well look at the devil himself. Walters, what the hell are you doing here. Thought you'd be sucking up to the generals. Isn't that how you got to be captain so quick?"

"Cool it, Brad. You're drunk."

"Not drunk enough to know you're one big suck up." Brad swayed far to the left.

Andy caught him before he crashed into a table. "If you weren't so drunk, I'd clean your clock right now!"

Brad swung his free hand at Andy but missed. His eyes rolled.

Andy shoved him forward. "You worthless piece of shit!"

Brad landed across an empty table and slid to the floor.

Andy reeled around in search of an empty table leaving Brad in a sprawl. *Why in the name of God do I keep trying to save this guy from himself. For craps sake!*

Sitting at a corner table was a familiar face, and at first Andy wasn't sure if he really knew her. She glowed in her red silk dress sprinkled with tiny white polka dots. He approached the table and a youthful twinge from a first crush surfaced. "Rose? Rose Martin?"

She looked up, startled. "Andy? I don't believe it. I haven't seen you since high school."

"Mom said in her last letter that you were over here somewhere. Small world. Red Cross?" He straddled the straight back chair and rested his arms between the posts.

"Yes, I left college in November and joined as a nurse. This war isn't just for men, you know."

"You're right. I left in December, right after Christmas. My, my, Rosie." Andy repeated the nickname he had given her years ago because of her china doll face and rosy cheeks. "You're not that little high school girl I remember."

"Pearl Harbor changed us all, I see," Rose said. "You look... good, Andy—more handsome than ever in that uniform. I see you still can't get rid of that dimple. I remember how you tried for years to scrub it off. "

"You don't forget anything."

"Not when it's about the boy I grew up with—only you're not a boy now." A serious look crossed her face.

Bulldog hustled over, "Andy. Why aren't you mixing? I thought that's why we came out tonight." He looked over at Rose. "Oh. Guess you are."

"Bulldog. This is Rose Martin. We went to the same high school."

He extended his hand. "Glad to meet you, Rose."

"Same here, Bulldog." Rose squeezed his hand.

Bulldog turned to Andy. "Where you been keeping this doll?"

Andy's serious face sent a message to Bulldog.

"Okay, y'all 'scuse me. I'm going back to practice the jitterbug. Sorry I interrupted, Andy." His face turned crimson, and he scrambled off.

Andy winked at Rose and smiled at his friend as he watched him scurry away. He gazed back at Rose, and they reminisced about old times at Fayetteville High. "I feel like I'm back home again." He flipped around at the sound of footsteps approaching.

"What are you doing at this table, Walters?" Brad spun the chair around and mimicked Andy's position. His eyes glazed with hostility.

"I invited him, Brad." Rose swished her hair back and nodded to Andy. "This is our time to reminisce."

Brad's lip curled. "Clear out, buster." He raised a beer mug to his mouth.

"Brad, Rose and I were going over old times."

"I'm her old times, and I'm back! Vamoose!" Brad set his mug down with a clunk and cracked his knuckles one at a time.

"Brad, excuse me? I invited him to sit at *my* table." Rose smiled sweetly and placed her hand over Andy's.

Brad jumped up sending his chair hurtling to the floor. He grabbed Andy's shoulder and whirled him out of his chair. Andy wheeled back around and planted a fist across Brad's left jaw. Brad fell backwards, catching himself against the next table. Andy hustled over and caught the front of Brad's shirt and stood him up.

"Now, apologize to the lady for creating a scene, and you had better hurry before the MPs join our party."

Before Brad could answer, Bulldog approached the threesome. "Brad, you 'bout to cause a problem, eh? You're drunker than a brewer's fart, buddy." Towering over Brad, he placed his arm around Brad's shoulder, faced him toward the center of the room and escorted him away.

Within Andy's earshot, Bulldog said, "Now, unless you wanna dance with *me*, you better find a nice young gal and dance on the other side of the room." He released his grip on Brad's collar and gave him a nudge.

Brad swung around and landed a blow on Bulldog's cheek. "You bastard!"

Bulldog shook his head and locked his muscular arm around Brad's neck. He bounced Brad's feet on the floor. "Enough?"

"Not on your life!" Brad's face turned blood red. He inserted a leg between Bulldog's legs and down they went with a thud—Brad under Bulldog. Brad gasped for air.

Andy dashed over and pulled Bulldog off Brad. "That's enough—both of you!"

Bulldog shot up, knuckles white, brushed himself off, and said, "Let me at him. I was just getting started. I want this fella!"

Andy caught Brad's jacket and flipped him back on his feet. "Cut it out! You'll have us all hauled into the brig."

Bulldog, with a quirky smile, resumed his old position of escorting Brad to the dance floor. Brad shook his fist at Andy, while craning his neck like a goose peering about for her little ones.

"You just wait. You ain't seen nothing yet!" Brad slurred. Now you're stealing my gal. Yeah, mine. What else can you take from me, huh?" Brad struggled to dislodge Bulldog's grip who nudged Brad along.

Rose sighed and glared after Brad. "I dated him a couple of times at college and he's been a problem ever since."

Andy glanced at Rose, "Sorry 'bout that. He's gone now." He straightened his uniform coat, reached for his hat, and picked up his chair. "You were saying…."

His thoughts drowned out her words. She was anything but frail. Her face revealed spirit, confidence, strength; a face that beckoned him softly. She captivated him with her southern charm. The overhead light reflected a soft halo around her pale blonde hair and full, luscious red lips, like the last red rose of summer. He reached across the table weaving her fingers between his, and gazed into her china blue eyes that sparkled like Christmas tree lights—eyes he knew would never give up youthful secrets. He lifted her hand and realized he hadn't heard a word she had said.

The conversation stopped, and the jukebox played, "I'll Be Seeing You." Andy turned to Rose, "Say. You wanna dance?"

"Thought you'd never ask." Rose caught Andy's hand, and he led her to the dance floor.

They turned toward one another, and their eyes locked. He caught her right hand, and she placed her left arm around his shoulder, her touch sending tingles through his body. Slowly, they moved to the music. Gently, he inched Rose's body against his and curled her soft delicate hand into his chest. She nestled her head onto his shoulder. His cheek rested on her silky hair. Her scent filled his being. No one else existed. Just the two of them. A flood of warmth flowed through him as her body formed itself to his. They moved as one to the music. Heaven. A new world to cling to. No war. Just heaven.

A wave of tranquility flooded him, like the hawk soaring, reaching out to the stars, to infinity. Rose fulfilled a dream beyond his tomorrow. A time for discovery—a turning point in his life. Before Rose, nothing existed after the war. She had the power to change his destiny—the power to calm his restless spirit.

The music stopped, but Andy and Rose danced in another world. She lifted her head and looked into his eyes and he into hers. It was as if he could see into her soul and she into his.

Whistles and shouts crashed into their world. Everyone cheered them on.

"I guess we'd better sit down," Andy muttered and squeezed her hand as he guided her back to their table.

Bulldog followed.

"This is embarrassing." Rose brushed her hair back revealing a crimson face, and slipped behind Andy.

"Yeah, I know." After pulling out the chair for Rose, he sat across from her—studying her—searching for a meaning—a relationship.

Bulldog plopped down and resumed his usual probing. "Boy! You two were the stars on the dance floor, Andy. Something special going on here?"

"Lose yourself, Bulldog." Andy transferred his gaze back to Rose where she teased with batting eyes; the corners of her mouth turned up in a sweet, innocent smile. His heart melted.

Bulldog hopped up, interrupting Andy's concentration, and backed away from the table like a whimpering puppy. "Okay. I know when I'm not wanted."

Andy grinned. "He's like a kid. Needs his hugs." He placed his hand on top of hers. "I don't want this evening to end."

"Neither do I." She turned her hand over and clasped his.

He raised her hand to his lips, kissed it tenderly and placed it against his cheek. "We knew each other so well back in high school that we took each other for granted. Look at all the years I've wasted."

"My goodness. That was so long ago. You've changed and so have I. We've grown up a lot." Her cheeks flushed.

"You were part of the boss's family. My dad was a tenant farmer, and I never thought I was good enough. Every time you rode by in that shiny black '39 Ford convertible with the rumble seat open, I said to myself, 'One day I'm gonna drive a car like that.'"

"Oh, Andy. You were the hotshot football player. The starrrrr…" She taunted him by moving her left shoulder forward and turning her chin over the shoulder Betty Grable style. "The girls swooned at your feet. I got so mad every time that happened. You were my friend, and those girls took you away. Who would play cowboys and Indians with me?" she teased. Her expression lost its smile as she reflected. "Look. Your family is no different than mine. They are hard-working, good people. The only difference is that your dad gets his hands dirty. Mine doesn't."

"A lack of education kept Dad from doing better, but he was never lazy. Hey, by the way, you didn't swoon at my feet. From what I remember, you had too many fellows hanging around to even notice me," he goaded her playfully.

Rose laughed out loud tilting her head in mockery. "It was you that didn't see *me*." She took a sip of her Coke and glanced over to the club entrance. "Andy, I've got to go. See that group of girls moving toward the door? The truck must be waiting outside for us."

Andy draped her sweater around her shoulders and held her close for a moment. Another song played on the jukebox, "Give Me Something to Remember You By." He didn't want her to leave. He wanted her, needed her—had desires beyond this war.

Once out on the street, Rose turned to Andy, stretched her five-foot-five inches, and kissed him warmly on the cheek. "Oh, I got lipstick on your cheek." She reached for her handkerchief to wipe it off. "There, now they won't rag you when you return to camp."

Quick as a snap, she scrubbed the dimple on his chin. "I've always wanted to do that!"

They both laughed, and Andy caught her hand holding the handkerchief, "Um. This smells like your perfume."

"Here. You keep it. Something to remember *me* by." She flashed *her* dimpled-cheek-smile and closed the handkerchief in his hand. Her expression became serious. "It's so good to see someone from home, Andy. Goodbye. I hope to see you again."

Andy pulled her close, took her in his arms, "You can't get away so easily again." He pressed his lips against hers. His passion blazed as she responded.

She pushed against his chest. "I must go." She turned and raced toward the waiting truck.

He stood with empty arms. Stunned.

"Goodbye, Rosie." He shouted. "I'll see you la…" A sudden realization hit him. "Wait! How can I get in touch with you?"

She never glanced back. He watched the truck drive off after she climbed in. A strange emptiness engulfed him for the first time since leaving Fayetteville. He caught his chin and squeezed his dimple between his thumb and forefinger. Alone with his thoughts, he wanted nothing more than to embed the vision of her loveliness deep into his brain—to savor the moment. Before placing the handkerchief in his pocket, he inhaled one final whiff of its scent—the deep fragrance of roses.

Andy discovered a new turmoil in his life—the desire to see Rose. Now he had someone else to worry about. Where was she? Could he be lucky enough to run into her once more? Would he ever see her again? What did that quick exit really mean?

# Chapter Nine

## Schweinfurt II

Almost two months had passed since Andy last saw Rose. Nothing. Maybe transferred? It was like a big empty hole that just got bigger. A hole that never existed before that night at the club. He had questioned everyone—even wrote home to ask his mom where she was stationed. Surely her parents, the Martins, knew. Still no Rose.

The monotony of summer ended, September slipped away, and now a cold, damp chill filled the air as fall eased in. Fog and drizzle. Nothing new there. When the sun dared to present itself, the brilliance of the October leaves, as orange as pumpkins, illuminated the landscape.

Flying came to a standstill—targets socked in by dense fog. The men grew antsy. After several days, the sky cleared, and the missions resumed. Not the usual milk runs—each mission tougher than the one before. More German fighter planes—more flak—more everything. More B-24s and B-17s lost every day. *When does it stop?* Andy's sense of immortality died with Schweinfurt. Life as he knew it changed. Forever.

*Dad, were you right when you said I was going off to get killed in this God-awful war? Should I have listened to you? Oh that's swell, now I'm doubting myself. What crap!*

The sound of silence annoyed him and allowed aimless thoughts to creep in. *Must I be perfect for my father to see me?*

\*   \*   \*

## October 14, 1943

It was 0500. Andy had scarcely slept three hours when he heard footsteps approach the hut. The door opened, and a flashlight danced around, interrupting the pitch-black stillness of the night.

The flashlight creased the darkness while Andy watched the orderly, wearing fatigues, make his way to the middle of the barracks invading the deep sleep of its occupants. His eyes followed the zigzag of the flashlight in the orderly's hand—the beam cutting through the dark like a searchlight. It stopped at the foot of his bunk.

"Captain," the orderly whispered and held up a paper that crinkled in the silence. "All officers report for briefing at 0630." He backtracked to the door, stood like a silhouette from the light outside, flipped up the collar on his sheepskin jacket against the morning chill, and slammed the door as if to curse the day.

Andy yanked the cord from the hanging light, pinched his eyes against the brightness, and then, slipped into his wools. "You 'bout ready Bulldog? Men? Shake-a-leg."

He ambled over to a window, shoved the blackout curtain aside, and rubbed the frozen condensation off the window with his sleeve. "Damn this fog. This British weather is pure 'T' crap." *Just like our morale.*

Only a few days before, Andy's superior officer, Col. Miller, said, "Morale in the bomber command is lower than whale crap on the bottom of the ocean." Andy knew why. Schweinfurt! It was a disaster two months ago and it was still out there. Waiting.

Something needed to change the attitudes of the men in the 125 air bases around East Anglia, and the colonel counted on Andy and the other command pilots to boost the spirits of their crews. *Yeah, but how, when names get scrubbed from the board after each mission?*

He mumbled, "Get hold of yourself, buddy boy. You've a job to do, so just do it."

"You say something, Captain?" Bulldog rubbed the sand from his eyes.

"Naw. Thinking out loud." He replaced the blackout curtain and leaned against the wall.

Matches blazed as the smokers lit up their first cigarettes of the day. Smoke curled to the ceiling as they sucked in the nicotine that helped open their eyes, got their hearts pumping faster, and allowed them to begin anew.

Andy watched Bulldog slide his feet on the icy floor which bit back when touched. He recoiled in shock and dove for his boots. "Hot damn! It's cold."

"How ya gonna put your pants on over your boots, Bulldog?" Andy flashed a smile he knew irritated his men that early in the morning. "Wake up! Let's get this day going. Tex. Pops. Get with it." He clapped his hands together.

While waiting for the men, Andy silently prayed for *"just another day." Please keep us safe, dear Lord.* His thoughts strayed, and his skin grew clammy as he questioned, *Is this our day? How can I lead a crew with such a negative attitude? All right! Shake it off, buster, your insecurities are showing again. Buck up!*

He'd force a smile, and he'd walk with a bounce—part of his job. He squared his shoulders. He was ready. He'd make sure his men were upbeat before the mission.

Cigarettes snuffed out, Andy flashed another smile, a smile so contagious that even Bulldog grinned as he grabbed his flight jacket, and the two men headed out the door. The others followed and once outside, everyone paused to zip their jackets, shutting out the early morning breeze, a preview of colder weather to come.

Banging doors rocked the silence as the men left the barracks. An opaque layer of fog hugged the ground, hid the trees, leaving the men to follow the well-worn path leading to the mess hall.

Pops scurried around them leaving Tex beside Bulldog. "Outta the way, big shots!"

"Oh yeah? Who needs the big cowboy hat on a 'big head' so the shine don't blind us? Pops, you can make a toupee next time I get a haircut." Bulldog shoved his gloves in his pockets and briskly rubbed his hands, blowing his warm breath on them.

Tex, wearing his cowboy boots, stepped into a mud hole. They all laughed, watching him do the Texas two-step, dodging a second puddle. "That's not funny. Back off, you hear." He hustled to catch up with Pops.

Bulldog turned to Andy. "Hey, you notice Tex yesterday? If his face could droop any longer, it'd drag the ground."

"Come on, pal. Leave the man alone. Who knows what's eating him and if he wants to talk about it, he'll come to me." He gave Bulldog a nudge toward the mud but pulled him back. "See, I didn't want that gunk in my plane."

A few minutes later, Andy noticed Bulldog's face change from a smile to a frown.

"Ever think this might be your last mission?" Bulldog asked.

"Naw," Andy lied. "What're you worried 'bout. I'm driving."

"You heard the scuttlebutt 'bout going back to Schweinfurt?"

"Hey, don't borrow trouble lest you know for sure. If we get real eggs, then we'll worry." Andy slapped Bulldog on the back, grabbed his arm, and shoved him toward the mess hall.

"Okay, if you say so, Andy. You know, all I want to do is get back home, buy a little farm, find a swell gal, get hitched, and have ten kids."

"Good luck. I think you'd better find a gal willing to have ten kids first. I just want to make it home, marry Rose, and live 'happily ever after.'"

"Oh, so it's that serious with Rose."

"She's the one for me. Can't get her outta my mind. My reason for making it home—staying alive."

"You've got it bad, Andy."

"Yep. It gives me hope for a future—something to plan for, to look forward to. At the end of all this, I know what waits for me—Rose."

"She feel the same?"

"Don't know."

"Where is she?"

"Don't know that either. Haven't seen her since that night at the club."

They arrived at the mess hall and lined up behind Tex and Pops. Andy and Bulldog reached for their tins from the counter—eggs. Real eggs!

Andy turned around to Bulldog. "Coincidental. Doesn't mean a thing." He knew real eggs had not been served since Schweinfurt.

Bulldog stared at the eggs—his face pallid.

"Come on, Bulldog. Let it go." Andy bumped his elbow against his bombardier's arm, nudging him along.

"Listen. It's too quiet in here. It's eerie. Somethin's up, I tell ya."

Silence prevailed during breakfast. After they finished eating, trucks and jeeps lined the roadway, waiting to drive the officers for briefing. Pops hopped a jeep for the navigators' building, while another jeep hauled Andy, Tex, and Bulldog to their briefing.

The clouds hung solid and low like a canopy over the base. The earlier stillness of the camp had erupted and the hum of engines and banging of equipment moving from one place to another echoed throughout the area. Preparations were in full swing. *But for what? Why this feeling of awe?* The arousal of old fears and uncertainties surfaced. Nauseating spurts of adrenalin coursed through Andy's veins. He shook his head as if to rid himself of the dark cloud hanging over it. He longed for the crisp autumn mornings back home—longed for mornings without dread—without fear.

Andy entered the briefing room, passed through the check-off point, and worked his way to a seat next to Tex. Pilots, copilots, and bombardiers packed the room. The noise reached a loud roar. Andy glanced over at Brad, and their eyes connected; Brad's lips curled in his usual mocking smile. The muscles twitched in his jowls.

Bulldog moved to a seat beyond Andy, blocking Brad's view. When he turned toward Brad, Andy figured Bulldog probably communicated a piece of his mind to Brad.

The men squirmed in their seats, and a sudden hush came over the room. All eyes forward, afraid to acknowledge the unknown. Staring at the blank screen which covered the map. Previous bomber losses had added up, and the Luftwaffe's strategy of extinguishing an entire bomb group ate at the core of the 8th Air Force. Andy observed earlier that some men refused to look at the log board with names erased—friends—gone forever.

Once everyone arrived, the operations officer rolled up the screen and the briefing commenced. Gasps echoed around the room. Eyes widened with alarm. Jaws dropped. No one moved. Their eyes stared as if glued to the board where the red target string stretched from Snetterton to Schweinfurt. Again. A dull, empty ache gnawed at Andy's soul.

The officer aimed his swagger stick to a location above the Danube and below Gotha, Germany. "I don't need to tell you, men, this is a dangerous mission."

"These three Schweinfurt factories produce 42 percent of the ball bearings that keep the German planes flying. One Ju 88 twin-engine bomber requires 1,056 antifriction bearings. Their 88mm antiaircraft guns use 47 bearings and searchlights use 90. Production slowed with the August mission but increased again, and now those factories must be taken out. They're sitting pretty—waiting.

"The August Schweinfurt raid was disastrous," he continued. "We can't afford those losses. We can do better. We must! If we unload enough bombs, it'll slow the Germans down to a snail crawl. They're hacking away at our men on the ground, stopping their forward progress. This is our chance to put this war behind us. Are you with me?"

"Yes sir," shouted the men as one by one they stood up from their seats, shaking their fists in the air—both fists. To Andy, it was as if inside they rebelled against the mission.

"I can't hear you!"

"YES SIR!"

"Fifty-six P-47 Thunderbolts will escort you into German territory, but when half their fuel is spent, you know the drill," he added. "Sixty B-24s will also accompany you. If heavy cloud cover sets in at the IP, there'll be a secondary target.

"Antiaircraft completely surround the factories. The flak's thick enough to walk on," the officer said, circling the factories on the board. "Luftwaffe will be in abundance." He indicated several points on the map and added, "Note the North Sea air rescue positions."

Next, the officer went over the flying formation.

Andy steepled his hands under his chin. *No Purple-Heart corner, please.* He knew the tail end meant death for sure. One day he hoped to fly in the high squadron position in the front—lead plane. The sweetest words came a few minutes later when the officer pointed to the *Alley Cat*'s position as the deputy plane. "Yes!" he whispered.

The operations officer expected 300 German fighter planes. He identified the Rally Point on the map for hookup formation and the return flight. Andy felt every tick of the clock as the room filled with the smell of sweat from men facing death.

"Targets are socked in now, but the weather should clear later in the day. A few clouds will remain and provide good ground cover." The officer finished with radio communications and questions. The men filed out and walked over to the building housing their flight gear.

They slipped into heat suits, stepped into fur-lined boots, and picked up their flight gear, helmets, earphones, oxygen masks, flak jackets, and heavy gloves. Though their bodies slumped from the weight of protective gear, no one objected.

Andy imagined he could hear the fearful heartbeats of the men as they made their way to the waiting trucks.

Brad caught up with Bulldog, grabbed him by the shoulder, spun him around, and shouted, "You dare mouth that shit to me. I hope you and your captain's numbers are up today, chump."

Bulldog wrenched away from Brad, "Would that make you feel less guilty?"

Andy moved between them. "Not now!" He caught the collar of Brad's sheepskin jacket. "I'll deal with you when I get back. Now go do your job!"

"I can't wait, CAPTAIN!" *If this mission doesn't take you out, jerk, I'll get you somehow. You can't keep taking everything from me. I deserve a lot better. Why do they hate me?*

After shoving Brad aside, Andy glanced back over his shoulder. Brad stood with clinched fists, face flushed and seething. Bulldog caught up with Andy.

Andy shook his head. "I've never seen a guy with so much hatred. It's gonna do him in. Maybe he's petrified about this mission. But you wouldn't think he'd say anything like that if he believed he might be wiped out today."

Bulldog stopped beside Andy. "One day, you watch, I'm gonna box his ears off."

Andy whirled around facing Bulldog. "Drop it, Bulldog. Everyone's touchy now. Keep a lid on. Now!"

"Yes sir!" Bulldog clicked his heels and gave Andy an arrogant salute.

They climbed into the truck that drove them to the fog-shrouded hardstands where the planes waited.

Andy observed the tires scrunched low from the weight of the bomb-laden planes. The crew arrived at the plane for pre-flight inspection. All wore their chutes except Billy, the ball turret gunner.

"Gather 'round, fellas." Andy briefed the balance of the crew on the mission ahead. "You know the risk, but close it out. We'll get through this."

Nealy and Billy looked down, eyes fixed on the ground, facial muscles tense.

"Let's go get 'em," Bulldog shouted, slapping his hands together. "Ready?"

"Okay, let's do it," Andy finished. He searched the faces of the crew for weakness but saw none. Most of their tension and fear hid behind masks of bravado. "Let's make America proud!" He passed out gum to each crewman to relieve stress.

Everyone clapped except Nealy and Whitie. The crew made their way to the starboard entrance giving the *Alley Cat* a slap on her exterior before entering. Andy watched the same routine before each flight. He climbed the ladder, gave the *Alley Cat* her customary name dusting, and mumbled, "Bring us back, old gal." He boarded through the hatch below the cockpit and delivered the maps to Pops, the navigator.

He worked his way to Nealy and Whitie, giving them a confident jab of encouragement. "Hey, we're number one! We're the best! Let's show these guys how it's done." They returned an assuring salute. After he spoke to the individual crewmen, he returned to the cockpit where Tex listened to the crew ready reports.

Andy slid into the pilot's seat, all set for the engine check-off list. Tex called out each item, making certain not to miss any. He waited for a loud and clear response from Andy.

Flight time, 0800. The dark heavy clouds swung low and threatening, squeezing any sign of blue sky into oblivion like a signal of what lay ahead. Latest information stated the weather remained socked in at the IP, six hours away.

The agonized minutes of waiting, five, ten, fifteen, twenty…. Andy and the men sat in their stations, sweating in their heat suits while checking their guns repeatedly. Friendly bantering filled the cabin and through the intercom in an attempt to calm the nerves.

Andy put his arm on Tex's shoulder. "What's the long, quiet mug about?"

"Nothing for you to worry about."

"Come on, fellow. Can't hide from me."

"Got a letter yesterday." Tex stared straight ahead.

"So, everyone gets a letter now and then. Your parents?"

"No. Wish it was that simple."

"Okay. You got a letter."

"Everyone doesn't get a 'Dear John' letter."

"Oh crap. Didn't see that coming. Thought you and your girl planned to marry as soon as you got leave or go home, whichever came first."

"Wedding, yeah. But not mine. She met a fellow who worked in the same factory with her. Now they're getting married and I'm over here stuck in this blasted war while this draft dodger is doing my girl." Tex beat his hands on the control wheel.

"Damn! What bad luck."

"Now I got no reason to go home. Why should I care if I live or die?"

"Whoa. Come on, Tex. Snap out of it. It's not just you in this plane. There's nine others with good reasons to live. Look at Pops. He's got two little girls waiting for him."

"Sorry, Andy. You know I won't let you down." His eyes met Andy's, "Tell me, what you think. Coupled with all the Schweinfurt losses in August, no fighters to protect us, what's our odds?"

"Odds are as good as any, but better if we work perfectly as a team—as brothers. You know that. I want to know for sure if you are ready."

"I said, 'You can count on me.' Maybe I'll get a minor injury, get sent home and my gal will come running back."

"There ya go. Now let's get 'er done." Andy shoved his fist into Tex's shoulder. "You ready?"

"Yep." Tex's eyes glistened.

The signal came at 1000 (ten hundred hours) indicating the mission was a "go." The silence broke, engines sputtered, smoked, and groaned, cutting the air with their three-blade props until each engine became indistinguishable, soaring to a loud roar. Andy realized the mission had reached the scrub point. It was now or never. Onsite visibility reached one-quarter mile. Weather information indicated a clearing over the continent and on toward the IP. Mission operational.

*Alley Cat's* third engine balked at the start, but with a belch of black smoke, caught on the second attempt. The Fortress lined up in position on the tarmac, ready for takeoff. Andy revved up the *Cat's* engines, released the brakes, and off they went.

A little later, Tex announced, "Approaching 10,000 feet. Put on your oxygen masks." One by one, he spoke to each crewman, assured of their mask's function.

Andy, eyes forward said, "You okay, fellow?"

"Yep."

*Not good—too automatic. Gotta watch him.*

Andy searched the sky for the British Super Marine Spitfire fighters who would defend the heavies to France, replaced by P-47 Thunderbolts, escorting the flying armada to the German border and slightly beyond before turning back. An empty, sickening feeling crept over him. His innards shook. Stomach bile rose in his throat. He choked it back.

He reached in his pocket and rubbed the buckeye. August 17 was not that long ago and permanently engraved in his mind. *Will this be a repeat? Dear Lord, please let us survive this mission.* Silent prayers continued in his head. *I know, God, that all these men are praying as well. Keep us safe. Amen.*

## Over Schweinfurt, Germany

Black Thursday. The slaughter commenced. One by one, the fifty-six P-47 fighters sent to defend the 291 big friends on the Schweinfurt mission turned homeward over Aachen. Now abandoned, the squadrons tightened into combat formation. The deputy plane, the B-17G Flying Fortress, *Alley Cat*, flew slightly behind and to the right of the leader plane. The mission—knock out the ball-bearing plants in Schweinfurt, Germany. Again!

Between the bombers and their IP, Andy knew the Luftwaffe lay waiting in the clouds, crouching like tigers, ready to turn the sky into an easel of color filled with firing planes.

"Brace yourself, men." Andy sucked oxygen. "Hell's on its way! Fighters closing starboard. Watch our backs, Tony."

Sully popped his head to the side shouting from the top turret gunner position. "Holy shit! Bogies headed straight at us... stick 'em! More at three o'clock."

Rounds crackled from his twin 50s. As the fighter exposed its belly above the *Alley Cat*, a final blast demolished the bandit.

Sully shouted, "Oh, God, that was too close. Here comes another one!"

*Whumpf!* Something hit the *Alley Cat*. A cannon. The plane shook violently. Air gushed into the plane. The engines clapped with irregular rhythm.

Andy waited for the explosion, like thunder expected after a bright flash of lightning. His senses dulled—numbed with shock. Nothing.

"What happened?" Andy shouted over the intercom turning to scan as far back as he could see.

"Gone," Pops replied, giving the area a quick look-see.

"Gone? Where?" Andy kept his eyes peeled forward, resisting another urge to turn around.

"The shell came in one side and barreled out the other." Pops said.

Andy held the intercom to his mouth. "Damage report?"

"No severe damage," reverberated throughout the plane, as each crewman accessed his area.

"No vitals hit, Captain," Pops said.

*Whew!* Andy breathed a sigh of relief. *Thank you, God.*

Andy performed mechanically, carrying out instructions as if a book lay in front of him. His brain was on autopilot. *Tight formation. Don't let the fighters slip in. The staggered formation's gun power puts up a mighty front. Must not deviate from the mission.* Andy completed his pep talk to himself. The ability to stay detached from fear during battle had served him well.

"Tex."

No response.

Andy shouted, "Tex."

Still no response.

Andy tapped Tex on the shoulder.

"Huh?"

"Hey buddy, where are you? You better damn sight be with us completely. Shake it off!"

"I'm here," Tex said after exhaling.

"Snap out of it—now!" Andy scanned the sky knowing *his* spirit was used up long ago. *I'll fight, but what about Tex? God help us!*

The brief calm ended. A mêlée of enemy planes peppered the B-17s. The mighty Fortresses held rigid. The struggle was on. Bombers dropped from the sky, some like paper floating to the ground, while others plunged straight down, spewing earth high into the sky on impact. As downed B-17s and B-24s left gaps in the defensive box formation, others closed the openings. Andy watched parachutes drift through the air, while visible sections of planes and debris plummeted below. He knew the men in floating 'chutes prayed not to be shot, hit by shrapnel, or clipped by a fighter plane. Dangling under their parachutes, they became easy targets for the Luftwaffe fighters. Andy's stomach scrunched as if he took the hits himself. *No homecoming for them.*

A yellow-nosed 109 flew at Sully, firing into the top turret grazing his head. "You son-of-a-bitch!" He spun around, aimed his .50 caliber and fired, missing the Meg. His left earpiece—blown off. He touched the top of his ear. Blood trickled down his neck.

Another blast caught Whitie in the right arm. "Yeowwwww!" He rotated his gun, but before he could fire, another B-17 detonated the FW 190. Fragments cut a small hole in *Alley Cat's* starboard wing.

"Bandits at 12 o'clock!" Andy yelled through the intercom. His stomach tightened and nausea flooded his body. A gaggle of fighters converged directly in front of the formation with their guns blazing like flaming meteors. They closed to ramming distance, then fired, unleashing incomprehensible destruction to the bombers. The mighty 8th fought with a barrage of gunfire from the tight solid formation and sprayed the bogies with everything they had.

Luftwaffe fighters, intent on igniting bombs in the B-17's bellies, closed on the formation with winking lights flashing from their wings as they fired cannon shells and rockets into the bombers.

Andy strained to hold rigid formation in an impossible situation. Through one explosion after another, smoke black as tar, chunks of hot burning metal dotting the sky, and splinters of steel, they held firm toward the IP. Perspiration dripped from Andy's face and overflowed his chin cup.

Fire poured from the *Alley Cat*'s machine guns. Two, three, four, enemy planes lost their fight, but not before three B-17s exploded in midair.

"Hold her, Tex, hold her," Andy shouted over the deafening sound of the *Cat's* guns while incoming hits scored intermittingly. His only air supply dangled beneath his chin, "Damn it! We need ten hands right now."

Another B-17 in front of the *Alley Cat* exploded spewing blood, guts, and a rain of steel crashing into her. Andy was beyond terror. A strange calmness crept over him. Six miles high with no foxholes and no place for a graveyard. Total chaos surrounded them. Blood dribbled on the cockpit windshield, forming a frozen spider-like web.


"I'm hit, I'm hit," came a shout from the belly of the plane.

Pops grabbed the waist high support rope and hustled over the six-foot-long, eight-and a-half-inch wide catwalk to reach Billy. He hoisted him out of the ball turret hole, and slit Billy's pants with a knife from the medical kit. Blood gushed from his leg. After applying sulfa, he shoved gauze into the oozing hole in Billy's upper thigh.

He braced himself in the jostling plane while reaching for more gauze. "It's not that bad, Billy. Gotta stop the bleeding."

When Pops applied pressure on the wound, tears from pain fogged Billy's goggles.


Back in the cockpit, Andy searched the skies. *Is this our Armageddon? I will not accept death!*

"Twelve o'clock, Sully, Bulldog." Tex shouted, fear reflecting in his voice. Guns rattled, and tracers raced above the starboard wing.

"Fire on engine number two," Bulldog called.

Andy feathered the engine twice before the fire snuffed out. He lunged forward and caught sight of a Me-109 firing a 20mm cannon into the *Alley Cat*. The *Cat* shuddered from the impact and the recoil of the .50 caliber guns firing simultaneously. The Me-109 exploded directly in front, and seconds later the *Alley Cat* flew through the disintegrating plane. More blood spattered the cockpit windshield and bombardier Plexiglas.

"I can't see—can't see," Bulldog shouted. "Need a windshield wiper!"

Andy shot a glance at the number two engine and made eye contact with the pilot of a Focke-Wolf 190 passing off the port wing.

"Pops! What's the damage?" Andy yelled, holding open his mouthpiece.

"We've got a hole in our portside roof, Capt'n. Nobody critical."

Another gaggle of fighters burst in waves through the smoke. "12 o'clock!" Andy bellowed through the intercom.

The .50 caliber guns poured into the fighter planes. Pops slipped down into Billy's ball turret gunner position to catch fighters sneaking in below. The *Alley Cat* shuddered violently but persisted undaunted on her course.

The slogging continued, and one by one, B-17s dropped from the sky, as did German fighters. Fireballs lit up the heavens like the fourth of July.

Pops looked up from below to see Nealy cowering against the wall of the plane. He climbed from Billy's bubble, caught the left waist gunner's front jacket and yanked him upright. Vomit oozed from Nealy's mouth. "What the hell are you doing, man? Get over there and do your job!"

Nealy slid back down. His oxygen mask dangled loosely. Pops slipped the oxygen mask over Nealy's face.

He bopped Nealy's head, "Come on, Nealy, we're depending on you." Pops' face turned crimson as he dragged Nealy to his feet, shaking him all the way. "We're all scared, man. You got a sick Dad back home who needs your help, don't ya? How about your mom? What would she do if you didn't come back? Come on, Nealy, buck up!"

Nealy shook his head as if clearing a fog. Trembling, he stretched out his arms, pushed his oxygen mask aside, spat the vomit down near his feet, and returned to the waist gunner section. He automatically reached out and clutched the machine gun after catching sight of a FW190 bearing down on them. Nealy was back. Robotically he spun his .50 caliber around and fired at the fighter.

"Way to go!" Pops gave him a pat on the butt, and returned to Billy's bubble, mixing it up, battling the fighters, and rejoining the maelstrom.


"Bandits, 2 o'clock…bandits 6 o'clock…bandits 10 o'clock…," flooded the *Cat's* intercom. The conflict continued for what seemed like hours to Andy. Undeterred, the *Alley Cat's* crew fought with all they had.

At intervals, Andy shouted to the crew, "We're gonna make it, fellas. I got a feeling." No reply was heard over the roar of the plane, the deafening sound of the guns, and the strain and groans of fighters diving in and out.

After persistent attacks, the fighters unexpectedly disappeared. Andy knew they were still attacking the tail end of the formation.

*Fighters gone!* Andy breathed a sigh of relief. *We're still flying, thank God. She's a tough old gal, this Alley Cat. Must be full of holes this time around. Thank God for this tank of a plane!*

"You okay, Tex?"

"Yeah, I suddenly realized I don't want to die. That mêlée back yonder scared the shit out of me."

"Welcome back, 'ole buddy."

Tex leaned forward. "Flak ahead."

"Yeah. Entering target area." Andy pressed his intercom. "Report damage assessment. Entering IP."

"Billy's okay, Captain. He's putting pressure on his leg. Think he'll be back with us before we reach IP. Bleeding's stopped. Minimal damage to the ball turret," Pops replied.

"No serious damage—reloading ammunition," Bulldog reported.

"All on go, no left earphone—holes all over top turret—air gushing through—manageable. Both guns operable," Sully reported.

"Tolerable…all guns working and ammunition boxes moved in and connected, no time to test them…operable damage in the tail gunner section," the reports poured in. Miraculous news to Andy's ears.

He noted no serious damage to the cockpit. Small fractures in the windshield but no major instrument damage.

The formation had crossed the River Rhine, and now approached central Germany. Andy scrutinized a wall of antiaircraft flak stretched out ahead such as they had never seen before—flak like a solid black carpet rolled out to greet them. Antiaircraft put up a "box barrage" in front of the squadrons—but the B-17s' engines hummed on.

No visual of the target site. Flak pinged against the *Cat* and some penetrated the fuselage.

Andy and Tex fought with all they had to keep the plane on target. Andy's arms ached from the strain and his stiff body begged for relief. The smoke from the exploding flak seeped into their oxygen masks and mingled with the stale air and oil fumes that filled the plane. Radio silence had broken from the moment they encountered the German Luftwaffe. A steady turbulence from bursting flak shook the plane.

A coded call came from the lead plane, "Visual target. Bomb bay doors open."

"Bomb bay doors open," Andy repeated through the intercom. "Bulldog. You got it!"

Bulldog switched the *Cat's* controls to the Norden Bombsight, which took over flying the plane, holding it rigid to the target.

He had already shuffled the stack of spare flak jackets at his sides and adjusted his flak helmet. He ignored the guns, pressed forward, readying the Norden Bombsite in front of him. The bomb selector box was mounted on the fuselage wall, and he had preset the bomb intervalometer, setting the spacing of the bomb releases.

"Bomb bay doors open?" Bulldog double-checked.

"Yes sir," a reply came from the waist section.

Bulldog's Plexiglas nose spattered with human fragments cut his visibility to fifty percent from the chin turret below his feet. The unattended twin 50s swiveled, rotated first left, then right.

With the lull in the gruesome battle, Bulldog watched for the lead ship's smoke bomb drop, signaling the formation to "lay eggs."

Bulldog spotted the smoke bomb. "Hold it! Pickles hot!" he announced. Once the leader salvoed, all B-17s dropped their loads. The bombsight released the *Cat's* bombs, and the Fortress bounced skyward as the ship's cargo whistled its way to an earthly destination.

Counting, Bulldog realized all bombs did not fall. "Captain. Got a stuck bomb. I'll grab a screwdriver and go trip the release mechanism." He attached a portable oxygen bottle to his mask and headed to the bomb bay. Encumbered with bulky clothing, he worked his way to the bomb bay, straddling the catwalk over the opened doors. He shoved the screwdriver in like a wedge, ready to unstick the catch but hesitated until a plane cleared below. He cringed at his vulnerable position with flak erupting beneath his feet near the belly of the *Alley Cat*. After tripping the release, the last of the 250-pound G.P. bombs took a destructive nosedive.

"Captain! Pull up! Pull up! B-17 climbing below!" Bulldog shouted.

Instantly, Andy pulled the controls with strained muscles and forced the *Alley Cat* up and to the right, narrowly avoiding a collision.

"Whew doggies!" Bulldog sighed. The screwdriver slipped through his bulky gloves. He stooped down to retrieve the tool when a huge jolt hit the Fortress throwing him into the side of the plane. He regained his balance and headed back to his section. A gush of air from the front of the plane blasted him square in the face, slowing his return to the bombardier section. Pops' papers on the navigator's table behind the bombardier section had blown away. Only a silk map remained, tacked securely to his desk.

Once Bulldog's section came into view, he felt blood drain from his face. He grabbed his mouthpiece.

"It's gone, Captain."

"What's gone?" Andy asked.

"The bubble. The Plexiglas. It's blown off. So's the back of my seat."

"Stay clear, Bulldog. No need to take any chances."

Bulldog shoved the clutter aside and checked the lower section of his seat for sturdiness. "I gotta strap to hold my ass in the seat, Captain." He strapped himself in, caught his twin 50s as a FW-190 made a head-on pass at the *Alley Cat*.

"Come on back, you bastards!" Bulldog swung the 50s around and clipped the wing of a 109, sending him in a blaze to earth, black smoke trailing.

Bulldog switched from the portable bottle to regular oxygen hookup. His stack of flak vests had disappeared. No more protection.

Andy brushed away any thought of innocent people dying beneath the black smoke. *Stop the factory production.* He knew the minute they cleared the carpet of black flak hell would resume. He kept his focus, squeezed the intercom, "Bandits hidden now—laying low. Heads up. Stay alert."

He checked the temperature gauge—it read minus thirty. Frigid air rushed through the fuselage like a wind tunnel. Frostbite now a real possibility. Fearful the men might be deprived of oxygen without realizing it, Andy reminded the crew over the intercom, "Squeeze your oxygen masks. Break up the frozen moisture. Shake out the ice."

"Out of formation now, heading for rendezvous spot. Starting evasive action," Andy continued. Minus the bombs, the plane responded with ease.

Seconds later, the Luftwaffe charged in, one wave after another, doggedly attacking the bombers.

"Tex. Hold her steady. Hang in there!"

"I'm holding with everything I got, Capt'n!"

"Look out, Sully!" Andy yelled into his mouthpiece. A Messerschmidt's belly whizzed above them—its wash rocked the *Cat*.

Sully shouted, "Missed, Captain, couldn't swing around in time."

The *Alley Cat* shook as if it might break apart any minute. Andy watched with horror. More B-17s dropping like autumn leaves in a windstorm.

A metal object burst through the windshield between Andy and Tex and buried itself in the floor. Andy felt the cold hand of death reach for him.

"You all right, Tex?"

"Ye gads, that was close." Tex felt for damage under his jacket. "We're sitting ducks. I don't want to die!"

"Don't you fall apart on me, buster. Get hold of yourself. NOW!"

"Bulldog. You still with us?"

"Yeeeeeaaaaaaah." He sprayed rounds at a FW 190 bearing down on them. The fighter exploded in midair, and the *Cat* flew under it. A lone piece of metal zoomed pass Bulldog and sliced into the navigator's panel.

Andy called to his right waist gunner. "Come in, Whitie. Come in, Whitie." Nothing.

"Pops. Check on Whitie."

The plane lunged while Pops struggled to the back. Shots spewed from Nealy's left waist position opposite Whitie. No sound from Whitie. Pops found him sprawled on the floor of the plane, blood seeping from his cap. He grabbed an oxygen bottle and hooked it up to Whitie.

"Mom? Mom?" Whitie whispered at the touch of Pops' hand.

"It's Pops, Whitie. Take it easy. You're gonna be all right." He removed Whitie's blood-soaked flight cap, split into two pieces. The puddle of blood quickly froze. Pops slipped off his gloves, grabbed some gauze, and wiped the top of Whitie's head. Shrapnel drove straight down the middle of Whitie's curly brown hair penetrating his scalp from front to back.

"Captain, Whitie's down. He'll be all right. Shrapnel knocked him out cold."

"Roger, Pops. Paulie, shift over to the right waist gunner position," Andy ordered.

"Whitie's oxygen mask...shot off. He's on a pieced together mask and portable bottle. Got an extra mask?" Pops asked.

No response.

"Pops. Keep changing bottles. How many extras?"

"Only five."

"After we get out of Germany, we'll drop down to 10,000 feet."

"Captain, that's totally against regulations!" Tex glared at Andy.

"I won't let Whitie die. He'll be out of oxygen in less than two hours."

"You could be court-martialed, sir."

"I know, I know. I'll take my chances. Watch it!" Andy shouted.

A piece of shrapnel came through the left windshield. It narrowly missed the radio system.

"Tex, they just don't give up."

"Yeah, and look at the price they pay. Us, too."

"Oh, my God!" Andy's heart sank as he watched the lead plane, piloted by Maj. Gaither, burst into flames when a 109 fighter on a suicide mission barreled head on into the plane. "It's going down, Tex. One, two, three...no, seven men bailed out! Do you see any more?"

"Look out," Tex shouted spontaneously to the men parachuting down.

A bandit made a pass and fired into three of them. Andy watched as the men went limp. Death in an instant. The chutes carrying their remains continued their descent to earth.

Andy turned away, focused on the situation at hand, and said in a barely audible voice, "We're lead plane now." He slipped the *Cat* into the lead slot and continued homeward, placing his emotions on hold. Air gushed through the entire body of the plane through holes in the cockpit windshield and the missing Plexiglas in the bombardier section. Intolerable cold penetrated their heat suits.

Andy's teeth chattered from the icy blast. He lifted his sheepskin collar on his flight jacket, marveling at the fact that during heavy battle, he never felt cold. Pressing his mouthpiece, "Navigator, need some help here."

Pops hustled back to his station calling out the position points to Andy.

"*Alley Cat* to *Big Bear*, come in. Come in, *Big Bear*," Andy called to Lt. Delinger's plane.

"Big Bear here," Lt. Delinger responded from the formation slot left of the *Cat*.

"We've got a problem. We have only five spare oxygen bottles for my injured crewman. In two hours, we gotta drop down to 10,000 feet. That'll put us over France. Be prepared to take the lead then."

"Roger, *Alley Cat*."

Though the fighting waned for the *Alley Cat* as the formation approached the Rhine, Andy knew "tail end Charley" battled for their very existence. He anguished over the fact that he could do nothing to help them—his friends—his buddies.

He swiped perspiration—frozen sweat—from his forehead and glanced at a ghostly white Tex. "How many planes do you think went down?"

Tex plugged his right gloved hand into a second gaping hole in the cockpit side wall. "Dozens. Don't want to think about it."

An hour and a half later, Pops advised, "Switched the last oxygen bottle for Whitie, Captain."

"I hear ya, Pops."

"We have about thirty minutes before dropping down to 10,000 feet. It'll be dangerous, but we should be near the coast of France."

"You sure about this, Captain?" Fear etched itself on Tex's face.

"Yes. I'll take the heat. We'll fly so low, folks below won't have time to react."

Thirty minutes later, Andy advised the crew, "Dropping down to 10,000 feet. After leveling off, remove your oxygen masks. Heading home, fellas. Bulldog?"

"Right behind ya. Had to get away from that surging wind below."

Andy relayed his situation to the new lead plane. Though against mission rules, he observed five B-17s dropped down to protect the *Alley Cat* on the flight home.

"Paulie, send a radio message to headquarters relaying our emergency."

"Roger, Captain."

The flight back to the base was uneventful until a new discovery. "Tex, the landing flaps aren't working. How about taking a 'look-see' from the top turret."

"Right away, Captain." Tex climbed to the top turret and reported, "The wings are loaded with holes and the landing flaps are shot to hell and back."

"Paulie, send another message. No flaps."

"Yes sir, Captain."

"This'll be rough, Tex." *Just when we were home free!*

# Chapter Ten

## Crash Landing

Andy sighted the airfield, and the knots in his stomach relaxed. But he knew they weren't finished. Not yet. He squeezed the intercom. "Brace yourselves. Rough landing coming up. Flaps almost gone. Need every bit of runway and then some. Hang tight!"

Red light on, the *Cat's* turn came soon enough with fire engines and medical trucks racing to the end of the runway. Andy checked the instruments, the B-17s circling the sky queued for landing, a couple of B-17s in front of the *Alley Cat,* and eyed the edge of the runway to hold the *Cat* steady for a balanced landing.

Bulldog sped back to the bombardier section as an extra pair of eyes. "Pull up, pull up! A flaming Fort's on the runway!"

"Whoa!" Andy firewalled the throttles and pulled the control wheel back.

"Hot doggies!" Bulldog shouted.

A thunderous explosion rocked the plane. "Hold it!" Andy struggled to regain control of the plane. "Pull Tex, pull!" *Oh, God!*

"Whew doggies! We missed it by a hair!" Bulldog watched the *Alley Cat* climb above the death trap below.

Settling into a cool controlled voice Andy said, "Well fellas, that was a close one—need another pass." He circled the field and slipped into the landing pattern once again.

"Without flaps, our runway just got smaller. Hang tight fellas!" Andy throttled back and when the *Alley Cat* touched down, he cut the engines and gently tapped the brakes.

"She's eating up the runway!" Tex's voice now shrill.

"Ride her out through the grass," Andy said. He steered the *Cat* left off the end of the runway, turning as sharp as possible without dipping the port wing. The tall grass cut the Fort's speed, and it gradually rolled to a stop—where the grass ended and the British airstrip began.

Fire and medical trucks arrived at the *Alley Cat*, lights flashing and sirens blasting.

Andy, knees shaking, dropped down through the hatch and yanked off his helmet. He brushed his hand over the tips of his hair and knew it stood as erect as needles in a pincushion. Waves of relief rippled his spine. He led the medical men to the starboard entrance closest to the crewmen. "Three injured—one serious."

Andy rejoined Tex in the cockpit for final shutdown checklist and left through the hatch after completing the task. Andy turned his eyes to the starless sky. He needed that moment to reflect—to realize he was alive—to give thanks. The mist coated his face.

Afterward, Andy climbed into the waiting truck with his other crewmen. "We need to take a moment to say a prayer for our fallen comrades."

Andy searched the faces of the remaining crewmen and it mirrored what was in his heart—fear for what they had just encountered—joy for coming through it—realization of the losses.

A short time later, they arrived at the debriefing building, where it was quiet as a tomb. Exhausted and hungry as they were, it was imperative that Andy and the other officers record information still fresh in their memories.

"Capt. Walters, what do you estimate our losses to be?" the interrogation officer asked.

"At least fifteen percent, I believe—maybe more. They dropped out of the sky like flies. Lots of aircraft crippled," Andy replied softly, afraid to believe his own voice. "Most horrible sight I've ever seen. A bloodbath. Remnants remain on my windshield—my friends."

"I'm afraid to ask. Do you know how many didn't come back?" Andy continued, head bent down, eyes staring at the floor. Not wanting to hear the answer, he closed his eyes, his mind, and the conversation.

"We estimate twenty percent, Captain. Sixty B-17s with possibly around 140 damaged. The worst ever. Maybe now, they won't fly missions into Germany until fighter planes can protect you fellows. All right. Go get something to eat and get some rest."

Andy heard the words, but refused to acknowledge them.

After forty-five minutes, Andy, Tex, Bulldog, and Pops were dismissed, loaded into a jeep, and taken to the mess hall. Andy could see his officers were visibly weak from the lack of food and shaken from their ordeal.

The aroma of baked ham filled the mess hall but did little to tickle his taste buds. No celebration that night. The mess hall was silent—like death.

"It's been a long time since breakfast." Andy lifted a spoonful of mashed potatoes and gravy. Flashes of friends blown out of the sky raced before him. Unable to shake the images, he shoved his plate forward, excused himself, and left the mess hall. Alone. He wanted time to think.

The distance from the mess hall to the field hospital gave him time to think. He'd check on his injured crew—Whitie, the most serious, then Billy, and Sully. "Thank you, God, for allowing us to survive this maelstrom," Andy said aloud, staring into the heavens. *He spared us only to die another day.*

Andy entered the base hospital, and announced at the desk. "I'm Capt. Walters here to check on three of my men who were brought in an hour or so ago."

"Sir, we have been swamped with injured men from this last mission. The nurses and doctors are overloaded at this point. I appreciate your concern about your men, but I would suggest that you wait until tomorrow to check on them. Here, write their names and I'll get a message to let you know if any are seriously insured regardless of the hour. Also, include your name and contact information. I'm sorry I couldn't do more for you right now, sir."

"Thanks, Private. I appreciate your help."

Andy flipped his sheepskin collar up, crammed his hands in his pockets, locking out the cold dampness and mist while pushing the limits of his energy to walk from the field hospital. Pain thrust itself through the depth of every bone in his body. The whole of his life rested on his own shoulders. He had been to hell and back. He'd been "baptized by fire" and survived and so had his crew.

The night fog rolled in, matching Andy's anguish. Distant giggles drifted through the dense fog toward him. He wondered how they could laugh as if there were no dying or killing anywhere.

He could not turn off his thoughts. *I want to laugh again. If I could only shut out this day, like it never happened. We did our jobs. But, God, how many lives did we lose? Yeah, and we saved many, many more by destroying those factories. That means fewer fighters, less bombing. That's good. Then why do I feel so bad?* He reached in his pocket, picked up the buckeye, and rolled it around in his hand.

Footsteps closed in on Andy, interrupting the gruesome reflections of the day's mission. Six Red Cross nurses broke through the fog immediately in front of him. Andy tipped his captain's hat, stepped aside, and continued on his way to the barracks.

"Andy?" one of the girls called after passing. He turned around and there she stood, waiting, wide eyed.

"Yes?" He took a few steps toward her.

"Andy. It's Rose."

"Good gosh!"

Rose moved closer to him. "I thought I'd never see you again."

Andy rushed in, wrapped his arms around her, and pulled her into his chest. "Rose, I couldn't find you anywhere—asked everyone. No one knew."

"I know, I know. What are you doing out here?"

He glanced at his watch and replied, "We've been up since 0500. Gotta be eighteen hours." He pushed back, lowered his head, and kicked a rock. "I was on my way back from the hospital. Three of my crew were injured today. I just left the hospital. We lost a ton of B-17s. A bloody massacre."

He tried to lighten the conversation—to put the mission behind him. "So, tell me. Where are you stationed? I wrote Mom to get an address from your family."

Rose ignored his question, stepped back as if checking him over. "You look good, and your dimple is still there." Mischief reflected from her eyes. "I'm really glad to see you."

Oblivious of the girls in the distant fog waiting for her, Andy caught her hands and stared into her eyes. "All I've been able to think about is seeing you in the club that night. I can't get you out of my mind."

Rose stared downward and gazed back into Andy's eyes. "I hope not. You're in my thoughts as well, Andy. I've been so worried about you—not knowing where you were—if you were dead or alive. Thank goodness I found you."

"That's my line." He smiled and pulled her close to him.

A call came from one of the nurses. "Come on, Rose. Now!"

"Andy, we arrived for our new assignment only an hour ago. The hospital is desperate for help. I'm on duty for the next twelve hours. Our shift will get back to normal after tonight. I've got to go. Don't you dare disappear on me again."

"No way. Now that I've found you, I'll never let you go again. Can we meet after you go off duty tomorrow? We won't be flying until they repair our plane; probably a week or so before the *Cat's* ready."

"Wait for me at the front of the field hospital at 1200 tomorrow. Oh, Andy. I'm thrilled to see you." She hugged him tight, and vanished in the fog.

Andy continued on to the barracks filled with nothing but thoughts of Rose. His pace quickened as he cut a path through the fog, hands in his pockets, rubbing the buckeye while his spirit soared.

The dangling ceiling lights greeted him as he walked through the barracks' door.

"Hey, you didn't eat your chow tonight." Bulldog wore a worrisome frown.

"Yeah I know. Not hungry. Tomorrow I'll make up for it."

Andy lay on his bunk, the mission still raw on his mind, and he longed for a day of peace and no dying. With Rose back in his life, thoughts of her softened the horror of the day, but could never block it out. No writing that night. Sleep came hard after his eyes closed.

The next day the grass wasn't less green because the men had died. The sky wasn't less blue because of the deaths under it. The birds didn't stop singing because of the dead. It was just another day unlike the day before. Andy refused to spend hours dwelling on the darkness of earlier days.

He jumped out of bed, anticipating his meeting with Rose. Though he could not see her until noon, he hurried with Bulldog, Pops, and Tex to the mess hall for breakfast. The country air smelled unusually clean. The unsullied wind blew the sadness from his soul. The sun burned off the fog early in the day, and the foliage glistened as the dew slipped to the ground below. A good day for walking.

Andy made a feeble attempt to contain his excitement. "Hey, fellas. You won't believe who I ran into in the fog last night."

"Who?" Bulldog turned toward Andy.

"Rose."

"What? That's not possible here in the boonies."

"Yeah. Rose."

"Andy, I swear. You're the luckiest son-of-a-gun I ever met," Tex drawled. He took off his hat and scratched his head. "How can this be?"

"I'm just a good man, fellas. That's all." Andy made light of the situation, slapping Tex on the back. "Hang in there, your day'll come soon."

"Well I'll be a monkey's uncle. With that kind of luck, I'll fly in your plane any day." Bulldog rubbed his hands together and looked skyward. "I guess yesterday was the *Alley Cat's* lucky day. I'm thankful to be here—to go to mess hall—even to eat those danged ole powdered eggs."

"Thank God, it wasn't our time." Andy had never seen Bulldog so serious. "Hey look. Let's shake it off. Our job is by no means done. Think of the lives we saved yesterday by destroying or slowing down the ball-bearing factories. Fewer fighters will fly."

"Don't know about you fellas, but I'm starving. Andy, that's great news about Rose," Tex said, lightening the mood.

"Yeah, Andy. That's terrific." Bulldog said. "When will we get a another glimpse of this doll?" He grabbed Andy's arm and ushered him along the dirt path.

They arrived at the mess hall, and the aroma of fried bacon and sausage filled the large building. The bright, airy room had rows of wooden tables and chairs, high white ceilings, and off-white walls displaying American graffiti. Andy smiled as he observed individual renditions of "Kilroy Was Here" decorating a small section of the wall.

"That looks like your drawing, Bulldog, oversized and out of proportions."

"Now, Andy," Bulldog replied.

"Hey, why the long face?" Andy caught Bulldog's arm. "One minute you light up like a Christmas tree, the next, you look as low as Kilroy."

"You know I ain't never run from nothin', but yesterday got too close to home. Look at Whitie." He wouldn't look in Andy's eyes. "I need to get home. Got a letter from my sister. Says Ma's got cancer. Don't know nothing else and God knows how old this letter is."

"Bulldog, I'm sorry about your mom. Glad you told me. Don't keep stuff like this inside." Andy continued. "You know they aren't allowing any leave now."

"I know that, and I ain't gonna leave the bombardier section empty."

Andy slapped him on the back. "We'll get through this, ole buddy. All of us have those thoughts. You wouldn't be human if you didn't."

"Awe, don't worry none 'bout me. I'll snap out of it as soon as my belly gets full."

Andy thought breakfast would never end, and the morning dragged on. After returning to the barracks, he worked off his excess energy by pacing back and forth until he finally decided to walk to the field hospital, visit his crewmen, and meet Rose. The old Andy had returned, and his heart beat a little faster with anticipation. *What a wonderful world! Just one day makes a difference. Far better than Black Thursday. Thank God, I don't have to write a letter to a crewman's family, and I pray I never will. Rose. That's it. Think about Rose. Yeah.*

At the field hospital, Andy went straight to Whitie's bed.

"Hey, fella. Looks like a white football helmet you got there. How ya feeling?"

The only thing showing on Whitie's head was his face. "Pretty good, sir. Except they shaved my head like when we first joined up." He lifted his head a tiny bit. "You won't believe the nurses making a fuss over me. I got my pick."

"Great, but whatcha gonna do after you get one?"

"Awe shucks, Captain. I was a lady's man long before this war. Bet you can't keep up with me."

"I would have never guessed. You're so quiet. I'm not trying anymore. Got the one and only."

"And if someone else came along, you'd pass her by?"

"Yes sir. You bet."

"Captain, you got it bad."

"Yep. But how about you?"

"I'm better than yesterday. How's the rest of the crew?"

"Billy has a tough thigh injury, but he can still walk. Sully had the tip of his ear clipped. He's fine now. They're in the back of the room. Guess you've been sleeping a bunch, huh?"

"Yes sir. I'll be back before you know it. Wouldn't want to miss the next mission. How many missions now? Twenty-five?"

"That's right. Listen, get some rest, and I'll check on the other men. See you tomorrow."

"Yes sir. Thanks for coming."

Andy shook Whitie's hand and made his way between the rows of beds lining each side of the spacious room. Sully sat on the edge of Billy's bed, dealing cards. A bandage the size of a grapefruit covered the left side of Sully's head. Billy's leg stretched out on the bed for support.

"What's this? You fellas aren't hurt. You just wanted an excuse to have a few days off," Andy quipped. "What a poor pretext for a crew. Y'all need to make room for injured men." He shocked himself by his own jubilation after the gut-wrenching events of their last mission.

"Morning, sir. 'Preciate you coming by," Sully responded. "I'm growing a new ear under this bulk." He moved his hand up to his bandage.

"How ya doing, Billy?" Andy asked as he moved over to peek at Billy's cards. "That's a full house if I ever saw one."

"You lucky stiff." Sully threw in his cards.

"I'm fine, sir. They said it's gonna heal real good." Billy pitched his cards down and chuckled. "You got suckered, Sully." He brushed his right fingers through his pompadour. His thin face disclosed every skeletal bone.

"Damn you, Billy. Drat it! I'll get even—count on it!" Sully gathered his cards.

"That's swell, Billy. We'll be waiting for you. What would I do without my best ball turret gunner?"

"Thank you, sir," Billy said, his mouth curving into a rare smile.

Andy squinted around the room searching for Rose. She was nowhere in sight. He checked his watch and noticed both hands rested on 1200.

"Gentlemen, I'll see y'all later. Take care." Andy shook hands with both men and walked away from the antiseptic scent of Mercurochrome and alcohol. He waited outside of the hospital...and waited. No sign of Rose. He resumed his pacing, back and forth, scuffing up the dirt as he walked. Still no Rose. *Maybe she's not gonna show. Maybe she doesn't care for me. Or maybe she pretended "nice" because I'm from her hometown. That must be it.* Hands clasped behind his back, he continued pacing.

"Andy!"

*At last!* He twisted around and was taken aback by her alluring beauty, eyes that sparkled even after twelve hours of work. Her navy blue cape flapped in the breeze, while her blonde hair streamed along with every step and shimmered in the noonday sun.

"Sorry I'm late," her cheeks rosy from the rush.

"Just glad you're here." He caught her arm and led her away from the hospital. "You tired?"

"We ran around like crazy last night. The ones who made it back from Schweinfurt are in critical condition. Six died, two during surgery and four more waiting surgery. It's been an overwhelming day with such suffering. I can't remember when I've seen this many severely injured men."

Andy put his arm around her shoulders, pulled her close to his side as they walked together. "I know. That's why they named the mission, 'Black Thursday.' I talked with the major briefly. He said of the 291 bombers on the mission, at least five crashed once they crossed the North Sea, twelve had to be scrapped because of severe damage and the rest had to be repaired before flying again. I've not been able to put it out of my mind. You've seen the injured. We lost sixty bombers again and 639 men. Can you believe it—639 men!"

"Oh Andy, I'm thankful you made it back. I'm terribly afraid for you." Rose slipped her arm around his back and looked up into his eyes.

Tears glistened on her cheeks and with his thumbs, he brushed the warm tears from her red cheeks. "Don't worry. "I'll always come back to you." He leaned down and lightly touched her lips with his. She reeled around choking back a sob.

"What's wrong?" Andy blinked, startled by her reaction.

"You haven't done anything wrong, Andy. It's me. I'm so frightened. I'm afraid to love you. What if you don't come back?"

She didn't wait for his answer. Like turning a page, she changed. She hooked her arm into his and taunted him with a playful smile. "Today's our day. Let's put everything serious behind us and have some fun."

Her winsome smile astounded him. "Come on," he said. "We'll hitch a ride into town, grab a bite to eat, and walk back. The white flag's up and we won't be flying tomorrow."

"Love it! I don't have to be back at the hospital until 0600 tomorrow. At least I'll catch up on my sleep tonight."

A few minutes later, Andy flagged a RAF (Royal Air Force) jeep headed in the direction of Dappleville.

"Heading to town?" Andy asked.

"Indeed. Hop in, mate."

"Step up, Rose," Andy said, as he helped her into the front seat and he in the back.

The olive jeep with no top was breezy on the cool October day. Rose removed her nurse's hat, while Andy secured his officer's cap. The jeep swerved right and left around and over potholes carved out of the partially paved road. Rose's hair flowed wildly as the jeep sliced through the air. She wrapped the blue cape tightly around her ample bosom.

Three miles later and a fair distance from the east coast, they arrived at McAllister's, according to the driver, the best pub in town.

"Thanks, buddy." Andy helped Rose from the jeep.

"That wasn't a minute too soon. I almost froze." She rubbed her ears and then pinned on her nurse's hat.

"Yeah. I should've put you in the back seat with me where I could have wrapped you in my arms." He put his arm around her shoulders as they made their way across the road to the pub, a large white house with tall red brick chimneys on each end.

They entered a huge room with tall ceilings, and the Wurlitzer Jukebox played Billie Holiday singing "I'll Be Seeing You." Cigarette smoke hung low and the scent of beer filled the air. Andy noticed a group of small snugs (booths) enclosed on three sides by curtains mounted above the seats. The front view faced an oversized brick fireplace with flames popping and cracking. They walked along the row of snugs until they found an empty one. The wooden floors creaked with each step.

"How'd you like this?" Andy slid the front curtain across a rod and back again. "We can close the front for privacy." He gazed at the rustic beams and the light paneling covering the pub's walls.

Rose glanced around the room. "So nice and cozy with those bright yellow and green floral curtains. Down right homey."

Andy removed Rose's cape, hooked it on a wooden peg, and helped her into the booth. "Back in a minute." He walked up to the bar and ordered a Shandy (ale mixed with ginger beer) and Bass Ale. While he returned to the snug, the song "I'll Be Seeing You" replayed and wove a worrisome pattern into a new relationship. *Hardly a promise of a future.*

"I love that song," Rose whispered and hummed along with the music.

"Let's make it 'our' song," he said, watching her twist a blonde strand of hair.

She sent him a smile that went straight to his heart.

Andy raised his mug, "To us!" He took several swallows and let the warm ale flow down his dry throat, calming his anxiety. He stared into the fireplace for several seconds before searching for Rose's hand. Their eyes met and a sensuous light passed between them. Euphoria swept over him. His gaze traveled her face in search of a small trace of mutual feelings.

"Oh, Andy. With all those girls chasing you back home, don't you have a special gal? You're probably just lonely." She smiled innocently and, with her free hand, pushed stray tendrils back from her cheek.

"Not so you'd notice. I've known you all my life and never dreamt I'd feel this way. Young and stupid—that was me. I've changed. War did that to me—to us all." He let go of her hand and wrapped both hands around his mug.

"You know, flying with the Luftwaffe raining fire on us, black flak, planes exploding in midair, others careening to earth disintegrating into balls of fire, parachutes becoming target practice for the bandits—that's what war does to a man. The thought of never loving you, never seeing your radiant smile, never touching your soft skin, would be unbearable. To leave this world in a burning ball of flame would be a tragic loss, if I hadn't fallen in love with you. Knowing you makes it easier to bear the horror of this bloodbath. It gives me hope." Andy swallowed a sip of beer, placed the mug on the wood carvings on the table, pulled her close, and cradled her in his arms. He kissed her gently on the forehead.

"That's so sweet, Andy. I'm so glad you came back into my life." She nestled into his arms, reached up and ran her fingers through his hair.

He leaned over and kissed her. Passionately.

Rose responded eagerly until a waitress wearing a white pinny (apron) interrupted them to take a lunch order. "Sorry my loves, for breaking in, but are you feeling peckish (hungry)? I've managed to get some nice cheddar for the ploughman's, but it's going fast."

Andy turned his head and smiled at the waitress. "Ploughman's lunch?"

"Never had it before? It's what ploughmen have when they're in the fields. Cheese, bread, onion, and pickle. A simple lunch to carry in yer handkerchief, see?"

"Not sure I want that, ma'am." Andy looked at Rose for her response.

The waitress wiggled her right forefinger left to right. "You must try it, darlin'. You'll love it. I'll put it all out special on me best china, of course. I've got a cottage loaf, which you'll like. White bread, very refined. And you'll love my apple and tomato pickle recipe. Go on. Have a go. It's delicious served with a pint of bitter."

"Oh let's try it, Andy. It'll be wonderful." Rose looked up at him with dancing eyes.

"All right. We'll have a go at it," Andy said, poking fun at the waitress. She acknowledged it with a mock curtsey and an impish smirk and swished away.

He smiled and once again focused on Rose. "I wish we could stay here forever. But there's a whole world out there—a good world. We have a future to plan for."

"Tell me more, Andy." Rose leaned back and rested against him.

With his right hand, he drew an invisible house on the table. "Our house." Then he drew two invisible stick figures arm in arm. "You. Me." Next, he placed two little stick figures in front of the larger figures. "Our children."

Rose smiled. "Girls or boys."

"A girl *and* a boy."

She reached up, put her arms around his neck, and pulled his head down to her. Andy's heart pounded in an erratic rhythm, sending blood spiraling through his veins. He reached over and closed the curtains across the front of the snug blocking the sizzling fireplace embers. As his body pressed against her breasts, his heart pounded against hers.

A short time later, the waitress appeared, peeking through the snug's curtain with two ploughman's lunches.

Andy looked doubtful at the food. "Okay. Shall we dig in?" He raised one eyebrow, forced a grin, and picked up the hard bread.

"Anything for afters?" the waitress asked.

"No thank you." Andy and Rose spoke in unison, then smiled at one another.

"Sure? Ma's done a lovely apple pie, my loves."

"It's tempting, but no," Rose responded.

After the last bite, Andy leaned back and rubbed his stomach. He looked at his watch. "If we're going to take our time walking back, we better leave now." He helped Rose on with her cape, grabbed his hat from the wooden hook, and left British pounds on the table to cover the food and drinks.

Rose shoved the leftover bread into her cape pockets, and as they were leaving, the jukebox played "There'll Always Be an England."

Andy strolled out of the pub with Rose, hand in hand, and came to a path winding its way well west of the North Sea. They walked, talked, and laughed on their way back toward the airbase, scarcely noticing the chilled air. He thought nothing could interrupt them.

Rose pointed to a seagull and pulled the bread from her pocket, broke it into tiny pieces and threw them into the air. The seagull swooped down catching a crumb before it landed. One seagull multiplied into ten. "Look at them, Andy. See how they swarm down and catch the bread in midair."

"You're really drawing a crowd. They're coming in from the east like a gaggle of geese." Andy took some crumbled bread from her hand and pitched it into the air.

"They're landing in droves, and we're running out of bread." Rose laughed and clapped her hands. "What fun! I never knew seagulls came so far inland."

"You forgot your history. Remember Salt Lake City, Utah, and the seagulls that saved the town from locusts?"

"I'd forgotten all about that. How come you're so smart?"

Before Andy could answer, a familiar drone coming in from the eastern sky sent adrenalin rushing through Andy's body. Antiaircraft bursts echoed like thunder.

"We've got to get out of here!" He grabbed Rose's arm, pushed her forward while scanning for shelter.

"Andy! What is it?"

"Luftwaffe! Hurry!"

Every muscle strained as they ran west. The land appeared void of cover. Andy glanced back in time to see the Luftwaffe armed with 20mm cannons start its descent, and in a matter of minutes, British Spitfires would be on the fighters' tails. Andy knew he and Rose weren't the low flying Luftwaffe's original target, but the planes would strafe the ground with .50 caliber guns at anything in their path.

"Gotta find shelter! Run!"

"I'm trying, Andy," she shouted with labored breath. He pulled her over clumps of grass, small dirt mounds, and short scrub bushes. "Whoa!" Rose tripped over a bushy stump and fell hard to the ground. Though Andy clung to her hand, he failed to break her fall.

He scooped her up in his arms and continued their flight. Ahead he spotted a shed. The planes droned on—the roar of the engines bearing down on them. Louder and louder. Andy's lungs expanded to near bursting just as he reached the shed.

He grabbed the wooden slab door, flung it open, and dove inside. A spray of ammunition riddled the ground behind them, showered the dilapidated shed as the planes continued on to targets beyond.

They plunged onto the dirt flooring, Andy on top of Rose. Neither moved. Exhausted and frightened, they lay there. Overhead, Andy heard the deafening roar of the RAF in heavy pursuit.

Finally, Andy stirred, glanced around and there it was. Blood. *Oh, God! Whose blood? It can't be. No!*

"Rose, Rose! Are you all right?" He rolled her over and patted her face. "Rose, can you hear me?" Anguish riveted his voice. The sound of explosions and the crackling of the 50s roared in his ears.

At last, Rose opened her eyes and gasped for air. "What happened?" She smothered a groan and winced when attempting to raise her left arm. Her eyes were sharp and accessing, brows arched high.

"I must have knocked the breath out of you. Can you sit up? We need to stop the bleeding." He reached behind her back and eased her up.

He ripped open her bloody sleeve exposing a sliver of wood and a path of torn flesh just above the elbow. "The bullet must have grazed your left arm just as we reached the entrance, hitting the wood and you at the same time when we dove inside. When we fell, the protruding end of the wood fragment evidently broke off inside your arm. It needs to come out."

He reached into his pocket, took out a pocketknife, a box of matches, struck the match, and burned the tip end of the blade, heating the metal. He shook the match when the flame scorched his fingers and wiped the soot off the blade with his clean handkerchief.

"Careful." Rose squirmed.

"Now, hold still. This will sting for only a second." Rays of sunlight peeked through the wooden slats of the windowless shed, creating zebra stripes on the dirt floor, where dust slowly settled from the abrupt attack. He spread his handkerchief under her arm, slipped the knife in alongside the sliver of wood, pinched the edge of the wooden dagger against the blade and pulled it out.

"Oh!" The blood drained from her face as she grimaced from the pain. Blood oozed from her arm.

"There. Now, let's wrap the handkerchief around it until we get back to the base." He examined the piece of broken wood covered in Rose's blood. "That sliver was larger than I thought."

"Are you hurt, Andy?"

"No, but you scared the fool out of me with all that blood. You up to leaving?" He realized they must be adjacent to one of the 126 small USAAF airbases in England, possibly the original target.

"I'm fine. Whenever you're ready." Andy helped her up, and they both studied the holes in the roof and sides of the tiny structure.

"Come here." He moved closer, placed his hand under her chin, lifted her face to his, and pressed his lips tenderly on hers. They stood motionless in the middle of the shed. His body responded to a growing arousal as she eagerly returned his kiss.

She pressed her hands against his chest breaking their embrace. Her chest heaved and her checks flushed. "Andy, I'm so afraid."

"Of what?" He swallowed his disappointment while his shoulders heaved with every breath.

"Oh Andy, you know what. Afraid of committing, of loving and losing. Of giving in and you not coming back."

Rose buried her head in his chest. Tears dribbled onto his shirt, and she gazed into his eyes.

"I love you Rose," he whispered in her ear. "I want to put you in a silk cocoon, and protect you forever, and bring you out only after each storm's end." She melted in his arms, too close for any man's peace of mind. His lips found hers in the sun streaks piercing through the shed.

"We need to go."

"I love you, Rose," he repeated once more.

Hand in hand, they walked out the door, leaving behind the shed that saved their lives. Andy heard the whine of a plane headed for a crash. "Sounds like the RAF got at least one of those dirty Krauts!"

Black smoke billowed skyward. Andy rushed west, pulling Rose along until reaching a knoll. In the distance, a small airstrip stretched before them, the target of the Luftwaffe. Fire poured from several planes. A funnel of black smoke curled upward from an exploding fuel tank shooting flames that spread a garish glow over the land.

"Sure 'nuf, those bogies had 20mm cannons. The FW-190 flew so low they used us for target practice with two MG-17 7.92 millimeter guns." Andy shook his head. "How many died this time?" He raged. "This has got to stop!"

Rose draped her arm around his shoulder. "There's nothing you could've done—nothing at all. You saved my life. That counts for something."

"I'm thankful you're all right." He reached for her hand, wove his fingers between hers and they retraced their tracks until the road came into view.

After walking a short distance, a British military truck approached. Andy flagged it down and they were on their way back to Snetterton.

He sat on the wooden benches in the back of the truck, his arm around Rose careful not to touch her injury. Cigarette smoke spiraled above several men in fatigues sitting near the truck's front.

"What happened back there, laddie?"

"The Luftwaffe targeted another American airbase." Andy discreetly relayed a smidgeon of information while resting his head on the wooden braces behind. The khaki canopy flapped endlessly in the breeze.

Andy's body released its tension as his mind spun wildly over the events of the afternoon. *What if I had lost Rose, now, after all this time—all this waiting for the perfect gal? She could've been snatched right out from under me! Thank you, God!*

The sun dipped out of sight below the horizon, while the truck jostled and bounced over the potholed road, spewing dust in their faces. Rose nestled in his arms, her head buried in his chest, exhausted from the events of the day and no sleep the night before. His lips grazed her silky hair, as he inhaled her cologne, the scent of a lilac bouquet. He tightened his grip around her shoulders, cradling her even closer. *What next? Is there another Black Thursday out there? Now, more than ever, I know what it means to be "baptized by fire."*

# Chapter Eleven

## Fayetteville, NC

"Betty Jane. I'm going to the barn. Back in a minute, you hear?"

"Okay, Mom."

Jane put the biscuits in the warming bin on the stove, slipped her sweater over her apron, and headed to the barn.

"John. John!" She stopped to listen for a response. Nothing. After entering the barn, she scanned the area. Still no sign of John. *It's not like John to be late for supper or continue working after dark. I'll go back and call Mr. Martin. Perhaps John stepped over to his house.*

"Mom, is that you?"

"Yes, Betty Jane. I can't seem to find your father." Jane's stomach crawled the same way every time she had thoughts about Andy—like an omen. She hastened her way into the hall and met Betty Jane.

"I'm going to call the Martins to see if he's over there."

"Mom, you know Dad would never go anywhere without letting you know."

"I know, sweetheart. That's why I'm concerned. He hasn't been feeling well lately.

"What? You never told me. Why not?" Betty Jane stomped her foot.

"We didn't want to worry you with all your school work, music practice, and part-time job."

"Mom! I'm not a little child, you know. Stop shielding me. I get more anxious knowing you and Dad constantly try to protect me. Please! I can handle things. Understand?"

Jane sat in the phone chair and dialed 2 for the Martin's partyline phone. She nodded her head to Betty Jane and held her finger to her lips.

"Hello." Ralph Martin answered.

Jane related her concerns.

"I haven't seen him in several days, Jane. I'll round up a few boys and we'll comb the fields."

Jane's hands trembled and her voice quivered. "Betty Jane and I'll grab flashlights and start on this end of the field. Thank you, Ralph." She placed the phone on its cradle and glanced at her daughter and read the fear draped over her face.

"Now don't go imagining all kinds of things, honey. We'll find him. Come on. Get your coat and hat while I find a couple flashlights and a heavy coat. It's getting colder by the minute."

Moments later Jane and her daughter walked in separate directions through the ploughed tobacco fields and made their way towards the Martin's side of the field. Flashlights sliced the darkness with streaks of light interrupting the virgin darkness while encountering new lights from the Martin's side. Jane called, "John, John," with Betty Jane crisscrossing her words, "Dad, Dad. Answer us. Please, Daddy," as they wove their way across the field.

"Don't miss a row, sweetheart." Jane continued shouting, "John, John. Joh....n." *Oh where are you darling? Where?*

Jane's heart pounded as a dozen lights from the Martin's side grew closer, and closer. The farther she searched, the louder the pounding in her ears. John's voice reverberated through her head—"Don't fear the worst until you know something." Try as she might, she couldn't calm her heart. "John. John."

"Mrs. Walters, we've got him." Ralph Martin shouted.

*Oh no. Is he dead?* The words raced over and over through her head. *Don't let him be dead, Dear Lord. Oh, please no.* She ran stumbling through the furrows. Mud caked on her shoes slowing her down.

"Mom. Mom. Wait," Betty Jane called out. "He's dead. I know he's dead. Tell me he is not dead, Mommy, please."

Her daughter's words instantly stopped her. *Be strong for our daughter. The same words John had said continuously over the past few months. I must be strong, but Dear Lord, I need all the help I can get to muster up for my daughter.*

Betty Jane caught up to her, grabbed Jane's arm helping her across the furrows.

"Honey, remember what Dad always said, "Don't think the worst. Wait."

"I know, but I'm so frightened."

"Be strong, sweetheart. He needs us."

They came upon John curled in a fetal position. He tried to speak but his words were not audible. Their eyes met for a brief moment and Jane watched them dart back and forth as she knelt over him. He had a look she had never seen before. He was her rock, her safe place, her everything. *And now, everything is up to me. Be strong, lady! Be strong.*

Without thinking, she tore off her coat, threw it over John, lifted his head and slid under, placing his head in her lap. She swallowed hard and buried the fear in her voice.

Jane glanced at Ralph pleading for assurance of some kind. "What's wrong with him, Ralph? Is he hurt?"

"Not sure. I've sent a boy to call for an ambulance. Ralph shouted after the boy, "Pronto!"

"John, Ralph Martin called for an ambulance. You'll be fine. Don't try to talk—save your strength." She stroked his forehead and lifted his right hand—ice cold. She could feel a little strength in that hand, but as she picked up his left hand, it was stiff—frozen like. She massaged it to create better circulation. Every time he tried to speak, she placed her finger over his lips.

Betty Jane, unusually quiet, lifted his right hand and massaged it. Tears soaked her scarf.

After what seemed like an eternity, she heard a siren approaching the field. The sound arrived long before the vehicle. A boy flashed his light signaling the direction to the site.

The ambulance pulled up and two medics worked on John attempting to secure his condition and ready him for the ride. They eased him onto the stretcher, slid him into the ambulance and secured him. Jane climbed in behind.

"Jane," shouted Ralph, "We'll bring Betty Jane and see you at Highsmith Hospital. Don't worry. We'll follow behind.

"Thank you, Ralph." Jane turned her attention to John as the ambulance bounced across furrows until the wheels connected to gravel in the Martins driveway and sped away to the hospital.

Hours had passed when a young man appeared wearing a white doctor's coat with a stethoscope draped around his neck. "I'm Dr. McBain. Mrs. Walters?"

Jane jumped to her feet as did Betty Jane and the Martins.

"Is he all right? Can I see him." Jane rushed questions one after the other.

"Mrs. Walters, your husband has suffered a stroke. How serious—we don't know yet. His speech is impaired and he is unable to use his left hand and we suspect the same for his left leg. Fortunately, you found him not long after the stroke and got him right to the hospital. Minutes count. That determines the recovery time, if any, of the speech and body movements.

He continued. "He'll stay in the hospital until I feel he's able to go to physical therapy and after that, home. Any questions?"

"When can we see him?" Jane asked.

"Family only can go in two at a time. Do not force him to talk. He'll get extremely frustrated with his situation. He needs rest…bed rest…and no excitement. Now, I am needed by another patient."

"Thank you, Dr. McBain." Jane reached for his hand.

An hour later, Jane and Betty Jane entered John's room. His eyes were closed.

Jane leaned over and kissed him on his forehead. "John, we're here. Don't try to talk. She glanced at teary-eyed Betty Jane when she noticed John's opened eyes.

For thirty minutes she talked to John blabbering about nothing. She ended with, "John, we're going to leave for a while. You need to rest. We love you, my darling." She kissed him once again.

"I love you, Daddy. Get better. We need you." Betty Jane spun around and rushed from the room.

Jane joined her outside the room and each wrapped their arms around one another. Their bodies racked with sobs.

Ralph and Theresa Martin hurried over. "Is there anything we can do, Jane?"

"No, Ralph. John's recovery can take a while and I don't know how we'll manage or who will take care of the farm."

*What's going to happen to us? What?"* Her body tensed as she began to understand  reality of the situation. *How are we going to survive without John's income? College for Betty Jane too.* "Oh, Dear Lord…."

# Chapter Twelve

## November 1943

"Transfer?" Andy asked. "Sir, we've flown twenty-five missions in less than six months. We'd like to finish out our mission quota here." He knew he had a good rapport with his squadron commander with full access and permission to speak freely as he deemed necessary.

Col. Miller flipped over a copy of *Yank* magazine on his desk; headline: LET 'EM HAVE IT, BUY EXTRA BONDS (1943). He stepped around the wooden desk to where Andy stood. "Son. The orders are to go to Foggia, Italy. Our squadron leaves at 0700 tomorrow."

"Yes sir." Andy looked straight ahead and snapped into his best salute. Before he turned to leave, he managed a weak grin to match the squadron commander's. He refused to leave a bad impression, like "uncooperative," with his superior officer—he'd worked too hard to avoid that kind of label.

He left headquarters concerned and tormented. *Not now. Just when Rose and I have something going. But Italy. It can't be worse than going back to Schweinfurt, or can it? I gotta get a note to Rose.*

He shoved his cold hands into his pockets, touched the buckeye, and remembered—*write Mom, too.*

The spattering rain added to the foggy murkiness of the day. He jogged the short distance to the officer barracks dodging and splashing through puddles. Water circled the brim of his hat and dribbled down the sides.

At 1500, he entered the barracks, where the crew lounged around in the warm, dry room. He took off his hat brushing as much water away as possible.

"Tex, Bulldog, Pops. We're moving out at 0700 tomorrow. Pack your gear. It's Foggia, Italy."

"No shit, Andy," Bulldog said. "That's better than Schweinfurt. I'll go!" He rubbed his head then slammed his closed fist into his bunk.

"Andy, that's not bad news. It'll be good to get away from this madness." Pops stood up and spoke with a hopeful glint in his eyes. "We'll adjust."

"Sure we will." Andy buried his feelings behind an improvised smile, while his chest felt like a slab of iron rested on it. No way could he reveal his conflict to anyone—torn between defending his country and being with Rose. At the sound of his own self-deprecating laugh, he decided not to go further with those thoughts.

Andy caught a jeep to the field hospital. He had to see Rose. Her shift didn't end until midnight, but surely she could speak to him for a few minutes.

The jeep drew up to the patched front entrance of the hospital scarred by the German blitz whose bombs spread death and havoc in 1940.

Andy stepped down from the jeep and faced the driver. "Thanks, Corporal. Can you wait a bit?"

"Sure, Captain. I'm finished for the day."

"Much obliged."

Andy dashed into the field hospital and stopped at the front desk. "Sergeant, where can I find Lt. Rose Martin?"

The Sergeant studied him for a moment. "Sir, I'll check." He left his desk and approached the head nurse. She shook her head, said a few words, and the sergeant returned to Andy and spread his hands wide.

"She has a critical patient in her care and cannot leave until her relief arrives. Sorry, Captain."

"Thanks. I'd like to leave her a note. Would you see that she gets it?"

"Sure thing."

"Swell."

Andy pulled a note pad out of his shirt pocket, shivered a little, and wrote:

*Dear Rose,*

*Tomorrow at 0700 the 96$^{th}$ is flying to Foggia, Italy. Don't know how long we'll be stationed there. I so wanted to see you and hold you in my arms once more, but now that's impossible now. I'd hoped you could step out for a moment, but you've a job to do. I understand.*

*Whenever I'm sad and depressed, I'll have our days in England to fall back on. They meant so much to me. Those memories will carry me through this war. Your face is the last thing I see at night. You are my lifeline, the music of my life, the song I hear, the stars I see.*

*I felt you were unreachable in high school—me a sharecropper's son, and you the rich tobacco businessman's daughter. But then I found you to be such a warm, caring person. Nothing like what I remembered. I was an idiot back then.*

*And Rose, always remember the words to this song:*

*"I'll be seeing you..."*

*I've never liked goodbyes. They're so final. Well, maybe that's a good omen, since I didn't get to see you. I love you, Rose, and I want to be with you. Always. I still carry your hankie, but it lost its fragrance long ago. It's in my shirt pocket along with you, tucked right under my heart.*

*I'll be seeing you...*

*Andy*

*P.S. I'll send you an address soon as I can. They might keep moving us around.*

Andy folded the notepaper. "Sergeant, do you have an envelope?"

"Let me see." The sergeant pulled the wooden desk drawers open until he found a blank envelope. "Here's one, sir."

"Thanks, buddy." Andy slipped his note into the envelope, wrote Rose's name on the front, and handed it back to the sergeant. "Please see that she gets it, Sergeant. 'Preciate it."

"Yes sir." The Sergeant's eyes cut a sideways glance and instantly saluted.

"Captain." Lt. Col. Lawing slipped beside Andy.

"Yes, sir."

"Are you in need of hospital care?"

"Uh…no, sir. Just leaving a note for a friend of mine. Good day, sir."

Andy glanced down the long row of beds in one last search for Rose. Nothing. After leaving the building, he lowered his head, thrust his hands deep into his pockets, and kicked a few rocks. The corporal flung the jeep door open, and after Andy climbed in, they sped off to the officers' quarters.

Col. Lawing fingered Andy's envelope on the Sergeant's desk noticing Rose's name as the addressee.

"Sir, that letter is entrusted to me." The Sergeant reached for the envelope but the Colonel held tight.

"I'm ordering you to remove your hand!"

The sergeant immediately released his hand, and the Colonel broke the seal, removed the note, and read its entirety. In spite of himself a smile crept over his face. *Now one less object to stand in my way. Rose, you'll be mine soon.*

"Sergeant, put this in another envelope and seal it. Be sure to give it to Nurse Martin." He tried to disguise his delight as he left the building.

In the barracks everyone busied themselves filling their duffel bags. Andy gathered his personal gear, packed all but his note pad, and wrote another letter—one that told his mom and dad of the transfer and more about Rose.

"I hear tell they got some hot tomatoes down at that new pub. How 'bout it, Andy?" Bulldog caught Andy's arm.

"Na. I got some thinking to do. Y'all have a good time."

In their excitement, the men rushed out and slammed the door behind them.

Andy pulled on his chin. If he couldn't be with Rose, he'd rather be alone—alone with his thoughts, his dreams of a life with her. *When did I fall in love with her? Maybe I've loved her all my life— the girl next door. The daughter of my dad's boss. Off limits. All I know is I'm miserable away from her.*

Her face flashed before him as if she stood a mere few feet away. He wanted to reach out and touch her but mused at the thought. *I must be losing it.* "Well, at least I can pull up her vision when I need to," he whispered. He laughed at the sound of his own voice and whistled in a melodic tone, "I'll be seeing you…."

After writing to his parents, he relaxed on the bunk, hands behind his head, preoccupied with memories of Rose in her red and white polka dot dress. He planned the day they would be together again. His eyelids drooped; he gave up the fight, and succumbed to sleep.

\*   \*   \*

The hands on Rose's watch slid together, displaying midnight. The relief nurse arrived ten minutes later. Rose updated the nurse on the progress of her patient, reached for her cape and made her way to the front entrance. Leaving the hospital, she opened her umbrella. "Good grief! It's quite a ways to the barracks in this soggy night air," she said out loud. She stopped and turned around after she heard a faint voice call her name. She observed the desk sergeant waving something in the air.

"Nurse Martin! Nurse Martin! Got a letter for you," the sergeant called from the entrance. "I almost forgot it." He splashed through puddles while rushing toward her..

She smiled as she watched him run. *Running that fast, he'll miss the raindrops.* She giggled at the thought.

He shoved the letter into her hand and dashed halfway back before she could say, "Thank you, Sergeant."

She glanced at the writing, but unable to see with the distant light from the building, she slid the envelope into her pocket and continued to walk the short distance to the nurse's barracks. Inside, nylons dangled on strings hung from the ceiling saving them from the rats. Panties and brassieres filled a line stretched across the back end of the barracks. Ginny stood at the table rinsing her underwear in a washbowl.

Rose slipped her cape off and heard the crinkle of paper in her pocket. *Oh, the letter. Hummmm....* She lifted the lightly sealed flap. *Andy! Why is he writing me?* Her heart flip-flopped in her chest.

She drew her hand up over her mouth. "Oh, no! He's shipping out!"

Ginny shook her wet hand over the wash bowl, rushed over to Rose, and asked in a strong Brooklyn accent, "Youse got your bubble busted?"

"Andy's flying out at 0700. I'll not see him before he leaves. This can't be happening. Not now." Rose buried her head in her pillow. Her body ached down to the bones after working sixteen straight hours. And now her heart tightened as if it would burst. She tried to hold back the tears, but the floodgates gave way.

Ginny sat on the edge of Rose's bunk, gently rubbing her back. A little later Rose sat up, wiped the tears away, and read the balance of the letter. After she finished, she clutched it close to her chest and smiled through tears. The moment she dreaded—lived in fear of— that moment was now.

"Nice letter, eh?" Ginny gave her another hug.

"Yes, it is. You're a great friend and thank you for being here." Rose remembered how the two had come over together from the States and remained good friends. "This is the very reason I wanted no part of love. I believed if I fell in love, he would never return. How I had fought that feeling! Then Andy came along—a kid I grew up with. Someone I looked to as a brother, nothing more—someone I felt safe with—someone from home. He barged back into my life where he intends to stay. Now I have fallen helplessly in love."

"You know, su...gar." Ginny mocked Rose's southern drawl. "Love is worth the gamble. Let's turn in. It's late now. You all right?"

"Yes, thanks." Rose reached for Ginny and squeezed her hand.

Ginny finished washing her dainties and went over to her own bunk. Rose read and re-read Andy's letter. *Oh, Andy. Be safe. I didn't even get to tell you goodbye or say that "I love you." How I wished I had told you before. When you drew the stick figures on the table at the pub, I wanted to tell you how much I loved you. When you held me in your arms at the shed, I wanted to tell you. And now, you're gone. Gone...and you might not return. Be safe my darling.*

Flashbacks of the escape from the fighter planes into the shed raced through her mind like tracers lighting the skies. She brushed her hand across the scar on her arm, slid back onto the pillow, and shut her swollen eyes. Thoughts of Andy darted through her head all night, interrupting her sleep like the intermittent pinging of ice in a frozen lake.

\* \* \*

It had been ten days since Andy shipped out to Italy. Rose's duty at the field hospital kept her busy and exhausted. Because she learned quickly, the doctors regularly requested her assistance. Her first training came from the Red Cross, as with many Red Cross nurses, they transferred her to the Army Air Corps Nurses Unit, though she remained in the Red Cross.

Rose rotated between the two field hospitals until December 1943, when she found herself and a group of nurses and Army medical personnel on a truck bound for Birmingham, England, with orders to report to the field hospital. Massive potholes caused by rain-wash and bombings rocked the truck as it slipped into one hole after another, jostling the nurses all over the back of the 4x4. Rose clutched the wooden bench as they slowed in front of a large, dilapidated, white building that looked like it had scarcely survived an earthquake. She noted that tents flanked its left side.

The truck stopped alongside several tents near a Nissen hut. The driver pointed to the white building. "That's the hospital. Nurses, out here! Watch your step."

Ginny glanced east. "Is that the sun fighting its way through the mist? I can't believe it. I thought it had vanished. Forever!"

"Wel…come sunshine! Come on, y'all, let's move into our new home." Rose picked up her baggage and hurled it across the threshold. "There. Home is now occupied! Where's my coffee?" The peeping sun did nothing to warm the frigid air for Rose and the shivering girls.

She watched seven of her fellow nurses pile out, lugging their belongings, and picking their path through puddles to reach the tent entrance. Rose made a beeline to the potbelly stove. She found some kindling, coal, and a box of matches to light the fire.

"It's freezing. Thank goodness we have a dry floor. Rough on the bare feet, but you know, it could be worse." Rose twisted around to see the girls standing motionless, still holding onto their bags as if they had no intention of staying. "Let's get busy. This is home. Our CO said to report to the field hospital an hour after we arrived."

Her hands, stiff from the icy cold, gradually thawed once they shook out mattresses, brushed away cobwebs, and made the tent more comfortable. Dust bunnies flew through every inch of the tent. She smiled while her fellow nurses moved like a movie reel set on its fastest speed. Family pictures soon mounted on wooden support posts. A clothing rod stretched across the back of the tent immediately filled up.

Rose hummed, "I'll Be Seeing You," as she smoothed out her wool blankets. "Hurry, gals, we need to be at the hospital in a few minutes."

"Be with you in a jiffy." Ginny grabbed her cape and headed out of the tent.

Rose and the other girls followed. They wove their way to the field hospital before spotting a sign that pointed to a Nissen hut next to it: NEW MEDICAL PERSONNEL MEETING HERE.

"Thank goodness someone placed wooden planks to bridge over the worst mud holes." Rose stepped off the last board into the entrance. The meeting was already in progress, and they hurried to find a seat among the crowded benches.

"I wish to welcome…" the commanding officer hesitated and glanced at the new arrivals… "all of you to the 879th Field Hospital. You are sorely needed. This is not an easy area to work in. We're on the fringe of Birmingham and Coventry, the German Luftwaffe's favorite bombing target. It's treacherous—more dangerous than most areas. You'll be safe only if you follow instructions. Lt. Walker is here to teach you how to protect yourselves." The CO shuffled papers in his hands before continuing.

"We minister to more than military personnel. Civilians injured by incendiary bombs come in droves. They're burned, some beyond recognition. Children, babies arrive daily with heart-wrenching injuries. Each day uncovers a new type of injury. No matter what is thrown our way, we must not become emotionally involved. We have a job to do. Our supplies are dangerously low. Food is critical—even the basic needs for the town people to survive.

"Don't think you're going to escape bombings. You won't. Depending where you are and when it happens, you'll need to make the best decision for the situation. Keep your helmet with you at all times."

He persevered for another hour with no sign of ending. Rose squirmed in her seat. *These benches are like sitting on a rock wall. Whew!* Rose glanced at Ginny.

"I'm growing numb. How about you?" Ginny whispered, lifting her body up an inch or so by her hands. After a few moments, she eased back down.

"Me, too. At least it's warm in here." Rose put her finger to her lips, signaling Ginny to shush.

The CO introduced Lt. Stevens, a tall, dark-haired, muscular man, who presented safety information briefly and concisely. Rose thought she heard women swoon at the sight of him.

The meeting ended with the CO inquiring, "Is there a Rose Martin in here?" His eyes searched the room.

Rose raised her hand and stood up. Her face burned. She knew it matched her name.

"Lt. Col. Richard Lawing needs you immediately after the meeting. Report to the Field Hospital, Room #7, make haste."

"Yes sir," Rose replied. She had assisted Lt. Col. Lawing in surgery numerous times in High Wycombe before transfer and he had told her before how astonished he was at her ability and requested her instead of other trained nurses.

Rose's hands trembled when she returned to her seat. Though pleased at the special request, her knees weakened as she thought about the CO's singling her out.

The nurses stood, moving in a stretching direction. "Oh, let me touch you, your highness!" Ginny teased.

The others joined in, not letting up. "You're so s.p.e.c.i.a.l," one girl said.

Rose headed for the exit door. "I'm out of here. Don't know when I'll see you, but maybe that's not so bad. Keep the home fires burning." She smiled warmly, purposely disarming her friends.

"Get outta here." Ginny laughed and tapped Rose on her rear end.

Rose dashed over to the hospital to find Lt. Col. Lawing. After a short briefing, they hurried into surgery. The operation was long and tedious. The patient, a little girl about two years old had a shrapnel injury to her stomach requiring extensive repairs.

After completing the surgery, Lt. Col. Lawing said, "Lieutenant, I couldn't have done it without you." He put his arm around her shoulders and stared deep into her eyes. "I've missed you, Rose. I need you by my side in more ways than one."

Rose blushed, and her heart raced as she twisted away from him. "I'm delighted to be working with you again, Col. Lawing. However, and I mean, *however*, that's all."

He caught her hand before she could move away and led her to an adjoining room. "Well, you can't fault a fellow for trying, lovely lady. I'm not giving up on you." He pulled her close and pressed his lips on hers.

For an instant, she felt good to be held in someone's arms. Realizing what happened, she pushed back to break his grasp. "Please sir." He held fast. "I don't date my superiors!"

"Since when? Who would know?"

She trembled at the thought of rejecting her superior officer. "I would! Now, I don't mean to sound prudish, but I care for someone else."

"How do you know he'll be around after the war ends?"

"That's it. I don't. But I intend to wait for him." She struggled to break his grip.

"I'm here and I don't quit easily."

"Try real hard, sir. Now, let go of me before I cause a real scene! I'm going to care for my little patient."

Rose broke his grasp and fled the room.

# Chapter Thirteen

Relieved to be out of the clutches of the colonel, Rose rushed to her little patient's bedside. With the success of the surgical procedure, Rose worked in the critical care unit the first twelve hours keeping a watchful eye over the two-year old and others in her charge. Instead of leaving at the end of her shift, Rose stayed with little Amy, the name they gave the toddler.

This went on for days while the little child struggled for her life. Rose could not tear herself away. A dedicated nurse, she felt a strong obligation to care for Amy, and later, attempt to locate her parents.

After each shift ended, Rose hurried back to the tent, bathed, changed clothes, and was ready to rush back to her patient.

"Hi, stranger. Got a minute?" Ginny blocked Rose's exit from the tent.

"Sure. What's up?" Rose draped her cape around her shoulders.

"Look. Aren't you getting too attached? You sing to her, cradle her in your arms, rock her, kiss her like you're her mother. That's against all rules. You know that!"

Rose did not look at Ginny. "I know, I know. You don't have to remind me. I can't seem to help myself. I wish I didn't know so much about medicine. Maybe I wouldn't be so frightened for Amy. The only thing we have left to fight infection is the sulfa powder. If she spikes a fever, she might not make it, and she needs to feel like she's loved. I'm all she has for now."

"You can't be everything to that child, I tell you. You're going to get in trouble with the colonel."

"I'm already in trouble with him."

"Now what? What about the colonel?"

"I don't want to talk about it now. I've got to run."

"You know what? You'll be forced to face that problem as well. Mark my word," Ginny shouted.

Rose rushed from the tent to the toddler's bedside where Amy's fever climbed above 104 degrees for the next three days. It became touch and go once again. Col. Lawing watched as Rose bathed the child with cool cloths to bring the fever down. Nothing helped. The infection ravaged Amy's tiny body.

"Look, you're wearing yourself to a frazzle. Take a break." The colonel caught her arm and pulled her away from the bed.

"She has no one else. I must stay." Tears welled in Rose's eyes.

"Okay, if you must. But I'm concerned that my special nurse is working herself into exhaustion. I'd pull rank except that I care too much for you."

"Thank you, sir. Now please let me do what I have to do."

The colonel gave her an affectionate hug and kissed her forehead.

Rose was too exhausted to resist and welcomed a strong shoulder.

With each day, Rose became more exhausted. When not helping another patient, she rested her head on her arms, propping them on the small child's bed. Her body ached, and only a good rest could relieve it.

On the fourth day, Amy's fever broke, and her eyes opened. She moaned and called in a barely audible, dry, raspy voice.

"Mummy? Mummy." Her eyes closed once more.

Rose jumped up and stroked Amy's forehead, occasionally patting her cheeks. "It's all right, Amy. I'm here with you." She sang "Rock-a-bye Baby" and other lullabies to her young patient.

Each day Amy's recovery progressed, and the lullabies changed to fun songs.

"Auntie Rose. Sing "Playmate."

"Yes, my darling." Rose sang Amy's favorite songs, "Playmate, Come Out and Play with Me," followed by "London Bridge Is Falling Down."

Amy's little face lit up, and she clapped her hands to the rhythm.

Rose rejoiced at the speed of her recovery. Col. Lawing allowed her to schedule daytime work so she could be near Amy during her waking hours. By the way the colonel's hazel eyes assessed her each time she entered the room, Rose knew he had more than a medical attachment to her, but that didn't matter, as long as she could choose her own hours.

Amy and Rose became inseparable, and Rose dreaded the day when Amy must be reunited with her parents. *Something dreadful must have happened to them. How could they neglect such an adorable child? Don't worry, baby, if they're alive, we'll find them.* She pulled back Amy's light brown, Shirley Temple curls and kissed her cheek.

Freezing rain tinkled against the windows, a sign of worse weather yet to come. The weeks clicked off, and now six weeks after Amy entered Rose's life, the day had come. No more putting it off. Time to find Amy's family.

Rose entered Col. Lawing's office. "Sir, I need a favor."

"Anything for you, my dear."

"Please, sir. Treat me like your other nurses. No special favors. I need a day off to search for Amy's family." Rose wrung her hands while standing in front of an immense wooden desk with gashes reminiscent of early bombings.

"That will be hard to do, but if that's what you want. Fine. Friday then?" A glimmer shone in his eyes.

"Thank you, sir." Rose smiled and scurried out of his office, fearful of a repeat performance of a few weeks ago.

Early Friday morning, Rose and Sgt. Roger Mallory, the medic who brought Amy to the field hospital and had a vague recollection of where they found her, headed to Coventry. Slowed by damaged roads from the numerous bombings and large transport trucks, they arrived on the outskirts of the city.

Low, gray clouds remained from the previous days of sleet, adding to the gloom, which resembled death itself. Rose's stomach churned in response to the horrific devastation—trees uprooted, buildings leveled, homes obliterated, chimneys left standing, and a schoolhouse flattened—scattered books, drenched papers, and only the school sign remained undamaged. She turned away, when her eyes rested on a white bone protruding from a demolished building. *Surely not! They would have recovered it by now.*

"This area remains under 'red alert,'" Sgt. Mallory said. "There's always a possibility of more raids. Don't take your helmet off." He added, "We'll check down the road and work our way back. Not quite the same. It looks weird. Three or four houses side by side charred, and the next few appear unscathed. That's an incendiary bomb for you."

"Let's hope the people in those homes made it to a bomb shelter."

He pointed beyond a mass of rubble. "Look! There's one behind that smoldering mess. See the sandbags piled high? That's one of those corrugated Anderson shelters Churchill provided for his people. It saves a few lives."

"It wouldn't protect them if it took a direct hit, would it?"

"No ma'am." He drove around holes, rocks, bricks, and twisted piles of wood. When the road disappeared, the sergeant created a new one with his jeep, right over the ruins.

"Let me out here. I'll check each of the houses. You go back to the other group."

Sgt. Mallory stopped the jeep. "You be careful lest you fall in a hole or pick up a nail, Lieutenant.

"Stay safe yourself, Sergeant. I'll need a lift back." She smiled over her shoulder after an unladylike exit over slippery bricks and rocks.

He tipped his hat and returned her grin.

Rose wove her way on a makeshift path to an English Tudor home that had suffered minimal damage. She reached to knock on the wooden door when, the shrill shriek of an air-raid warning blared. The door sprung open, and a woman with a young baby and an elderly man ran out.

"Come!" She caught Rose's arm and hastened her along. "Hurry!"

Rose rushed with the threesome, dodging debris and glancing back for her driver. He was nowhere in sight. They came to a little knoll with a pile of camouflage over sandbags, scooted down dirt steps to a dank, dirty, and musty hole in the ground. The ceiling was lined with boards and supported by thick posts to hold the dirt back—a crude makeshift shelter.

Two children whimpered but no one said a word. The old man lit a candle. Rose counted fifteen people crowded into the small shelter. *Where did they all come from?* She sat on the ground next to the woman and baby. The earth shook as the buzz of planes and the unforgettable noise of whistling bombs landed in the near distance. The ack-ack of antiaircraft artillery on the ground penetrated their ears as the retaliation commenced.

The eerie whistling of a bomb grew closer and closer. Rose held her breath, her body rigid as she waited for the impact. The bomb sounded right over them. They dove for the ground, even the children. The entire shelter rocked, the candle flickered and lost its battle. The woman next to Rose made a canopy of her body over the baby. Not a sound came from the infant.

Dirt slipped between the boards overhead as the ground shifted from the bomb's impact. Yet, in spite of the dampness, dust filled the shelter's cavity, choking its inhabitants. Helpless, trapped like in a massive grave six feet under, Rose's heart pounded as if it could fly out of her chest.

The old man relit the candle. Eyes turned upward and watched the wooden supports hold back the dirt. They expected the structure to collapse at any moment. Faces ashen, hearts pulsed, waiting for the next strike. Another whistle. Rose held her breath. Gasps resounded throughout the shelter.

The whistling faded. The bomb, with its ferocious wreckage, landed farther away. She sighed with relief. Voices rose up in joyful shouts. "Thank God!"

The Luftwaffe doggedly unloaded its destruction without letup. The woman on the ground next to her wept.

Rose placed her arm around her. "It'll be over soon. It's all right."

"Thank you, lass. Those bloody Krauts will get it one day." She shook her fist in the air. After gaining control of herself, she picked up the baby, cradled her in her arms, rocking back and forth.

Rose found it hard to disguise her own trembling body and queasy stomach. "How often does this happen?" Rose swept the hair out of her eyes.

"Every bloody day and some at night. When there's a good cloud cover, the fighters are beastly brave."

"You must be exhausted." Rose reached over and pushed the blanket from the baby's face.

Another whistling sound rushed closer than before. They dove once more to the ground. A momentous explosion rocked the earth surrounding the shelter disintegrating one wall collapsing it within. Everyone scrambled on knees and bellies to the other side— everyone except the old man and two young children—the wall collapsed over them—like a silent grave. For an instant, no one moved.

Again, someone relit the candle.

Mothers screamed for their children. Rose lunged forward and dug with her bare hands. She pulled out a partially buried little girl— all but her feet. Everyone joined in sending dirt flying. A small boy coughed and cried after they rescued him from under the pile.

"There's a foot!" Rose said. She clawed at the earth harder than ever.

"Hurry," someone else said.

The woman with the baby scrambled over. She clutched the baby to her chest. "Grandpa!" she screamed. "Grandpa…"

It seemed like hours as the digging ensued. Too many minutes passed. "There…there's his head," Rose shouted. They uncovered his head and body brushing the dirt from his face. He wasn't breathing. Rose, checked the pulse in his neck. Nothing. After flipping him over and turning his head to the side, she pushed rhythmically on his back, stopping only long enough to check for a pulse. Pumping…pumping…pumping. Nothing. The boy brushed more dirt from the back of his head That's when she noticed it. A deep gash on the backside of Grandpa's head—it was like a wide wedge had been driven into his bald scalp. She glanced at the woman and baby. The woman sobbed uncontrollably.

"I'm sorry. He died before we reached him. We can do nothing for him." Rose put her arms around the weeping woman.

"Blimey! The bombs 'ave stopped!" another shouted in a high-pitched voice. Concerned with the attempt to rescue the old man, no one had noticed when it stopped.

"Those wretched Germans won't leave us alone! There's naught left to keep bombing!" a man added.

"We need to get you home. By the way, what's your name?" Rose asked the bereaved woman.

"I'm Elizabeth Chandler. My grandpa was Waddell." She popped her hand up to her mouth. "Can't believe I said 'was.'" The tears flowed again.

The locals in the shelter gathered around her. They assured Elizabeth they would handle the body and funeral for Waddell. "What, with you and the baby…" a lady said.

Slowly Elizabeth regained control. "I must post a letter to his sister." She wiped her tears on a sleeve. "You rapped on my door?"

"Yes, I am trying to locate the parents of a little girl. We call her Amy. The medics brought her to the hospital from this area. She's about two years old, with curly, light brown hair and large brown eyes."

Elizabeth broke down once again but soon regained her composure. "You 'ave her? I didn't know what came of her. I searched everywhere. She's my sister's daughter. Sis named her after me. I call her Lizzy. Her mum was killed several months ago. Same as her father. I always kept Lizzy with me, but one day the air-raid siren wailed, and we rushed toward the shelter. Lizzy ran away in search of her mother. I couldn't run after her carrying my baby. She didn't understand the danger. Where is she? Is she all right?"

"Yes, she's fine now. She had extensive stomach injuries but is recovering very nicely. Where's your husband?"

"Shot down." Elizabeth gazed down at the floor. "A pilot in the RAF." She abruptly changed the subject. "When can I fetch her? I don't have a motorcar. If I did, where would I get petrol?"

"Well, I think in a week or so, she'll be well enough to come home. I'll bring her."

They climbed the steps of the shelter to the acrid smell of smoke saturating the bomb-scorched earth.

Once outside, Rose shielded her eyes from the brightness.

Elizabeth jumped up and down with the baby in her arms. "It's here! It's still here!" The bombs missed her home completely.

Rose realized that Elizabeth forgot about Waddell after discovering her home intact. "In spite of all you've been through, someone above is watching out for you." She gazed at Elizabeth through humid eyes.

"Not so's you'd notice. Our men are gone, and so is my sis."

"I'm sorry. You're a brave woman, Elizabeth." Rose followed her back to the house.

"Come in," Elizabeth said, while scanning the front room. "It's not much but, I say, it's a roof over our heads."

"Thanks, but no, I've got to find my driver. I hope he's all right. He drove down the road searching for Amy, I mean Lizzy's home."

"There's a shelter down the road that's not hidden like this one."

"Oh yes. The sergeant pointed it out."

Just as the words flew from her mouth, the jeep drove over a new pile of rubble and stopped.

"You okay, Lieutenant?" Sgt. Mallory cupped his hands and shouted. "The doc will kill me if I let anything happen to you."

"Yes. Be right there." Rose turned to Elizabeth. "I'd better get back to the hospital. Injuries from the bombing will be heavy. I'll be in touch when it's time to bring little Amy…Lizzy back home. Will you be all right?"

"Yes, I need to feed the baby and put her to bed. I say, my friend, you're so kind but you haven't told me your name. You're American aren't you?" She smiled at Rose.

"Rose Martin, Red Cross/Army Nurse Corps. I'll see you in a week or so. Bye-bye." Rose scurried along, dodging debris. Her thoughts turned to Lizzy. *How do I let go of a little girl I've come to love? Especially to live in such danger. I thought most children were evacuated to safety. Oh, Andy, I wish you were here with me. I miss you so. It was much easier when I had only my family to worry about. Now you and Lizzy. Dear God!*

Over the next two weeks, Rose prepared Amy to go home. "You know what, Amy? You've never told me your real name." Rose took off her blue cape, sat down on Amy's cot, and cradled her in her arms.

Amy sent Rose a loving grin and flashed large twinkling eyes up at her. She brushed Rose's cheek with her pudgy little hand.

For a two-and-a-half-year-old, Amy had mastered much of the English language.

"I found your Auntie Elizabeth last week. She told me your name is Lizzy. Yes?"

"No! Amy!" Lizzy poked out her bottom lip.

"Okay. Well, that's all right. But now, let's pretend your real name is Lizzy." Rose squeezed Lizzy and kissed her forehead.

"Mummy and Daddy?"

Rose held Lizzy tight. She had dreaded this moment for a long time. *Oh, dear God. Please let me say the right thing. I knew this day would come. How do I tell her? How will she react? I wish I could hold her in my arms forever—protect her—not let her hurt anymore.*

Rose ignored her question. "Lizzy, your Auntie Elizabeth wants you to come home right away. Her baby needs someone to play with."

"Millie wants to play?" Lizzy clapped her hands and bounced up and down on Rose's lap.

"That's what she said. You ready to go?"

Lizzy shook her head "yes," crawled out of Rose's lap, and grabbed her white yarn doll with yellow hair. "Take Rosie?"

"Of course. Ginny made her just for you." Rose knew that Ginny helped Lizzy name the doll after her. It had two black beads for eyes, one for a nose and a row of beads for a happy smile. Rose picked up a spool doll strung together with parachute cording. Nurse Sally had painted a cute face on the top spool and tied yarn around the head for hair.

Rose thought about the hours she had spent with Lizzy and her dolls while her tiny body healed. She loved the way Lizzy hugged her neck every time she leaned down over the bed to kiss her rosy cheeks.

She shoved the child's other things into a pillowcase. Nurse Mary had knitted a red jumper for Lizzy to wear over a white, long-sleeve blouse. After Rose slipped the jumper over Lizzy's head, she twirled her around.

"Perfect! You look lovely, Little Princess." Rose's heart sank at the thought of their separation. "Come here; let's put your coat on."

Rose watched the moist-eyed nurses swarm around Lizzy stealing hugs and kisses.

"Youse better come back and see us, baby." Ginny gave her a big squeeze.

Lizzy waved goodbye as she walked with Rose to the front of the hospital and a waiting jeep.

"Well, Sgt. Mallory. Nice of you to be my driver again."

"You knew I had to see this through. So, this is Lizzy."

"Can we ride in your jeep, Mr. Soldier?" Lizzy asked, looking up at Rose for approval. She tightened her grip on Rose's hand.

"You bet." He jumped out and took the pillowcase from Rose and flipped it into the back of the jeep.

Rose climbed into the front seat, and Sgt. Mallory lifted Lizzy onto her lap. He pulled a wool blanket out to wrap around them. "Once we start moving, she might get cold."

"Thank you, Sergeant. That's very thoughtful."

"Anything for the Lieutenant, ma'am." Sgt. Mallory beamed.

The jeep wove through the same path traveled two weeks earlier. For a long time Lizzy sat straight up in Rose's lap and didn't say a word.

She pointed to partially shattered houses and buildings. "Houses broke."

"Yes, they are. But not yours. Auntie Elizabeth's home is good." Rose pulled her in close and Lizzy leaned back and relaxed for the rest of the drive.

They arrived at Elizabeth's house, and Rose helped Lizzy out of the jeep along with her pillow sack. No one would have guessed that Lizzy's life hung on the fringe a few short weeks ago—not from the way she bounced down the now cleared path to the house with Rose right behind.

Lizzy knocked on the door after Rose removed her hand from the door handle. Except for the hum of the jeep motor, the community reflected death. Rose heard footsteps approaching the door. Lizzy jumped up and down with excitement.

Rose dreaded the moment. Since early that morning, her heart felt extra heavy. Even before she took Lizzy home, emptiness engulfed her entire body.

Elizabeth partially opened the door then flung it back with a smile that made her face glow. "Lizzy!" she shouted. "Oh Lizzy, I was so worried about you. I'm glad you're home." She caught the child up in her arms and tears streamed down her cheeks. She glanced at Rose. "Thank you for taking care of her. I don't know what to say."

"Just take good care of Lizzy. That's all I ask." Rose handed Elizabeth the pillow sack.

Lizzy squirmed down, ran to Rose, and wrapped her arms around her legs. Rose pushed her back, knelt down, and cradled the toddler in her arms.

"No, Auntie Rose!"

Tears welled up in Rose's eyes as she fought back her emotions. "I love you, Lizzy. Now you must go in with Auntie Elizabeth. I'll come by to see you often. You be a good girl for Elizabeth. You hear?"

Lizzy shook her head.

Rose peeled Lizzy's arms from around her legs and nudged her over to Elizabeth. "Bye-bye, the two of you."

"Thank you," Elizabeth said. Lizzy's chubby cheeks glistened with moisture.

Rose hurried to the jeep. She dared not look back. Not once, though she wanted to. She knew for Lizzy's sake and her own, it would be the last time she would see Lizzy. Once out of sight of the house, she let loose, buried her head in her hands.

Sgt. Mallory stopped the jeep and pulled Rose over to him. He caressed her hair and then wrapped his arms around her. "Let it go, Lieutenant. You've given your heart to this kid. I know it's hard. I care for you both and hate to see you hurt like this."

"Thanks, Sergeant. That means a lot. I know how much you care about Lizzy."

"Not just Lizzy."

"You're sweet, Sergeant." Rose sat up, wiped her cheeks, and smiled. "But I'm already spoken for."

"Dag nabbit! I'm always too late. If you ever change your mind, ma'am, think of me."

"You'd be the top name on my list. Thanks for your kindness." She planted a kiss on his cheek.

When the jeep returned to the barracks, Rose rushed inside the tent and crashed on the bunk, where she buried her face in the pillow. *Oh, Andy, the love of my life, and now Lizzy....* She was glad the barracks was empty. After a few moments, she pulled out a pencil and pad of paper:

*Dear Andy,*

*I've just had my heart torn, ripped from my body. I don't remember when I hurt so bad except after I found that you had shipped out before I could tell you good-bye. Remember little Amy? I wrote about her earlier. Her real name is Lizzy, and it was time for her to go home. Of course, there's more to it than that, but I'm so devastated that I can't write about it now.*

*I became too involved—too psychologically attached. I grew to love her as if she were my own. How did I let that happen? Nurses cannot become close to their patients. I knew a bond was forming and I did nothing to stop it. Now I am paying for it. But I'll make it through this, somehow.*

*I know I haven't written as often while I took care of Lizzy. I was exhausted during her critical days.*

*Andy, I think about our walk thru the meadow, the tenderness you showed me, and how frightened you were for me when the Luftwaffe strafed us.*

*I don't even know if you're getting any of my letters. I worry about your safety. You're what's in my heart. Please hurry back to me.*

*All my love,*
*Rose*

Rose scooted under the covers instead of addressing the envelope. Fatigue drained every ounce of energy from her body. She clutched the letter to her chest. Tears dribbled from the corner of her eyes into her hair. Her last waking thoughts were of Andy and Lizzy. Finally, she drifted into a worrisome sleep.

Later, Rose felt someone lightly caressing her hair and forehead. *I must be dreaming. But it feels so good. Soothing. Lips pressed on mine. Oh Andy.* She reached up and embraced him. He eased the covers back and in seconds was on top of her pulling at her clothing…

# Chapter Fourteen

## Foggia, Italy - December 1943

Andy watched Tex step off the runway into muddy gunk that devoured the bottom half of his boots.

"Holy shit! This is nothing but a mud hole." Tex shook and kicked at the mud on his boots to no avail, grabbed his gear and pitched it into the truck.

They left a dreary, wet England and now the same in Foggia— cold, wet, and miserable. Andy observed that nothing had changed except the mud, and no lush countryside with bicycle trails.

"For crap's sake. We just left this mess." Bulldog stomped his shoes before climbing into the truck.

"Wait 'til you see our living quarters," Andy replied. "You're not bringing that mud inside my tent. It's fit for a king." He gave Tex a jab, pitched his duffel bag onto the truck, and climbed in. "Come on, fellas."

The crew followed Andy, eager to get out of the rain—the eternal rain.

Several crews, all from England, packed into 6x6 trucks. Once off the runway, the canvas-top truck occupied by Andy and his crew swerved around mud holes, slipped into deep squishy ruts, and struggled to emerge without becoming stuck.

Three miles later, the truck came to a slippery halt. "Officers' quarters," the driver advised.

Andy, Tex, Bulldog, and Pops scrambled out of the truck. The others pitched the duffel bags to them.

"See you after briefing tomorrow," Andy shouted to the rest of the crew.

Andy stopped at the tent entrance and noticed a trench surrounding the tent to keep the water out. "Thank you!" he said under his breath.

He dumped his duffel bag on the first bunk. Bulldog took the bunk next to him. Tex and Pops grabbed the two opposite them. A coal-fired, potbelly stove sat in the middle of the tent with its pipe jutting through the highest center point of the canvas. Wooden structural reinforcement surrounded the interior of the tent, and a center post supported the top.The crossbeams doubled as clothing racks.

"Well fellas, this is home for a while. We've lucked out—better than most tents. Men with ingenuity must've worked hard. Look. We actually have flooring. Say, don't our bombs come crated in this floor stuff?"

"When ya need something and don't have it, ya make it. Ain't that right, Pops?" Bulldog affectionately tapped Pops on his half-bald head.

Andy hung up his best uniform and shoved other things wherever he could find a spot. *I need a picture of Rose.* He mounted his family's picture on a wooden tent support.

Later he settled in for the evening, hating the damp chill—the sickening sound of the never-ending rain beating down on the tent.

His thoughts got the best of him. *Everyone's grumpy and Christmas is in fifteen days. I am so depressed and homesick. Except for Pops, these guys are just kids. They've got to be homesick, too. If only I had someone to talk to—someone I could honestly share my fears with. I'm so alone. Can't talk to my best friend. It would destroy him if he knew the fright in my gut. Heavenly God! No one can know. It's eating me alive.*

December and January rolled in and out with numerous milk runs—simple missions—uneventful bomber flights. The USAAF increased the number of missions for squadrons in Italy to complete the requirement for reassignment home from thirty-five to fifty. Andy assumed they deemed flights out of Italy held less risk than those from England.

He discovered Foggia, Italy, located on the eastern coast of the Adriatic Sea, desolate and poor. Noticeably absent were English pubs and the friendly faces of locals drinking with American flyers. Italians refused to fraternize with the Americans who had bombed them only a few short months ago. R & R (rest and relaxation) disappeared in Italy. Nothing but poverty everywhere as far as Andy could see. The language barrier, coupled with the country's customs, made it less desirable to venture into the villages. With only a small officers' club on the base, Andy and his crew had little to do during the days of no flying.

## Middle of February - 1944

Andy checked the mission flags—no flag up. On boring days, they kept the mess tents busy and their stomachs filled. And then the long, endless evenings rolled in. The rains plummeted, deepening the mud holes, as if that was possible. Farther north, ice and snow shut down all missions where ice clung dangerously to the planes.

"Bulldog, you realize we got only four missions to go before reaching our fiftieth? We go home then. I'm going back to England, get Rose, go home, get married, and get my law degree. How about you?"

"I'm going back to that little gal in Kentucky, buy a farm, and raise ten kids. My mom's doing a lot better now. You, Tex?" Bulldog pumped his closed fists together and stared at him.

"I'm going back to school…get me a medical degree." Tex spit on his boot and rubbed it till it shined.

"Pops, you got family waiting for you, right? Andy asked.

"I can't wait to get back to my wife and two beautiful daughters. What's coming up next, Andy?" Pops asked, cards spread all over his bunk where he played solitaire.

Andy sat on his bunk, elbows propped on his knees. "Don't know yet, but hear tell something big is in the works. They got those new P-51 Mustang fighters that can fly the entire missions with us. We'll stop losing lives and planes now."

"Where were they when we lost all those planes over Schweinfurt? Ever notice all our missions have been milk runs since we got here? Yeah, all those milk runs. Fly out on a mission, drop our bomb load, no danger, return for another day—another milk run. How long can this last? Four more to go to our 50$^{th}$. Who gets to that number? I don't know of one crew that made it." Bulldog slipped his boots off and rubbed his feet. "This rain is pure 'hell.' Can't even dig a foxhole without drowning in it, and there ain't no air-raid shelters. They'd fill up with water. What crap."

"Would you rather fly to Schweinfurt?" Andy asked.

"Hell no, you know better 'n that. I'm hitting the sack." Bulldog rolled over on his bunk.

"Come to think of it, I don't know either. What's our chance? We got four missions. Which one's gonna take us out?" He wrung his hands. Perspiration dribbled on his temples. "I saw the names scrubbed off the mission boards before they sent us to Italy," Tex said, his drawl reached a higher pitch.

"Hey, fellas. I can navigate you through anything. Don't get so worked up." Pops paced back and forth.

"Come on, men. We've been a great team. Think positive. We're going home soon. Snap out of it." Andy turned away fearful his men could read his face.

Andy had never seen his crew this uncertain and grumpy. Instead of commenting further, he stretched out on his bunk and let his own thoughts run rampant. *No shelters, no foxholes, no place to run. We're sitting targets. Leastways, we're not six miles up in the sky.*

## February 20, 1944

Andy listened intently. The CO laid out the entire week's missions. "The 8th USAAF will merge with the 15th USAAF to engage in one of the largest battles of the war. Combat wings from England and the balance from Italy will join in these missions. During the week of February 20 through 25, 1944, plans for Big Week, also referred to as Operation Argument, will dispatch one thousand planes to destroy twelve major enemy assembly and component plants for German fighter planes.

"With twelve targets and the new P-51 US fighter planes to accompany the P-47s and P-38s, these little friends can split off to specific assignments leaving few for actual shared defense of the bombers. The Luftwaffe will scatter to defend each point of attack, leaving small groups of fighters to assault the B-17s and B-24s."

The CO ended after another forty-five minutes, and Andy and his crew hustled out of the briefing room.

Andy observed the uneasiness of his crew. "Come on, fellas. I know what you're thinking. Any one of the next four missions can do us in. Remember how we got here. A tank of a plane, a superb crew, and we are brothers—brothers who watch our backs—brothers who work together as one."

"Yeah, but we had all those easy milk runs. And now the tough ones." Tex fumbled with his cowboy hat dragging his fingers round and round its rim.

"Well, you'd better bet if we have real eggs, we'll know this is it." Bulldog grabbed each side of his head and rocked back and forth.

"No, no, no. That's not right. How many times did we have real eggs? Several times and we're still here." *Please God, don't let them know how frightened I am. And please, Lord, help me to overcome my fright and be the leader I know I can be.* Andy added, "Tex, you're ghostly white. Where's your faith? Faith in God and your brothers? Pops. How about it?"

"Well boys, I'm as afraid as you are knowing 20% of lost men on each mission is an unthinkable number, but I plan to beat those odds. How about you?" Pops clapped his hands.

Andy joined in. "Yes, sir! We'll not be defeated! Our loved ones are waiting for us. Thanks, Pops." He pumped his right arm.

"You are welcome. Need I say that I re-iterate your exact fears. I want to return to my family ASAP—just like the rest of the men. I don't want my name scratched off the Roster Board.

"You're a good man, Pops. Let's do it!" Andy added an extra step in his gait.

"Damn it, Cap'n, why ain't you afraid. Sometimes I shake in my boots and I ain't afraid to say so." Bulldog stepped into Andy's space.

"I have my moments, but we have a job to do. Our freedom is at stake. We must defeat Hitler and win this war. That's our duty." Andy stared at the men studying their demeanor.

## Operation Big Week

All hell broke loose. Andy and his men encountered the most harrowing experiences since Schweinfurt, flying the early missions of the week—numbers forty-seven, forty-eight, and forty-nine.

The crews that made it back to Foggia Airfield during Big Week would have kissed the ground upon their return—most especially Andy and the crew of the *Alley Cat*, had it not been so saturated. Andy had reached the point that he would not fly without his seasoned crew. No splitting a family of brothers. They worked as a team, and if one crewman was missing, it put the entire crew in jeopardy. After forty-nine missions, a sense of their good luck surfaced. No way would they break that streak. They were one.

On the evening of the 23$^{rd}$ day of February 1944, Andy prepared for yet another early morning mission. He pulled out his note pad once more.

*Dear Rose,*

*As I lie here listening to the rain beat down on the tent, my thoughts turn to you and the weeks we spent together in England. Oh, how I miss those days—the warmth of your smile, the twinkle in your eyes, and your bubbling enthusiasm that drew me to you like a magnet.*

*Yes, the sun will come up tomorrow, well, maybe not in Italy, but surely somewhere winter will fade into spring. With the change of seasons, the birds will return, filling the air with their beautiful chirping. Bluebirds will bring twigs for nests to cradle their eggs—he with his bright blues and rust browns—she with her subdued colors, but just as beautiful.*

*Rose, from the moment you walked back into my life through the evening fog in Snetterton, I knew that you were the one for me, just as I am sure the sun will rise, somewhere. The vision of your face is what brings light into this dismal bleak war—the warmth just when I need it. You are God's promise of a better life. A promise that I fall back on. It gives me hope for the future—our future. The thought that I might have missed the chance for something lasting and precious is unthinkable.*

*My dearest Rose, I believe that our love is the union of two spirits destined for lasting happiness. You are the light of my life in this dark, gloomy world. We are a pair of bluebirds waiting to build our nest, and one day we shall. It's our destiny.*

*All of these things are beyond my control. The last three missions have been traumatic. We were fortunate to make it back. Tomorrow's mission is another perilous one. It's our 50th mission and we all know the Alley Cat has been one lucky ship. Only God knows the outcome of this mission, but He also knows what's in my heart. I pray He will bring me back safely to you, my love.*

*If you receive this letter, you know I didn't make it. Do not grieve for me. I want you to go on with your life,*

*a full life, with a husband and children—just as we*
*would have done. You only live once. Don't waste it.*
*I will love you forever, my darling.*
*Andy*

Andy folded the letter and placed it in his best uniform's shirt pocket. He prayed it would still be there when he returned. His thoughts turned to his family, and he wrote a second letter. When he looked up, he noticed the other fellas pushing pencils on pads of paper.

He slipped a second letter into the same best uniform pocket giving it a pat before turning in for the evening. When he lay on his bunk, the same bunk that another flyer never returned to, he looked at the top of the tent and imagined a sky full of stars looking down on him. He prayed to God for a safe return and safety for the entire squadron. Before he shut his eyes, he envisioned a million twinkling angels watching over him.

Andy scarcely slept. Insomnia wasn't the problem. Lonely thoughts crawled like maggots in his mind—of self-doubt—of life itself. He tossed his knobby cotton pillow aside after numerous attempts to find the right spot against his cheek.

Wakeup call came at 0500. Andy and his men stretched and yawned, and like his body, rejecting the hour.

Rising up, Andy said, "Hey, y'all. Know what today is?" He forced a jovial upbeat sound, lost his balance, and fell back on his bunk as he attempted to be spunky before his body agreed to the task.

Tex, Bulldog, and Pops looked at Andy as if he had lost his mind.

"What you talking 'bout?" Bulldog said. He pulled on his socks.

"Our 50th mission, fellas! Don't tell me you forgot. Where's the enthusiasm?" Andy slipped into his wools.

"You're right. I 'bout forgot. Fact is, don't talk about it. It'll jinx us. I'm bailing if we have real eggs today. No joke." Bulldog glanced around to see if Andy was paying attention.

"Think about that. What difference would it make? We've had real eggs for the last four breakfasts. I believe we'll make it all the way. You wait and see. Let's go! Real eggs await us!" Andy snatched his flight jacket and hat from a hook.

The rain had disappeared. Fog locked in the entire airfield. The men followed a trail of muck and oozy mud to the mess hall. Vehicle exhaust fumes lay trapped in the stagnant fog that choked their lungs.

"Remember all the times we actually flew within a couple of hours of our IP only to have the mission scrubbed? Also, the times we had to salvo our bombs before landing? All those wasted hours toward number fifty. Don't be surprised if it happens this time as well," Andy said. He dodged a deep mud puddle by cat-walking a nearby log. "The man upstairs has looked after us so far."

"We hear ya," Bulldog replied weakly.

Andy entered the oversized mess tent, where steam curled above boiling pots. He fell in queue and worked his way to the food.

Bulldog gazed at a tray before him. "Damn it! What'd I tell ya, Andy. Eggs. Real eggs."

Andy stepped in front of Bulldog's face, "Get over it, Bulldog. Let it go! You're gonna upset the rest of the crew. Now go sit down and eat your *real* eggs and enjoy them. Nothing more and nothing less." Andy popped him an affectionate tap.

"Sorry, Andy. You're right. Just uptight today."

Andy moved closer to Bulldog and whispered in his ear. "If it helps, Bulldog, you're not by yourself."

Bulldog shot a glance into Andy's eyes.

Andy did not make that statement lightly, and realized Bulldog got the message. "We've been through a lot together, and we'll make it through this. I have faith, and you need to depend on your faith as well." Andy urged Bulldog forward. "We've got eight other men watching out for us. They need us as well. Okay, ole buddy?"

"Yeah, Andy. I'm okay. I ain't gonna let ya down." Bulldog lifted his tin, and the cook dropped a large mound of scrambled eggs on it. He stopped, transfixed on the eggs. "That don't look like no five eggs."

"Count 'em." Andy flashed his white teeth and nudged Bulldog on.

After breakfast, Andy and Bulldog hastened to briefing. Sounds of moving equipment penetrated the camp with its hustle and bustle in the early morning. An officer stood at the tent entrance to check off their names. The benches overflowed. Mixed squadrons crowded in with some sitting on the floor, others standing around the edges.

Andy scanned the faces and listened to boisterous words that echoed throughout. *This is something big. Obviously these guys have not witnessed tragic missions. Reality has not set in for some of them. They're too eager. Reminds me of myself ages ago. Where'd they all come from?*

The noise built into an earsplitting crescendo. Restless men, shouting, smoking, and drinking coffee. The CO stood next to the covered map, waited until all the men were inside, then uncovered the map. The flight pattern led straight to ball-bearing factories in Steyr, Austria. Others led to Regensburg, while the balance of the 8th still in England, directly to Schweinfurt, Gotha, Bernburg, Oschersleben, Aschersleben, and Halberstadt. A riveting hush came over the room. Smiles disappeared. Ridges formed on brows. Men shifted in their seats. None took their eyes off the board, faces deadpan, beads of perspiration forming.

"I need not tell you that this is a long dangerous mission. You will incur a wall of flak like you've never seen before. P-38s, P-47s, and P-51s will defend you. It is imperative that you maintain extreme close combat formation. The gaggles of enemy fighters you've experienced before will be scarce. They'll hold back to defend their factories. Remain in tight formation to put up a barrage of firepower from all the B-17s to knock out the first row of fighters. But that won't stop them. It'll slow them down because some of those bastards will turn away. They'll be back though. Don't allow *one* bogie into the formation. You're doomed if you do.

"Stay the course toward your IP. If you veer away from the protection of the formation, you *will* be picked off. Some of you flyers are sleeping on the bunks of a few poorly flown squadrons, careless with their formation and lack of attention to the sky. If your crew works closely together, you stand a better chance than they did. Watch out for each other." The CO ended abruptly.

Pops stood up and rubbed his backside. "Those benches need a little padding." He walked with Andy and the men to the equipment building.

"Well, I'll be dogged. The fog has dissipated. Our lucky day," Tex said, with a smile that covered the entire lower half of his face. He shoved his cowboy hat above his forehead.

After they picked up their flight gear, donned their heat suits, flak vests, and parachutes, they hopped on one of several jeeps waiting to transport the crews to their planes. At 0730 the early eastern sky cleared for the first time in weeks.

A second jeep pulled up behind Andy with the balance of the *Alley Cat's* crew.

"Y'all look like penguins waddling over here," Andy joshed in an effort to relax his men.

"I say, I feel like I'm wearing a corset. Is this what those bloody Victorian women suffered through with their cinched waists?" Paulie broke into an exaggerated hip swing.

"Those ole broads had it pretty rough, I'll wager. Bet a fella had a hard time getting to skin." With that Bulldog got the entire group's attention and took a cue from Paulie and followed suit with the same hip shaking. A tad more jovial, they climbed into the plane and set about their tasks.

Andy slipped on his helmet, completed his walk around the plane, climbed up a ground crew ladder, and dusted the *Alley Cat's* name, a ritual that stuck with him from the day they acquired the *Cat*. He talked to each ground crewman and pulled himself up through the pilot's hatch. Instead of climbing into the pilot's seat, he stepped over to Pops, the navigator, clasped his hand, on to Sully, the flight engineer and top turret, grasped his hand, and then gave Bulldog a couple of thumps on his back. Before crossing the narrow catwalk, he gave Paulie, the radio operator a thumbs up. Andy pumped Billy's hand and noticed his stashed parachute next to the ball turret.

"Thank you, sir."

"We're counting on you." Andy continued on to Nealy and Whitie, waist gunners, and grabbed their hands. Last, he tapped Tony's back. "You watch our backs, Tony!"

"Gotcha, sir!"

Andy observed the crew of the *Alley Cat* as he headed back to the cockpit. He caught his chin between his thumb and forefinger. Tightness squeezed his chest. *They are my family now. We are truly brothers. I would have never made it without them.*

Andy settled into his seat, hooked his helmet strap, and began the long checklist with Tex. He forced himself not to let his mind wander. *Concentrate. No fatalistic thoughts today. We've not lost one crew member. Not today either!*

The list continued nonstop, one item after another:

…Master Switch - ON

Battery switches and inverters – ON and CHECKED

Parking Brakes – Hydraulic Check – ON CHECKED

Booster Pumps—Pressure – ON and CHECKED

Carburetor Filters – OPEN

…The list hummed on until the *Alley Cat* rolled down the tarmac with the final checklist. Andy and Tex touched each instrument called out on the lists. Everything by the book.

The four engines revved up to 1,500 rpm clearing out gunk, tail wheel locked, gyro set, generators on, they waited in a set pattern at the edge of the runway for the signal. The flag signal was given. Andy removed the foot brake pressure, and at 100 mph, the *Alley Cat* took off into the blinding sun. They bounced and jostled down the tarmac until the air lifted them up and away. He knew once he raised the landing gear, it was a dangerous time with bombs loaded to the maximum. The plane built up speed to 150 mph. He throttled back and eventually reduced the rpm to 2,300 feet per minute.

"Approaching 10,000 feet. Put on your oxygen masks," Andy ordered.

Tex squeezed his intercom for a call to each crewman confirming oxygen mask functions. Replies of "operational" reverberated through the intercom system.

Andy didn't like what he heard. *I hear tension in their voices. They need to relax. Yep, soon as the first bogie is spotted. Our 50$^{th}$ mission looms heavily over all of us—the only crew going for their 50th. I'm nauseated, and my stomach is rumbling. We're so damned frightened; this will be our doom if we don't shake it. I pray to God we make it!*

On the way toward their IP, they flew in and out of cumulus clouds as Andy began the slow process of maneuvering the *Cat* into the formation. Perspiration dribbled down his forehead. The close proximity of a combat formation proved harrowing, considering the combination of the entire formation's bomb load.

"Test your weapons," Andy ordered. A barrage of weapon testing commenced as they flew up the Adriatic Sea. The *Cat* vibrated from the expulsion of .50 caliber shots. He knew the test helped release tension for the crewmen.

Approaching the enemy coast, Andy ordered, "Refrain from unnecessary chatter." He knew enemy tracked them with radar that detected every sound as they pressed forward to their IP. He turned to Tex. "Our little friends above look good. Let's hope they can stay with us. We need more little friends."

"Yeah, you better believe the Jerries are ready to pounce on this *Cat* like a ferocious dog." Tex scanned the sky.

"Yep, they always seem to know our where 'bouts." No sooner had Andy spoken when the P-47s and P-51s peeled off one after another, to intercept Luftwaffe fighters. "So much for the speech about fighters staying home to defend their factories."

The first row of bogies raced in to attack the defenders in a fierce battle. The formation of bombers droned on toward their destination, undaunted with the mêlée going on above.

"Bogies 6 o'clock," Tony shouted, taking aim with his .50s. The *Cat* shuddered violently from the rounds.

Bandit 3 o'clock, Tony. I got 'em," Sully shouted, while pouring a stream of fire blasting a FW-190 to smithereens. "Nine o'clock, Billy. He's sneaking under."

Billy swiveled around, but missed only to see another B-17 send the ME-109 spiraling to the ground.

Andy gripped the control wheel tighter. Eyes darted from side to side and above, searching for bogies. His internal autopilot took over. Fear vanished. Determination took its cue.

"I need help," Tony yelled from the tail gunner position. "They're coming faster than I can shoot." Directly in front of him hanging upside down, poised for the kill, another ME-109 with flashing lights suddenly disintegrated before his eyes after Tony hit the ME's fuel tanks. His body shook in rhythm with the .50s.

One P-47 plummeted to the ground, while a P-38 collided with a JU-88, exploding and sending debris cascading onto the *Alley Cat*.

"Damn!" Sully shouted as a metal piece crashed through his bubble and cut into his left arm. "Pops! Need your help!"

The six remaining Luftwaffe fighters continued unmercifully after the Purple Heart section—not enough of them to attack the side of the formation. Andy knew their goal was to pick off the tail end of the formation. One plane at a time. Tail-end Charlies—doomed.

"Three o'clock, Whitie." Sully shouted as Pops slit the sleeve of Sully's jacket, dumped sulfa into the wound, and applied pressure to slow the bleeding. The intense cold reduced the blood flow. He applied a tightly wrapped bandage to Sully's arm.

Whitie fired wildly from the starboard waist gunner position as another ME-109 closed almost within reach. He connected with the fighter unable to bring it down.

Tony showered another gaggle of 190s coming in at 6 o'clock and missed.

Two more Fortresses went down, one spiraling and the other on a fiery glide to an earth-bound grave. Andy's mouth was so dry he couldn't swallow.

"Nine o'clock, Billy," Bulldog shouted, his voice shrill.

Billy swiveled around in time to unleash rounds from both 50s at two 190s. He hit one dead center, shredding it to pieces. Fire spewed out from the wing on the other.

Tony struggled with a Ju 88 coming at his tail position. He sprayed a pair of twin 50s. Missed.

"Sully! Coming 'round. Two o'clock, he's yours," Nealy bellowed while pumping rounds on the port side at a ME 210 on the attack.

"Yeow! Where'd that son-of-a-bitch go?" Sully said, swinging his guns around in time to fire at two FW 190s, missing them both. The 190s discharged numerous rounds whizzing past Sully. Firing in bursts, Sully spotted a FW 190 with its belly tank attached. He took dead aim and hit the tank, blowing the plane to bits. Slivers, like metal nails, flew toward the *Cat*.

The skirmish persisted for forty-five minutes with no letup.

"Barrage of flak ahead. Hang on!" Andy ordered. They entered the deadly black flak as they neared their IP, and the fighters turned away but not before the *Alley Cat* took hit upon hit.

Two simultaneous 20mms hit the side of the *Alley Cat* and the 2nd waist gunner position. Nealy slumped to the floor of the plane—a piece of metal in the side of his throat.

Whitie spun around and ran to Nealy's aid but froze at the sight.

"Get back to your guns," Pops yelled, as he rushed to Nealy and knelt by his side. There was nothing he could do. The blood gushed until it froze on the outside of Nealy's body. He lay lifeless on the fuselage floor.

"Watch out," Andy shouted as a metal object ripped through the cockpit, struck his shoulder, careened up toward Sully, clipped his earphone, and severed the wires to his intercom. "You okay, Sully?" Andy yelled.

"Yes, sir," Sully shouted, audibly shaken.

The number three engine ground to a halt and burst into flames. Andy feathered the engine. Nothing stopped the fire. "Number three's gone." His throat scraped like sandpaper when he swallowed. The smell of fear filled the *Cat*.

"Andy! They're ripping us to pieces." Tex clung solidly to the control wheel as a jolt from beneath rocked the ship.

"Hang tight, Tex. We're as helpless as geese over a blind." Andy was beyond terror.

A jarring burst of flak ruptured the pilot's hatch, slicing the flesh in Andy's upper left thigh. It went numb. Another piece hit the control console and forward side of the instrument panel.

"Whoa!" One jolt after another. Andy looked down to see Bulldog's extra flak cushions tumbling from the plane. His Plexiglas nose plummeted into obscurity. He secured his guns, dangling precariously while swiveling with the twin 50s firing randomly until he regained control.

The next incoming blast severed the main oxygen line. Andy tried to focus, but his vision blurred. No oxygen. He reached back and tapped Sully just as he slipped from the top turret to the floor. Andy dragged his left leg; fell onto the cockpit floor as he noticed Tex's head drooping.

Gasping, Andy reached for an oxygen bottle, fought to hook it to his mask. After taking several deep breaths, he gathered additional bottles, and linked up Tex, leaving him at the controls. Pops lunged for one of the bottles. Andy knew he had a limited time to reach the others, fearing they would not realize the oxygen supply was gone. After connecting each man, he placed two fingers on Nealy's neck to check for pulse. None. Dead. A cold chill flooded Andy's body. His actions became automatic. He limped back to the cockpit, not wanting reality to set in.

"Bail out! Bail out!" Andy shouted through the intercom. Switching to radio communications, he called, "Come in Leader Plane. Come in! This is *Alley Cat*. Mayday! Mayday!"

Ink-black smoke flooded the mortally wounded B17G Flying Fortress bouncing helplessly out of control between antiaircraft bursts high above Steyr, Austria. A 20mm blast burst through the starboard side of the plane. Acrid smoke poured from the control panel in front of Tex. Andy gawked at the instruments for any sign of life—then at Tex. All controls...gone. This was it! The *Alley Cat*, fully loaded with 4,000 pounds of bombs, would crash short of their target.

Andy pushed the bell—no response. Nothing worked. "Bail out! Bail out!" he shouted again over the thunderous rush of air, roar of engines and exploding flak.

Tex rushed through the plane passing the word along, Sully behind him.

Boom! Another hit. Smoke rapidly filled the cockpit. Bulldog groped his way to Billy, pulled him from the turret bubble.

"Here, you're shaking too much." Bulldog struggled with Billy's parachute "Hold still!" Finished, he spun Billy around and shoved him in the direction of the exit door. "Hurry! Get outta here!" By then, the smoke saturated the plane, forcing the crew to feel their way to the back of the plane.

Andy's quaking hands fumbled over a gap in his oxygen tank. He snatched a cord away from the stationary tank and yanked another portable oxygen bottle mounted on the cockpit's sidewall. He slid from his seat, crouched low, and groped his way to the bombardier section. Bombardier, navigator, and radioman—gone. His breath came in terror-stricken gulps. *Oh, God. Only seconds to get the hell out of here. The Cat's going down!*

Ebony smoke seeped into his mask, absorbing precious oxygen. He dropped to his hands and knees, gasping for air. The crippled plane drifted in a wide spiral beyond the torturous flak zone. He wrestled back to his feet. The deafening buzz of Messerschmidts and Focke-Wulf 190 fighters surrounded the plane, closing in for the kill. Guns crackled, penetrating the plane, and the sputtering belches of the remaining fourth engine propelled him forward.

In search of his crew, he stumbled toward dark shadows scrambling to the rear exit. His chute's ripcord snagged. He jerked to a stop. The parachute burst open—inside the plane. Blood drained from his face—he stood motionless. "Oh, Jesus!"

He broke into a cold sweat—smelled the scent of death. Numbness overtook his entire body as if he was already dead. He grappled with his chute, gathered it up, and cradled it in his arms.

Whitie cowered in a fetal position by the door. "Whitie, get up! Jump! Plane's going down!" Andy shook him, but White refused to move. He sat there—frozen. Andy had no choice. He had to jump or go down with the plane. Death was imminent. If he jumped, his chute might not soar. Only seconds left.

Adrenalin shot through his veins and pressed him forward. He lurched to the exit—parachute in arms. He jumped.

"May God have mercy on my soul!" His life snapped in front of him like the pop of a rubber band.

# Chapter Fifteen

Startled, Rose's mind cleared and she became fully awake—her body shuddered. In the dim light seeping through the tent, she realized it was not Andy, huskier.

"Get off me," she screamed. "Help!" She pushed with all her strength until he grabbed both arms and shoved them above her head.

"Anybody. Help! Help me!"

The man tried to drop his elbow across her mouth. Kicking and screaming, Rose clashed, clawed, and clobbered the man with all her might. Rolling her body side to side he became unsteady on her. "Get off me! Now!" *Oh, God. Get him off me!* Her heartbeat matched her breath in short rapid spurts.

Rose screamed so loud, she could hear nothing else. She waited for the proper moment, arched her back forcing him to slip lower on her body, twisted to get a leg free, and thrust her knee into his groin. Her arms freed as he withered in pain, she shoved him to the floor.

Just as the man hit the floor, Ginny rushed in. "What the hell is going on in here? Are you all right, Rose?" She raced over to wrap her arms around Rose helping her to sit up.

"Colonel!" Rose and Ginny shouted in unison. They both studied the man on the floor in astonishment watching him roll in pain until he was able to speak.

He raised his arm and pointed a finger at Rose. "Now, now, Rose. I knocked, but you didn't answer so I walked in. When I saw you sleeping so peaceful and beautiful, I couldn't resist you. And when I kissed you, you responded. What was a fella to think?"

"Get up. Now! Get out of here!" Rose, sitting on the edge of her bunk, could not control her trembling body.

He struggled unable to stand straight, brushed off his clothes, and leaned over Rose. "You enjoyed it, and you know you did! I'll not give up."

"Leave now, sir. Now!" Rose followed him to the entrance returning to her bunk once he retreated from the tent.

Ginny had not moved. Her jaw drooped—eyes followed Rose.

Rose sat on the edge of her bunk and caught each side of her temples. "I fell asleep and the next thing I knew, he was all over me, kissing and trying to go further. I thought I was dreaming, until he tried to take my clothes off. He's my superior officer. What'll I do now?"

"You've got to report him...tomorrow! It's no telling what he might do next."

"How can I do that? I've been able to schedule my time with Lizzy whenever I wanted. Nobody else gets these privileges. But get this, Ginny. I was enjoying this in my dream when I thought it was Andy until I realized it wasn't. Oh my gosh! He probably could tell I wanted it and thought I knew it was him."

"Gal, you got a problem, but a Lt. Colonel slipping into his nurse's tent and taking advantage of her? That's serious." Ginny sat on her bunk rolling her white stockings down.

Hot tears scorched Rose's cheeks. "I miss Andy so much and wanted to commit my love to him, but the possibility of him not coming back stopped me. I dared not let him know how I felt, how quickly I fell in love with him, how I delighted in his open admiration. Was I so wrong?"

"No, daa…ling, as you say," Ginny grinned, "not if you really love the Captain.

Look at me, I don't commit, just have a grand time when my fella's around."

"I wish I could be like you. Perhaps if I didn't fall in love, I could fall for the Doc. Andy just touches me and a ripple of excitement races through my body. He's irresistible and when I'm with him I am blissfully happy, fully alive."

"Gal, you got it bad, really bad. I might sound flippant about love, but the truth is I'm envious of you and your captain."

"Well, sir. I'd a never known if you hadn't told me. Friend, you never fail to calm and set me straight. What would I do without you?"

"Them's good words to hear from a Southerner to a damn Yankee. By the way, I've never heard screaming like that. I almost peed in my pants."

"Thank goodness you appeared when you did. My throat is raw, let's continue this conversation in the morning." Rose plopped on her bunk staring at the tent top. Chills ravaged her body when she thought about what almost happened.

The next day Rose reported for duty as usual at the base hospital. Lt. Col. Lawing was nowhere in sight. *How can I report the Colonel when, though I didn't realize I wasn't dreaming, I definitely responded. What does that say about me?*

Rose went about her duties as usual until a tap on the shoulder caused her to suck air. She spun around with a fist and connected to the Sergeant's upper arm.

"Whoa! What's going on? Did I miss something?" Sgt. Mallory stepped back expecting another blow.

"Oh no! I am so sorry. I thought you were someone else, but I'm glad you weren't.

"What caused all this? I've never seen you this upset. Hey, you owe me a cup of java for that greeting. Can you get away for a few minutes?"

"Sure. I 'do' owe you. Don't mind having a cup of coffee with a handsome Sergeant." She sent him her infectious over-the-shoulder smile.

A few minutes later Rose and the Sergeant sat opposite each other, coffee in hands, while nurses bustled around, some taking a break, others reporting for duty. Rose observed several strange looks.

"Now tell me, what the hell happened to put you on defense like that?" Sgt. Mallory took a sip of coffee.

"Something happened last night and I simply don't have a clue how to handle it. I'm afraid I led someone to think I cared about him, when I was sleeping—dreaming of my fella. He took it as a come on when it wasn't. In the first place, he had no business slipping into my tent while I was sleeping and the other girls were away on duty."

"Who was the louse and I'll take care of him? What the hell was he thinking? You need to report him."

"You're not listening. Yes, he should not have entered my tent. But once in and while I was asleep, he kissed me and I responded. Did you hear that? I responded! Can you believe it?"

"Who was the bastard? Who?" The Sergeant set his cup down hard.

"I can't tell you. He went too far which woke me up and I fought him off. Now who would believe me, a lowly nurse, against a high ranking officer?" Rose reached in her pocket for a hankie.

"You know I believe you." He reached over and pushed back a lock of hair that slipped from under her nurse's hat.

"I knew you would, but in reality, it's a man's world and that's why women don't come forward with things like this. And now since I feel partially responsible..."

"Stop right now! Did you invite him in? Of course not. Whatever you decide to do, don't ever blame yourself. Only a louse would walk right in, see a woman sleeping and take advantage of her."

"I know, I know, Sergeant. But there's more. He allowed me to stay with Lizzy as much as I wanted, arranged scheduling so I could be with her during the day after she got better—whatever I needed." She picked up her cup, swirled the coffee around, and without a sip, set it back down.

"Oh, brother. You've got a mess. So, if you don't report him, what are you going to do when you see him?" A nurse swished by after tapping him on the shoulder. The Sergeant twisted around, "Hey, Marla."

"You've got fans," Rose teased.

"Nothing like you. You've got a B-17 pilot madly in love with you, a sergeant madly in love with you, and now a high ranking officer is madly in love with you. How could you be so lucky?"

"Surely you jest, Sergeant?" Rose joked until seeing the look on the Sergeant's face. She squirmed in her seat.

The Sergeant's eyes locked with hers. "I've never been more serious than now. I'm crazy about you, Lieutenant. Whenever you hurt, I hurt. Whenever you smile, I smile, and whenever you love, I love, and I love Lizzy."

"Sergeant, you are a terrific friend and I don't know what I'd do without you. But you know where my love is." She shifted from serious to light hearted. "But be assured, if I ever change my mind, I'd be looking for you." She tapped him on his arm.

"Sure, but don't look for me to hold my breath 'til then." He returned Rose's smile and clasped her hand.

"I've got to get back and face the big guy. You've helped by putting everything into perspective, and I appreciate it. You're a good friend."

"I'm always here for you."

They both stood and she gave him a kiss on the cheek. "I know."

Later, while checking on her patients, Lt. Col. Lawing caught up to her. "Lieutenant, may I see you in my office?"

Without glancing up, Rose responded. "Yes sir." She completed changing the patient's bandages and headed for the Colonel's office wringing her hands as she bustled along.

After entering his office where the Colonel sat behind his paper filled desk-top, she said, "Yes sir?"

"About last night…"

Standing at attention in front of his desk, Rose interrupted him. "Sir, let me speak. Number one—last night you had no business entering my tent most especially while I was sleeping. Number two—you should not have attempted to take advantage of me in a situation like…"

"I didn't take advantage of you. You wanted it. You responded eagerly. Don't you go blaming me, young lady." The Colonel's brow creased.

"Sir! I thought I was dreaming and that it was someone else. Not you! You had absolutely no right to even be there." Rose felt the blood rush to her face.

"You wanted it. I know you did."

"All I'm going to say is, I apologize if I led you on but don't you ever forget you will never take advantage of me like that again, never!" Rose pounded her fist on his desk and stormed out of the Colonel's office.

She clomped back to her patients. *Andy where are you? What's next? Oh what have I gotten into now? Lizzy baby, have I ruined it for us? I've got to work this out—now!*

# Chapter Sixteen

## Austria

A burst of frigid air slapped Andy's face. He was in a free fall. After tumbling far enough to clear the plane, he thrust the cradled parachute above him. The silk drifted skyward. A strap buckle flapped, hitting him on the cheekbone directly below his eye. His body never flinched. The pit of his stomach contracted into a ball.

A severe yank and blast of air forced him skyward. Andy looked up. Overhead floated the most beautiful white silk he'd ever seen. His body went limp. He laughed hysterically—uncontrollably. It was like floating upward to heaven. He waited for the descent. The numbness in his thigh turned to sharp pain.

Glancing backwards, he searched the sky for his crewmen. If they made it out, they were well below him. He prayed a fighter would not pick them off. Now he turned his attention to the Luftwaffe and flak. Antiaircraft fire peppered the sky with black splotches of exploding flak that threatened his very existence.

As his eyes focused through the haze, the ground far below appeared covered in snow. Andy strained for a backward glance and sadly watched his beloved *Alley Cat* glide into extinction, sending up a ball of fire in Steyr, Austria's industrial area. Not the intended target—just short of the IP.

Minutes later, the distant ground erupted, spewing mushroom-like debris high over the IP—the ball-bearing manufacturing plants. A sense of accomplishment rushed over Andy, even though the *Alley Cat* did not participate in the bomb dump—did not complete its mission. The sounds of battle picked up as the bombers headed to their RP—Luftwaffe blasting B-17s, the USAAF defending its airspace—and the whine of the whistling bombs gradually faded while Andy glided away from the foray. He searched the sky back to the IP target for other parachutes, but opaque black smoke obscured his vision.

The blustery wind propelled him far from his target and his earthly descent. A 190 swooped down to get a closer glimpse at him. He played dead, dangling his arms and letting his head fall forward, legs limp. Andy realized the pilot took one look and peeled off, ignoring him. He watched the pilot head toward a target in the *new* Purple Heart section.

The western wind shift sent him toward Salzburg, Austria, near the German border, but far out of the dreaded flak and IP area.

While descending, he memorized the countryside to establish an escape route. The snow-covered ground brilliantly contrasted with the dark clothing of people below. He knew the locals would scramble to find him the minute he touched down. His pulse roared in his ears, and a sickening wave of nausea rose up from his belly.

An abrupt force of air gushed up from the ground, propelled him skyward. He sailed toward the mountains and once again studied the landscape for possible hiding places or new escape routes. The sun spread its smile over the mountains, and Andy, having just left hell, found it hard to believe that this war with death and destruction could exist beyond this heaven. A barn sighting interrupted his thoughts, and he pulled on his chute cords to maneuver his landing closer. His feet skimmed the top of the snow. The chute dropped him within a hundred feet of the barn and tangled in the bushes and smaller trees. Pain shot through his left thigh like he'd just been hit—the numbness long gone. He unhooked himself from the line and wrestled with the silk until it released itself from the entrapment. The bright yellow Mae West suddenly caught his attention—like announcing his arrival to anyone within eyesight. Quickly he ripped off the life preserver and rolled it into a small bundle inside his parachute. He broke the upper crust of ice with his heel and shoved the snow aside to bury the telltale bundle.

Andy crouched among the bushes like a wild animal stalking its prey. Nothing moved. All appeared like a perfect picture postcard. Virgin territory over the ice covered snow—no footprints.

Moments later he decided it was safe enough to charge the barn. In his haste, he skidded clumsily into the wooden side of the barn banging his head. He shook the stars from his head until his vision cleared. His tense body shivered from the glacial wind that seeped through his clothing.

Andy flattened himself against the side of the barn, easing to the end for a look-see. He slipped around the corner, noting a shoveled path leading to a small cottage where smoke curled skyward from the chimney. The smell of burning wood sent a cold chill through his body, and he longed to approach the warm house but knew he dared not.

He scanned the snow-covered fields leading up to the house and peered around to the barn door. A large wooden plank, normally seated in two slotted racks, one on each door to hold the barn doors closed, rested on the ground. *Is someone in there?* Andy stiffened and listened. Not a sound. He edged his way around to the entrance, eased the creaking door back enough to squeeze through and haul it shut.

Once inside, he flashed nervous glances about the spacious barn. Two horses munched on hay in wooden fence-like stalls on the opposite side of the barn, while chickens pecked the dirt floor. A piece of straw drifted down from the loft. Andy paused and looked up. After a few seconds, nothing had moved—absolutely nothing. But he remembered the unhooked door.

He spun around and met a solid object against the side of his head. His body stiffened, and he felt himself slip into a black hole.

The ack-ack of a distant antiaircraft gun penetrated Andy's ears. The hum of plane engines sounded from above. Light slipped between his fluttering eyelids. He tried to force them open but lapsed into darkness. Again his eyes sprang open—a world unknown to him—three people surrounded him and a young girl wiped a cold cloth over his face.

"Umm," Andy moaned, rolling his head from side to side struggling to stay awake. He closed his eyes once more, popped them open wide, and bounced to a sitting position. "Where am I? What's happening?" Pain riveted his left thigh matching his headache.

"You are in Weinsberg near Salzburg." The young girl spoke in broken English.

Andy thought her dirndl dress typical alpine clothing. The tight-fitted burgundy wool bodice and long, navy wool skirt cinched at the waist accented her girlish figure.

Andy gave his body a once-over and snatched the blanket up around his waist. He wore only a grungy white undershirt and skivvies.

"Where's my uniform?" He grabbed his dog tags, relieved they remained around his neck. He studied the room. A fire crackled in a black cast-iron stove, and the pipe jutted through an outside wall. Cozy and warm. The window across the room had a blanket draped over it. An older dark-haired bearded man limped into the room. Andy thought him to be the father. His arms rested on a beer-belly covered by pants held up with suspenders.

"Mein brother landed a nasty blow on your head. You surprised him." The young girl pointed to a four-drawer chest to the right of the bed and nudged him to lie down. "Uniform and everything are in that drawer. Amerikanisch?"

"Yes," Andy replied. He rubbed his head until he came to a huge lump on the left side. "Oh!" he winced. *American sympathizers, huh? Can't figure why he gave me this knot. What's wrong with me? I'm burning up!* He wiped the perspiration from his forehead.

The father left the bedside and returned with a shot glass. His belly shook as he laughed contagiously and shoved the drink toward Andy.

After studying it for a moment, Andy turned up the glass and swallowed the contents. In a raspy voice scarcely able to spit out the words, he said, "Much obliged."

The four people glanced quizzically at each other.

"Danke," Andy said forcing out more volume.

They broke into a hearty laugh and nodded their heads. The boy who stepped forward appeared to be younger than Andy. He caught Andy's hand with a firm grasp, "Maybe too strong, uh? We help you—nein hurt you."

Andy pulled his hand back and propped up on his elbow. "Why? Why would you risk helping an American?"

"Hitler not friend. He mörder. Mein bruder and vater (father)." The boy spread his arm out, palm up, toward the older man, "this Uncle Rouel." He moved his hand indicating, "Mutti (mother) Maria, and sister, Anna." He curled his hand into his chest. "Karl. Mutti sprechen nein English. Soldiers steal food and kill animals. They not find underground food bin. I were down there when you came in barn. When better, we help you go."

"But you'll be shot if they discover you helped me." Andy sat all the way up and slid his legs down the side of the bed. He cringed at the pain in his thigh.

No one responded until Uncle Rouel said, "We help you." He grinned under a wide mustache that spread all the way to bushy sideburns.

"Now, you rest. We cook." Anna picked up a white apron, tied it around her tiny waist brushing it smooth against her dress. Andy watched her lead the group into another room and noticed that her long blonde hair flowed down her back. His thoughts immediately turned to Rose. *Will I ever see her again?*

When he scooted down in the bed, pain shot from his thigh. He traced the pain to

a bandage covering the wound.

The flickering fire danced through the opening on the stove and created a sense of peace and security in Andy. Before drifting off to sleep, he stared into the fire suddenly reminded of the flaming end of Nealy, Whitie, and the *Alley Cat*. He drew his hands over his eyes as if to shut out the vision.

Exhausted from the events of the day, he fell into a deep sleep.

Several hours later, Anna returned to the room where Andy stirred from a much needed rest. "I came to check your injury. How do you feel?" She pulled back the blankets.

"I've had better days. I need to be getting out of here."

After lifting the bandages, Anna responded, "You're not going anywhere until the infection subsides. The redness is spreading."

"It feels numb…

Karl dashed into the room. "Anna! Anna! Hurry. Heinz rushed over to tell us that the Gestapos are checking every property within a three-mile radius to find the Amerikanisch. We must hide him."

"Quick, Karl, grab all of his things from the drawers. Check everywhere. Make sure we don't leave anything that shows he was here." Anna raced to the door. "Mutti! Bring bedding." She helped Andy out of bed as Uncle Rouel entered the room.

Karl and Uncle Rouel caught each side of Andy and helped him bundle up. "Where…where are you taking me?" *Is this for real? I don't know these people.*

"To the barn where I find you. We hide you where we hide our food. They never find it." Karl's breath came in short spurts.

Andy wrenched free. "I can walk. Don't need tracks showing someone helped me."

"Good! We walk over your foot prints once we get you down with the food." Uncle Rouel's face flushed. He took Andy's clothing, the parachute, and pistol from Anna as they made their way to the barn.

"Damn!" Andy slipped and slid trying to steady his foot on the ice-covered snow. "Thank goodness for ice—no tracks or at least few tracks."

"Jawohl! Come along." Karl sat the lantern down as he unhitched the barn door. He hustled into an animal stall and grabbed one end of the feed trough and swung it around.

Uncle Rouel scraped back the straw with his foot and a small slit large enough for a man to slip through appeared. He set Andy's things in the trough and forced the jammed cap opened.

Karl led the way down the ladder with the lantern. "Come." He motioned to Andy.

Andy backed up to the opening, and placed his good leg on the first step of the ladder and continued down to the straw-filled flooring. The musty smell slapped him in the face as he glanced around at the closet-like space observing the food supply.

"Here." A familiar bundle floated down the hole. "Don't have time to burn it."

"Thanks, Uncle Rouel."

"You make no noise. Whatever you hear, do not move. Do not try to rescue anyone…make worse. Do not come up! Do not come up," Karl said in broken English. "We know risks and are doing what we believe good for our Austria." He climbed up the ladder and handed down excess food supplies from the house.

Andy winced with pain from his shrapnel injury as he reached for each load. He took the last batch and said, "Good luck. Don't take chances."

Anna shouted down the hole. "Captain, be safe."

* * *

Karl closed the minuscule opening, spread old straw over the lid, and moved the trough back over the underground cover. "Good?"

Uncle Rouel inspected the area. "Needs old straw to cover trough scrape lines." He gently nudged and patted down the original straw. Good. "We must hurry out of the barn to see things the Nazi's would see. Work out problems—cover tracks if there."

"Uncle Rouel, tell me it will be all right—everyone will be all right—the captain will be all right." Anna caught his arm as they stepped out into the blinding sunlight reflecting off the white snow.

"My dear, no one knows. We have done well so far with others, and suffered only one loss. We must keep our eyes and ears open." He gave Anna a hug.

Late that afternoon Anna heard motor vehicles pull into the yard. She peaked from behind the dark parlor curtains and whispered, "Here they are. Looks like they might have driven over tell-tale footprints. Hurry, here they come." She jumped into her chair, picked up her sock darning, and wove the needle in and out of the repair area.

The dreaded knock pierced Anna's spine. She stiffened. Uncle Rouel opened the door. Karl stood close by.

"Güten Morgan, bitte (Good morning, please). Amerikanisch here?"

"Nein, nein," Karl said.

"Ja. Here." The Gestapo clicked his heels and ordered his men to search the home and surrounding areas.

"Jawohl (Yes sir)." The soldiers scattered over the country home and seconds later a Gestapo hustled out of the bedroom with a blanket in hand pointing to a blood stain..

Anna's heart pulsed erratically and she tried to swallow with no success. "Mine," she uttered. "That time of the month."

"When?"

"Last night. Thought I washed it out.

The Gestapo walked over to his officer. "Okay (German). Take it back."

"Jawohl."

Another Gestapo searched the kitchen. "Nein food—very little."

The Officer clicked his heels again and pointed to the front door. "Barn."

Deep down in the food bin, Andy listened intently for footsteps probably searching every inch of the barn. It was too quiet. The pit of his stomach ached and nausea threatened to erupt. *What's happening to the family in the house—the loyal and kind family who rescued me—the family who, due to my very existence brings on a death sentence if I'm discovered. I couldn't live through their demise.* His body trembled from the realization of "what ifs" once again.

Engrossed in his own fears, it took the bashing of the barn doors against the walls to drive him out of his thoughts. He dowsed the lantern and moved closer to the ladder. Heavy boot steps tromped across the barn—nothing until what he thought were bayonets thrashing through the straw in search of an opening. He heard chickens squawk as they flew from one side of the barn to the other. Angry shouts in German seeped from above. Footsteps moved into the chicken coop area shooing chickens sitting on their eggs. Moments later he listened as knots twisted in his belly. The Gestapo searched one stall after another pushing the unwilling horses aside until the last stall leading down to Andy. The trampling did not belong to the Gestapo. Obviously the horse wanted his hay, sparse as it was, and the Gestapo wanted to check under and around the trough.

Andy grabbed the sides of his head, struggling to remain calm. He remembered Karl's instructions, "Do not come out no matter what. Wait until we come get you." He sat back down, his back against the cold, damp wall.

The thrashing and banging continued what seemed like hours to Andy. They were getting closer by the minute. The sound of a moving trough hit Andy's stomach like a bullet from a gun. He held his breath. More bumping and thrashing caused straw particles to fall from above. So close…too close.

He tried to stand but it was as if his body refused to move. Like something pushed him down. *Don't come up. Don't come up,* echoed through his head. Loud shouts again. Scampering above him. *What's happening? Did one of the family come to the barn? Karl? Anna? Oh, no! Please no!*

Slowly the scampering grew less and the shouts seemed farther away. Andy exhaled. He hadn't realized the heat his body generated in fright. Leaving the safety of the bedroom he did not take time to dress in warm clothing. With stillness of the animals above and the exit of the Gestapo, silence set in for the moment, and the dampness of the 'hole' sent chills rippling through his body.

He heard engines crank and vehicles move away from the family house. *Surely I'm safe now—the family is safe—no gunshot sounds. Don't come up. Don't come up* rolled over and over in his head. *Someone might be waiting...waiting as long as it takes for me to rise up. I'll wait. I'll wait as long as it takes to keep the family safe.* He swiped his forehead with his sleeve as he felt control over his body return.

After what seemed like hours, he grasped the lantern in his hands and knew without a match, he could not light it. *What about mice? Light would keep them away. I've got to find a match.* He felt around for his uniform. "Damn it! Where is it!" He laughed at himself. "I've lost it already—the sun didn't rise and set before I lost it." He came across his flight jacket, slipped it on and checked the pockets—came up with a box of matches, and lit the lantern.

"Light. Light. Hot damn! Well, there's nothing to do but rest. Somebody will come and tell when I can come out of here." He ate bread from the food sent down, and later pulled over his parachute, gathered the bedding, and doused the lantern once more.

Hours passed and what seemed like days crept by, and it became more puzzling to Andy why nobody came for him. Perhaps Gestapo watched the home place and they didn't dare go to the barn. Perhaps they were dead and no one would come for him.

As the hours and days dragged on, food was not his problem and he had used the lantern sparingly. It was his wound. Heat radiated from his entire thigh. His appetite disappeared and his head throbbed. He checked his forehead; *I'm going to die right here. My head is hot as a hot water bottle. I'll sleep a while and then I'm going up. Yes, up.*

Karl opened the trap door to the food bin. "Captain! Captain!" Nobody answered. "Anna, hurry. He no answer." He handed Anna the lantern and moved away from the entrance.

Anna scurried down the ladder and rushed over to Andy who hadn't stirred. She shook his shoulder. His eyes opened, covered them with his arm shielding them from the light of the lantern, and sat up.

Anna set the lantern down and felt his forehead. "You are hot. We must get you to the warm house and in front of the heater." She put her arm under his shoulder, helped him onto his feet, and steadied him as they made their way to the ladder. "You are weak, my friend."

He reached down. "My pistol?"

"Karl will bring it when we get you to the house and in bed."

Is everyone all right...Mutti...Uncle Rouel? The Gestapo gone?" Andy's knees buckled slightly as he grasped the ladder.

Anna strengthened her grip. "Yes. We waited those days to make sure the Gestapo had left the entire area. Heinz let us know when the last vehicle drove away and made sure no Germans remained." Anna breathed heavily under Andy's weight. It was too much for her petite frame. "Karl...," she called, "...help me."

Karl climbed partway down the ladder, reached for Andy's hand, and pulled him up the ladder while Anna pushed from below.

Anna and Karl lugged Andy into the bedroom and onto the bed. Anna removed the old bandage, cleaned the wound, and wrapped a new bandage around his leg. She realized the infection had spread over his entire thigh.

A while later, Anna brought Andy a bowl of hot soup. She fed him spoon after spoon...the first hot food he had had in days.

"Now you rest," she said and pulled up the patchwork quilts around his neck.

After a short doze, Andy woke up kicking the covers off. He had spiked a high fever and while cooling off, chills took over. His body shook, his teeth chattered. He curled into a fetal position and pulled the patchwork quilts around his neck. The chills escalated.

Anna came into the room. "Would you like to join us for abendessen (supper)?" Seeing Andy wrapped in blankets barely responsive, she called in German, "Mutti, Mutti. More blankets!" She reached over and felt his forehead and shouted, "Aspirin?"

Mutti glanced into the room but quickly hurried for the covers. As she returned, Anna grabbed the blankets.

"Thank you, Mutti. His thigh injury is infected and causing a high fever. Get the sulfur, bitte."

Uncle Rouel bumped into Anna in her haste. "What's going on? Thought we were ready to eat."

"Our captain is burning with fever from his leg injury. Infection from shrapnel spreading." Anna's hands shook. She surprised herself with 'Our captain.' *The last soldier died under my care and I'll not let it happen again.* "Bitte, Uncle Rouel, find some aspirin."

"Shall we wait supper?" Mutti's years of hard times revealed in the lines on her face. She handed Anna the sulfur.

"No, Mutti. I'll stay with our patient tonight. We need to save his leg."

Uncle Rouel disappeared in another room and returned with a clear bottle of white pills and a cup of water.

Anna reached under Andy's back and raised him high enough to swallow the pills. "Here, Captain." She shoved the aspirin into his mouth. His eyes fluttered long enough to swallow the medication when she placed the cup to his lips. "There now, rest. The chills will subside soon."

She whispered to Uncle Rouel, "Go eat. I'll stay here for a while."

He smiled and backed out of the room.

After applying new sulfur, Anna watched Andy's chest heave up and down. She couldn't take her eyes off him—not for a moment—fearful something dreadful might happen. The chills shook the bed. She slipped into the bed and wrapped her warm body around his.

Soon Anna felt his body relax. The chills subsided and he slipped into a deep sleep.

Sunrise forced a speck of light through slits in the curtains as Andy tried to open his eyes and focus. *Where am I? How'd I get here?* Something warm rested against his back. He rolled away, sat straight up, and noticed blonde hair flung over a face. He shook her shoulder. She jerked up and hopped out of the bed.

"Oh, I'm so sorry." Anna's clothes revealed wrinkles pressed in from perspiration when Andy's fever broke.

"What are you doing in here?" Andy struggled to remember.

"I… I… You could not stop shaking from the chills and I tried to help warm you with my body. Mutti did that with us when we were feverish." She glanced at the door as if to escape.

Andy felt his face flush.

"Your thigh infection grew and needed treatment. That's what caused the high fever.

How do you feel today?"

"Much better, danke! That was mighty sweet of you, Anna." He stood too quickly and the blood drained from his head. Black specks danced before his eyes.

Anna rushed to him, eased him back down on the bed, and forced him to lay flat. "You are too weak. You must wait until you get your strength back." She tucked the covers around his neck and stared into his eyes.

Moments later she backed off. "I'll fix you some porridge. It'll give you strength."

When Anna returned with the porridge, Andy was asleep. She set the bowl on the chest, walked over and felt his forehead. *A slight fever.* She caressed his face running her fingers over his dimple, and leaned over and kissed his cheek. *Mother of God, what am I doing! Such a silly lass. What's going to happen to us? To him? Why can't this horror end? How long can we continue to be safe?* She thrust her hand over her face and darted from the room.

Hours later, Andy rolled over and touched his thigh. *Hum. It's still hot.* He pulled up on the bed, and punched the pillow for support when Anna came bursting through the door.

"Brought you some souper (dinner). Potato soup. Stick to your bones so you Amerikanisch say."

"You look lovely today." Andy was flattered by her cheerful smile and eagerness to care for him. *Rose, Rose, Rose.* Guilt seeped into his brain.

Anna sat on the edge of his bed and spoon fed him.

"I can do it myself."

"Save your strength. I'm here with nothing to do but care for you."

*Umm. How lucky can a fellow be.* Andy swallowed the warm soup savoring every gulp.

Finished, Anna stood with the bowl but Andy caught her arm. "Stay. Please."

She sat back down and the two of them talked for hours—laughing, joking, teasing.

Once Anna left the room, Andy's guilt surfaced. *But I love Rose—deeply love Rose. What if I never make it back to her? Anna…*

Evening came and Andy dozed off again. A stir of the blankets woke him. Anna slipped into his bed once again. Andy reached over and pulled her to him kissing her forehead, cheeks, and her mouth—deep arousing kisses.

Each morning Andy went through the guilt trip. *I'm so sorry, Rose.* And each night Anna came to his bed. *Resist? This is war and we might not survive.* Anna was there.

The day came when Andy knew that it had to end, night after night of Anna—lovely Anna. With her splendid care, he had grown much stronger. It was time. Time to return to uncertainty—escape—possible capture—looming death. Lingering brought on a great danger. To him. To the family. He hopped gently out of bed, took the clothes from the drawer, and put on a brown flannel-like shirt. He eased the pants over the bandage on his injured thigh and limped into what they called the esszimmer (dining room). He gazed around the room. Treasured heirlooms sat on hand-tatted doilies all around the room, much like his mom's doilies. He joined the family in the parlor.

Hours later in the dining room, Karl pulled a chair out for Andy. "Bitte. Sit down."

"Uncle Rouel, Mutti wants you to say the blessing for our guest." Anna poured red wine into all the glasses.

Everyone bowed their heads as Rouel began, "Baruch atah Adonai elohenlu melech haolm…b'ra pri hagofen." *"Blessed art thou, oh Lord…who brought forth fruit from the earth."*

The glasses clinked around the table. Anna tapped her glass to Andy's. "No, no," she said. "You must look into the person's eyes when you touch glasses."

Andy made a point of looking deep into her eyes, much to the delight of her family.

"I don't know how to thank you, friends." Andy smiled and raised his glass to each of them, after viewing a spread described by Anna, of twisted egg bread, sweet, saucy stuffed cabbage and crisp potato pancakes with applesauce. An aroma of strudel and mandel bread filled every crevice of the home. He rubbed his hands together ready to dive in, but hesitated before turning to Anna. "That blessing sounded Jewish. Was it?"

She glanced at Rouel before responding. "Ya. My Großmutter was a Jew."

"How about your grandpa?"

"Nein, Opa, Anglo Saxon." She stared down at her plate.

Andy noticed tears filling Mutti's eyes and decided to change the subject. "I'll have some potato pancakes—they look great. Oh, applesauce, too."

Mutti smiled as she passed the food to him.


Before turning in for the final night and the last soft, warm bed for a while, Andy spied his buckeye on top of the chest of drawers. He picked it up, rubbed it, and bowed his head. *Thank you, God. You've brought me this far, now don't let me down.*

The family treated Andy kindly, and he grew to trust them bug tomorrow he would leave. He searched for his uniform, officer's hat, and sheepskin jacket, only to discover Anna had neatly packed them in a stack.

"We must burn." She stood at the door watching and reached for the stack of clothes. Andy held firm. "If they find them, we'll be killed."

"No, no! I understand, but they will think me a spy without my uniform." He refused to let go of his uniform.

She released the sack and walked over to a chest, opened a drawer, pulled out his wallet, gun and holster, a pair of long johns and placed them on the bed. "Tomorrow, you wear." She curtsied and left the room.

"Tomorrow, Anna, tomorrow," he shouted after her.

That night Anna slipped back into his bed. "I miss you all ready."

"You've known from the beginning that I have a girl...a Red Cross Nurse.

"I know, I know." Anna refused to look into Andy's eyes.

"But Anna, we fell into this because of the uncertainty of war. I'm sorry I took advantage of you. If Rose did not exist, it would be you. I'll miss you."

"No need to say more. I wanted to make you happy before you left. We do not know if you will escape or be captured."

"I know, but I feel very guilty because of Rose."

"Do not. I decided when you arrived, we would be together because tomorrow might never come. It is okay. I shall be fine. Anna smiled sweetly and kissed Andy on the cheeks.

"I won't forget you, Anna. You'll be forever special to me."

She wrapped her arms around him and slid her body on top of his.

*If I die tomorrow*...he was powerless to resist.

The next day came too soon for Andy but nothing good would come from his lingering. He picked up the long johns and laughed recalling how he chuckled when he saw his dad's flapping on the clothesline. After slipping into the long underwear he muttered to himself. "Aw, shucks. These actually feel warm. Should have thought about them sooner."

Karl entered the room. "Here. You wear over uniform." He handed Andy a dark green shirt and suspenders to hold up brown wool pants.

Andy noticed tiny moth holes in the pants. He slipped into a heavy, black wool coat and picked up a black flattop wool hat. Ready for another journey, he stepped into the parlor. He and Anna had their goodbyes the night before. Andy admired his new appearance. He stretched out his arms, "I look like y'all now." He realized that only Anna understood. "Me," he pointed to himself, "You," he spread his arms out to them.

"Ja." Mutti smiled. She strolled over and caressed his coat. A chunky woman, with hair pulled back in a bun, she appeared dumpier in her burgundy dress, which draped to the floor.

"It was my father's coat." Tears boiled up in Anna's eyes.

Andy knew her tears were not all about the coat.

Karl caught Andy by the arm and pulled him to the early morning light. "We found parachute and hide it in food bin. Burn tomorrow. Smoke cause attention. Now," Karl said pointing at the map he held in front of Andy, "when get to Klobensdolf, see cobbler here." He pointed to a location on the map. "Go in shop and tell cobbler, *'Spring is coming. The robins will be here soon.'* He know then." Karl pointed to Andy's boots.

"Yeah, that is a problem. GI stock."

Uncle Rouel walked over, placed his left foot beside Andy's right foot, and immediately exited the room. A few moments later, he returned with a pair of beat-up black boots. "You wear." A pleasant grin spread across his face as though he was proud of himself.

Andy winked and smiled at the man while Anna clasped her hands together in delight. "This completes you," she smiled through glistening eyes.

"Much ob…," Andy remembered, "Danke schöen!" He sat on a wooden, straight-back bench and changed the boots. "No need to take these with me," he said, shoving them into Karl's hands.

"We burn with parachute."

"Here." Anna gave Andy a cloth drawstring sack. "You're taking potatoes and cabbage to a friend in the next town. Understand? Your jacket's in the bottom."

"Good idea, Anna. Thanks. I'll miss the aroma of your cooked cabbage." He looked into her deep-set blue eyes and kissed her.

She sent him an embarrassed smile and handed him another knapsack. "This will feed you for a few days. Make it last."

Andy sauntered over to the mother and said, "Danke schöen! Mutti." When he hugged her, a rush of pink flushed her face, and she returned the hug, kissing him on each cheek. The bandanna covering her graying hair slipped down.

"How lucky can a fella get." Andy said.

Anna drew closer and kissed Andy on both cheeks. "Stay safe and do not forget about us. A hay wagon awaits you behind the barn."

Andy wrapped his arms around her and held her tight. "How could I after all y'all did for me. Thank you!"

"Oh yes. This is something you might need." Anna handed him his flight survival kit.

He grabbed the kit, shook Karl's and Uncle Rouel's rugged hands. "Thank you so much! Danke schöen!"

He caught the door handle and peered around before stepping outside. The early morning sun blinded him until his eyes adjusted. The snow clung to the trees like frozen clumps of cotton. He stepped onto the glazed snow and promptly lost his footing, landing on his sore thigh. Quickly he hopped back on his feet, tipped his hat, and waved to the smiling family.

"Auf Wiedersehen," he shouted, performing a silly two-step to show he had gained his balance, though his thigh ached.

Andy headed down the path toward the barn, feeling secure about his disguise.

The sun-glistened-ice surface covering the snow made his eyes sting. He leaned into the frigid wind and pulled the kerchief Anna gave him higher over his cheeks, covering his nose and mouth.

When he stepped behind the barn, a one-horse hay wagon waited. He waved at the stranger holding the reins. A man, dressed much like himself, pointed to the back of the wagon. Andy shoved his cloth bags into the hay. The wagon jostled with his weight as he sat on the edge of the wagon, spilling precious hay from the pile. He shoved the hay aside forming a tunnel, turned himself around, and slipped his feet in first. He pumped his feet in and out until he had moved the hay enough to slide under the mound. The hay covered his body except for his face. He slipped off his hat and pulled down some hay, only slightly covering his head, leaving it thin enough for visibility.

Heavy wagon tracks had created icy grooves on a snow-covered road that appeared to lead to nowhere, weaving its path through the flat lands surrounded by mountains. Andy pulled out his survival kit and opened his compass, which indicated they traveled in a westerly direction. He rode for more than an hour under the hay, dozing now and then. For the first time since he left Italy, Andy felt warm while outdoors. The straw blocked the bitter wind. Occasionally, the driver broke into song—nothing recognizable to Andy, but nice. Thoughts of Anna, her family left behind for God knows what, and his family back home ran rampant through his mind. *Wonder if they even know I'm missing yet? What about Rose? Oh, Rose. How will you and my family deal with it when all of you get word? How could I have let Anna into my life? Forgive me, Rose. I don't know if I'll ever get back to you. Oh crap! The letter in my uniform pocket. They'll think I'm dead. Why did I ever write such a letter? Well, fool, you didn't know if you'd ever come back. Hey, you're not back yet! Come to think about it, can I trust the wagon man? Hmm.*

The bouncing wagon startled Andy. It was as if the wagon crossed ruts in the road, instead of riding in them. The hay blocked his entire view. He pushed aside a small opening and surveyed the area after the wagon came to an abrupt stop. He hauled out his compass and checked the direction. It still pointed west. Andy sighed. Nothing to do but wait. He felt the driver slip from the wagon and heard him crunching over the snow.

Andy wrestled himself farther out of the wagon and observed a row of quaint, little shops. After spotting two men approaching, he slithered back under the hay, fearful of being seen despite hearing the men clamor beyond the hay wagon. Everything grew quiet again except for the horse snorting and chewing on the bit.

He eased out from under the hay, grabbed the knapsacks, and searched the area for movement. Nothing. He brushed himself off, threw the bag of cabbage and potatoes over his back, and walked down the row of shops. A sign in a front window stopped him in his tracks. It read NEDDLES… He couldn't read the second German word, but the picture of a shoe painted below the name removed any doubt.

Andy reached in his coat pocket for the map. Snow clouds had moved in, and the temperature dipped even more. He set his bags down and steadied the flapping map from the gusty wind. The roar of a truck caused him to turn. From a distance, silhouetted against the snow, a military truck loomed ahead. Andy quickly shoved the map in his pocket, grabbed his bags, and rushed into NEDDLES Shop.

Once inside, the smell of new leather saturated the air. Behind a worktable stood a man wearing a leather apron, hammering the sole of a shoe mounted on a last. His lips pressed against a row of tacks protruding from his mouth. He nodded to Andy and continued removing the tacks from his mouth, one by one, seating them in the shoe sole. Tiny metal-framed glasses slipped down his nose, exposing eyes spaced closely together under a sparse patch of gray hair.

A young tow-headed boy sat at a table staring out the front window. Several books lay open in front of him. He slipped a glance at Andy and then returned to the window.

Snow began to fall. The force of the wind kicked up, blowing the snow sideways—blizzard style.

Andy waited until the man finished hammering the tacks into the shoe soles. "*Spring is coming. The robins will be here soon.*"

The man looked up, startled and spoke something in German.

"Nein," Andy responded. "English."

"Ja."

"German military truck." Andy pointed west of the shop.

"Ja." He motioned hurriedly to Andy, "Come!" The man hastened to a large back room that doubled as living quarters. He reached a wall of shelves lined with shoes and boots of all types, and touched something on the inside wall. Slowly the shelves moved, and an opening appeared. Andy's mouth dropped. A dark, dank hole. The man shoved him through the opening. Immediately the entrance disappeared behind him, closing out any form of light.

Andy reached out with his hands feeling his way when he heard a vehicle door slam in front of the building. He took a few steps forward and ran into a wall. *This is a closet.*

A voice, several feet away, brought Andy quickly to attention.

"Well shit! Of all the people to be stuck with. What luck! Sounded like you through the wall."

Andy recognized the voice instantly. "Keep it quiet, Brad. A military truck pulled in front of the building. We're both lucky to have a place to hide," Andy whispered, ignoring Brad's real meaning of luck. "How long is this area, anyhow?"

"It runs the depth of the building. Cripes! What the hell are you doing here?"

"Look, buster. Work together or we'll never get back home!" Andy's eyes slowly adjusted to the darkness with the help of a few cracks between the exterior wooden boards. He guessed the 'closet' to be four feet by twenty.

Loud voices drifted from the room he had recently passed through. Chairs scraped, which indicated to Andy that they were pulling up to the table. It sounded like liquid being poured into containers. Glasses clanked as if in a toast. Laughter and boisterous sounds seeped into the secret room. Occasionally Andy understood a word or two. He heard footsteps inch toward the shelves of shoes— close to the secret entrance.

"Holy shit!" Brad said. "We're trapped!"

# Chapter Seventeen

Three weeks later, John had recovered enough to return home. Jane had prayed for this moment, but realized he was not back to his old self.

"Mom, I can't wait to bring Dad home."

Jane noticed that Betty Jane had finally outgrown showing excitement by jumping up and down. "Me, too, sweetheart. You know, if it hadn't been for the Martins and Andy's check coming in, your dad's homecoming would not be good." She glanced at her daughter and smiled as she drove the green Pontiac to the physical therapy wing of Highsmith Hospital. "I can't wait to bring him home!"

She pulled up to the entrance and said, "My stars, there he is sitting in a wheel chair waiting for us!"

"Mom, why is that nurse standing beside him?"

"Honey, a nurse always has to wheel patients going home to their transportation to make sure nothing happens to them on the hospital property

Betty Jane popped out of the car and hugged her dad. "Oh, Daddy, I've missed you so much!"

Jane walked around the car.

"I'm Nurse Williams. He's really doing great. I wish all my patience were as motivated as he is. If he keeps up his exercises and follows his new diet, he should have no problems."

"That'll be my job, Nurse Williams. No more fried chicken and gravy." Jane leaned over and kissed John. "I'm just glad he's coming home. Thank you for such excellent help."

John slowly got up from the wheel chair and walked to the car a few feet away.

Jane gazed in amazement. "John. You've been hiding something from us. How long have you been walking?" She noted a mischievous smile on John's face.

"You didn't know?" Nurse Williams laughed. "You old teaser," she addressed John.

"Daddy! I'm so happy for you."

Jane opened the car door and John motioned her away as he slid into the passenger seat of the car. Though his speech had almost returned to normal, he remained quieter than usual.

Once home, the three of them embraced in a circle of joy as Jane prayed—usually John's job. "Dear Heavenly Father, once again you have blessed our family, our John, our son, and our home. Most especially our John. You have not given us more than we can bear and we pray that You will restore John's health completely and bring our son, Andy, home.

"Please keep all the boys safe as they defend our freedoms. Also, please bless the families who have suffered losses.

"We pray in Jesus' name. Amen."

John kissed her on the cheek.

One week, two weeks, more weeks passed and John slowly returned to his routine, though modified.

While sitting at the supper table one night John shouted, "I'm starving for fried chicken, mashed taters, and gravy. Don't think I can work another day without real food, Jane. This diet is killing me."

"John, think about all our boys in POW camps with little or no food. It might be our son."

"Okay, okay. If you fried a chicken after that statement, I'd have too much guilt to eat one bite. See what you've done?" John caught her hand and kissed the back side of it.

# Chapter Eighteen

Andy lunged for Brad clamping his hand over his mouth. He held it securely until Brad quit struggling. He then placed his index finger over Brad's lips. Brad spun away.

"Jawohl (Yes sir)!" the German said. He continued speaking in German and ended with a laugh when he dropped something on the floor.

A boot, Andy thought. A pair of boots—maybe. The possibility of being captured raced inside his brain. The German stood so close; Andy imagined he could hear the soldier breathe. His heart raced like a runaway horse.

The German's footsteps retreated, and he scuffed his chair over the wooden floor once more. For an hour or so, the ramblings continued in the next room. Andy sat on the floor with his back against the outer wall and locked his arms around his knees. Brad crouched within Andy's reach.

Forks or spoons clanked against plates until, finally, the Germans pushed their chairs back, laughing, ribbing, and left the shop. Andy sighed with relief when the truck engine started up. He turned and whispered to Brad, "You 'bout gave us away back there. What the hell were you thinking?"

"I thought you had been followed, and I'd be captured because of you."

"It's still all about you, right? Well listen up, buddy boy! We're stuck here together, and there's not a damn thing you can do about it!" Heat flooded Andy's face.

"Yes sir!"

Andy applied all his skills to calm himself and be civil. The rush of blood slowly retreated. He spoke in a near whisper to encourage Brad to do the same. "What happened to your plane?"

"It was badly damaged from a barrage of antiaircraft fire. The starboard wing tip blew off and we were going down. I rushed to the back of the plane and bailed out."

"What about the other men?"

"Don't know. I left."

"You son-of-a-bitch! You mean you didn't check on the others?" Andy rammed his right fist into his left palm.

"Hell no! They didn't mean nothing to me. I'd never flown with them before."

"You're unbelievable, Brad. You don't give a damn about anybody but yourself. One day you'll get yours! Count on it!" The hair bristled on the back of Andy's neck. He knew he had to control the anger.

"Don't give me that crap! I made it out. I escaped. I'm alive."

"Button your lip!" Without seeing Brad's face, Andy felt the heat of Brad's rage. "Okay? How'd you get here and when?"

"Several boys in their late teens brought me here last night. How the hell are we gonna get out of here?"

"Don't know yet. What's this guy's name?"

"Ludwig. That's all I know."

"You hungry, Brad?" Andy bit his lip trying to remain calm. He pulled out his small sack. "The family that helped me escape gave me a sack of grub."

At that moment, the hidden entrance opened, and Ludwig came in carrying a lantern and squatted down beside Andy.

"Me, Ludwig. You?" He pointed to Andy.

"Capt. Andrew Walters, USAAF officer." He reached over and shook Ludwig's hand.

"Officer?"

"Yeah. A pilot."

"He a pilot?" Ludwig pointed to Brad.

"No. He's a bombardier. Ludwig, how we gonna get back to Italy or somewhere safe?"

"Not easy." Ludwig's broken English missed many words but Andy understood.

"Look. We haus big underground. We help Amerikanisch military. Tomorrow a group cycle to Salzburg. We haus two, how you say, bikes ready before sunrise. You must leave then. It only my son and me here. He be in danger if you stay."

Ludwig continued, "A pot of potatoes on stove. You like? The German SS men come eat two days a week. They like."

"Sure," Andy said standing up. "Come on Brad. We'll eat while no one's in the shop."

Brad followed Andy and Ludwig into the large room, where the natural wood walls had aged over the years to a deep brownish gray. Steam spiraled to the tall ceiling from the boiling pot.

"This is good stuff, Ludwig." Andy and Brad devoured the potato soup and brown bread.

After they finished eating, Ludwig gave Andy an old tattered quilt and sent them back into the hidden room.

Andy removed his jacket from the knapsack and wrapped himself in the worn cover while trying to get comfortable on the hard floor. Brad said nothing all evening.

The next morning arrived with Andy propped against the wall struggling to keep warm. Even his sheepskin jacket, wool coat, and blanket did not keep out the horrendous cold. Pain rippled up his stiff legs and sore thigh as he stretched from the fetal position.

Ludwig entered the secret room before daylight. "Gûten Morgan (Good morning). Bitte."

"Gűten Morgan to you, sir," Andy said slowly rising to his feet. He folded his quilt and handed it to Ludwig. After he picked up both sacks of food, he extended the large sack of potatoes and cabbage to Ludwig.

"Danke schöen!" Ludwig replied after he peered into the knapsack.

Andy turned to Brad. "Did you bring everything with you?" He observed Brad's empty hands, rubbing his eyes as he adjusted to the light.

"What stuff, *Captain* Walters?"

Ludwig stood beside Andy, while Brad went back into the secret room. "He big trouble."

"I can handle him, Ludwig." Andy looked over at Ludwig's son sleeping peacefully in the double bed in the big room. The only window had fogged over and frost trimmed the window edges. "Keep him safe," Andy said nodding toward the young boy.

Ludwig smiled and shook Andy's hand. "I go watch for cycles. You stay back. I call."

"Ja." Andy said. "Come on, Brad. You ready?"

Brad meandered out of the room, dragging a sack over the floor.

A faint sound like a bell grew closer. "Now!" shouted Ludwig. He wrapped a brown scarf around each man's neck as they left the shop.

"Danke schöen!" Andy said.

"Danke schöen, Yankee!" Ludwig smiled for the first time, showing laugh crinkles at the corners of his eyes.

Brad walked past Ludwig without a word.

The bell stopped ringing. Once outside, Andy counted five bikes. A girl with blonde hair, protruding from under her wool bandanna, and two young men straddled three bikes while steadying two additional bikes.

"I haven't ridden one of these in years. Never in snow!" Andy chuckled. "Thank goodness it's not pitch black out here." His eyes slowly adjusted to the darkness.

"You mean there's something you can't do?" Brad sniped, while hopping on one of the bikes. "How the hell are we going to ride them in this snow?"

"We must go!" The blonde girl spoke in English. She fell in behind the larger man with the bell mounted on his bike. He rang the bell steadily, as the tiny village faded in the early morning darkness. The mantle of snow illuminated their way. Andy and Brad had a difficult time staying in the tracks carved by earlier vehicles and wagons.

Brad rode his bike beside Andy. "Hey, Walters. That damn bell is gonna give us away."

Andy realized the lead cyclist understood a little English when he remarked something to the girl and they all stopped.

"What the hell…" Brad said.

"Sir, I'm blind, and the sound of the bell indicates how far the object is in front of me. It leads my way. The local people pay little attention when they hear me riding with friends. Thanks to Franz, I can participate in the underground. My keen sense of hearing is a distinct advantage. They know Franz goes to work in another town where I go to school, and we ride along with him," the girl said.

Astonished, Andy stumbled for words, "Thank you for the risk you and your friends are taking." He cut an "if looks could kill" glance at Brad.

"Thank you, sir, for trying to save our country from Hitler's Third Reich. Now, let's go!" The girl mounted her bike once more.

What seemed like to Andy an hour had passed, when vehicle lights crept over the eastern horizon as the morning light slowly squeezed out the night. The leader shouted to the girl and signaled the group to hurry behind a small cluster of evergreen trees and thicket of underbrush. The bell stopped. They dropped their bikes in the bushes. Andy watched Franz and the other young man rush back to the road, working backwards, smoothing out the bike tracks and their own footprints.

"They think of everything," Brad said.

"It's life or death," the girl whispered. "Someone's yelling!"

"I don't hear anything," Andy said, while watching the boys back into the small clump of trees after covering their tracks.

The truck inched closer—headlights spread wider. Andy shot a glance at the girl who mouthed "don't move," and she held her finger up to her lips. The truck slowed. It came to a stop about ten feet from where they left the road.

Andy's heart pumped a little faster, and in spite of the cold, perspiration formed on his brow. They huddled behind the bushes. Andy prayed not to be discovered.

Two men jumped from the back of the canvas-covered truck. They scoured the area just traveled. Headlights reached dangerously close to Andy's group.

Shouts came from the truck cabin, and one of the men down the road replied, "Jawohl."

The girl translated, "A German in the truck shouted at the two men searching for something. 'Come on!' One replied, 'yes sir.'"

A soldier on the road bent down, picked up an object, and waved it high in the air, laughing and running to the truck. The other followed.

Andy held his breath and felt his pulse beating in his throat. He knew that if the men sitting in the truck followed the spread of the headlights, they would be exposed.

He mouthed to Brad after glancing at the girl's finger placed on her lips. "Don't move."

Everyone exhaled after the Germans hopped into the back of the truck, and it slowly drove away.

Andy stepped over to the girl, "Look, I'm not sure this is a good idea—with the bell ringing constantly, it announces our presence."

The blonde turned her face in the direction of Andy's voice. "The people know I ride this way twice a week to school. They look for me. They're convinced I'm perfecting my riding by following the bell. Trust me. I've done it many times. The Germans know me—listen for me."

She pleaded her case. "There are times when we must avoid the German military at all cost, and other times we'll go in their midst. You'll see. Germans are all over Salzburg. You must be careful."

"What's your name?" Andy leaned over, picked up her bike, and placed her hands on the handle.

"Liesel." She reached her hand out, and the lead bicyclist caught her hand. "This is Franz, and the other is Kurt."

"I don't know how to thank you." Andy patted her shoulder. He reached for the hands of the other two and shook them.

"Let's go!" Liesel said, impatience reflected in her voice.

Franz pressed the bicycle bell and took the lead. Liesel followed, then Andy and Brad, while Kurt brought up the rear.

Daylight arrived with the sun reflecting iridescent sparkles from the snow crystals. Andy traveled along in the five-some and watched people wave and shout to Liesel as she followed flawlessly behind the bell. He'd never seen anything like it. He shut his eyes for a few seconds to see what it was like to listen for the bell, but lost his nerve after the bike swerved over a rut, forcing him to regain control quickly. *This girl is blind. She knows everyone for miles—recognizes their voices. And she chooses to spend her life working for the underground. They want desperately to remove the Third Reich and take back their country. Talk about bravery!*

Andy stared at the distant snow-covered mountains with patches of trees on the hillside and a frozen lake nestled below. Something out of a picture book. Birds with radiant white feathers (Österreich Seagull) flew over the lake, some landing on the ice. The road wove through the valleys between the shadows of the mountains. Now and then soft patches of snow gave way to the hard surface of the road as they approached the town.

Franz stopped, Liesel narrowly missing his back wheel. In the far distance at the edge of Salzburg, Andy observed two military trucks with soldiers standing guard at the edge of town. He assumed they were German SS or Gestapo.

Kurt walked over to Liesel and Franz. Andy approached the group.

"We can't take you any farther," Liesel translated for Franz. "Remember your contact words? Inside the square, the middle of Salzburg, you'll find an old pastry shop, Bertha's. In fact, it's so dilapidated many people don't know it's still in business. The

Germans keep it stripped of most sweets. Franz will give you a layout of the square, the open areas near the monumental horse statues, and other places suited for hiding. I suggest you enter through St. Peter's Cemetery. The tombstones are quite close together. Tombs are adequate for cover and moving between."

Franz opened a map and spewed instructions in German. Liesel continued to translate for him, while Franz pointed his finger, drawing imaginative lines around Salzburg's St. Peter's Cemetery. "That's near Residence-Square and St. Michael's Cathedral. Hide there until you hear the ringing from the Belfry Tower. They clang the thirty-five bells three times a day—seven and eleven in the morning, and six o'clock at night. Six o'clock is your signal. There'll be Krauts everywhere. You must work your way down to Bertha's Old Pastry Shoppe. If you stay on the outside of the Square, there are several cathedrals to slip into."

"I can't thank you enough," Andy said. He reached for the map.

"It's not over yet," Liesel said. "You will leave the cycles here and go by foot—get off the main road."

Two boys in their late teens appeared unexpectedly. Andy felt uneasy at their presence.

The tall one tapped Liesel on her shoulder. "Liesel."

"Oh, Joel. You're here." She turned to Andy. "They've come to ride the cycles back with us later today."

Andy checked the young men out. "They're dressed like us, Liesel."

"I hope so. We planned it that way. Now, you must leave before we draw too much attention," Liesel said.

Joel pointed to Andy's coat and then back to his own jacket. He then proceeded to take off his jacket.

"Exchange coats?" Andy retrieved the map from his pocket and changed his coat for Joel's jacket. Brad swapped his with the other fellow.

Andy reached over and hugged Liesel, tipped his hat to Franz and Kurt, and nudged Brad to do the same.

"Thank you," Brad said to Liesel. He held her hand not wanting to let go until she pulled away. *Why can't I say the words, damn it? She risked her life and I acted like a jackass. What in hell is wrong with me? She's blind—I'm not. What a jerk I am.*

Andy and Brad handed over the bikes and began their walk into Salzburg.

After leaving the road, crossing open fields, and hugging a tree line, Andy spotted a military car speeding down a side road.

He seized Brad's sleeve, pulling him in the direction of a small building. "Hurry!"   "Oh God!" Brad's voice cracked.

They reached the ramshackle structure, and Andy jerked the door. "Locked! Move out! Check for a window or an opening."

A gunshot whizzed past Andy. A second bullet halted their forward movement. They hit the ground.

"That didn't come from the road…" Andy swung around to see an elderly man wielding a rifle with both hands.

The man shouted "Hände Hoch!" pushing the rifle barrel upward signaling them to raise their hands and stand.

"He's got us, Brad. Put your hands up."

"Oh shit," Brad said. He threw his hands high over his head.

The stooped man limped over to them, patted Brad down searching for weapons.

Andy lunged forward and grabbed the old man's rifle. "Hände Hock!" he shouted.

The old man's face grew pale as he raised his hands.

Andy shoved him toward the back of the building. He nudged the man once more when they discovered a tall double door slightly ajar.

Once in the shelter, Andy scanned the area until his eyes rested upon a couple of horse bridles mounted on the wall. It looked and smelled like a makeshift barn—two horse stalls but no animals.

"Brad, hand me that leather strap dangling in the bucket next to the halter." Andy pointed outside the end stall.

"How you gonna tie him with that?"

"You'd be surprised. Reckon that strap is probably wet."

"Yes. But it's frozen."

"Bust the ice with the rifle butt. We can't go until he's restrained."

The white-haired old man trembled—his body spent with arthritis. His eyes darted back and forth at each man.

Andy handed the rifle to Brad, freeing himself to pull and stretch the leather. He stretched it as far as it would go and shoved the man's hands behind his body, walked him into one of the stalls, and backed him up against the wooden slabs. He wound the leather around the man's wrists, crisscrossed it in the middle, and looped it through the stall post as an anchor. "There, old man. I mean you no harm, but this will keep you quiet."

Andy took the man's boot off, removed his sock, and shoved it in the man's mouth.

"That'll hold ya. Let's get out of here, Brad. We'll toss the rifle in the woods."

Brad walked over to the man and with the butt end of the rifle, slammed it upside the elderly man's head. The man went limp.

Andy reeled around, "What the hell did you do that for?"

"Insurance."

Andy seethed. His face flushed and his body stiffened. "Listen buster, I outrank you, and I gave no such order. You *will* follow my orders."

"I don't gotta listen to you. We're not flying or at the base. You're just a jerk!"

"Wake up, Brad. You *are* under my command. Get used to it, buddy." He snatched the rifle from Brad and shoved him out the door. "Head for the woods. Now!"

When they reached the trees' edge, Andy removed the bullets from the rifle and slipped them into his pocket. He buried the rifle beneath a patch of snow and underbrush.

"Got your pistol?" Brad asked.

"Yes. Do you?"

"Yep. Won't catch me without it."

"Okay. Let's plan our trek into the city." Andy pulled out the ragged map and smoothed it for better readability. "If we stay at the base of this mountain, we can weave in and out of the trees especially where snow has melted. We'd stand out like a bold target in the snowy areas."

Brad pointed on the map. "Look at that large open spot. How do we cross it?"

"We've got a couple of miles before we get there. It looks like a lake. Don't run. Causes suspicion. Watch for farm people. Some apparently not friendly."

"Yes sir," Brad sneered.

Up ahead loomed a lake, much larger than they had expected. It was not completely frozen—a sign of fast flowing water, Andy surmised. A group of German soldiers stood around a fire outside a shabby hut at the water's edge.

Andy and Brad stood well back in the woods and analyzed the situation. A rustling in the woods behind startled both men. Andy reached for his pistol, but found it buried in his layers of clothing. Before he could pull it out, two young boys appeared.

Andy, somewhat relieved, waited for them to speak.

*"Spring is coming. The robins will be here soon."* The smaller boy spoke in broken English.

"What?" Andy studied him. He was barely old enough to shave. His voice had yet to change. "Yes, that's right," Andy added. The other boy simply nodded.

"Come," the first one said. Andy and Brad followed in silence for about a half mile around the lake moving closer to the water. Thick underbrush offered scant cover. A small "john" boat lay secured on the bank.

"Help flip the boat over and into the water. We'll row you to the other side, but you must hide in the bottom of the boat."

"Sure thing. Come on, Brad." Andy and Brad caught one side of the boat, and the two boys grabbed the other side, heaved it into the water, and broke the frozen edges.

Partially in the water, the pair signaled for Andy and Brad to climb in.

Andy stepped back, "Go ahead, Brad."

Brad got in and the two curled up in the bottom of the small boat—one on each side of the wooden seat in the center.

The boys hopped in and took the middle seat, sitting side by side. One of the boys took off his hat. Long, light brown hair unfolded from beneath.

"What the...no wonder 'he' wasn't old enough to shave." Andy chuckled.

A smile crossed Brad's face as well, which surprised Andy. He chose not to make a comment.

The girl and boy picked up the oars and began rowing. The girl started singing and the boy harmonized with her.

"Oh, I get it. Two lovers taking a boat ride together. Smart." Andy whispered to Brad.

"Real cute," Brad responded with sarcasm.

The girl and boy rowed and sang. Once they became parallel to the Germans, they waved. The boy leaned over and kissed the girl.

"Die Wonnen der Liebe!" (The joys of love!) a German shouted. Boisterous laughter broke out from the water's edge.

The two continued singing for another half mile, Andy estimated. The boat's bow broke through the ice and rested in a shallow cove on the lakeshore. The singing abruptly stopped, and the girl shouted, "Go! Go! Hurry! Germans are all around the edge of the lake. Don't stop."

Andy and Brad jumped out and raced for a thicket. Andy's breath came in short bursts. The singing resumed. He turned around to see the two pushing off with their oars.

Andy's knees wobbled from the cramped position in the boat, and his thigh burned. He retrieved his pistol from his shoulder holster. Brad followed.

A sudden fluttering of birds from the trees alerted Andy. He placed his finger to his lips, "Shhhhh!"

Brad readied his gun.

They crept toward the area. Movement sounded only a few feet beyond the thicket. Andy moved forward once more, Brad immediately behind.

The rustling of underbrush came closer. Andy froze. He stepped behind a tree. The object continued its movement. He aimed his pistol. His stomach knotted.

# Chapter Nineteen

## St. Peter's Cemetery

Andy threw a quick glance at Brad. The blood had rushed from Brad's face and his gun hand visibly shook. Andy held his breath.

The branches crackled and crunched as the object came closer. Into the clearing burst an eight-point buck.

"Good God!" Brad shouted. "I almost pissed in my britches."

"What a beaut," Andy said. They watched the buck dart away.

Andy continued, "We're on our own now, and I don't mind telling you, I'm scared stiff. I know nothing about this city or where to go next. Let's work together best we can. That's the only way we'll survive."

"Yep," Brad half-heartedly replied.

"It gets dusk dark around 1800. We got four hours to get to the square." Andy motioned Brad to move on.

"How the hell are we going to get through all those Krauts? They've got the entire area cordoned off." Brad threw his hands up in the air and then slapped them down on his sides.

"Buck up, Brad. Come on." Andy led Brad deeper into the forest hiding behind trees and clumps of underbrush along the way.

Twenty minutes later they heard screams from what sounded like a female. Loud shouts from a masculine voice and whacking noises were followed by hysterical screams.

Andy signaled Brad to slow down. They crept closer to the commotion. A barn loomed ahead. They slipped around to the entrance. The screaming drowned out the squeaking from the rusty door hinges. A Gestapo officer sat on top of a struggling young girl, brutally beating and forcing her into submission.

Andy rushed in and wrenched the man off the girl, yanked him to his feet, drove his fist into his jaw, and slammed him against the barn wall. He turned to help the sobbing girl to her feet.

Brad plunged into the skirmish as the German recovered sufficiently enough to lunge at Andy. Brad wrestled the German to the ground. Andy caught the glint from the German's revolver as the soldier struggled to turn it toward Brad.

Andy snatched his gun, took aim at the soldier's head, and fired. An explosive flash erupted from the barrel. The German slumped on top of Brad. His gun fell from his hand.

The young girl watched in horror.

"Go! Go!" Andy shouted motioning her away.

She fled the scene in hysterics.

Brad shoved the German's body aside, and looked up at Andy.

Andy noticed Brad's ghostly white face, reached down and caught his hand. "Hurry, any second they'll be swarming on us like bees after honey."

After Andy shoved the German's gun into his pants, they raced from the scene. Near the edge of the forest, he saw the girl flee the area until a car of Gestapo men stopped her. He watched them question her briefly and let her go. The Germans drove over the field to the edge of the woods and abandoned the vehicle to search by foot.

Andy swiped his sleeve over his brow, and held his breath.

"Andy," Brad began when Andy interrupted him.

"We've got to survive. There's nothing more important. Concentrate and stay alert."

"Thanks." Brad said.

Andy knew what he meant but refused to dwell on it. No time.

They raced through the woods, eyed possible new routes, their chests heaving with each gasp of air. Germans from all locations moved toward the woods searching for the source of the gunshot. "They're following the sound of the shot, Brad. This might give us a better chance…" A second later he landed sprawled on the ground face first.

Brad raced over. "You all right?"

Andy rubbed his nose touching a tender spot. He cringed. His hand came away bloody. "Damn!" He jumped to his feet, glanced at the vine that tripped him, and resumed his running.

The bulky clothing needed for warmth slowed him immeasurably. He wasn't sure the perspiration came from overdressing or fright. Andy's uncertainty of their future took its toll on both men, propelling them forward like wild animals. They wove their way to a doubtful ending.

Through miles of underbrush and trees, up the sides of mountains and down into the depths of valleys, Andy and Brad reached the end of the forest. Andy studied the area. A road with buildings on one side. "Brad, look between those two buildings. Is that the St. Peter's Cemetery?"

"Can't see from here. Better check it out."

Andy held out his arm to keep Brad back until he scanned the area. "All clear. Go!"

They hustled across the road, keeping an eye out for Germans. "Yep, this is it," Andy said, after struggling to interpret the sign: *Peterfriedhof.* "Liesel was right. Those are huge tombs. Find one near me and stay there until we hear the bells at 1800."

Andy hid behind a large tombstone, reached in his cloth sack, pulled out a hunk of cheese, broke a piece off, and pitched it to Brad. "Heads up, Brad." He sailed a chunk from a pone of bread across to Brad.

"What I wouldn't give for a hot meal!"

"And a hot stove." Andy's body had cooled from lack of activity, and sitting on ice didn't help. "Thank God the cemetery is empty."

No sooner had Andy spit the words from his mouth when two men came out of St. Peter's Cathedral. Andy's heart thumped so loud, he put his hand over his chest as if to stifle its beat. The men read a couple of tombstones and then crossed the cemetery and walked down the road.

The sound of marching feet set off an alarm inside Andy. His stomach churned. The clomping boots approaching the cemetery sent chills through him. His feet told him to run but his brain said, *stay.* "Brad. I think we better move. Sounds like marching soldiers. Let's go—inside the church." He didn't listen to his brain.

"People may still be in there, Andy."

"Our chances are better inside than out here." Andy eased toward the church portico, slipping behind one column then another—Brad on his heels.

Dusk had settled in and cast shadows on the monuments and darkened the area behind the numerous pillars buttressing a long alcove across the back of the monastery. Andy's body shivered from the frigid air as they waited for the right moment to enter.

"Psst! We need to get the hell out of here," Brad said.

"No! Hold your position!" Andy peered around the pillar. The heads of the approaching platoon marched up the hill and came into view.

A German officer barked orders to the men. The platoon picked up their pace and were now adjacent to the cemetery.

Brad was well hidden, and Andy didn't exhale until the men marched beyond the cemetery. "Thank God," he mumbled.

A couple exited the door of the cathedral—Andy's total concentration still on the soldiers. Their footsteps caught his attention. He moved to the pair's blind side of the pillar. Brad followed Andy's move.

Once the duo left the alcove, Andy breathed easier. His brain stayed in high gear. *Time to go inside now and work our way to the front entrance.* Andy waved his arm, signaling Brad.

The two men opened one side of the tall, ornate, double doors and slipped in. The sheer artistry caught Andy off guard. The sculptures, the magnificent architecture, the brilliant gold trimmings—all in the middle of a war-torn nation—it was awesome.

Brad's eyes scanned the enormous cathedral. "Where did all of this come from?"

"Guess we're in the old section of Salzburg. I never knew this artistry existed…" Andy's attention shifted to a group of men huddled in a corner.

"Best move behind the statues." Andy led Brad beyond the main section of the cathedral down a side passage with exquisite sacred statues with handrails surrounding them. Candles, some lit, others not, filled the step-type tables at intermittent points inside the church. Andy chose to stay away from the extra light and slipped into the darkest corners, weaving his way to the front exit of the church. He tasted bile. Any little noise triggered the surge of adrenalin raging through his body.

"What's that?" Brad turned sharply to Andy.

"Hold it!" Andy slunk behind a towering statue. The sound of scuffling shoes inched closer by the minute. Andy's legs quivered and perspiration dribbled down the sides of his face. He dared not move to wipe the trickle of sweat.

An elderly woman, hair covered with a cloth, emerged into the light. She stopped, stared into the shadows and glanced across the church.

*What the hell is she looking at?* Andy's eyes stayed peeled on the woman while his hand rested on his pistol.

She turned back to Andy and motioned him to follow her.

Uncertainty flooded over Andy, but at this point, he took the gamble. "Brad," he whispered, "Let's do it."

The old lady caught Andy's arm, holding it as if *he* were helping *her* along. Brad scurried up to catch her other arm, taking Andy's lead.

The threesome made their way through the arches that stretched the depth of the church and provided minimal cover. The woman said nothing and it became obvious to Andy she was determined to leave the church.

They left the shelter of the arches to the front exit which took them squarely into the center of the church near the narthex.

Andy scrutinized the area for suspicious looking people. Only a few visitors and several men in the center section of the church huddled together. "Watch that group of men, Brad."

"I see 'em." Brad watched from the left of the woman when they turned right, heading for the massive double doors that touched the ceiling. The woman had not spoken a word.

They entered the foyer, and the woman picked up her pace. Andy and Brad kept in step.

*What are we doing? Who is she? We have no idea who she is and what she wants.* Nevertheless, Andy continued to walk with her. They had no other choice. They cleared the church entrance and found themselves in the pitch-black evening. After walking a short distance, the old lady stopped.

By then their eyes had adjusted to the darkness.

The woman spoke. *"Spring is coming. The robins will be here soon."* Her voice was raspy, and she reached up and removed the cloth and wig from her head.

"What the …" Andy gasped. "Who are you?"

"I'm part of the underground. You were about to get in trouble. Didn't you see that group of men in the middle of the church? They are my countrymen but loyal to the Germans. Their job is to spy on possible escapees. They don't realize we know exactly who they are—just like they know who we are." His English was flawless.

"So that's why the disguise, huh. Now what?" Andy sputtered the words out of his mouth as the Belfry Tower clanged its penetrating countdown.

"It's 1800 hours. Brad, we need to make haste." Andy continued. "Sir, how can we find Bertha's Old Pastry Shoppe?"

The man didn't reply but stopped long enough to put his wig and cloth back on. "We waited for you. Catch my arms and follow me. My name is Dietrich."

Andy, Brad, and Dietrich wove their way around the square of buildings, clinging as close to the walls as possible for obscurity. A monk in a dark robe, belted with a rope, and a hood covering much of his head and face, crossed in front of them. He hobbled along with the aid of a cane.

Andy glanced to the right at a tall, yellowish stone cathedral. "According to the map, that must be St. Michael's Church. See the fountain? We're in Residence Square. The greenish building on the right is Belfry Tower." He had memorized each building's identity before dark.

"Seems to me you're not lost. Figure you don't need my help," Dietrich joked.

"Don't bail out now, sir. I'm just not quite clear about the pastry shop."

Brad pointed and said softly. "Andy, two Nazis—one's coming from our left,"

Andy reached for his pistol.

"Find a side street. See if he follows," Dietrich said.

Andy motioned right. "Turn here." The trio turned into an alleyway with numerous shops bordering each side. He and Brad readied their guns.

"Hold your fire. No need to attract attention," Dietrich said.

Andy saw the glimmer of Dietrich's blade. Adrenalin raced through his veins as one soldier pressed closer. The click of the German's boots magnified his footsteps on the cobblestone street. Andy's heart raced twice as fast as the soldier's steps.

Dietrich moved slightly to the front of Andy and Brad. The blood vessels in Andy's head pulsed violently.

"Herausgekommen! Direkt! (Come out! Immediately!)," the German shouted. The soldier raised his Lugar and glance down the alley.

Dietrich inched to the corner of the building. He burst out, swatted his hand over the soldier's gun knocking it away. He lunged with his other arm wrapping it around the soldier's neck. Dietrich pulled him against his own body and shoved his knife deep into the soldier's jugular vein.

Andy rushed over to assist, but stopped when blood spurted from the side of the soldier's neck into Dietrich's face and dribbled down his cheek.

After Dietrich shoved the German to the ground, his wig slipped off during the scuffle. Brad picked up the wig with the cloth still draped over it, and handed it to Dietrich after he sheathed his knife. Dietrich took the head cloth and wiped the blood off his face.

"Let's get out of here before the other one follows," Dietrich said—calm like nothing had happened.

They slipped around another building, entered the square, but waited for the German sentry to search for his comrade before they took cover in the shadows of each building.

"How is it that you speak such perfect English, Dietrich?" Andy asked.

"While a young lad, my American mother taught me your language and spoke only English when my father was not home."

They increased their pace. "Are your parents living?" Andy asked.

"No. My father died several years ago at the hands of the Gestapo. The same Germans killed my mother not long after my father when they discovered her American heritage. She refused to be arrested, fought them off until they killed her. My sister, Liesel, witnessed my father's brutal death. I was not around when they murdered my mother. Liesel heard Mom's terrified screams but was well hidden and muffled her own screams. She wanted to help our mother, but knew she would be killed herself. The Gestapo did not see her which seemed strange at the time. She and I went underground to survive."

"Liesel?" Andy asked while wondering if that was the same Liesel.

"Yes. Why do you ask?"

"Is she blind?" Brad joined the conversation.

"Yes. Oh, that's it. She helped get you to the outskirts of Salzburg."

"That's why she spoke such perfect English. Now it all makes sense. How long has she been blind?" Andy lifted up his wool hat and rubbed his head.

"After witnessing our father's death, she went into shock and her vision disappeared. The doctors knew of no medical cause for her lost sight. They agreed that someday her sight might return, since the reason for her blindness was most probably mental. She was only fourteen when it happened. Before my mother died, she tried hard to help my sister become independent. Liesel succeeded, but not during my mother's life." While he spoke, Dietrich looked at neither Brad nor Andy.

"Well, she certainly rode her bike like a real pro. She followed that bell perfectly." Brad took a couple extra steps to keep up.

"When hiding, her exceptional hearing saved us many times," Dietrich responded.

"No wonder the underground chain is so coordinated," Andy added.

"Not really. If it hadn't been for a Catholic priest, Roman Kark Scholz of the old Augustinian monastery of Klosterneuburg, we wouldn't be doing this today. I'm hoping he won't get caught. Many have been beheaded since 1938. You can't imagine."

Dietrich continued. "Hurry now. Danger awaits around the corner. We don't expect to be here tomorrow." He caught Brad's coat and pulled him in closer to the buildings.

"Holy shit!" Brad whispered. "There's a group of, looks like…Germans soldiers heading this way."

"Come!" Dietrich signaled them to duck into yet another side street.

"Didn't we just pass the pastry shop?" Andy asked while keeping pace with Dietrich.

"Yes, but we dare not go there. The Germans will kill everyone in the shop whether they are involved or not. There is no mercy in this war." Dietrich motioned them along, zigzagging to areas of shelter until they came to a car. "Get in," he said.

"We're directly behind the pastry shop, right?" Andy hopped in the passenger seat, and Brad jumped into the back.

"Yes! Now, let's get the hell out of here!" Dietrich pressed the ignition. Nothing. He tried again. Still nothing.

"They're coming!" Brad yelled.

# Chapter Twenty

## Birmingham, England

The screaming blast of warning sirens sent Rose and the nurses scrambling. She grabbed her helmet and slapped it on her head. Piercing voices penetrated the room as the women doused the lights and rushed over the path to the field hospital's basement air-raid shelter. Before entering the building, Rose glimpsed the searchlights scanning the sky for enemy aircraft.

Her friend, Ginny, clad in pajamas, sat next to Rose on a crowded bench. A dim overhead bulb provided the only light in the large concrete tomb.

"You look so silly in a helmet and petticoat." Ginny teased.

"Like you've never seen this combination before?" The loud ack-ack from bursts of antiaircraft guns drowned out further conversation.

Ginny removed her hands from her ears between intervals of penetrating sound. "You know, I hate the close sound of that gun."

"Yes, I know." Rose placed her arm around her friend's shoulders. Fear invaded Rose's thoughts as well, but she forced herself to remain calm and struggled to ease the trembling of her own body. A vision popped into her head of Andy doing the same in a critical situation.

Rose observed how the nervous chatter of women in the shelter competed with the drone of planes overhead.

"Let's hope those planes are ours," she said, remembering the new P-51 fighter planes.

Ginny became a little more confident, shook her fist, and shouted in her Brooklyn accent, "Youse guys high tail it!" She turned and mocked Rose, "Y'all hear now?"

Rose smiled at her friend. "Now y'all know we don't sound like tha..a..at."

Twenty minutes later the all-clear siren wailed, and Rose and Ginny returned to their tent near the hospital.

"Lt. Martin." The call came from outside the tent. "Lt. Martin. Are you all right? A...the other nurses too?"

Rose recognized Lt. Col. Lawing's voice and cut her eyes over to Ginny. She whispered, "The nerve of this man."

"Yes, we're fine," she called out. She whispered to Ginny again, "I'm *not* going out there."

"Please, Lieutenant, come out and talk with me."

"I'm not dressed, sir."

"Throw on your cape. Please."

Ginny said, "For gosh sakes, gal. Do the man a favor and let him take a gander at you. Give him a thrill. Wish someone felt like that about me!"

"Really? You've no idea about him. And he's my superior officer."

"Sure, sugar. Go. Let us get some rest."

"Lieutenant…."

"I'll be there is a minute." Rose brushed her hair and sent an annoying glance to Ginny. She slipped on her cape over her petticoat, hooked it, and stepped outside.

"There you are. I was worried about you." He wrapped his arms around her until she struggled free.

Rose knew he could make it hard for her about Lizzy. Though she never led him on, she had to play nice.

"Thank you, sir, but I can take care of myself and my girls. We'll be fine." She backed away but he pulled her into his chest and kissed her.

She pounded his chest until he let go. "Sir. You must stop this. It is *not* okay." After wrenching away, she cold cocked him on the jaw and stormed into the tent.

Ginny, Myra, and the other girls were hanging on the edge of the tent opening.

She was greeted with cheers beyond the tent door.

"Well, what do ya know. Our little kitten is really a tiger." Ginny gave her a pat on her rear.

Others shouted, "You told him, babe!"

"Atta girl!'

"That's our Lieutenant," Ginny chimed in.

Rose flopped down on her bunk. *What have I done? He's my superior! Oh, God! What next. He can forbid me to see Lizzy. What will they do for food? How do I handle this man? There's nobody a woman can complain to. Even if there were, he could turn on me and ruin my nursing career.* She buried her face in her hands.

Ginny walked over, sat on Rose's bunk, and rubbed her back. "Seems we've been here before, sugar. Take it easy, doll. It'll be better tomorrow. This fella is smitten by you."

"I know, but he needs to leave me alone."

"You can't have it both ways—use him at times and reject him other times."

"I only used him to have time with Lizzy. You know better than that."

"Yes, and he has taken advantage. How you gonna change that?"

"Oh, Ginny. I don't know. I always lead with my heart, not my head!"

"It'll be better tomorrow."

"Thanks, Ginny. Gotta few things to do before turning in. Don't know what I'd do without you." She laid there for a few more minutes and knowing how much she had to do, went methodically through her routine, washing white stockings and other personal items. Her thoughts flowed back and forth from Andy to Lizzy—her two loves.

She had received no news about Andy and feared for his life. No mail from either set of parents. Her father had promised to check regularly with the Walters family, and she knew they would immediately relay a message—good or bad. A tight knot within her begged for some release—some information—any information about Andy. She wrapped herself in a cocoon of anguish and prayed that she and Andy would be together once again. *Will this wretched war ever end?* She wanted to scream out but knew better than to upset the girls.

"You still dreaming of the captain? It would be much easier if you cared for the Doc. He's got big eyes for you, and he's here. I hate to tell you this again, doll, but he ain't going to ever give you up. You said you didn't want to get attached to a flyboy because he might not come back." Ginny immediately put her hand to her mouth when she saw Rose tear up. "Oh Rose. I'm sorry. I was just kidding. You got so many boys going goo-goo-eyed over you. You're the envy of half the dames in England."

"It's all right." Rose brushed the tears away and looked up from washing her dainties. "I haven't heard from Andy for so long. You're right. I didn't want to fall in love. I'm glad I'm not back at Snetterton where names are wiped off the roster board after every mission. I don't know what I'll do if Andy doesn't come back. We planned to spend the rest of our lives together."

She squeezed out her stockings, carried them to a string dangling from the ceiling, and tied them loosely to dry. Andy's words "a love for eternity" danced through her head. *Someone to spend the rest of my life with—to celebrate our fiftieth wedding anniversary with—someone to watch our children grow up, marry and bring grandchildren into the world—someone to count gray hairs with and share a lifetime of love.*

Ginny remained speechless.

Rose was conscious of Ginny's eyes following her around the tent. She turned to her friend. "Don't you wonder if this war will ever end? How about your fellow?"

"Oh William? He's lucky. The RAF seems to fly only at night out of England. Less danger. That's okay by me."

"Enjoy him while you can, Ginny. Who knows what tomorrow will bring."

Rose hung her brassiere and panties over a line strung across the back of the tent.

"What about Lizzy? Have you seen her lately?"

"Oh yes. *Lizzy*. I promised Col. Lawing that I'd stay away from her, but you know I couldn't keep that promise. They had no food. I have to fess up. I take them food when I'm not on duty."

"Did you really think we didn't notice? And if the colonel wasn't sweet on you, he'd never let you get away with it."

"You knew? Guess I'm not surprised. Elizabeth has no money and even if she did, without transportation, how would she get food home? With a babe in arms and holding the hand of a small child, no way could she manage."

Ginny shook her head without replying.

"Fact is, I got a message from Elizabeth yesterday. Tomorrow, I'm biking over to Coventry to see her." Rose wrung out a pair of gloves, picked up the wash pan, pitched the water outside, and returned to hang the last items. She glanced at her bunk, "That bed looks inviting. I'm gonna hit the sack. Night."

Once in bed, Rose tried to shut out the thoughts racing through her mind—the incident with the colonel and the conversation with Ginny later. *A promise broken to my superior officer. He knows my plight, but he didn't stop me. With all those days spent with Lizzy, I let it get out of control. Now Lizzy's such a part of my life I can't let her go. First it was Andy, now Lizzy. Why do I let myself get so attached?* She wrapped her arms around herself pretending they were Andy's. Her brain finally rested, and she fell asleep.

The next morning, a mild summer day, started out misty as usual, but around ten o'clock the sun ate away at the foggy haze, exposing a vibrant blue sky. After dressing, Rose slipped her feet into her white tie shoes.

She loaded the front bicycle basket with food and hooked cloth sacks like saddlebags over the metal rack above the rear wheel. *Elizabeth and the girls can eat for another week.*

She climbed onto the bike, wearing her summer gray uniform and a white armband with a red cross on it, which designated her as a noncombatant. She knew this allowed the Red Cross, under the Geneva Convention, access to many areas and protected the workers from attack. She tucked her skirt tight under the bicycle seat to keep it from being caught up in the rear wheel spokes.

Rose had memorized the route. The British kept most of the roads cleared of rubble, and she felt safe, except for air raids. Her feet pumped the pedals up and down in unison like pistons, building speed, straining her legs for the next upgrade. With every mile her attention centered around Andy and Lizzy. Andy, if still alive, had no idea of her transfer to Birmingham. If he hadn't received her letters, he knew nothing of Lizzy—her second love. She had dreamt of war's end, going back home, marrying Andy, and bringing Lizzy to live with them in the States.

Rose steeled herself against the ugliness of the flattened buildings, shattered houses, and what remained of a church steeple that partially blocked the road. She forced herself to ignore the thoughts of families torn apart, lost lives, and orphaned children resulting from catastrophic bombings. The man responsible for this, Adolph Hitler, had brought on the same bombings to his own people, and she hated him for it. She remembered reading that Hitler once exclaimed, "Gods and beasts, that's what our world is made of."

"He's the beast," she said aloud. *And now the Brits and we Americans are creating havoc on his country.* The wind blew against her face, as she shook her head to clear it like a dog shaking water from its back.

Rose arrived at Elizabeth's house, propped her bicycle against a pile of bricks, and removed the cloth sacks from over the rear tire. A fire smoldered beyond the outside perimeter of the house where she assumed Elizabeth had cooked something for the children.

Her knock on the door brought a red-eyed Elizabeth to the entrance. "Oh Rose. I'm so glad you're here. I don't know how long I can keep this up."

Rose set the cloth bags down and put her arms around Elizabeth, whose tears flowed. They stood arm in arm for several minutes until the sobs subsided. Elizabeth moved back from Rose and smoothed down the straight lines of her floral shirtwaist dress.

Upon hearing Rose's voice, Lizzy ran from another room and wrapped her arms around Rose's legs. Her wet tears dribbled on Rose's stockings.

She leaned down, caught Lizzy's arms, prying them away, and picked her up. "

There, there now Lizzy. Nothing can be that bad. Look what I brought you." She reached down into one of the cloth sacks and pulled out a piece of chocolate. Lizzy seized the piece of sweet, devouring it like a wild animal. Rose sat her in a chair and returned to Elizabeth.

"We were stretching our food until you got here." Elizabeth dried her tears.

"Elizabeth, we need to get the three of you out of here, somewhere more suitable to live. Between now and my next visit, I'll try to find you a better place to live."

"I'm so sorry I can't help you. Blimey! Even if I had a motorcar, how and where would I purchase petrol?"

"I know. I'll do everything I can." Rose crept over to the crib where Mary Beth slept with her thumb in her mouth. She smiled at the ten-month-old. "How adorable."

Elizabeth looked at Rose with sad, pleading eyes. "I must talk with you, love."

Rose moved closer to her, her own mind reeling in bewilderment. Her heart pounded faster. *It must be about Lizzy.* She cringed at what it might be. *Oh no! She's going to send her to one of those orphanages that house children whose parents are missing or have perished—a place far into the country—a place safe from bombings—a place to be picked up by a family who lost a child—a place for her to disappear from my life forever. No!* Rose grabbed the sides of her face. *Stop!*

"If we make it through this war, would you take Lizzy to the States?"

"What?" Rose flopped down on an unsteady chair, losing her balance. She swung her right arm to the side to stop from tipping over. Unable to digest what she had just heard, she resisted jumping up and shouting for joy. "Go ahead."

"Lizzy would have a better chance in America. I love her dearly, but it'll be a long time before I can take care of myself, much less her and the baby. She loves you, Rose."

"You don't know how many times I've hoped for something like this." She glanced at Lizzy emptying the food sacks on the floor, oblivious of the words concerning her future. Rose could scarcely contain herself. She took a deep breath and swallowed her excitement.

She continued, "I don't know how long I'll be stationed here and doubt that I could take her home when I leave. However, I *will* come back for her."

"Sis would like that, I'm sure. I'm buggered here." Elizabeth stooped down to pick up the remnants from the sacks unable to shield her tear-flooded eyes from Lizzy and Rose.

Observing Elizabeth's grief, Rose struggled up from the teetering chair. "I know this is a heart-breaking decision for you, Elizabeth. It shows just how much you love Lizzy. I'll not let Lizzy forget that." When she hugged Elizabeth, all the pent-up worries exploded. Rose stroked Elizabeth's hair until she regained control.

"Well, let me get the other things from my basket. I'll be right back." Though she wanted to believe that Lizzy would come to live with her, she knew rough waters were ahead before that could happen. She reached in the front basket and pulled out several Red Cross packets and a book she found in the road when returning from her last trip; THE LITTLE ENGINE THAT COULD, a book she recognized. She hurried back into the house with the packages.

Lizzy stood by the door, behind Elizabeth, waiting for Rose to return.

"Here, love, let me take those." A dry-eyed Elizabeth took the parcels and placed them on the table.

"Come, Lizzy. Want me to read a story?" Rose swooped Lizzy up as she ran into her arms. They sat in a sturdy chair, and Lizzy wrapped her arms around Rose's neck, her little cupid mouth and brown eyes glinting with pleasure. Rose lovingly kissed her on both cheeks and then opened the book.

Lizzy pointed to the train and squealed with joy. "Train."

After reading the book several times, Rose said, "It's getting late and I must go."

"No, no, Auntie Rose." Lizzy clung to Rose's skirt until Rose reached down, picked her up, and cradled her snug in her arms.

Lizzy put up a terrible fuss, and with each visit, it became more difficult to leave. *I can't bear this. It's tearing my heart out piece by piece. I must be strong!*

Elizabeth smiled and gave Rose a hug. "You're so grand with Lizzy. You'll be a splendid mum." A second later, her expression changed. "Don't mind me, love. I'm just a blubbering fool. It's such a beastly war, and I miss my husband and sister. And now with Grandpa gone too, I don't know what to do." The tears swelled again.

Rose gave Lizzy a hug, handed her to Elizabeth, and stretched her arms around both of them. "I'll be back on my next free day. Love y'all."

She retraced the steps to her bicycle and headed back to the hospital. The sound of Lizzy's wailing rang in her ears. She dared not look back—her own cheeks wet.

A prayer almost answered—Lizzy could stay in her life. Andy and Lizzy—the three of them—a family, sent her feet pumping as if she were an angel flying through the sky—*oh please, let Andy be alive.*

# Chapter Twenty-one

"Keep your britches on, buster!" Dietrich said. "We're not done in yet!" After pushing the ignition again, grinding it, laboring it, he floored the gas pedal, and the engine finally caught. He slipped into gear and accelerated from the area.

Brad fell back on the seat.

Andy's foot pressed imaginary brakes while they sped out of town. With scant lights, the feeling of an imminent crash loomed ahead.

"Dietrich, what's wrong with the lights?" Andy absorbed every bump from the broken pavement that threw his body from one side to the other. His knuckles turned white. "They're taped over halfway down to make the light less visible. The back lights are taped completely over." Dietrich said.

A light caught the corner of Andy's eye as he glanced back over the road just traveled. Two headlights burnished in the far distance—unmistakably their pursuers.

"They're behind us, Dietrich," Andy said. "Can you see okay?"

"Yeah. I can drive these roads blindfolded." Dietrich shoved in the clutch and shifted to second gear, releasing the clutch simultaneously to pick up the speed needed to climb the steep grade ahead.

The lights trailed behind, slowly closing in on the trio. The car's momentum propelled them over the hill into utter darkness as Dietrich whipped the vehicle to the right, which sent Brad sailing across the back seat. Andy grasped the dash, knuckles strained. Dietrich's hands froze to the steering wheel, swinging it right, then left, and back again as necessary. Low limbs brushed against the windshield. The auto fled the area and abruptly came to a screeching halt after it turned into a mountain overhang that covered an open garage door. Dietrich set the brakes, leaped from the car, raced to the rear, and dragged the garage doors closed. He flipped a handle. "This releases a wooden plank on the outside of the garage doors which slips the plank into a slot that locks the doors."

Andy had bounded out of the auto behind Dietrich, feeling his way to the garage entrance to check the security of the "locked" doors. "Won't they see strange doors with no house way out in the boonies and get suspicious?" Andy whispered to Dietrich.

Dietrich let out a boisterous laugh—Andy could not see his face, "When I pulled the doors down, winter vines fell into place draping over the brownish doors. Hear their motor approaching? They'll whiz past in mere seconds."

Andy didn't know enough to have confidence in Dietrich yet. "Here they come." He held his breath listening to the vehicle swish past—no slowdown. "Whew! Thank you, God! Now what?"

"Shall we grab a bite to eat?" Dietrich headed toward the back of the garage. He fumbled his way around the wall—for a door, Andy suspected. "Ah! Here it is. Come in, gentlemen."

Dietrich opened the door, and a tiny light on a battered table greeted them. The light glowed no brighter than a flashlight with waning batteries.

"Whoa!" Brad, the last one to enter, stumbled on an upraised doorframe. He caught himself against Andy's back.

A cast-iron stove on the opposite wall beckoned Andy. He backed up to the heat and rubbed his hands behind. "How'd you vent this thing, Dietrich?"

"A pipe goes up through the top of the ground with a metal screen cover. There's no heat during the day—the smoke would be too visible. At night, someone comes in to start the evening fire, unless it's a bright moonlit night. They also check the food supply."

"A well-oiled machine," Andy said marveling at the splendid coordination of the underground. Once his eyes adjusted to the sparse lighting, he could see steam rising from a pot on the stove. "Smells like rutabaga soup." A lopsided table with benches sat precariously in the middle of the small room, and open shelves supported a variety of foods like potatoes and cabbage. Brown bread was stacked in a corner of the shelf. Blankets teetered against the wall beneath.

"Afraid the Germans confiscated all the locals' meats. Sit. Have some chow. Tomorrow, I promise, will be a busy day." Dietrich threw his leg over the bench and sat down. Brad and Andy joined him.

"You married?" Andy asked Dietrich.

"Was. My wife and two-year-old daughter died in a house fire many years back. I had gone to a pub for some spirits and met up with some lads. Ever since, I swore to stay sober and help the underground."

"That must have been heartbreaking. You appear to be engrossed in your work—helping strangers—people not belonging to your country."

"I can never forgive myself for not being home with my family—protecting them." Dietrich's voice cracked. "For a year or so, didn't care if I lived or died. Took irresponsible chances. My mother's death brought me to my senses."

Brad, listening quietly to the conversation, drifted back to his own mother's death. *I've never been the same person. It changed my entire life—anger, hate, revenge—I got it all. But why?* His lip curled. *Why do I need to hear this crap? It's not going to help me none. Who cares, Dietrich? Nobody cares. Nobody gives a dam. No one!*

After eating, Andy spread a blanket and stretched out on the hard floor between Dietrich and Brad. His first thoughts were of Rose and the possibility of a future after all. Before drifting into a deep sleep, he wondered about his family and how they coped—not knowing if he was dead or alive. *The stress must be more than they can bear....*

Morning came too soon, though Andy didn't think daylight had arrived. He watched Dietrich fetch some brown bread, and each man pulled off a section and spread a spoon of fruit jam over it.

"This is good jam, but what is it?" Andy held out the spoon to Dietrich.

"They didn't have enough of one kind of fruit so they combined several. Let's get moving." Dietrich picked up three knapsacks, handed one to each of them. He opened the front of the stove and scattered the remaining embers.

Andy and Brad slipped into their jackets and followed Dietrich into the garage.

"We're heading out to Lienz. Near the coast of Italy. But the tough part is yet to come...crossing the Alps. I can take you only so far in the car. Petrol is a real problem. It's possible the underground can help you get into Italy. As of now, I've been unable to make contact. I must tell you, this is dangerous."

"I understand. But we've gotta try. Right, Brad?"

"Damn straight. *I'm* not gonna be captured," Brad said.

"What's the odds, Dietrich?" Andy stared into his dark brown eyes, searching for answers.

"Not good. I'll do everything I can, but there's no guarantee." Dietrich opened the garage doors with a handle that retrieved the wooden plank and peered into the darkness. He walked to the auto, climbed in, started the engine, and backed out.

Andy closed the garage doors and hopped into the vehicle. The air smelled like snow. Wet and raw. "Just what we need," he muttered.

Brad was already in the back seat. The black of night still clung on, waiting for the dawn of day.

"How'd you get this '38 Renault, Dietrich?" Andy asked, but decided that since Dietrich didn't respond, it wasn't that important. Their goal—make it back to Italy.

The early morning chill spread into the unheated vehicle. Andy caught the sides of his jacket and pulled it taut over his extra clothing to trap much needed warmth.

He glanced up and down the road for headlights. "Don't see any other vehicles on the road. Think you could pull the tape off now?"

Dietrich drove at the speed of the night before. "I got this road memorized. Relax. Save your worry for something serious." He smiled as he reached over and tapped Andy on the back of his head.

They rode in silence for several miles until Andy observed a hint of the eastern sun playing peek-a-boo over the jagged mountaintops, spilling rays of glistening light dancing on the snow. "Awesome. God sure knew what he was doing when he created the Alps."

"Well, he messed up damn good when he created Hitler." Brad spun around to check the road behind.

Andy leaned to the back at the same time, "What the hell is that? It looks like a train."

Dietrich held the rearview mirror tight to steady the vibration. He aimed it at the area Andy pointed. "Good Lord, that looks like a convoy—a German convoy. Our luck might be running out."

"Get us off this damn road," Brad shouted.

Andy turned and noticed Brad's ruddy complexion suddenly ashen.

"We're close to the town of Mondsee. There's a rather large cathedral that's always open." Dietrich pointed up the road. "Do you see that clump of trees a couple miles ahead on the left? The town is just beyond there."

"What about the car?" Andy glanced forward and back.

"It's not unusual to see an empty vehicle parked in a town. If we try to hide it that would definitely be unusual. Germans own this town."

"Is this a German car? Can't this bucket of shit go any faster?" Brad sat on the edge of the back seat, staring out the rear window.

"No need to attract attention. Andy, how about keeping that joker calm?" Dietrich's impatience showed.

Andy reached back, caught Brad's shoulder, and pulled him forward. "Button your lips." He stared into Brad's eyes until Brad signaled he got the message. Andy shoved him back on the seat.

"We gotta be in their sights, Dietrich." Andy turned back around.

"Definitely, but when we get to town, there'll be other staff cars, and unless they get close to the engine, they won't know which one is warm under the hood. We'll stop a good distance from the Mondsee Cathedral."

"Holy shit! This is a German staff car!" Brad grabbed the sides of his head.

"Shut up, Brad! We've got enough problems." Andy felt his face flush.

Dietrich rounded a curve and the town of Mondsee appeared—almost out of nowhere. Andy noticed a yellow stone cathedral seated at the base of a mountain. It overpowered the area with two tall towers; at the top, a clock adorned the front of each tower. "Is that it?" he asked.

"That's it! We'll pull in on the left of the cathedral among other cars. Soon as we get out of the car, rip the tape off the front and back lights." Dietrich shoved the gearshift into reverse, cut the engine, and jumped out. "Hurry!"

The three men hustled out of the vehicle, snatched the tape off, avoided snow patches that left telltale tracks, and rushed down the road and into the cathedral. Once inside, the dim lighting gave them ideal places to hide.

Quietly, Dietrich said, "Can you believe that this is where Maria and the Baron von Trapp were married? They fled the country when

Hitler annexed Austria in 1938." He slipped into one of the elegant alcoves along the left side of the cathedral.

Andy noticed the emptiness of the cathedral. "Did you see any people outside?" His eyes scrutinized the area.

"No. How strange is that?" Brad asked, following Dietrich's example hiding in the shadows.

"They must know something we don't," Dietrich whispered.

"We can't be sure there's nobody around, right?" Andy said in a low voice from the alcove beyond Dietrich.

The rumble of the convoy seeped inside the cathedral sending a tremor through Andy. Gunfire resounded and shouts in German echoed from the trucks, signaling their arrival in town.

"What are they saying, Dietrich?" Andy rubbed his face with his sleeve.

"They're warning the people to stay inside. No need to worry. The Austrians would never even peek out of a window. They would surely be shot."

"Jawohl, jawohl, jawohl," worked its way down the convoy with instructions shouted from one vehicle to another as the Germans replied, "Yes sir."

Andy strained to see Brad shifting from one foot to the other, hiding behind a pillar following his lead.

The back door they had entered a few moments ago opened. Andy's heart sank as the thunderous noise of the convoy penetrated his ears.

A thin, bald man wearing a white robe appeared. Dietrich held his finger in front of his lips. Andy and the two men stood frozen for what seemed like hours. He assumed the man in the robe was a priest but suspected it might be a trick.

The rumbling of the convoy stopped. Voices sounded in the distance. Andy realized a heavy odor drifting into the building came from the motor oil and exhausts of the vehicles just passed.

The man in the robe turned and walked down the aisle between the alcove and the pews, getting closer by the minute. Andy held his breath.

The man stopped abreast Dietrich. He kept his head forward and said, "My sons, you're safe for now, but you must leave. The convoy stopped and began searching all the buildings." He spoke with a strong German accent.

"Danke," Dietrich replied.

Andy watched the priest continue to walk, circle to the back entrance, and leave the cathedral. Andy rushed to the door, partially opened it, and stuck his head out in search of the man. He was nowhere in sight. "How could he disappear like that?"

Dietrich said, "We've more to do than worry about an unknown. Let's get out of here."

Once in the car, Andy said, "It's gonna get worse than this, right Dietrich?"

"Yeah. It's about fifty miles to Lienz near the Italian border. Don't know how long the petrol will hold out. Probably have to ditch the car at some point."

Brad's intense stare and anemic face set off an alarm inside Andy. His eyes darted rapidly from one place to another. "Brad, you all right?"

"Hell no! How can I be all right when we're running for our lives, fat-head? Tell me."

Dietrich looked over at Andy. Neither responded. They continued winding their way around the base of the Alps and the Salzkammergut Lake District.

Andy glanced at the road behind. No vehicle following. The beauty of the peaceful Alpine peaks laden with snow reflected rainbow colors and made it difficult for Andy to believe he was in the middle of a war. *If my life ended today, this would be the chosen spot. The letters in my uniform pocket might be necessary after all. Freedom has yet to come.*

A shout from Brad broke into Andy's thoughts. "A car is gaining on us!"

"Get hold of yourself, Brad. You don't know they're after us. Calm down." Andy turned around in his seat glancing from Brad to the road behind and the speeding vehicle closing fast.

"Turn around, both of you. Don't make us look suspicious!" Dietrich had a serious edge in his voice.

Andy and Brad faced forward. Dietrich's eyes held fast to the rearview mirror. "That son-of-a-bitch is flying. He'll pass us in a couple of minutes."

Dietrich steadied the car at about 80 kilometers. Andy's stomach crawled—not from the lack of food. "Where's it now?" He asked Dietrich, his face straight ahead.

"It's about to pass. He hasn't slowed down a second. He's sailing."

The car sped past like a bullet whizzing by.

"Phew!" Brad sounded. He brushed his hands all over his face, "Do either one of you know whacha doing?"

"Quit your bellyaching. I've about had enough of you!" Andy slid down in his seat and stretched out his legs.

The car disappeared from sight, and the kilometers clicked away as Dietrich sped onward. He reached over, shielding the sunlight from the petrol gauge. "Shit! We're empty—traveling on fumes."

"Damn! Now what?" Brad shouted.

"There's a small village up ahead. If we can make it there, we'll seek help. The underground is stronger now than two years ago—a new résistance."

The worried look on Dietrich's face sent Andy's heart racing. "God, I hope so."

They arrived in a village near Giezendorf where German military vehicles, trucks and cars, lined the streets.

"Where to now, Mr. Know-it-all!" Brad scrunched down in the back seat.

"Don't attract attention, Dietrich. Just drive through the town and keep going." Andy squirmed in his seat.

"Can't. Not enough petrol to go much farther, I tell you."

The alarm in Dietrich's voice continued to set off bells in Andy's head. "Pull down that road to the right!"

Dietrich turned, and a village church with its tall steeple emerged on the hillside on the left of the road.

Andy pointed. "Whip it in there." He glanced around in time to see a car follow from the road they just abandoned. "See if you can get behind the building." Andy prayed the tire tracks would not be visible. Only one car was parked in front of the church.

Dietrich wheeled behind the church.

"Cut the engine, quick!" Andy said. The sound of the car passing soothed his ears. "There's a door. Get inside." He hurried to the door, as the sound of another vehicle grew closer. "Oh, God, let it be open."

Andy pressed his thumb on the door handle. It moved. He pulled the door and held it open. Brad shoved his way in front of Dietrich. They found themselves in the pulpit section of the church.

"Preacher's entrance, huh?" Andy whipped his finger up to his lips. A lady cradling a baby in her arms sat in a third-row pew—her head lowered in prayer.

She looked up.

"Marta? What are you doing here?" Dietrich's face filled with surprise. He walked over to her.

She spoke in German, and Dietrich translated. She said, "Hans was killed three months ago along with eight others while working with the résistance."

Dietrich lowered his head. "I had heard."

Andy smiled back at the cooing baby. He suddenly became aware of the danger the three men heaped on this innocent woman. "I'm sorry, ma'am, but this will put you and your baby in serious danger. You must leave."

"This is Marta." Dietrich motioned toward the two. "Andy. Brad. She understands a little English."

"How'd ya do, ma'am," Andy's eyes scanned every crevice of the sanctuary.

"Hello." Brad said.

"Come," Marta said in broken English. "Pulpit. Hide." She hurried up to the oversized pulpit and pointed to the bare floor directly under the three-sided podium.

Andy reached down and touched a ledge on each side to lift the wooden square. When opened, a ladder extended below.

"Andy, you and Brad go below. I'll stay here with Marta. Hans was a great friend of mine. I'll close the top."

Andy stepped back for Brad to climb down the ladder, then followed. He noticed Brad looked waxen.

Dietrich called to them, "I'll be down shortly." He gave them a few minutes of light, before replacing the block that closed the escape hatch.

Andy spotted a lantern, rushed over, and grabbed it before the light disappeared. "Gotta a match on you, Brad?"

Brad reached into his pocket. Nothing. He checked another and came up with a box of matches. Without a word, he handed them to Andy, who lit the lantern as Dietrich closed the hatch.

"Hey, I'm not liking this. How do you know Dietrich won't turn tail and run? We don't really know him."

"Brad, he got us out of Salzburg and this far, didn't he? He's risking his life for us."

Loud footsteps resounded overhead. Running feet. Shouts echoed from above. Then a scream—female scream.

"My baby. Don't hurt my baby!"

"That's Marta!" Andy jumped up knocking over the wooden keg he sat on.

"No men here! Give back my baby!"

Though he couldn't understand all her words, Marta's screams triggered Andy's panic button.

He heard Dietrich shouting in German. A scuffle sounded above.

A shot penetrated the sound and a thud came from above. Marta let out a blood-curdling scream.

"Oh, God! Brad, we've got to go up. They shot Dietrich. They'll kill Marta and the baby unless we give ourselves up."

"You idiot. She's nobody. Don't you move!" Brad stepped in front of the ladder.

The screams grew louder, and the commotion grew more violent.

Andy knew enough German to understand Marta was fighting for her baby. With his right hand, he landed a blow to Brad's jaw. "Get out of my way, scum!"

Brad swayed then rushed forward. "No way!"

Andy thrust his left fist at Brad's nose followed by another blow to the gut. Brad fell to the floor. Andy shoved him out of the way, reached in his own holster, removed his gun, and placed it on the keg.

Guarded, he stepped over to the ladder and clamped his hands over his ears to shut out Marta's screams. He heard his own breath shudder. *Dear God, don't let them kill her and the baby. Please.* His hands grabbed hold of the ladder.

After reaching the top, he lifted the trap door aside and climbed out. The baby's crying grew louder, and Marta's screams reached a higher pitch.

Andy's veins pulsated. He stepped from behind the pulpit, hands held high. Marta's screams stopped. She wrestled away from her captors, who had turned their attention to Andy. She grabbed her crying baby from the pew. Then she leaned down over Dietrich. The blood puddled beneath his head. He lay still—like death.

"I'm your prisoner," Andy said. He kept his hands high over his head. "She didn't know I was down there."

Marta turned and said in German, "I do not know this man or how he got down there. I came to pray."

A German rushed up and grabbed Andy. He bellowed something in German then looked at Marta.

"He say, 'More?'" Marta translated for him while holding her baby snuggly against her breasts.

"Yes. One more. I'll get him. She does not know us or why we were down there."

Marta translated for him.

The German hurled Andy around toward the pulpit. His shoulder slammed into the wooden structure knocking it over while sending him sprawling on top and flattening the pulpit. Andy scrambled to his feet, shoved the pulpit pieces aside, and called below to Brad. "If you want to live, get up here. Now!"

Brad emerged reluctantly from the ladder, hands behind his head. Immediately the German officer seized him.

# Chapter Twenty-two

## Fayetteville, North Carolina - March 1944

John Walters and Ralph Martin stepped out of one of the numerous tobacco curing barns on the Martin farm. They faced the rich, naked sweep of earth awaiting planting.

"John, you look great. Gave us a scare a while back. Have any lingering problems."

"Thank you, I'm doing good thanks to my wife and you. I notice a slight weakness on my left side, but it's improving."

"Say, what do you hear from Andy?"

John removed his straw hat and slapped it on the side of his overalls. Dust genies floated over the hat and on to the tall, pale, clean-shaven, gray-haired man in a business suit. "Got only one letter since he shipped out to Foggia, Italy. Arrived January—nothing since. Jane's pretty uneasy. You heard from Rose? Where is she?"

"Rose hasn't heard anything from Andy either. She's still in Birmingham, England. Hopes she can stay there 'til the end of the war. Seems there's a little orphan girl she's become attached to."

"You don't say. That sounds like Rose. I pray they get home safe from this hellish war." John walked around the first tobacco barn, carrying a pad and pencil, examining the structure, and noting repairs. "I got a crew coming in next week to shore up the barns. The winter wind weakened them and most of the clay seals need to be replaced." He caught hold of a post supporting an overhang which moved under his pressure. "Yup, I guess this is the year we spend all spring reinforcing the barns."

Ralph followed. "Well, whatever it takes. Let's fix them up before May planting. Fields plowed and sufficient rain during March. If April continues the same, it'll be a good planting year. By the way, how's that teenager of yours, Betty Jane, isn't it?"

"She's a big girl now. Singing at school a lot. Fact is, she's got solos Saturday night in some kind of play."

"Congratulate her for me. Maybe the Missus and I'll catch the play. If not, I'll stop in and see you and Jane in a week or so. You've taken a load off me and now that you are in good shape, I don't worry with you around. I know it'll get done. You're a good man, John."

"Thanks, Mr. Martin. 'Preciate it." John shook Ralph's hand and watched him make his way across the furrows. Occasionally he reached down to pick up a handful of dirt and sprinkled it back over the field as if checking the richness of the soil.

John headed back and opened the door leading into the barn. Once inside, he scanned the tall straight walls searching for light penetrating through openings. More dust particles danced in sparse rays of light. "Okay, more repairs—can't have that light," he muttered to himself. He glanced at the poles lining the upper part of the barn that would support wooden sticks strung full of tobacco leaves. *Two rotted. Need to make a note.*

The thought of harvest time brought him back to Andy and how he diligently helped with never a complaint. *Dear God, let him be all right*. The nagging memory of how he pushed his son to excel beyond reason and his anger at him for dropping out of college to go to war plagued him every day. John knelt down in prayer—he could do this in the privacy of the barn. *I can't let Jane know how worried I am.*

As he pressed his hands together, he noticed for the first time how the rays pouring in between the slats resembled the rainbow colors of stained glass.

*Dear Heavenly Father, we've been so blessed, and I am grateful for everything you have done for us. I don't ask for a lot, but today, I'm asking for a big one. Please, dear Lord, let Andy be okay. He's such a good boy. Please bring him home safe and sound. If I could have gone in his place, I would have, dear Lord. His whole life is ahead of him—please keep him safe. Allow me the opportunity to beg my son for forgiveness for how I pushed him all those years. I am truly sorry. I ask in the name of Jesus, Amen.*

He got up from the dirt floor, brushed off his knees, and left the barn. Once he stepped into the warm March sunshine, a peace came over him as he observed spring in its fullest—redbud trees blooming near the edge of the woods, and distant cherry trees in a soft array of pinkish white blossoms decorating the grounds of their home. *Andy helped me plant those trees. Oh, what I would give if he were here to see spring in its finest and to smell the freshly plowed fields.*

After completing a few more chores, John headed back to his house to wash up. Suppertime. Betty Jane would be home from school, bouncing with excitement of the day. She brought sunshine into his life when he needed it most.

"Hello, dear. How was the meeting with Mr. Martin?" Jane asked. She untied her yellow-bibbed apron from her green plaid dress and shook the white flour out the back door like shaking off a tablecloth. John stepped back from the white dust.

Chicken spattered and popped in the frying pan, cabbage boiled, and cornbread baked, sending a pleasant aroma throughout the cozy home.

"All this fresh weather stirs up my appetite. Smells good, honey. Everything's fine with Mr. Martin. He likes an update now and then. Where's Betty Jane?" John pitched his hat on a hook at the back door and slipped out of his jacket and boots. He pulled at a strap on his denim overalls.

"She's doing her homework. After supper she's going back to school for rehearsal. She's a ball of fire with excitement. Doesn't appear nervous in the least. Remember when I sang in my first play, I couldn't stay out of the bathroom. I was afraid to drink anything before my part—then my throat felt like sandpaper as the song came out."

"But you got through it fine. I remember well. Even back then, you were a beauty." He walked over to where she stood, turning the chicken. He placed his arm around her shoulders. "You're still my gal." He planted a gentle kiss on her cheek.

"My, my, John. What's gotten into you? You melancholy or something? What happened today?"

John gazed into Jane's troubled eyes, knowing she searched his for a sign—a sign of anything about Andy.

"How about being my date Saturday night for the school play?" He moved her away from the frying pan, pulled her close to him, and cradled her in his arms.

"Why yes, I'd love to, Prince John." She smiled mischievously.

"Thank you, Cinderella. I'll have you home before midnight."


Saturday night Betty Jane sashayed into the parlor in a silk, pastel blue gown with a simple, sleeveless, V-neck bodice decorated with hand-sewn pearls. Her chiffon, tiered skirt flared delicately as she swished around the room.

"You never looked prettier." John beamed with pride at the sight of his daughter, no longer in pigtails. "Is that what your mother's been secretly working on for weeks?"

"Yes, Daddy. You like it?" Betty Jane twirled with her arms spread out.

"You know I do."

"Thought you'd like it, John." Jane sauntered in from the bedroom.

"Well, look at you, too. That pink suit is beautiful. I didn't see you sew either of these."

"That was our little surprise," Jane said, mimicking Betty Jane's twirl.

A horn blew.

"That's my ride. Peggy and her mom—we have to be there early. Daddy, I'll see you and Mom at the play. Love you two." Betty Jane ran over and kissed them goodbye.

John caught a whiff of the same perfume Jane used, like a bouquet of spring flowers. He smiled as he watched Betty Jane close the door. "She's the spitting image of you when you were that age, Jane."

"I'm so proud of her. I wish Andy could see…" The phone rang and interrupted Jane's sentence.

"I'll get it." John crossed the room to the phone in the hallway. "Hello?"

"This is Western Union," the voice on the end responded. "I have a message for you."

"Go ahead."

WASHINGTON DC 1944 MARCH 15 AT 6:30 PM:

THE SECRETARY OF WAR DESIRES ME TO EXPRESS HIS DEEP REGRET THAT YOUR SON, CAPTAIN ANDREW EDWARD WALTERS HAS BEEN REPORTED MISSING IN ACTION SINCE TWENTY FOUR FEBRUARY OVER AUSTRIA STOP LETTER FOLLOWS=
ULIO THE ADJUTANT GENERAL

The blood rushed from John's head. He felt his knees buckle. He dropped onto the phone chair.

"Would you like a copy, sir?"

"Yes, please." He eased the phone back on its hook.

Jane raced over to him. "John! What's wrong? Oh, no! It's Andy, isn't it? I knew it, I just knew it. Oh, dear God! Don't let it be! No! No!" Her face collapsed.

Jane's anguish jarred John back to reality. He braced himself for what he knew he had to do. Regaining his composure, he stood up, swallowed the lump in his throat, and embraced his wife. "Jane, the telegram said 'missing,' not 'dead.'" His own voice quivered.

"You don't know that, do you?" The tears rolled down streaking her makeup.

John knew from her pleading look she searched for a positive response from him. She needed a sign—even the tiniest glimmer of hope.

"Now, let's get hold of ourselves. We know nothing more than what the telegram states. For three weeks, they have not located him, so possibly he bailed out." His own words began to calm even himself as his faith came through for him.

"But what if the Germans capture him? They might kill him. Horrible stories are all over the newsreels, and the radio tells us every day how brutal the Japanese are to our POWs and…"

"Listen to yourself. You said Japanese, not Germans. Andy flew in the European Theater, not the Pacific." John surprised himself at his sound of confidence.

"Oh, dear. What about Betty Jane?"

"You've got thirty minutes to straighten up your face before we leave for school. We'll not say a word to her until we get home. You hear?"

"But John. She'll know when she looks at us." Jane reached in her suit pocket and pulled out an embroidered handkerchief. She dabbed her eyes.

John caught her shoulders, moved her to arm's length, and stared her square in the eyes. "It's up to you and me not to spoil her special night. We *can* do this. We're stronger than we think. How 'bout it?"

"Okay, John. For Betty Jane. I'll do my best."

"Atta girl. You'll do fine." He twirled her in the direction of their bedroom and gave her a gentle nudge. "Now, touch up your makeup. We don't want to be late."

John drove into the parking lot of Fayetteville High School, slipped into a parking space, got out of the car, and hurried around to open Jane's door. He caught her hand and helped her from the car.

She reach back for the bouquet of roses for her daughter. When she stood, John took her in his arms, "We can do this for Betty Jane. This is her night. Let her enjoy it." He leaned his cheek on her soft, gray hair.

She turned her face up to his and gave him a reassuring kiss. "John, you look positively handsome in your navy, pin-striped suit."

"Thank you, my lady." He gazed adoringly at his wife.

"I'll do what I must." She smiled sweetly, and arm in arm, they wove their way through the rough dirt and rock parking lot to the school entrance. The sun had long since given way to the coal-black sky.

"Are my eyes still puffy?"

"No, my dear," John lied. He stumbled up the first step in the darkness.

Freddie, Betty Jane's friend, met them at the door. "Betty Jane saved y'all a couple of seats near the front."

"Thank you very much, Freddie. That was sweet of you to watch for us," Jane said. Freddie escorted her to their seats.

"Thank you, young man," John said.

The school band belted out the song "Don't Sit Under the Apple Tree With Anyone Else But Me," and continued into a medley of "In the Mood," "String of Pearls," "Always," and ended with "White Cliffs of Dover."

By the last song, John had to force back his emotions and change his mood. "What's this play all about?" he asked. He already knew but wanted to engage Jane in conversation lest her thoughts matched his.

"Jane plays the lead role. A young couple is separated by WWII, and the fellow is based in England. They postponed their wedding until he returns…Oh John…" Jane reached for her handkerchief. "She has several solos. I'm so proud of her."

"You know, my chest is so tight I think I'm gonna hyperventilate before she starts singing. How about holding my hand—keep me calm."

"You ole teaser. You think I'm the one that needs to be calm. I'm fine for the moment."

He squeezed her hand and raised it to his lips to kiss. "I'm serious, Jane. I'm more nervous than Betty Jane. Is it possible for a father to be that anxious?"

She turned and stared at him. "John, you weren't kidding. You'll relax as soon as she comes on stage. Trust me!"

John smiled, grasping her hand tight. *Trust is what we've always had. Jane's been my life. But what if I'm wrong this time? I can't let her down. In my heart, I know God is looking out for my boy. He'll be all right.*

Annie, played by Betty Jane, sent her lover off to war and sang, "Somewhere Over the Rainbow."

John and Jane sat in their seats and wept. Chills flooded John's body while he listened to the melodic sounds coming from his own daughter's throat. His chest swelled with pride. He reached in his pocket for a handkerchief and blotted his eyes. "She's absolutely angelic!"

"That's beautiful…sniff…little does she know. Oh, John. How are we going to tell her?"

He gazed at Jane struggling to control her sobs. He knew she would never spoil her daughter's special day.

John let go of her hand and placed his arm around her shoulders, drawing her close. The fragrance of her perfume drifted up. Her head rested on his shoulder—the same shoulder he had kept there for her during their twenty-five years of marriage. "We'll get through this, honey. Let's don't think the worst until we absolutely know better. Betty Jane will need hope, and it's our job to help her through this."

Betty Jane ended the song in scene one, "…If happy little bluebirds fly beyond the rainbow, why, oh why can't I?"

The audience sprang from their seats and broke into a resounding applause.

Jane and John marveled at the packed room. Jane clasped her hands together near her chest. "Oh, John. How wonderful for Betty Jane."

When the next scene opened, Betty Jane sang, "This is the Army, Mr. Jones," and then ended with "Smile the while, you kiss me sad adieu, ("Till We Meet Again")." The audience rose from their seats, caught hands, and joined in the song, swaying to the music.

The last scene ended, and John watched people rush to the front and throw roses onto the stage. Betty Jane beamed with delight as she took her bows and curtsied to the audience, sending them into another round of earsplitting applause.

John and Jane wove their way through the audience to backstage. Betty Jane exuded confidence as she smiled at the well-wishers.

John noticed an opening and rushed in, placing the bouquet of roses in Betty Jane's arms. "You sounded like an angel." He hugged his daughter and clung longer than usual.

"Thank you, Daddy. I'm so excited. It's a night I'll never forget."

"You enjoy it, baby. We'll wait in the lobby."

Jane moved in to hug her daughter.

"Mom, I know you're happy, but you don't need to cry." Betty Jane patted her mom on the back.

"You were breathtaking—positively divine. I'm so proud of you. We'll see you in a bit."

John and Jane meandered on but glanced back at Betty Jane greeting a line of people who presented congratulations and hugs.

"Come on, dear." John caught Jane's arm and ushered her along.

John and Jane remained quiet during the ride home, allowing their daughter the spotlight. Betty Jane bubbled over with chatter about the play. The car shook as she bounced excitedly on the back seat and leaned over the front seat, first glancing right and then left. Her mouth engaged in nonstop babble.

They pulled into the long driveway, which split a path between two freshly plowed fields. With the windows closed in his 1938 Plymouth sedan, John imagined the fresh scent of the dirt turning over—the same field hidden by the darkness of the night.

The headlights revealed Ralph Martin's car, with engine running, parked in front of

John's house. His wife, Theresa, sat beside him.

John pulled up next to them, cut the engine, and stepped out of the car. "Come in folks." He motioned his arm toward the house.

"We came by to congratulate Betty Jane instead of wading through that mob surrounding her," Ralph said. He walked around and opened the car door for his wife.

Jane stepped out of the car without waiting for John and walked up the steps to the porch. She pushed open the door. "Y'all come in. I've got a cake, and we'll put on a pot of coffee—or maybe you'd prefer hot cocoa." She brushed a hand over her puffy eyes and smiled. "Come on in," she urged again. She entered the house and flipped on the lights.

Once in the parlor, Theresa hugged Betty Jane, "You were simply magnificent, Betty Jane. I never knew you could sing so beautifully."

"You look lovely," Ralph chimed in. "Andy would be so proud of you."

A sob exploded from Jane as she hung up the coats in the front closet. John rushed over to her.

"Mom, what's wrong?" Betty Jane waited. Nothing. "Dad, what's going on?" Her face drained of all color. She rushed over to her mother.

John moved Jane over to a chair and sat her down, Betty Jane on his heels. Jane trembled uncontrollably.

"John, did I say something wrong? Do we need to leave?" Ralph asked. His wife covered her mouth with her hands.

"No. Please stay. I've got some bad news. Betty Jane, sit over here beside me." He patted the sofa seat next to him.

Betty Jane's breath came in short spurts. John feared she was gasping from the sounds coming from her throat. She sat down and their eyes connected.

"Just before we left for the play tonight, we received a telegram over the phone."

"It's Andy, isn't it? Tell me no, Daddy. Say no." Tears overflowed their boundaries. Her eyes fixed on John's.

"Yes, but it only said he was 'missing in action.' That's all. Only missing." He pulled her over to him. Her tears spilled onto his shirt.

"Andy's gone, Daddy. I know it. He's gone." Betty Jane howled.

Her mother, after hearing Betty Jane's outburst, attempted to comfort her. "Let's don't jump to conclusions, darling. Dad said 'missing in action.' We should know more in a few days. Andy will be fine. You wait and see."

John couldn't believe how Jane pulled herself together. He stood and turned to Ralph. "That's all it said, 'missing in action.' A letter would follow."

"Oh John. We're so sorry to hear this. How did you get through tonight?" Theresa asked. She pulled a handkerchief out of her purse, dabbed it to her eyes, then twisted it round and round in her hands.

"Does Rose know?" Ralph asked. He joined John pacing the floor.

"I don't know. They would notify the family first. Say, Ralph, just because I'm pacing, doesn't mean you have to." John smiled and motioned for him to sit down.

"Thanks, but we need to go home. Y'all need to be by yourselves. I wish I could help. You'll let us know if there's anything we can do, won't you?" Ralph reached in the closet for Theresa's coat, held it for her to slip into, and then gathered his coat and hat.

"We'll be praying for Andy, you can be sure. We're here for you." Theresa hugged Jane and Betty Jane before she left the house.

As soon as the door shut, John, Jane, and Betty Jane huddled in the middle of the floor, arms entwined, weeping and praying as a family. They depended on John's strength. His own tears scorched his face.

"We can only pray and wait. There's nothing else we can do. Our faith must take over and keep us strong until our boy comes home." John broke away from the family and walked over to the window. He gazed out into the darkness, but it didn't matter. The agony of his goodbye at the train station fifteen months ago reared its ugly head. His thoughts were with his son. *Dear Lord, please take care of my boy.*

# Chapter Twenty-three

"No!" Andy swung around yelling, "She had nothing to do with us! No, no!" He held his hands to his head, absorbing the horror in front of him. Marta spun away from the pistols pointed at her by the Gestapo and fought like a mama bear desperate to shield her baby from the inevitable.

Spine-chilling screams filled the sacred building. Prickly hairs covered Andy's body. He lunged toward Marta but a German officer shoved him back, toppling him to the floor. Andy bounced up. A rifle stretched out in front held him back.

Two shots rang out and Marta dropped to the floor. The bullets penetrated her back and traveled through her body into the baby. She lay in a pool of blood struggling to reach her daughter. The baby's crying stopped—a slight whimper followed. She kicked and gasped for air as Andy watched the life drain form her tiny body. Marta and her baby—neither moved.

Andy grabbed his head. *Oh my God! How could this happen? How could they kill a mother and baby. I couldn't even help them. Oh, Jesus! This was my fault—all my fault!*

He crumpled to the floor.

Brad dashed over to Andy. A German struck Brad's shoulder with his rifle butt driving Brad down. He stepped over Brad, and rammed Andy's cheek with the same rifle butt.

Andy staggered up, unable to see, tumbled down the two steps that led away from the pulpit, and landed on the first pew.

The Gestapo grabbed Andy and Brad by their jackets, heaved both men onto their feet, and shoved rifle barrels in their backs.

Andy covered his face in muffled anguish. "She came here to pray. That was all!" Stunned and sickened, he reeled in desolation, unable to accept his part in this terror.

Brad responded to Andy without hesitation. "You caused this, Captain. You got her killed!"

A rifle barrel dug deep into Andy's back, propelling him forward toward the church exit. *Brad's right. I caused Marta and her baby's death. Oh, God!*

Andy's eyes cleared somewhat. The Gestapo marched he and Brad into the hamlet where the townspeople gathered, staring, and yelled unfamiliar words—German words that Andy wished he had taken the time to learn—or maybe not. The crowd's shouts grew more ferocious. They threw sticks, rocks, and spat on them.

Totschläger, spione, mörder, attentäter! (Killers, spies, murderers, assassins!)

Andy's stomach drew up in knots. The village people moved in closer, some brandished sticks. *We're going to be slaughtered right here, and how're the guards gonna stop them? They wouldn't give a damn.* His heart pulsed in his neck—his breath quickened.

Soon they arrived in front of an aged brick building with black window frames. Andy breathed a little easier at its sight. As they moved toward the structure, the town's people pushed and shoved in close. He feared at any moment they would wield their sticks and beat him to death. Brad's teeth chattered. A strapping German officer met them at the entrance, pulled out his Lugar, and relieved the Gestapo of their captives.

Andy assumed this was a jail or holding place. *Well, at least the rifle barrel is out of my back.* A different fear took over—fear of the unknown. He turned for one last glimpse of the outside area.

The village appeared small with snow-covered roofs. Another church towered at the end of a group of scattered houses, its steeple the tallest in the village. The German officer shoved Andy and Brad into the building, where two officers sat in chairs, each at different tables, the only furniture in the room. An oversized swastika draped the wall behind the two tables. "Empty pockets," the German officer with the Lugar ordered in broken English. Andy reached for his wallet. Within seconds, the officer with the gun shouted, "Hände Hoch!" Andy responded instantly, raising his hands high.

The officer emptied Andy's pockets and repeated body pats. The guard spread a small flashlight, an army pocketknife, and a few other non-essential items including Rose's embroidered handkerchief, his buckeye, and his wallet on the table. An officer picked up the buckeye, examined it closely, bounced it on the table, and dropped it on the floor. Satisfied that it had no value, he picked it up and returned everything except the pocketknife and flashlight.

The officer motioned for Andy's wristwatch.

Andy pretended not to understand.

"Armbanduhr! Armbanduhr!" (Wristwatch!) The officer stripped the watch off Andy's arm.

Andy rubbed his arm and decided to make an issue of the watch. "I want that back!" *Thank God they didn't find the silk map of Austria hidden in my wallet. They probably won't keep me here anyway. The dirty Krauts. What next? Dad, were you right?*

"Nein! Tell me. Where are the other men from your plane?"

"My name is Andrew Walters, ..." Andy repeated this over and over regardless of the leutnant's (German spelling) retort.

The leutnant jumped up from his chair sending it sprawling against the back wall. He slammed his hands on the table, demanding a response.

"My name is Andrew Walters, ..."

"Answer my questions!" The veins in the leutnant's neck pulsed as if they would rupture at any moment.

He questioned Andy for hours, and eventually the leutnant grew weary of the repeated response.

"Take him away!" The leutnant slammed his fist on the table causing Andy to jump.

The guard marched Andy to a dark cell and shoved him inside. It reeked of urine and mustiness and had the closeness of a tiny room. He flinched as the officer slammed the door and secured the lock.

His eyes had not yet adjusted to the jet-black hole when he heard something move. He stepped back. Blood drained from his head. His chest tightened and his body shivered from more than the cold. He searched for a wall and backed against it.

He heard something move toward him. He shifted away from the noise and waited for the unpredictable. The loud, pumping beat of his heart throbbed wildly in his ears.

He blurted out a weak, "Who's there?"

"Well, I'll be John Brown," a familiar subdued voice said. "Andy? It's Bulldog. Thank God, you're safe."

"Bulldog! Unbelievable!" Andy fumbled for Bulldog's hand.

"Gee willikers, Andy. Shuuush. Don't want the guards to find out we know each other. They'll separate us."

"Trust me. They probably already know. How long have you been here, Bulldog?"

"Two days or so. I saw you jump with your parachute in your hands. I never thought you'd make it, ole buddy." Bulldog wrapped his arms around Andy.

"Gosh, it's good to see you. Didn't know if I'd ever see any of you again." Andy heard a sound from his left.

"Andy, this is Charlie. He's from the 15th."

Andy couldn't see Charlie but acknowledged him anyhow. "Glad to meet you, although not under these circumstances."

"I've heard all about you, Captain."

"How big is this cell anyhow?"

"About 10 x 10." Bulldog had moved away from Andy. "You're eyes will adjust, but you still won't be able to see much."

"Shhhh!" Andy found the door and put his ear to a small closed wooden window. "They're discussing what to do with us." A one-sided conversation ended with "Heil Hitler!"

A short time later the sound of footsteps grew near, and the cell door opened. For a fleeting moment, Andy could see his surroundings. A guard shoved Brad into the cell. Bulldog moved to the rear.

Andy walked over to Brad and guided him into the darkness before the door closed squeezing out the last rays of light. He saw blood around his mouth. "What happened to your lip, Brad?"

"The guard didn't like my looks."

Andy let the comment go. "Brad, this is Charlie from the 15th, and Bulldog is in the back."

Brad barely grunted. "If it weren't for the captain, I wouldn't be here!"

Andy lowered his head. Brad's right. *Marta and her baby might be alive except for me. Dietrich, too. Dad, you win!*

The guard returned, opened the door, and motioned the four men to move out. Once outside of the building, the men were loaded into the rear of a military truck along with four other Americans. Two guards jumped into the back. One carried a rifle and a Lugar, and the other lugged a MP40 Schmeisser machine pistol.

Andy recognized fear in the faces of all the captives and hoped they couldn't see through his pretext. A few carried their parachutes and used them for warmth from the bitter wind rushing through and around the canvas top.

The excitement Andy felt from finding his old friend temporarily blocked out the guilt about Marta and her baby. He turned to Bulldog and spoke just above a whisper, "Nealy died before we bailed out. My parachute release snagged on something and it opened inside the plane. Whitie froze. He huddled on the floor next to the door and refused to budge. I couldn't force him out."

"No need to feel bad. Me and Pops tried to push him out, but he clung to anything he could grab. Couldn't pry him loose. He took one look at that flak and made his choice."

"I know, but I'm responsible."

Bulldog tilted his head and moved closer to study Andy's face. "What in the hell happened to your eye?" He roared with laughter. "What'd the other guy look like?"

"I caught the butt of a rifle." Andy reached for his cheek and felt it puffed out covering part of his eye. "No wonder. I thought I was going blind in that eye."

"Sure, Andy. Sure." Each man took a turn poking fun at him.

"All right, fellas. All I can say is, they did a fine roundup when they caught the likes of you."

For hours, the truck wound around curves, struggled up steep hills, and pushed forward to the unknown. Without his watch, Andy had no idea of the time, but sitting next to the truck's cab, he raised the canvas for a look-see. "We're headed north. Not good. Probably inside Germany by now."

The sun had retreated behind the evening clouds, casting elongated shadows over the rolling, snow-covered hills. *How can something so striking be in a world so ugly?* A gust of frigid wind tore the canvas from Andy's hand, and an unhappy guard rushed toward him. Andy struggled to close the flapping canvas. The angered guard carrying the MP40 Schmeisser machine pistol gave Andy plenty of incentive to hurry.

The temperature dropped rapidly, and the men inched closer for extra body heat. Andy's stomach growled from emptiness, and fatigue set in.

Bulldog rubbed his stomach. "I got belly cramps. How 'bout you, Andy?"

Andy nodded followed by a barrage of food discussions between the men. The guards ignored the conversation.

Late into the night, the military truck pulled into Frankfurt, Germany. The guards shuffled the men from the truck into a partially bombed, poorly lit building for interrogation.

Andy's turn came, and he followed the guard into the interrogation room. He welcomed the warmth of the sterile room. Outwardly he displayed confidence, but inwardly his body prepared for the worst.

Through the entire questioning, Andy kept repeating his name, rank, and serial number to the displeasure of the German officer.

He motioned Andy to sit down and slid a pencil and paper in front of him. "You must sign this paper," the interrogation officer said in broken English.

"Jawohl!" (Yes sir!) Andy said. He proceeded to recite his name, rank, and serial number and slid the paper back to the officer.

The officer's face turned a bloody vermilion and he shouted once again, "You must sign the paper!" He shoved it back at Andy.

Andy looked the paper over and pushed it back to the officer.

"Your family in Fayetteville, North Carolina, will not be notified that you are alive. Sign…the…paper!" The officer shuffled the pile of papers in front of him.

After repeating the same procedure several times, the officer snatched the paper up in disgust, bolted out of his chair, turned to a guard and barked in German, "Take him away!"

With deep furrows in his brow, through clenched teeth he said, "You *will* sign the paper."

The guard shoved his rifle butt into Andy's injured left thigh, knocking him out of the chair. Andy reeled on the floor in excruciating pain. Two guards picked him up, dragged him down the vile smelling hallway, and dropped him on all fours in front of one of many doors. The larger guard unlocked the metal door, stepped back, and placed his foot on Andy's rear, and heaved him inside. The clanging echo of the slammed door vibrated in Andy's head. He listened in relief as the footsteps faded.

No lights. Nothing. Only darkness. Andy fumbled his way around the wall, pulled himself up, and discovered it was a tiny cell, no larger than a double closet. No furniture. Empty. With his back against the wall, he slid down to the cold concrete floor. He wore his jacket, several shirts over his uniform, and the long johns the Austrian family had given him. Before long, the cold dampness of the concrete seeped through his wool pants and into his aching bones. He reached down to his left thigh. Sticky. He raised his hand to his nose. Blood.

He rested his head on his arms, bruised and in pain; he shook from the wintry cold. Total defeat racked his body; his spirit waned. A suffocating sensation tightened in his throat as he searched for hope. Feelings of desertion and abandonment came easy when imprisoned in a pitch-black hole. For the first time in his life, he was helpless to control his destiny.

By his own calculations, twenty-four hours had passed when footsteps approached. A key turned in the lock. Andy lay on the floor—his shivering body curled into a ball. The door opened, and something soft and bulky tumbled in. A parachute. Immediately the door slammed shut.

He jumped up, pulled it over to the wall, wrapped it around his body, and tucked the silk under his chin, not believing the guard's kindness—very unusual. Not enough warmth, but better.

Andy tried to sleep, but cold and hunger prevented any rest. His brain rendered him powerless as he sought to close out all thoughts. They spun wildly through his mind. Helplessness engulfed him. He tried to picture Rose and her smiling face—she was the voice in his head, his reason for living—but he couldn't. Instead, an inner torment gnawed at him. Marta's face. Her horrified screams. Blood oozing from her back. His heart flip-flopped as he re-lived the revulsion—over and over. He grabbed the sides of his head. *God, help me!*

It was impossible to know if daylight had arrived. The sound of footsteps and a key slipped into the lock sent a wave of icy fear through his body. *Is this the end?*

A large square of black bread landed on the floor and Andy scrambled on his knees to the bread before the darkness closed in again. A sharp pain shot through his leg, the shrapnel injury had reopened. Once the pain eased, he devoured the hard crusty bread though his throat grew raw from swallowing.

An hour or so later, a guard returned. Andy's stomach clinched tight waiting for the next move.

The guard led him outside to the latrine. He was happy for any reason to get out of the dank closet. When he stepped out of the building, the bright sun bore down on the glistening snow temporarily blinding him.

He scanned the area for Brad and Bulldog and glanced at his watch only to remember the Germans had confiscated it. *Judging where the sun is, it must be around 1400 hours.* The guard returned Andy to his dark hole before he caught sight of the other men.

Another guard arrived later and took him back for interrogation. Same officer—more interrogation. Andy politely looked over the paper and slid it back to the officer.

Frustrated, the officer slapped his hand on the stack of papers in front of him.

Andy marveled at the information the officer spewed forth. The *Alley Cat*, the name of the B-17, names of crew members, which squadron and group, Andy's sister's name, his family, Fayetteville High School, etc.—the officer didn't leave out anything, including the fact that his father had a stroke.

"What?" Andy who prided himself for staying in control of everything lost it.

"Your father." The officer deliberately stalled.

"My father…what about him."

"He suffered a stroke. Don't you want to get home and help him?" He shoved the paper in front of Andy.

Andy forced control, said nothing, and slid the paper back refusing to confirm any statements. The process continued over and over again.

The officer hoisted a walking cane over his head and whacked Andy across the left hand. Andy yanked his hand back, bit his lip refusing to show pain. The German officer jumped to his feet and shouted, "Out! Out!" The veins in his neck swelled to the bursting point or so Andy thought. The guard rushed in quickly and removed him from the room and back to his cell.

The German officer jumped to his feet and shouted, "Out! Out!" The veins in his neck accented his rage.

Hours passed before a guard took Andy out of the building once again, where at least a hundred POWs had lined up. Sunshine had succumbed to damp, bitter cold. When Bulldog saw Andy, he let out a yell, clapped his hands, and whistled. A guard rushed over and busted Bulldog on the side of his face with the butt end of his rifle.

It didn't stop Bulldog. "Andy, you made it. We was worried 'bout you." He reached for Andy's swollen hand. A guard stepped in and blocked him.

Andy fell in line behind Bulldog. "Button your lip, fella. Don't make it any harder on yourself."

Bulldog nodded.

A guard ordered the men to march. German guards with fully automatic MP40 Schmeisser Machine pistols suspended by straps over their shoulders, fingers resting on the triggers, lined up on each side of the marching POWs.

Bulldog mouthed, "Where're we going?"

"Probably to the train station. Shush! You'll anger the guards," Andy said.

An infuriated crowd gathered as the men marched through the town. The angry townspeople shook fists with vile hate and shouted indistinguishable words of vengeance. The meaning was ever so clear to Andy.

On the outskirts of town just beyond a demolished train station, lay bent tracks and shards of iron in piles where once smooth rails stretched ahead.

They marched on through the snow in the frigid temperature beyond the townspeople. Andy envied the guards wearing heavy coats, boots to keep the wetness out, and hats with muffs covering their ears. His own body shivered uncontrollably, unable to produce warmth.

After marching for two miles, they arrived at a train idling far from town; its smoke hovered above the engine.

Andy eased up to Bulldog. "This train can't go south. The POW camps are north."

"What's that mean?"

"Let's pray we don't get sent to Stalag III or IV." Andy inched away from Bulldog.

The guards moved the men forward, stopped at the fifth car, and loaded the men like cattle into the boxcars—forty-some men per car.

After one car filled, the line moved along to the next, passing occupied cars, then the next, until they filled all the cars. Andy and the last group of men squeezed into the end boxcar. Guards locked each car as it overreached its capacity.

Andy, Bulldog, and Brad confiscated one end of the boxcar. Grimy, filthy straw covered the floorboard and the smell of human waste saturated Andy's nostrils. Cracks in the wooden walls allowed a visual of the outdoors while traveling farther north—farther away from Foggia Airfield and the end of their 50th mission.

Andy leaned back on the boxcar wall. Arctic wind gushed through the large cracks, while the train slowly picked up speed.

Unable to sleep, he spoke to the men around him. "You fellas bailed out recently? I noticed you're wearing your uniforms."

"We flew in BIG WEEK. Some military called it ARGUMENT," a Lieutenant replied. "Soon as I landed, they caught me. Didn't have a chance. They watched me all the way down. Locked me in a building for weeks until a few days ago. How about you?"

"We flew our 50th mission during BIG WEEK. Didn't even get to drop our load. Flak and a couple of 20mms from 190s took us out. Ended up near Salzburg and tried to work our way back toward Foggia, Italy. Got captured at a small church in an Austrian village." Marta's face flashed in front of Andy, and he lowered his head. "We're lucky to be alive."

Soon the conversation diminished, and the cold ravaged Andy. *We're all POWs now. Prisoners of War, Kriegsgefangenen or Kriegies. An attempt to escape now means sudden death, even if we could break the locks of the boxcar doors.* He had watched the guards secure vital positions on the train.

The thunderous drone of engines above pierced through the humdrum sound of the train clanking down the tracks. Ears of the boxcar boys perked up and they pressed into the sides of the boxcar to catch a glimpse of the skies as the reverberation came closer and closer. Smiles broke out on their faces when one yelled, "It's our boys up there! Must be on another mission. There's gotta be two hundred of 'em. Looks like a bunch of fighter escorts this time."

"Hurray!" The cheers came from Andy's boxcar with echoes of the same up the track.

"Go get 'em, men!" Andy shouted and shook his fist over his head. "The sooner we'll get home."

"Go get 'em." The words traveled along the track drowning out the monotonous clickety-clack.

Within a minute or so, a couple of P-51s swooped down sending a spray of gunfire pelting what sounded to Andy like the front of the engine or tracks ahead. Another sweep failed to destroy the tracks or stop the train's forward momentum.

The P-51s scurried back up to guard their bombers, and, when the planes disappeared from view, Andy and the men settled back down. For one glorious moment, they forgot their hunger pains and the bleak winter numbness.

The train rolled on for two days and two nights on a northward path, stopping only to load coal. It sat for hours without allowing the men to leave the cramped, revolting, putrid boxcars. By dawn of the third morning, the train pulled into the station in Barth, Germany.

Guards unlatched the outside of each boxcar. "Out! Out! Out!" a German officer shouted. With ice on their beards, fellow prisoners helped carry the weak and others with frozen feet from the boxcars. The guards divided them into groups: healthy, injured, and sick.

Though weak, the blood from Andy's thigh froze, and he felt no pain. He walked without a limp fearful the guards would place him in the injured group.

A guard rushed up and pointed to Andy's trousers. "Blut!"

"Nein! Nein!" Andy pointed to a man with blood on his clothes. "Sein (his)!"

The guard signaled Andy to move on with Bulldog and Brad in the healthy group. The unhealthy and injured men were loaded into trucks and whisked away.

"God only knows where they're going." Andy watched the trucks travel down the road until clear out of sight.

"You're damn lucky they didn't notice your thigh injury." Bulldog rubbed his shoulder. "How is it?"

"Numb. Those dark khaki wools don't show much. How about your shoulder?" Andy remembered Bulldog telling him that a shell had grazed his shoulder.

"I grabbed a medical kit before bailing out, and once I landed, I did the doctor bit. It's good. A guard confiscated the stuff before we left the village."

"I got a sulfa tablet or two, Captain. The guards never found them. Don't know if you can swallow them since we're all so dry." Charlie handed Andy two tablets.

"Gee, thanks, Charlie. I'll wait a bit to see if we get some water. Think they'd choke me now."

Again, the Germans divided the men into groups, lined them in columns of four, and surrounded them with guards.

After counting each man a minimum of five times, an English-speaking officer warned the POWs not to talk, shout, or sing. It would provoke the village people.

That was all Bulldog needed. "Okay, they asked for it," he muttered under his breath then belted out, "Praise the Lord, and pass the ammunition…"

The entire group broke into song. Heads held high, chests out, the men bellowed in unison. Guards planted their rifle butts into the men, but the POWs remained undaunted. Determination set in as Andy and the men moved into the village of Barth.

German men, women, and children came running, lining the sides of the road spitting, shouting, and throwing rocks.

As the rocks met their targets, Andy and the men pushed onward through numerous hamlets without a flinch while residents glared, shrieked, and bellowed at them.

They arrived at Stalag Luft I (Stalag means prison, Luft means air). Andy knew of this prison and that it housed only officers. A second group of one hundred men stood in a line outside of the gate—POWs, Andy guessed.

"Where the hell are we?" Bulldog asked.

"We're still near Barth; on a peninsula north of Berlin and on the Baltic Sea. Sweden is sixty miles across the water. I think this is Stalag Luft I for officers."

"Capt. Walters," a shout came. "Capt. Walters!"

Andy followed the sound to the other group of POWs. Tex and Pops stood waving frantically. "Hey fellas! I don't believe it. Bulldog. Look." Andy pointed to Tex and Pops.

"Hot damn!" Bulldog slapped his legs just as a guard stepped up in his face. Bulldog immediately jumped to attention.

The Germans divided Andy's group, separating officers and non-officers. Charlie and many others fell in line with the POWs heading for a prison for non-officers, Andy assumed.

He spoke softly to Bulldog. "Must be Stalag Luft III or IV. I hear it's brutal over there."

Andy stepped out of line, but immediately a German guard stuck his rifle in front, restraining him. The new men of Stalag Luft I nodded their heads to their fellow captives and watched them march away.

The icy winds of March barreled in from the sea and pierced their bodies, as the weather greeted Andy and the men to their new home. The dark, cloudy sky appeared ready at any moment to dump rain, sleet, or snow and add more misery.

Andy stood in front of North 1 Compound and scanned the prison as far as visible, first right and then left. Stalag Luft I stretched approximately half a mile each way on a flat terrain with the Baltic Sea discernible beyond the North 3 Compound sign. Double, ten-foot-tall barbed wire fences surrounded each compound, with a four-foot wall of tangled barbed wire between the two fences to discourage escapees should they manage to cut through the first fence.

He turned for one last glimpse at the other POWs marching to who-knows-where. Some men looked back, despairingly. He prayed that the men had *not* embarked on their death march. Powerless to help, Andy navigated through his own emotional minefield. The unknown might as well be a knife stabbing him in the back.

*I couldn't stop the murder of Marta and her baby. I can't even protect Bulldog or Brad. I've let them all down. And now, how are we gonna get outta here? Maybe Dad was right. Did I do my best? I've let you down once again, haven't I?* Andy wrung his hands ending with a scrub over his face. He wanted to wash all his thoughts of horror away, but instead they grew…and grew.

# Chapter Twenty-four

## Fayetteville Tavern

Betty Jane rushed into the house. "Mom, Mom! Where are you?" Her brown pigtails abandoned, replaced with long soft curls, and tendrils that tickled her no longer chubby cheeks.

"What in the world's going on? You flew in like your shirt was on fire, sweetheart?" Jane Walters covered her mouth waiting for the next shoe to drop. Something she'd grown to expect since no word from Andy.

"Mom. We saw a news reel at school about North Platte, Nebraska, and we've got to do something—something like what they're doing for our soldiers. We have a train station just like them."

"Child. Slow down. You're not making sense. What're you talking about." Jane slid the frying pan off the stove and wiped her hands on her apron.

"Mom. We can do it. Just like the women of North Platte."

"Do what? Something this exciting must be really great." She placed her arm around her daughter. "Here, sit down and let's have some hot cocoa. I heated the milk in case you wanted some. Tell me. What is North Platte all about?"

Betty Jane continued. "They're a small town similar to ours except for the military base and a train depot running through town just like ours. As soon as they heard about the troop trains passing a bunch of times each day, a lady had an idea to bake cookies for the military men from her town. She got several other ladies to bake cookies, and when the first train came through, the women yelled for men from North Platte. There was not one soldier on that train from North Platte. One lady determined to pass out her goodies shouted, "I'm not taking these back home. Cookies for everyone." They got mobbed. And from that day on, they baked cakes, cookies, everything they could make with the rations allotted them by the government."

"Well, I swan. That's a great story and good for our military men."

"Mom. That's not all."

"You don't say."

"We can do that too. We have a depot and our men from Fort Bragg and Pope Field coming in and leaving all the time for new military bases."

"Yes, you might have something there. It would take more than the two of us."

"I've already thought about that. Mrs. Martin would help and she has a lot of relatives here."

Jane Walters perked up. "My quilting party ladies. That would be a good start. A lot of your girl friends from church and school can help too." She smoothed the kitchen table cloth and took a sip of her cocoa.

"Oh, Mom. Do you really think we can do this?" Betty Jane bounced on her chair while holding her cup of cocoa spilling a couple of drops.

"Okay. That's enough. Look at your plaid skirt. Go get a damp cloth and wipe it off." She smiled at her daughter's excitement and how eager she was to help the soldiers.

Days flew by as Jane Walters lined up her friends to help with the Fayetteville Depot military feeding effort.

She lead a group meeting under the old Market House on Hay Street giving the ladies suggestions and recipes.

"Look at you—all of you. Thank you for coming." She spread her arms wide. "My, my, I didn't expect it to be this windy today. We'll hurry." She wrapped her coat tight around her body and continued.

"If half of you bake cookies doubling and tripling the recipe, each of you can come up with around 450 or more cookies. The other half can bake cakes, cut them into squares—or use your imaginations and come up with something unique. I heard a lady in North Platte baked ten Angel Food cakes a week using turkey eggs. Mix it up, ladies. See you next Monday at 8 a.m. with your baskets full. We'll cheer up our boys before they go to battle."

Jane overheard Theresa Martin (Rose's mother) talk to her bridge club about bringing tons of brownies—as long as the chocolate, sugar, and lard lasted. "What with rationing…"

She knew she could always count on Theresa Martin.

"I have extra stamps for sugar this week. We've stopped using it altogether in our coffee and we don't eat sweets like before the war. Don't you think we're better for it?" Theresa whirled around.

"You look amazingly trim, Theresa. Think I'll try that with my family. Could use less sugar for all of us." Jane shouted to her.

"Mom. Tell me you didn't mean that. No more pies or cupcakes for us? I'd just die." Betty Jane's face turned into a pout.

"Why Betty Jane! Wouldn't you give them up for the boys? Wouldn't you want other people to do the same for Andy?"

Betty Jane wiped her hand over her face. "Gotcha, Mom. Of course I would. Don't you remember whose idea this was?"

"My stars, child. I never know what's coming out of your mouth next. Speaking of food, come on. I've got to start supper before your dad comes in from the field."

During the week, Jane had no problem working in the kitchen but after school…

"Mom, where's the vanilla? I need your pan."

"Sorry little one. I'll be finished in about twenty minutes and it should be cool enough for use. Looks like we need a restaurant kitchen for this kind of baking."

"You betcha. I can't wait for Monday to come. Wouldn't it be amazing if Andy happened to be on one of those trains?"

Jane stared into space. "Yes, it would." Smiling, she changed the subject. "You know, I can't remember when I've had this much fun since Andy left. You have brightened our days, sweet daughter. And guess what? Dad's sampling too many sweets. We'll have to hide a lot of the chocolate cake squares. He's got a sweet tooth and it's not good for him when he can't get the exercise on the farm like he used to."

Monday arrived with a hustle and a bustle like John had never seen. He helped the girls load all their goodies in the car and off they went.

"Help me find a place to park, Betty Jane. I've never seen such a crowd. Oh, here's one." She pulled into a sandy spot.

Betty Jane flew out of the car and ran for a baggage wagon.

Once loaded, Jane heard the train whistle. "Here it comes. Hurry. Must be early."

The roar of the engine arrived long before the train and as it prepared to stop, the hissing wheels and steam pouring from the smoke stack, sent chills up Jane's spine. She and Betty Jane inched their way through the crowd over to the makeshift 24 foot table made of saw horses and plywood. Red and white checkered tablecloths covered the long table and baskets of homemade goodies spread from end to end.

"Betty Jane, just look at the number of ladies helping." Tears came to her eyes.

"I know, Mamma. I hope someone is being good to Andy like this."

Jane shook it off and shouted. "Come on, boys."

The train came to a stop, and soldiers, sailors, air force men, and marines jumped from the train, grabbed cakes, cookies, donuts, turkey sandwiches—everything imaginable.

One air force fellow grabbed Jane and hugged her. "God bless you," he said.

"I have a boy overseas and I know he'd like this. I'll be praying for your safe return to your family."

He kissed her on the cheek with glistening eyes. "Thank you, ma'am. I hope your boy returns home soon."

A sailor next to Jane grabbed Betty Jane, kissed her and said. "I'm on my way home for two whole months. Hot dog! Thanks for the cookies."

In a flash he was back on the train with his hands full. "What was that?" Betty Jane asked.

"One happy sailor." Jane was immediately swamped by other soldiers.

An air force man slowly inched over. "I wish we'd had this before my buddy got shot down. A bogie took him out before his parachute could land. I miss him."

"I'm sorry to hear that and I know you miss him terribly. God bless you for all your service and we'll all pray for you and your safe return home." Jane walked up close to him, gave him an extra long hug. "Do you have someone in the service you're close to?"

"Just Barry and now he's gone. It's not worth making friends. They'll be gone tomorrow. Thank you for the food…and the hug. I don't have much family left and it meant a lot."

"You're quite welcome, son. We love you." Jane couldn't believe she said that so freely. "I hope and pray for your safe return."

A marine stepped off the train, arm around the waist of a fellow marine with one leg and a crutch.

"Oh my gosh. It's Bobby Miller."

Jane watched Betty Jane rush over to him.

Betty Jane ignored the marine helping Bobby. She wrapped her arms around Bobby and kissed him on the cheek. "Bobby. It's so great to see you. You made it back."

"Yeah. Most of me. Hey, Betty Jane. Damn! You've grown up."

Betty Jane's face flushed. She grabbed her mom and introduced them. "Bobby graduated two years ahead of me."

"Yeah, and only part of me returned." He dropped his head. "My buddies were not so lucky."

"Bobby," Jane said, sensing his despair. "You were the brave one. You have nothing to be ashamed of. You made it home and you have the opportunity to do something big for your country once again. There are lots like you around. Hold your head high and you will be an inspiration to them. We love you! Fayetteville loves you! And I'm proud to know you. Welcome home."

An elderly gray-haired woman hobbled over to him. "Bobby, I'm sorry I'm late. My car didn't want to start but I didn't give up. Welcome home, love." She glanced at the marine with his arm around Bobby. "And thank you for your help, sonny."

"I gotta get back on the train, ma'am." He turned to Betty Jane. "Can you help him to the car?"

"I'd be honored. Mom, can you pick up his duffle bag?

The marine grabbed a handful of cookies, headed back to the train only to be stopped by Jane. "Son, you have a heart of gold and a kindness beyond life."

"We take care of our own, ma'am."

Jane reached up and planted a kiss on his cheek. Tears reflected the sunlight. She could say nothing more and turned away lest he read her mind.

The ten minutes ended, the train whistle sounded, and the conductor shouted, "All aboard!"

The gigantic mass of iron blowing its smoke down on Jane, chugged, chugged, chugged up the silver track with soldiers hanging out the windows blowing kisses, waving and shouting:

"I wanna marry you."

"I love you."

"Adios beautiful."

"You're in my dreams."

"You cook like my mom."

"Thank you. Ten minutes of heaven."

"Farewell Fayetteville Tavern."

"We love you, ladies."

Jane's eyes found the airman looking out the window and she followed him until out of sight. *Dear Lord, that could have been my son shot down. Please keep Andy safe and bring him home soon.*

# Chapter Twenty-five

## Stalag Luft I

Andy, Bulldog, and Brad watched the horse-drawn wagon pull away from the camp carrying two wooden boxes. Andy couldn't take his eyes off the coffins. *What had they done? Did they try to escape?* He slammed his fist into his other hand. *Those Krauts are pure evil!*

Once he realized that, like him, all of the new POWs had focused on the wooden boxes, he forced himself to put the wagon out of his mind. "Come on, fellas, think positive. Don't assume what happened to those two men." *Do as I say; don't do as I do. What crap! Okay, keep beating up on yourself.*

The men pivoted away from the wagon. "You gotta admit, that's a shocking first image," Bulldog said.

"Yes. But this might be home for a long time. Least ways 'til the war is over." Andy fixed his gaze on the sandy soil, kicking it up and observing the fine grains. He surveyed the buildings, counting nine barracks stretched out in front of him: the North Compound. Armed guards with powerful spotlights occupied the five towers and kept eyes honed in on the prisoners day and night. Andy noticed that each strategically placed tower covered the entire fence line of the compound, making escape next to impossible.

"They got wooden barracks jacked up on blocks, maybe two feet off the ground. How we gonna tunnel with that gap?" Bulldog rubbed his hands together for warmth.

Andy lowered his head and whispered. At night, a guard slips under the barracks to spy on us. Some ferrets—German spies—I hear, use stethoscopes, hoping to pick up crucial military information."

"Oh yeah?" Bulldog stared at the up-raised barracks.

Within a few minutes, the guards marched the prisoners through the central gate where the check-in process began. The men were photographed, fingerprinted, and given a Kriegsgefangenen (prisoner of war number).

After check-in, the guards marched them to a building where they stripped and showered. The vile smell of soiled clothing pervaded the building. An enormous round metal barrel adjacent to the wall held the water. Andy and the men took turns pumping water from the barrel.

The showers streamed full blast. He slid under one. "Yeeoow!" He hopped back and slowly moved under the icy water once again. Teeth chattering, he hollered to Bulldog, "How long has it been, Bulldog? Weeks for me."

"Before our 50th." Bulldog danced under the shower as if he thought that would keep him from freezing. "Holy crap!"

Once showered, the guards issued clothing—wool pants, long-sleeved cotton shirts, and jackets.

Bulldog picked up his stack of clothes. "How we gonna keep warm in these?" Bulldog complained.

"Get used to it." Andy searched the pile of clothes for his old sheepskin jacket.

Next, the guards lined the men up for barrack assignments.

Andy motioned to Bulldog, Pops, and Tex. "Hurry! If we line up together, maybe we'll be assigned to the same barracks."

"See that guard with the papers. He's assigning the barracks numbers. Stay close. Here he comes." Andy stared straight ahead and waited for the guard to work down the line.

Brad stepped in line in front of Andy.

The guard farther up the line checked his papers and counted off men. He shouted in broken English, "Barracks #4."

He motioned to the men in front of Brad, making another division. "Barracks #3."

Another guard moved in and led those men away.

Next, the officer with the papers pulled Brad, Andy, Bulldog, Tex, and Pops from the line. "Barracks #2."

Andy swallowed hard, forcing himself to keep quiet. *Yes.* Inside his mind, he pumped his right arm. *Not everything's all bad.*

A guard hustled over to the five men. He pointed to himself. "Lt. Heinrich." He said in German, "Komm schon!" (Come on!) "Bewegen Sie sich heraus!" Move out!

He led them into the #2 barracks, where a wide hallway split the two rooms, leaving a communal room at the opposite end of the entrance. Visible cracks in the wooden flooring allowed the raw, damp air to squeeze in from the sea. Heinrich pointed the men to the right into a huge room. Without another word, Heinrich did an about face and left the building.

Eight sets of bunk beds lined the walls in front of Andy. He noticed that three sets near the heater already had possessions scattered over them. Andy and Bulldog secured a bunk in the left corner near a window diagonally opposite the cast-iron heat stove.

Andy poked the burlap mattress for softness. "It's straw and woodchips. That's better than just straw. No need to open it up every two weeks to change the straw. You gonna be able to climb up those slats on the end, Bulldog?" He bumped the two by four posts, testing the wooden structure.

"Sure, Andy. It's colder than an icebox at the North Pole. Heat's supposed to rise, ain't it? Should be warmer up there, you think?"

Tex and Pops grabbed a set of bunks next to Andy.

"Well, the way I see it, we're inside," Tex said. He punched the mattress and fluffed an imaginary pillow.

Andy scanned the room for Brad. He was nowhere in sight. "Y'all seen Brad?"

Pops stopped smoothing out his mattress and glanced up with a quizzical look on his face. "Thought he followed me in." With a shrug of his shoulders, he returned to his task.

Later, a jovial man burst into the room and immediately everyone stopped talking.

"I'll be dogged! It's Johnny?" Bulldog rushed over to greet him.

"Johnny! You made it. How long you been here?" Andy remembered he was Mitch's copilot before the plane crashed.

"Bulldog, Andy. All you fellas. I'm not believing this!" Johnny's eyes became fluid. "I been here a couple or so months. Lost track by now. Mitch wouldn't bail out until everyone bailed."

"Yeah, we only saw eight men bail out. Figured Mitch would be the last." A sudden rush of sadness flooded Andy.

"Eight? Hummm. We only had nine crewmen that mission. Soon after we bailed, the plane blew up over our heads. Don't guess Mitch had a chance." Johnny rubbed his hands over his face.

"Do you think there's a possibility that Mitch bailed?" Andy stepped back. The sound of footsteps at the door caught his attention.

Johnny followed Andy's gaze. "Eight you say? Thought our radioman was dead before we bailed. You sure you didn't count someone else's parachute?"

"Can't be positive. Maybe there's hope for Mitch." Andy pinched his chin.

Bulldog glanced at the door as Brad entered. "Well lookie here. Look what the dog done drug in."

Andy leaned over to Bulldog. "Watch it! I don't want any trouble, you hear? God only knows how long we'll be here, and we gotta make the best of it."

Bulldog spun around, and Andy heard him mutter something under his breath.

Brad threw his clothing onto the bunk over Johnny. "Anybody sleeping here?"

"Empty." Johnny rested his hands on his hips.

Andy caught site of Brad's lips curling with disgust while his eyes glared at Bulldog.

Bulldog whispered to Andy, "Thank God, he's no closer." He spread his only wool blanket and tucked the end corners under the mattress.

"Cut it out, Bulldog! Brad is a big enough problem, and we don't need you adding to it. End it. Now!" Andy shook his head.

Bulldog rammed his fist into his mattress.

Tex removed his wool cover from the bunk and wrapped it around his shoulders. "I just *thought* I was cold before. We need more blankets."

"I want my heat suit. I used to hate that thing," Bulldog said. "Some dirty Kraut's wearing it now."

"Can't we jazz up that heater?" Johnny said, blowing into his hands and rubbing them together.

"I'll check it out, but one of the guards said we're allowed one briquette per man per day. That's it." Andy said.

He walked over to other occupants of Barracks #2. They sat on wooden benches as close as possible to the stove. "I'm Andy Walters."

Each man stood, and Andy gave them his famous movie star smile, shook their hands, and repeated each name. "Rudy, Art, Jack, Roy, Gino, and Simon. Glad to know you."

"Welcome to you and your men, Walters." Jack said. "We've been here since November—all from the RAF. So far, it's not too bad, just cold as hell. Four of us are Brits, one Italian, and then Simon. We dare not say what he is." Jack cupped his hand, leaned over to Andy, and whispered, "He's Hebrew."

Jack looked at the quizzical expression on Andy's face and let out a belly laugh loud enough to reach the Baltic Sea. Then softly he said, "Yes, he's Hebrew—with blue eyes. Before capture, he bailed out, tore off his dog tags, and threw each part in different directions."

Andy smiled and sent a wink to Simon.

The crewmen from the *Alley Cat* joined Andy and, after introducing themselves, mingled among the men exchanging stories.

Later they moved to the wooden table and benches in the center of the room.

The door opened, and four men came through the door. Andy and Jack walked up to meet them. They were from the 15th USAAF out of Foggia, Italy, and had flown the same mission BIG WEEK over Steyr, Austria, as Andy and his crew.

Jack continued his conversation. "I say Captain, in a day or so, you'll fit right in. I piloted a Lancaster bomber all over Germany; Berlin, Hamburg, Wilhelmshaven, Bremen, Cologne, Essen, Nuremburg, Munich, Stuttgart, Frankfurt, Düsseldorf, and Peenemunde. Flew at night. Fewer planes lost then."

His accent reminded Andy of good days spent in Snetterton, England, and the British friends left behind. Andy pointed to Johnny. "Guess you already know him. He's a …"

Jack interrupted, ignoring Johnny. "Your men told me about your ship, the *Alley Cat*. They are proud to have served under you, Captain."

Andy's chest puffed out once again. "Thanks. I had the best crew ever. Some didn't make it."

"Sorry to hear that, old chap. I say, did you know that Col. Brawley is in Barracks #1?" Jack sat down on his bunk and offered Andy a seat motioning with his hand.

"Son-of-a-gun! He sent me to pilot's training in the States. I'll go see him tomorrow."

"He's a good old bloke," Jack said.

"Y'all digging any tunnels now?" Andy asked as he sat down on the bunk.

"We had a lively good run at tunneling in Barracks #9. It's lower to the ground. No digging since the third tunnel caved in a few weeks back. Last week two chaps tried to hide in a delivery wagon while some of us distracted the guards. They got caught and sent to solitary for thirty days. We've made a bloody lot of attempts, but nary a one has worked."

"Tough luck."

"We haven't given up. One chap went berserk one day and tried to climb the fence. They shot him dead. Don't try that."

"What's with the dogs? Noticed them when we came in." Andy said.

"They bring those bloody beasts in at night to sniff under the buildings. It's a fright to go out at night." Jack reared back on his bunk.

"What do you do for food around here, Jack?" Andy smiled at his men, knowing food would perk up their ears. "We're all about to starve or is that a bad word?"

"I say, we've been fed pretty well. Civilian volunteers at the mess hall prepare the German food with the guards watching them. The Red Cross sends in parcels once a week, one per man. Sometimes we prepare food right here in our barracks, but mostly we combine it with the German food for a jolly good meal."

"Talk about food is making me hungry. They tried to starve us on the trip here. We'll eat anything right now." Andy rubbed his flat stomach. "Think the mess hall's open now?"

"By the time we get over there, it will be. They feed us two meals, breakfast and dinner. Guess you say 'supper.'" Jack turned to his group and waved his arm in the air. "Let's go, mates."

"Come on, fellas. Let's get some grub." Andy motioned his men to follow. The entire room emptied. Johnny left with Andy's group.

"Walters, the mess hall is that building down on the left. The North 1 Compound housed Hitler's Youth; that's why we have a communal mess hall, inside latrines and running water taps. Those chaps were lucky, and, I say, so are we. The South, West and North Compound #2 aren't nearly as lush."

"So Hitler had the best for his young men, you say." Andy observed the well maintained buildings.

A shrill sound of an air-raid warning sent men scampering everywhere.

"Captain, hurry!" Jack motioned to the men. "We're closer to the mess hall than our barracks."

The alarm pierced the calm with a deafening sound driving the men to cover their ears.

"By golly, they want to make us deaf as bats," Jack said, as he rushed along. "If we don't go inside, the guards have orders to shoot to kill. Two weeks ago, they shot a Kriegie because he didn't hear the alarm. That's why they revved up the volume. They claim it's disrespectful for us to wave and applaud the planes. It's the Americans on another mission. They can't pass us without dropping a few scattered bombs just to keep the Germans alert. That's how they let us know they haven't forgotten us. By Jove! It makes a man feel good to know that. Just wish they would hurry and end this blasted war."

"Has a bomb ever hit the camp?" Breathing heavily, Andy rushed through the door with Jack at his side.

"Not yet, and I don't think they would. The bombers stay well out of the range of the German antiaircraft guns. Well, you know what? We might as well eat while the guards are shooting at your Air Force."

Bulldog's face lit up for the first time since their capture. "Andy, did you see our boys? Wish I was up there with 'em."

Andy tapped Bulldog's shoulder. "They'll be back for us before you know it."

He studied the room partially filled with men from other barracks. The floors followed the same wooden pattern of the barracks. At the end of the room was a cook stove with a tall round metal pipe protruding through the back wall. Pots large enough for a young toddler to hide in covered the surface of the wood stove. Steam curled high as the ceiling and the smell of boiled cabbage saturated the air in the mess hall. Jack told Andy these were the usual food—potatoes, cabbage, and turnips. No meat.

The men lined up with metal bowls in hand, while the cooks wielded a dipper to serve their supper. Andy's group squeezed in around wooden tables and benches, huddling to keep body warmth from escaping. Jack joined Andy and his crew, and the conversation continued on until the air-raid alarm signaled the end of the raid. No sound of exploding bombs—only the ack-ack of antiaircraft guns.

"Hot damn, these boiled potatoes and cabbage never tasted better." Bulldog clanged his tin bowl. "I'm ready for more."

"Lad, you're not allowed seconds around here," Jack said, beating his tin with his spoon and mocking Bulldog. "We'll get Red Cross food packages tomorrow, and that'll fill your gut."

"Now that the air raid is over, let's pop over to the library." Jack strode toward the door.

"A library?" Andy asked.

"Yeah. It belonged to the German Youth training camp. Before you ask, yep, some books are in German, but the Red Cross regularly sends books in English. It's quite a selection now."

Andy shouted to his men, motioning them to come on. "Y'all want to check out the library?"

"Right behind you," Tex replied, pushing Pops in front of him.

"Hey, look at that," Bulldog said, pointing to a flatbed wagon parked at the camp gate and stacked with bread. "That's our food."

A horse pulled the wagon through the gate and on to the mess hall, where the cooks rushed out and unloaded the bread.

"I should help 'em," Bulldog said. "I'd slip me some extra grub."

"Don't hold your breath, Bulldog. It won't hurt you to cut back a bit," Jack quipped, slapping Bulldog on the back.

"What do you mean by that, sir?" Bulldog patted his flat stomach. "All of this is muscle."

Jack ignored him but Bulldog didn't stop. "Take a gander at this." He held up his arm and flexed his bicep."

Jack continued to ignore him.

"What? I'm not good enough for you to look at? Hey, you." Bulldog pursued.

Andy stood next to Bulldog. "Hey, let it go. Come on, let's go to the library." He left the mess hall area followed by Bulldog. He leaned into Bulldog and whispered, "Forget this guy. He cares nothing about us."

"Easy for you, Andy. He can't mouth off like that to an officer and get away with it," Bulldog whispered.

"Let's go, fellas." Andy grabbed Bulldog's arm and hustled him on to the library.

Entering the library Andy's face brightened. "This is swell." Bookshelves lined the walls, and others jetted out in row upon row of shelving filled with reading material. He noticed a small law section. "That's a surprise." He ran his fingers over the books.

"Best in town," Jack added. "Here's my section." He pointed to the sports books.

"Yeah, mine, too. But right now I'm more interested in this law section." Andy pulled out a book.

Long wooden reading tables with benches filled the center of the room. Andy sat down on one of the benches and thumbed through a book in front of him.

"Come on, sir. We're going back to the barracks," Tex called over to Andy.

"Think I'll stay here for a while. Y'all go ahead." Andy flipped through the book pages.

Only a few men remained in the library, and a while later, Andy was the last to leave. *This is great! This will help pass the time.*

He turned up the collar on his jacket and meandered back to the barracks. *I'm wiped. Wonder if my family even knows I'm alive? Does Rose know? So many questions and no answers. I'm hitting the sack soon as I get back.*

He arrived at his barracks not a minute too soon. All the POWs had lined up outside for roll call. The wicked wind from the Baltic bore down on the men, whipping their pant legs and jackets. Two German officers walked back and forth, counting each man. If the count differed between the officers, they counted until their numbers matched. After they eventually verified the count, Andy and the men hustled into the barracks for the evening.

Daylight had long since vanished, and ebony clouds slid under the heavens. Andy lay in his bunk long before lights out at 10 p.m. His conscience took over, and he struggled to replace Marta's face with Rose's. Anna's face intruded now and then, which kept beating up on his guilt. The busy day and newness of the camp had dominated his thoughts, but no matter how hard he tried at night, they could not deaden the pain he carried for Marta's death. The events leading up to and during her murder flashed before him like a newsreel at the movies. He rubbed his hands over his face. *Make it stop!*

Early the next morning, Col. Brawley sent for Andy, who left immediately for Barracks #1.

"How'd he know you wanted to see him?" Bulldog asked, brushing his hands through his hair.

"He must be a mind reader. See ya later." Andy snatched his knit cap from the nail on the wall.

He entered the barracks, where a paper sign posted over the door in the center back of the building indicated the colonel's office. A lieutenant sat behind a small table outside the office. Andy walked up to the wooden table, and the lieutenant stood and saluted him.

He returned the lieutenant's salute. "Capt. Walters here to see Col. Brawley."

A frail man appeared at the doorway. Andy looked twice before recognizing him.

"Col. Brawley." Andy raised his hand in a salute, trying to disguise his shock at the amount of weight the colonel had shed.

"Capt. Walters. Glad to see you again. I got wind of your presence yesterday, and it didn't take me two minutes to assign you a job." His eyes lit up as he shook Andy's hand.

Andy pulled his hand from the colonel's grasp. "Your grip is still firm, sir. Now what might that job be, sir?"

"Except for the Brits and one other man in your barracks, everyone is new. They need a leader, and because you are an outstanding leader and outrank these men, I'm placing you in charge of Barracks #2." He grinned broadly and reached over, patting Andy on the back. "I've followed your career and watched you grow, son. You make me proud."

"Thank you, sir. I'd be honored to be their leader. But tell me, what about 2nd Lt. Jack Newton. Might there be some flak from him?"

"No British officer will lead my men!"

Surprised at the response, Andy said, "Yes sir!"

A pleasant demeanor returned to Col. Brawley's face. "We meet here two or three times a week, depending on what's going on in and out of the camp. My lieutenant will let you know when the meetings are scheduled. Welcome aboard."

"Thank you again, sir." Andy saluted once more.

The colonel retreated behind his desk. "Here, take this order with you. Post it so there will be no doubt about who is in charge. You're dismissed, Capt. Walters."

"Yes sir."

Andy returned to his barracks, handed the paper to Tex, and told him to post it.

* * *

Black evening clouds squeezed the balance of light from the sky, closing another wretched endless day.  As the days plodded along, Andy created a tracking calendar, marking off each day one at a time. He reached over and marked an "X" over the current day. *The same pointless routine. Line up every morning, get counted, line up every evening, get counted again.*

Andy lay on his bunk, thinking of his family and how worried they must be. He thought about Rose and what she must be going through. Sitting up, he reached for a pencil and pad of paper furnished by the Red Cross. The picture of Marta and her baby flashed before him. Tormented by her vision, he swallowed in despair. His throat ached in defeat. For the first time since arriving at Stalag Luft I, he could no longer deny to himself that he caused Marta and the baby's death. He alone was responsible.

The note pad slipped from his hand, and he let the pencil fall to the floor. The shadow of the bunk above shielded his face from the others. He locked his hands and placed them over his eyes, thumbs resting on his temples. No letter to Rose.

The morning light rushed in as the guards threw open the shutters, launching another day. Though it was March, the weather remained cold as hell to Andy, someone used to a mild climate. A fresh snow pasted a new cover over the compound during the night.

"Ain't this like the an-artic? We need more coal." Bulldog folded his arms close to his belly.

"This is as good as it gets, buddy. Stop your whining and accept it," Tex said. "You got more fat to keep you warm."

"I'll have you know that's pure muscle. You're just jealous."

"Hush, Bulldog," Andy said. "Go stand next to the stove." *If it's not him, it's someone else—always complaining when they damn well know there's nothing we can do about it.*

"I've an idea. Bulldog, go dig a ditch. That'll warm you up." Tex grinned and slapped on his cowboy hat over his knit cap.

Except for the twice-a-day countdown, a breakfast and supper of black bread and barley soup—the gourmet standard for the day— enough to make anybody puke, drained Andy of the enthusiasm for another day. Why bother? He and the men remained inside, sheltered from the arctic air. He tired quickly of endless card games. Day after day, he studied the German language. After a few weeks, he mastered numerous words. *Might need this when we get out—some day.*

The next morning, the men stirred, and eventually fell in behind Andy, making their way through new snow to the mess hall.

"Will we ever get warm, Andy?" Bulldog flipped up his collar and tightened it around his ears.

"Maybe when we get home," Andy said. He swung around to investigate the commotion behind.

"Yeah, if I had a knife, I'd slit the throat of every Kraut in this camp!" Brad said to the man walking beside him.

"You're full of crap. You couldn't stab one before the entire guard unit came down on you," the other man said.

"Bullshit! You just watch me!"

Andy hustled back to Brad, caught him by the front of his jacket, and threw him on the ground. He planted his foot in the middle of Brad's chest.

"What in Sam Hill do you think you're doing? Do you know the penalty for making threats against the guards? Death! Did you hear that? DEATH!"

Brad grabbed Andy's foot and attempted to move it aside. Andy dropped his knee down on Brad's chest and Brad let out a loud grunt.

"When will you ever learn?" Andy eased off his knee. "Now, can it! Do I make myself clear?" In one sweep, he lifted Brad up.

Brad warbled and Andy steadied him. "Yes, sir," Brad said, scarcely audible.

"I can't hear you!" Andy got into Brad's face. He tightened his hands on Brad's jacket.

"YES SIR!" Brad pealed Andy's hands off his jacket and hustled to catch up with the other POWs.

Andy lingered behind. He pressed his lips together and squeezed his chin between his fingers. He realized he was no longer hungry. *Why do I feel so responsible for this man? Yeah, I know. I caused his capture. How many more times do I save him? He better be worth it!*

Brad glanced back at Andy. He curled his lip and drove a fist into his palm. *One day I'll show them. Show them I'm somebody. Somebody to reckon with. Somebody not to mess with. Not one of these fellows gives a crap about me. Not one! Why? Just because I'm different doesn't make me unlikable. If we survive this war, I've nobody to go home to. Nobody cares. I listen to them talk about family, girlfriends—I've no one.*

*I can't keep a girlfriend. Once they get to know me, they bail out—gone. Don't have a chance. How will I ever have a home—a family—a kid or two?*

# Chapter Twenty-six

## Fayetteville, North Carolina – Late April 1944

John Walters drove the tractor under the shed and headed for the house. He turned the knob on the kitchen door where weeping sounds drifted from the living room. John rushed into the room.

"Jane, what's going on?" He hadn't had time to wash up yet, his overalls dusty from the tobacco fields.

A uniform lay beside Jane on the sofa. Without a word, Jane handed him a letter.

John began reading:

*Dear Mom, Dad, and Betty Jane,*

*I miss all of you terribly. We are in a real hell hole with mud and rain that just won't let up. Well, England's Nissen huts were palaces compared to Foggia. We were fortunate enough to draw a tent that is ditched around, but others were not. It won't stop raining long enough for them to gutter around and they can't leave anything on the floor.*

*This is our last mission, we hope. Our 50th. Most of the missions here have been easy except the last three. An earlier one proved disastrous for an entire squadron. We occupy their tent now. What an eerie feeling.*

*Betty Jane, you must be growing into a young lady by now. You keep those boys at arm's length, you hear. Listen to Mom and Dad. They know best. Study hard and practice your music.*

*Dad, I can't wait to get home and help on the farm. Maybe after this mission, I'll be there in time for spring planting.*

*Mom, I miss your good cooking and the hours we spent talking. It seems like so many years ago.*

*If you should receive this letter, you will know by then that I didn't make it. Always remember, I died fighting for my country, so people all around the world can be free. I like to think I left this world a better place. Many have already died for freedom, and I hope everyone will remember that. Don't let them forget.*

*Please don't grieve for me. This was my choice. I wanted more than anything to be a pilot and do my part. Yes, and I did it. I hope I've made a difference.*

*Be happy for my life, though short, that I lived it to the fullest and gave it for my country. Rejoice, don't weep.*

*Thank you for everything you have ever done for me. I should have thanked you sooner, but I've had more time to reflect.*

*Mom, I still have my buckeye, and I always wear clean underwear.*

*You all are forever in my heart. I love you very much.*

> *Your loving son and brother,*
> *Andy*

John's chest compressed as if a boulder had dropped on it. Slowly he refolded the letter, careful to follow the same creases. He couldn't bear to look at Jane. He felt her eyes steady on him.

"Where did you get this?" His voice quivered.

"From the pocket of Andy's uniform. There's another—to Rose. Oh, John. Does this mean our son is gone?"

"No, no, no. I'm sure they send home their personal items, even if they're missing in action. We've had no final word. Not even a letter." John glanced toward Betty Jane's room. "Is she home yet?"

"No, she's eating with Peggy and her family. She'll be home by eight." She swiped at the tears flooding her cheeks.

John's gaze rested on Jane's questioning eyes. "Look Jane, devastating as it is, we still don't know any more than we did in middle March. There's no need to upset Betty Jane. Hang Andy's uniform in our closet and put his other items on the top shelf. Can you hang one of my coats over his uniform? Betty Jane doesn't need to see it right now." John placed his hand, dirt and all, on Jane's shoulder. She leaned her cheek against the backside of his hand.

A few moments later, she pulled the second letter out of the uniform pocket and handed it to John. "This is his letter to Rose. Can you take it to the Martins tomorrow?"

"Leave both on the sideboard, and I'll take them after supper. They need to read Andy's letter as well." John attempted to appear unshaken. Once through the bathroom door, he closed it and walked over to the window. The dam burst and tears flowed freely, no longer held back. His body shook. He muffled all sounds and allowed the emotional release.

John pushed his chair away from the supper table when Betty Jane burst through the door.

"Hey, Dad, Mom."

"You're home early." John meandered over toward her.

Betty Jane noticed the letters on the sideboard. "What's this? That's Andy's handwriting. Oh my, God! He's alive!" Hands shaking, she opened the envelope.

John reached for the letter only to have Betty Jane spin around dodging his hand. Nothing he could do now but let her read the letter. *How stupid of me to tell Jane to leave the letters there!* He glanced at Jane whose eyes had already teared up.

Betty Jane raked her sweater sleeve across her eyes. "He's dead, isn't he?"

John took the letter and held her in his arms. "Sweetheart, this is just a letter written in case, remember, in case, he doesn't return. We don't know anything new yet so don't read anything into this. Mom found the letter in his best uniform pocket which was sent home when he did not return after the mission. That's normal policy for the military in this situation. Understand?"

Betty Jane replied, "Yes, sir," then broke away and rushed into her room.

Jane started after her.

"Wait. She needs time to be alone, honey. She'll be all right. I'm sorry I didn't put the letters in my pocket before supper." He gazed at the floor and shook his head. "I'm sorry."

"Oh, John. You're only human. She'll be out of her room soon." Jane stepped over to John and hugged him.

Days turned a thousand shades of gray, spilling into the darkest nights—those dreaded nights. John fought the evenings, fearing what might lie ahead. Waiting took its toll on the family. No longer did they laugh and kid around. Everything became excruciatingly serious. From the moment John entered the house, his ear stayed glued to the radio, searching for any hint of progress in the war. One way or another, he knew they would hear something. Then it came. The timing was never good.

John returned early from the field. Jane was listening to "Stella Dallas," her favorite radio show. He walked over to the console radio and switched to the news station.

"John, what are you doing? That's my show. Bob was about to ask Stella to marry him!" Jane rushed to the radio and turned it back with no apologies.

"I'm sorry, darling. I wasn't paying any attention to the time. Any mail?" At the sound of Betty Jane bouncing in, John spun around toward the door.

"Mom! Dad! Look! A postcard. Look!" Betty Jane jumped up and down. Her brown hair draped in soft wavy curls around her shoulders.

John rushed over and snatched it from her, his heart skipping beats. Jane leaned over his shoulder, tears already streaming.

April 29, 1944, postmarked May 1, 1944:

*Berlin Short Wave just transmitted a message from Andrew W. "I am now in Germany, safe and well, do not worry, letters limited, can receive unlimited mail, get in touch with Red Cross about packages, love"*
   *Hope this message will be a comfort to you.*
     *Mrs. L. F. Miller*
     *36 Mollybranch Road*
     *Middleburg, Conn.*
*S.W.A.M.*        *Please acknowledge!*

John and his family gathered in a circle, clung to each other and wept. Through the tears and shouts of joy, months of tension, worry, and frustration vanished in their little tenant home. John wiped his eyes with the palms of his hands and reads the postcard once again.

"Andy had to tell them how to reach us. It must be him. We'll have to send Mrs. Miller a telegram." Without another word, John walked out the front door and looked up into the heavens. He locked his hands in prayer, "Dear Lord, thank you, thank you. I knew you'd never let us down. Please continue to keep him safe."

Late June another Western Union telegram arrived:

CF61 34 GOVT-WUX WASHINGTON DC 50 651P
1944 JUNE 30 PM

REPORT JUST RECEIVED THROUGH THE
INTERNATIONAL RED CROSS STATES THAT YOUR
SON CAPTAIN ANDREW E. WALTERS IS A

# PRISONER OF THE GERMAN GOVERNMENT LETTER OF INFORMATION FOLLOWS FROM PROVOST MARSHALL GENERAL- ULIO THE ADJUTANT GENERAL

Several days later, a letter arrived. Jane waited until John came in from the field to open it. John's hands shook and a tremor slid down his spine as he tore into the envelope.

*Dear Mr. and Mrs. Walters:*

*Under date of March 15, 1944, The Adjutant General notified you that your son, Captain Andrew E. Walters, had been reported missing in action over Austria since February 24th.*

*Further information has been received indicating that Captain Walters was the pilot of a B-17, (Flying Fortress), which departed from Southern Italy on February 24th, on a bombardment mission to Steyr, Austria. Full details are not available, but the report indicates that as our planes were making their bomb run they were attacked by hostile fighters and in the ensuing battle your son's craft sustained damage. Immediately thereafter the bomber was seen to leave the formation and to go into a wide spiral glide to earth, and as it was descending two or three parachutes were seen to leave. The report further states that the intensity of the action prevented further observation of Captain Walters' Fortress, therefore, there is no other information available at this time.*

*Due to necessity for military security, it is regretted that the names of those who were in the plane and the names and addresses of their next of kin may not be furnished at the present time. The great anxiety caused you by failure to receive more details concerning your son's disappearance is fully realized. Please be assured that any additional information received will be conveyed immediately to you by The Adjutant General or this headquarters.*

> *Very sincerely,*
> *CLYDE V. FINTER,*
> *Colonel, Air Corps,*
> *Chief, Personal Affairs Division*
> *Assistant Chief of Air Staff, Personnel*

"Well, sir. It's obvious Andy was one of the two or three parachutes. Now we can't let this worry us. One day our boy will be home again." John took Jane into his arms to comfort her. He needed her as much as she needed him.

"Life is a precious gift, and every day is a blessing," Jane said. She moved away from John and smiled back at him, "It's dinner time, and I'll continue setting a fourth plate on the table until Andy comes home."

# Chapter Twenty-seven

## Late Spring 1944

Andy stepped into the barracks after returning from the compound library. "What the hell's going on here?" he demanded. Smoke clouded the room.

Shouts rang throughout the barracks and the men had formed a circle around Brad and Simon physically going at each other.

"Hit him, Simon. Take him out!" Randy slammed his right fist into his left hand chewing his lip at the same time—his eyes intent on the confrontation in front of him.

Simon's head rocked from another blow by Brad. Simon followed with a lunge into Brad.

Andy noticed the fire in Jack's eyes and the eagerness for the fight.

"Jack! What's going on here? Why haven't you stopped it? Damn!" Andy rushed into the center of the scuffle, separating the two men. Blood poured from Simon's nose, and a cut over his eye gushed. Brad's lip spilled blood.

Andy held them at arm's length and shouted, "Cut it out! Both of you! Get a grip." Brad kept swinging at Simon. Andy flashed his eyes at Brad. His voice, cold and exact, commanded authority. "Break it up, I said!" He shoved the men toward opposite sides of the room.

"I'll not have that in here. Do you understand?"

"Yes sir!" Brad's lip curled

"Yes sir," Simon said, head bowed.

"Now, who started this mess?" No answer. Andy threw up his hands in disgust. "Why would you fight with someone so much larger than you, Simon?"

"He threatened to expose my heritage, and you know what would happen then," Simon said.

"Brad, what the hell's going on?" Before Brad could answer, Andy turned back to Simon when he heard him stuttering.

"He…he…he keeps telling me I'm going to hell because I don't believe in Jesus." Simon's face clouded with uneasiness.

"Brad, I'm telling you for the last time, leave Simon alone. What do you *NOT* understand about that?" Andy felt the blood rush to his face.

"He asks for it. Such a shrimp!" Brad spat on the floor.

Andy grabbed Brad by his jacket and slammed him against the wall. "You listen here, buddy boy. You keep your damn hands off Simon! Got it?"

Brad twisted out of his grip. "Yes sir!"

Andy caught a glimpse of the table filled with scattered cigarettes and personal items. "And what's all this on the table?" Andy's jaw muscles tightened as he clinched his fists. He turned to Jack. "What do you know about this? You part of it?"

"The fellows were simply having a jolly good time, Captain. Where's the harm?" Jack said. A peculiar smile slid across his face.

"Not at the expense of a Jew. And you will *NOT* place bets on fights again. Is that understood?" Andy took one sweep of the table items and raked them onto the floor. He made glaring eye contact with each man before moving on. "Got it?"

Bulldog, Pops, Tex and Johnny popped in on the scene.

"What's going on?" Tex asked.

"It's okay now. Where've y'all been?" Andy asked.

Bulldog rubbed his hands together. "We been watching that broad, uh…uh…uh…. Oh, Betty Grable at the compound theater. What a dish!" He looked around at Tex. "You see those gams?"

"Sure did. She's a looker all right." Tex got serious and asked, "What's Brad done now?"

"It's over. Forget it." Andy moved over to Brad and caught the sleeve of his jacket.

"And you, fella…" Andy, Brad in tow, moved to the other end of the barracks, depositing Brad at his bunk with a shove. "You make another move toward Simon, and I'll have your head."

Brad didn't respond except to reel away from Andy's grip.

Bulldog turned to Andy, "Hot damn. I've been waiting for a long time to hear that."

Andy glared at him and chose not to respond. He propped his hands on his hips and shook his head. *God almighty! Dad, I'm gonna prove you wrong yet. I'll not let Brad get the best of me! Not on your life!*

Jack mumbled something to his men and items on the floor disappeared. Andy became the brunt of a few disapproving glances from Jack, but pretended not to notice.

Soon after, the air in the barracks turned thick, and a quick division between the RAF and the USAAF formed. He regretted Brad had drawn this imaginary line. But, Andy knew this division had roots earlier, even before that day.

Pops strode over to Andy and knelt down beside him. "I don't mean to butt in, Captain, but I smell trouble. The Brits resent our liveliness and playfulness, except in a bloody fight."

"Yeah. You've gotta wonder how they can carry that same theme 'The Yanks are overpaid, oversexed and over here,' even into the POW camps. Have you noticed some of them are almost too friendly with the Krauts?"

"Some of their ancestors are Germans, didn't you know?"

"I'd heard that. Well, let's hope it calms down soon. I don't like the smell of this. Look, I need to get outta here for a spell."

"Yes sir," Pops said and went back to his bunk.

Andy, still wearing his flight jacket, stepped outside and headed for Col. Brawley's barracks to check the BBC radio for news on the progress of troop movement into Germany. He shook his fists in the air.

Week after week, the POWs made one attempt after another to escape, mostly through tunnels, only to be brought back when the dogs chased them down, scarcely to the thicket of the woods. Andy believed as long as they were not killed, this kept the men occupied and hopeful. Once all hope disappeared, he knew they would surely be in trouble.

Daily, Andy marked the makeshift calendar on the wall next to his bunk. He refused to lay idle. That's when the vision of Marta and her baby usually surfaced to an unbearable state. *Thanks to Pops, I'm getting better. Believe it or not, Dad, I'm strong, capable, and extremely determined.* He pulled on his chin.

Andy teased Bulldog for becoming a master at swapping cigarettes and other Red Cross items for radio parts. He accused him of being buddy-buddy with Heinrich, the guard. "You've got them bamboozled all right."

"I get what we need, don't I?" Bulldog bragged. "Johnny assembled a radio, scant as it is, but it works. Can't knock that, eh?"

"The colonel appreciates it, and thank God it hasn't been discovered yet." Andy changed the subject. "Have y'all seen the colonel lately? He resembles a walking skeleton."

"I saw him yesterday at the mess hall. He didn't eat enough to keep a flea alive." Bulldog ambled over to Andy, standing in front of the heat stove warming his hands.

"Don't know if he'll make it. He looks severely jaundiced." Andy stepped back to let another man back up to the stove.

"I saw him walking to the latrine building yesterday. Wobbled like a drunk. Too bad they boarded up all the barracks' latrines. He wouldn't have to walk so far." Bulldog shook his head.

"We have no one to blame but ourselves, but our job was to escape any way we could. Boarding up the latrines was each POW's punishment. Do you realize that not one man has successfully escaped this place?" Andy didn't wait for an answer; he didn't want to dwell on the fact that he and his men were prisoners and had lost total control of their own lives. *How can we bear another day of this? I want my life back. I want Rose back in my life. We are helpless here—totally helpless. We're at the mercy of the Germans.*

## June 1944

The days dragged on, and Andy continued to mark his calendar. Spring had seen its last days, and summer pressed into being. The entire camp engaged in numerous sports, mostly baseball—anything to pass the time and be outdoors. Sex and food continued to dominate the conversations.

"Hey skinny," Bulldog joked with Andy. "Your ribs are beginning to show."

"You should talk. You're looking more like a bean pole with a knot tied around the middle of your gut!" Andy said.

"What do you expect? They ain't feeding us half what they used to when we got here."

"Our boys are bombing everything that moves. Trains, tanks, and trucks. The Red Cross supplies can't get through like before."

Bulldog rubbed his stomach. "Splitting my packet is like cutting out half my grub."

"Get used to it, Bulldog."

Andy and Bulldog finished eating and meandered back to the barracks. As they neared their building, a runner bounded out of Col. Brawley's barracks. He rushed toward Andy waving a paper.

The runner clambered up in a military gait and back-pedaled to contain his excitement. "Here, sir. Look at this!"

"The Normandy invasion started today! Gather 'round, fellas!" Andy didn't have to force a smile. He waved the paper in circles above his head.

The men converged outside shouting and dancing. Bulldog broke into song, "God Bless America." A spray of gunfire over their heads squelched their joy and sent them dashing into their barracks.

Andy joined in the celebration, which resumed inside the barracks, temporarily removing the overwhelming hopelessness of the men.

This hint of expectation served Andy and the men well, but by the end of August, despondency returned. The June bounce in each walk faded, and Andy stood outside, gazing through the double fences and triple rolls of barbed wire. He forced himself to believe that one day he would be free again.

At least two times a month the horse-drawn wagons pulled through the gates, and the guards loaded a wooden box or two and hauled them away. Andy watched while intense anguish and desolation swept over him. Defeat and resolution saturated his being. *Rose, I can barely see your face. Where is it? I can't get through this without you. You are my future, my life, someone to come home to.* Slowly her face came into focus.

Brad's concentrated hatred for Simon escalated. Andy dreaded getting up each day to face another skirmish between Brad and Simon. He used every relationship skill known to him to defuse the problem between the two, but if Brad didn't instigate it, Simon did. It was a bomb waiting to explode. Only a matter of time.

Brad treated Andy with respect—no more dirty looks and no more nasty comments, except when Andy had to break up fights. Andy realized this was Brad's way of saying, "Thank you," for saving his life in Austria. Since they first arrived at the camp, Brad had yet to mention Marta and the baby.

The edge between Andy and Jack remained cordial once the air thinned after the first ruckus back in April. The Brit's resentment of the USAAF surfaced now and then, but Andy saw no major problem develop—only man against man—sports rivalry and educational competitiveness. Something to whittle away the time and set goals for improvement. He knew it kept them out of trouble. *Nothing wrong with that.*

## September 1944

"Andy! Andy! Wake up!" Bulldog whispered loudly, while shaking Andy's shoulders. "There's a body outside of our barracks."

The night clouds had begun their ascent, making way for a brilliant red, gold, and orange sunrise. A dull, gray light seeped into the barracks through the closed shutters.

"Oh Bulldog. Is this another one of your pranks? I'm not in the mood. Go back to bed." Andy turned toward the wall and pulled the khaki blanket over his head. He knew the men rarely rushed out of bed before the guards called for the morning countdown, making sure no one escaped during the night.

Bulldog jerked the covers back, grabbed Andy up by the shoulders. He spoke in a low voice. "Listen to me, sir. I ain't foolin'! There's a…a body outside. Got me an urgent call to use the latrine and slipped through the hole in the flooring of our old latrine. On the way back, I saw it—behind the barracks' pinning—facing inward." His breath came in short spurts.

Andy slipped into his pants. He checked the barracks for anyone missing and glanced at Brad in the top bunk. Brad did not move. "Who else knows about this?"

"No one. I came straight to you."

"Shush! Ease out before we alarm the others. Check to see if the guards unlocked the barracks door yet." Andy headed out of their room as Bulldog pushed on the entrance door.

"Hot dang!" Bulldog said.

"Quiet!" Andy reminded him before closing the door behind. "They forgot to lock it last night. Otherwise, wouldn't they have discovered the body?" They shuffled down the steps, and Bulldog led Andy to the left of the barracks, where a body lay sprawled under the edge of the barracks, facing away from them. "Get the colonel, Bulldog."

"Yes sir." Bulldog scurried to Barracks #1 and quickly returned with a half-dressed barefooted Col. Brawley. The colonel twisted one side of his white mustache as he approached.

"We have a dead body here, sir. I haven't touched him. I climbed under the barracks to see his face. It's Simon." Andy lowered his eyes.

"What happened? Can you tell?"

"No sir. I don't see any blood. It's important that we secure the area just in case it's foul play of some sort." Andy used his hands to suggest a perimeter of protected area. Bulldog stepped back from the vicinity of the crime circle.

By then several guards had gathered, and Kriegies poured out of their barracks as the news traveled.

Heinrich stepped forward and leaned down as if to turn Simon over. Andy blocked his path. "Nein! No! Don't touch! Get the commandant. Bitte (please)." Andy knew Heinrich had picked up a little English language over the last few months. He stepped back.

"Get the commandant. Immediately. Bitte." Heinrich barked the order in German to a guard. The guard hastened to the commandant's office.

Two minutes later, Commandant Scherer arrived. "Take this man away!" he ordered in German.

Andy had learned enough of the language to understand the order. "No sir. You can't do this until we take photos and sketch the body position and everything of importance."

The commandant spoke somewhat comprehensible English. "This is not your concern. You have no voice here."

Andy realized the commandant's patience grew thin. "The Geneva Convention allows us to determine the cause of death of a fellow prisoner."

"Gibberish!"

"Capt. Walters is right. Reserve a room to place the body and keep the perimeter secure," Col. Brawley ordered.

"Ja, Ja. You Yanks still think you can run this camp." He removed his officer's hat and scratched through his salt and pepper hair. Deep pock scars resembling pounded beefsteak covered his full jowls and neck. Wild gray hairs protruded from his ears and matched the hairs growing from his nostrils.

"Take the body to the interrogation room. Place it on the long table. Col. Brawley, you have total access." He clicked his heels and turned to leave.

"Commandant. Bring your camera, bitte," Col. Brawley shouted, his knees buckled slightly before he leaned against the barracks. His eyes followed the commandant.

Andy caught his arm. "You okay, sir?" The colonel looked at him strangely as if he had no idea what he was talking about.

"Of course, Captain." As an afterthought, the colonel managed a weak smile on his jaundiced skeletal face—his corn-silk hair, prematurely gray. He gazed at Andy with deep sunken blue eyes.

He continued, "Take over this investigation, Capt. Walters, and have a report on my desk by morning."

Andy watched the colonel until he entered his barracks—a shadow of the man he remembered from early training. "Bulldog, fetch my note pad and pencil. On the double!" He smiled at the extra hustle Bulldog, exerted like a torpedo. *Fastest I've seen him move since we got here.*

A few seconds later, Bulldog returned. "Here ya go, sir."

Andy stooped down, placed the pad on his right knee, and sketched the body angle and body position in relationship to the barracks. He drew a pencil drawing of Simon and his surroundings—even boot prints in the damp sand.

Heinrich returned with a box camera and snapped numerous photos.

After detailing everything possible, Andy nodded to Heinrich that he had completed his work and to take the body to the assigned room.

Heinrich signaled two guards. They lifted the body and headed for the interrogation room. Andy followed on their heels when an American officer arrived.

"Capt. Walters? Lt. Chandler here. Col. Brawley thought you might need a medical evaluation on the deceased. I'm not officially a doctor, but I've had extensive medical training. Best we can do for now." A thick patch of black wiry hair protruded beneath his khaki knit cap. He scratched the black stubble covering his lower face,

Andy shook Chandler's hand and returned his friendly grin. "Thanks. I can use the help."

An air of discomfort rippled through Andy upon entering the interrogation room. The guards had  placed the body face up on a rectangular wooden table. Lt. Chandler proceeded to remove Simon's clothing, checking for signs of unusual marks. He zeroed in on the neck.

Andy moved closer. "Appears to be twine markings around his neck."

"Possible strangulation, sir." The lieutenant lifted Simon's shoulders to view the back of the neck. "Yep. See here. A rope, cord, or wire—twisted in the back. Here's where it caught his skin. Strange." He laid the body down and searched Simon's neck. "There are no scratch marks whatsoever in the front. Evidently, he made no attempt to free himself from the cord. His build is small. A larger man overpowered him. Someone caught him off guard. That's my guess, Captain."

"Sounds plausible, Lieutenant. Stay available." The lieutenant left the building, while Andy sketched another set of pictures showing the twine marks and scribbled multiple notes before leaving the room.

On the way back to the barracks, a thought flashed intermittently through his mind. *Who would murder a fella like Simon? Who?* An unsettling answer crossed his mind. *Who regularly instigated a fight with Simon? Brad! The others appeared to get along well with Simon—even protected the fact that he was Jewish. My God! Not Brad!*

# Chapter Twenty-Eight

## POW Camp

"No, no, please no!" Andy shouted in a grief-stricken, tormented voice. He lay on his bed staring at the wooden slabs under the bunk overhead. The torture of his actions sent him into severe despair.

*I broke all military rules of avoiding capture and now I'm trapped in my own defeat.* He hadn't eaten in two days. Food brought on nausea. He preferred to be alone in the solitude of the empty barracks, where he mulled over the mindless isolation of his failure.

Thoughts of Rose surfaced only to be shoved aside. "I don't deserve anyone like her." He continued his own verbal abuse. "Especially after Anna!"

"Oh, God!" he cried out grabbing the sides of his head. "Take me away from this torment!"

The image of Marta and her baby, riddled with bullets, lying in a puddle of blood on the sanctuary floor, flashed before him. He knew Brad battled his own hell, leaving Andy to his. The fact that Brad remained close-lipped, never mentioning Marta and her baby, puzzled him. Yet, Brad's stinging words at the sanctuary piled more guilt on Andy.

He continued to search Brad's eyes, but he never made contact unless forced to. Brad avoided him like poison ivy. *What a miserable failure I've been. This is the fella I was determined to win over.* Andy scrubbed his hands up and down his cheeks and twisted them as if he could squeeze the anguish away.

The barracks door swung open, and Andy sat up sliding his feet to the floor.

Bulldog approached him. "Andy, you gotta eat. I brung ya a slab of bread."

"Thanks, but don't think it'd stay down."

"Look. We all got captured. Don't be so hard on yourself."

"Just drop it, please!" Andy knew that so far, no one knew of Marta with the exception of Brad, but that only deepened his guilt. *They wouldn't be so nice if they knew!*

Andy quickly brushed past Bulldog, after picking up the chunk of bread. The sting of Bulldog's eyes burned on his every movement. He snatched up his flight jacket, exited the room, and headed to the library.

He realized that those who knew him were puzzled at the change in his behavior and lack of camaraderie. They would have to live with it as far as he was concerned until he found a way to cope, to survive, to get through it.

Pops caught up with Andy just before he reached for the library door latch. "Andy. Let's sit out here for a spell. How 'bout it?"

"Sure thing, Pops. What's your problem?"

"It's not mine, Andy, it's yours. What's eating you?" Pops voice was soft, not accusing. Sincere.

Andy looked at him—his insides pleaded to spout out the truth, but he dared not let this kindly man share his burden.

The two of them slid down against the exterior south library wall into a sitting position on the frozen sand, away from the biting wind.

"I can't close it out. I made a severe mistake, and this is my punishment, I guess. For other things, too. Did you ever have an affair with someone after you were committed to marry someone else?"

"Men do many things when facing the possibility of death in war—women as well. The uncertainty of life, an attractive person, all of this creates an atmosphere of desire in the face of death."

"When I was taken care of by this Austrian family after bailing out and landing near their home, the daughter took a fancy to me and I didn't refuse. We both thought we might not make it out of this war but I knew it was not right. I was committed to Rose."

"Many men fall into the same circumstance, Andy. Impending death does serious things to people."

"I've done worse and can't get the incident out of my head."

"Look Andy. You're not the only one that carries a burden. This is war and unbearable things happen. Your damn perfectionism doesn't serve you well under these circumstances."

"You don't understand, Pops. I've fought insecurity all my life. That's why I give more than 100 percent. I can't do any different."

"You're allowed to fail occasionally. Quit beating yourself up. War is about life and death decisions, and not one fella calls it right every time—even the generals."

"Did *you* ever kill anyone or get them killed by accident?"

"Yep. And I regret it to this day. An innocent boy. A hunting accident. The vision of his mother kneeling over him will stay with me until the day I die. But I had to go on and here I am."

"How'd you get over it?"

"I …" Pops abruptly stopped his sentence.

Before Andy realized it, he spewed the words out—uncontrollably. "I caused a young mother and baby to be murdered by the Gestapo. The image of her face as she struggled to reach her infant, and watching…listening to that tiny baby whimper and gasp its last breath, won't leave me. It's with me every waking moment."

Pops stared into Andy's eyes. "I poured myself into work, did my job, and before I knew it, the vision of the boy and his mother dulled, but never left."

"It's so hard to get into anything here as a prisoner."

"Weren't you studying law before you joined up?"

"Yeah." Andy thought for a minute rubbing his chin with his thumb and forefinger. "I need to bury myself in books and keep my mind busy. You're right. Thanks, Pops. Thanks for listening. I needed that."

"Don't you ever forget, *you* did not pull the trigger. The Gestapo did."

Andy stood up, reached for Pops' hand, and pulled him to his feet.

"You know, we all have crosses to bear. Always remember, you're not by yourself, son."

"Pops, you really know how to jump start a fella." Andy chuckled inwardly at the word 'son,' an endearing, consoling term, though scarcely a decade separated their ages.

"I'm back at the barracks now if you need me." Pops stood and reached a hand out to Andy before leaving.

"Thanks again, Pops." He turned to go into the library but stopped and glanced skyward. There it was, dipping his wing before soaring higher. The hawk. Andy reached into his pocket and rubbed the buckeye.

# Chapter Twenty-nine

Clouds rolled in from the north like a great tidal wave off the Baltic Sea. Gusty winds picked up, spiraling around the wooden barracks, sending blasts of moist air through the open windows—a welcome change from the hot muggy heat of summer. Andy took the four steps up to the barracks by twos.

He entered the room to find two groups of officers huddled in serious conversation—the Brits and the Americans. Brad had stretched across his bunk, stoically detached from either group.

Bulldog and the men rushed Andy, who opened his mouth to speak, but instead paused. He quickly brushed the men away. "Graham!" He motioned Brad to follow him. "Out here!"

Brad stormed out of the building, matching Andy's stride.

The cool mist dampened Andy's face. He spun around and beat his fist against the wooden sidewall until the pain shocked him back to reality. From the corner of his eye, he spotted Lt. Jack Newton leaving the barracks and heading toward the main gate.

Andy asked Brad. "What do you know about Simon? Did you leave the barracks last night or early this morning?"

"Are you accusing me of Simon's death?" The color seeped from Brad's face, leaving a chalky white pallor.

"Damn straight, Brad. Didn't you know you would be the first suspect?" Andy's eyes narrowed as they exchanged dubious glances.

"I never left the barracks all night." Brad sniffed with haughty denial. He raised his hands above his temples, beating his head repeatedly.

"Can you prove it?"

Brad recoiled at the thought. "Hell no! Can you prove you didn't leave last night?"

Andy continued his tirade of questions. Brad's frustration grew.

Heinrich, two other guards, and Commandant Scherer marched beyond Andy and Brad and entered the barracks. Andy ignored them and focused on Brad.

"Look. You've been after Simon ever since we got here, and now I've gotta know exactly what's your beef with him. It's gotta be more than a personal dislike." Andy shuddered at the thought of anyone in his barracks killing a fellow officer.

"What do you care? I'll end up taking the rap just like I've done all my life." Brad's face turned to stone. A wicked smile crossed his lips. "Hell, you might as well lock me up now."

"I need to know what we're dealing with. And that means now! Stop acting like a loser and help me. Did you kill Simon?" Andy stared into the depth of Brad's eyes, searching for the truth.

"No. Absolutely not!" Brad shouted emphatically. "I didn't like Simon, but I would never stoop that low."

Angry shouts, in German and English, and resounding crashes inside the barracks caught Andy's attention. He and Brad rushed inside. Commandant Scherer stood next to Brad's bunk.

"Lt. Graham? This yours?" Commandant Scherer held up Brad's jacket.

"Yes, that's my jacket."

Scherer then held up a length of twine with sticks anchored to each end like handles.

"This yours, too?"

Brad approached the commandant and sounded off indignantly. "Positively not!"

"This was found on a hook beneath your coat." Scherer nodded his head to Heinrich.

Heinrich shouted, "Take him away." The guards moved to each side of Brad, caught his arms, and ushered him out the door.

Brad recoiled in horror. From a backward glance over his shoulder, he shouted, "Andy, I had nothing to do with this. Nothing!"

Andy faced Commandant Scherer. "The Geneva Convention prevents any summary execution! You will grant Lt. Graham a fair trial, right?"

"Who says I have to obey this Geneva stuff?"

"The entire world says so."

"Poppycock! Is that how you say it?"

"A prisoner accused of murder against a fellow prisoner has the right to a fair trial, sir."

"So you say. What does your Col. Brawley say?"

"I need to talk to him. Right away." Andy watched in dismay as the guards hauled Brad off. "Tex, I'll be at the colonel's barracks." He bolted from the building.

"Capt. Walters to see Col. Brawley," Andy said to the lieutenant at the entrance of the colonel's room.

"The doctor's with him right now. Shouldn't be much longer."

"I'll wait. Thank you." Andy took a seat on a wooden bench. The commandant's words echoed in his mind. *Poppycock my eye! That's what my dad said—a few days before I left. Wonder what he would say now?*

Minutes later Lt. Chandler, the temporary doctor, left the barracks. The colonel motioned Andy to come in. "What are we dealing with?" He appeared ghostly frail—his voice strained.

"Sir, may I speak freely?"

"By all means, son."

"I've had my difficulties with Brad, but we've made a decent effort to work through them. Perfect? No. But my gut tells me he didn't do this..." Andy continued to speak with grave deliberation.

Behind Col. Brawley's haunting eyes, Andy thought he absorbed his every word. "The commandant wants to meet with you, Colonel. Are you up to it, sir?"

"Yes. I want you to go with me." The colonel stood precariously on his feet. Andy rushed to assist him.

"Once we're out of the building, don't hold on to me." The colonel eyed him gratefully.

"Yes, sir."

The pair left the barracks, the colonel under his own steam and Andy ready to assist at a moment's notice. The mist falling from above had a salty taste when he moistened his lips.

Beyond the prison entrance appeared the commandant's office. The two gate guards expected the colonel, flung open the mesh wire gate squared by strips of wood, and signaled them through.

They entered Commandant Scherer's office, where he sat behind a highly polished wood desk. The commandant motioned with his hand for them to have a seat. An oversized swastika draped the wall behind him. Andy removed his hat. He stared at a picture of a much younger officer standing with the commandant and a young blonde woman. It was hard for him to think of the Germans' having families. That became Andy's shield against the reality of war.

"Your son?" Andy nodded to the photo.

The commandant glanced over to the photo. "*Was* my son. You Yanks killed him at Normandy." He focused back to Andy. "My daughter, Christa. You have family, no?"

"Yes." Andy slipped his right hand into his pocket; his fingers automatically closed around the buckeye.

The commandant rested his arms on the desk and locked his fingers together. "Colonel, you look peaked."

Col. Brawley spoke first. "No need for concern, Commandant. I'm assigning Capt. Walters to defend Lt. Graham."

Andy snapped his head toward the colonel. "But sir, I've yet to complete three years of college and am not ready for this. Lt. Graham needs an official lawyer."

Col. Brawley placed his hand on Andy's shoulder. "You've kept legal books flowing through this POW camp library. It's settled."

The blood rushed to Andy's head as self-doubt once again reared its ugly head like an octopus attaching itself to every brain cell and demanding control. He twisted the khaki hat in his hands.

"And whom do you expect to be the acting judge, Col. Brawley?" Commandant Scherer flashed a quirky smile across his face as he steepled his fingers to his chin.

"You're looking at him," Col. Brawley said while mustering the strongest voice possible.

"Very well. The trial will take place in the library. You have ten days to get ready." The commandant stood.

"What?" Andy and the colonel spouted in unison.

"Ten days." The commandant raised his hand and waved to the guard to see the two men out.

Andy and the colonel followed his action, excused themselves, and left the office.

Once Andy made sure the colonel returned to his barracks, he headed to the building where Simon's body lay. Questions drummed through his head. "This murder does not make sense—not by Brad," he said aloud.

Andy arrived at the building. He stepped across the threshold, and his eyes fixed on the body spread over the table. Already, a stench seeped from the room. *Maybe my imagination's working overtime. After all, September has yet to turn cold.* Andy covered his nose with his hand.

The wooden walls, darkened with age, smacked of isolation. The room brought back a sense of discomfort, uneasiness— memories of hours spent during interrogations. A sense of guilt, riddled by the death of Marta and her daughter, resurfaced at the sight of the room. Guilt at his weakness in his attempt to save Marta and her baby and causing Brad to become prisoner. "If I can't forgive myself, how can anyone else forgive me?" Andy said aloud. *How long am I going to navigate this river of hell? How long?* His hands moved up to the sides of his head covering his ears as if shutting out his words. He shook his head to purge the thoughts.

He methodically walked around the table, checking the body as he went along. Once he reached the upper body, he lifted the head from the table. In his hand, he felt a round protrusion on the lower backside of the head near the brain stem. Gently he eased Simon's head back down.

Andy hustled back to the door, flung it open and motioned the guard to come.

He urged the guard to help him turn the body over. The guard hesitated. "Nein."

"Ja, bitte." Andy responded emphatically. "Then call Commandant Scherer?"

"Nein."

"Then I will." Andy moved toward the door.

"Nein, nein." The guard moved toward the lower body, while Andy reached for the upper. They eased the body over.

"Danke," Andy said. He leaned over Simon's head, separated the thick, curly hair, and examined the injury.

"Arzi, bitte? *Doctor, please?* Lt. Chandler, Barracks #4. Danke." Andy watched the guard leave the building and shout orders to get Lt. Chandler. The concern for his discovery overrode the unpleasant smell. He struggled to imagine what type of instrument could land a blow such as this and by whom. A noise startled him, and he moved away from the body. The rustling happened again. Andy's eyes followed the sound. In a dim corner, a large rat nosed around a dead rat—most likely the source of the odor. He stomped his foot, and the rat scampered through a hole in the wall.

Several minutes later Lt. Chandler entered the building. He hurried over to Andy.

"Lieutenant, check this out. Look at the lump on the back of Simon's head. What do you make of it?"

The lieutenant studied every inch of Simon's head, separating the curly strands of black hair. Andy gazed on as Lt. Chandler slowly traced Simon's skull down onto the neck and the first vertebra and then back up to the brain stem.

"No wonder no scratch marks appeared on this fellow's neck. He died before someone wrapped the twine around his neck. But why?" Lt. Chandler stood up straight and scratched his head.

"What kind of object could kill with one blow?" Andy pinched his chin between his thumb and forefinger in a deep study.

"It couldn't be a hefty size because it would have damaged a much larger area. Must have been exceptionally strong, perhaps a long piece of iron. An iron blow to the base of the head, the cerebral base, causes internal bleeding, which produces swelling. Blindness comes first and then death. Sometimes external bleeding occurs as well." The lieutenant looked down at the floor and paced back and forth. "But then a blow of that nature should have left some blood. The hair is slightly matted."

"None of our men have access to anything as strong as iron—nothing that I can think of. What about the guards?"

"Hell, they would just shoot the man."

"You're right, Lieutenant. It's got to be an inside…" Andy walked over to the lieutenant. He raised an eyebrow. "Let's keep this between ourselves. Can I count on you?"

"Sure thing, Captain. You done with me?"

"Yes, and thanks. You're dismissed."

"Yes sir." After saluting, Lt. Chandler hurried out the door.

Andy pulled out his pad and pencil and recorded the examination before he returned to the barracks. He would give a report to Col. Brawley tomorrow—not today.

The chaos of the long day slowly dwindled. Food had not crossed his mind—missing barley soup and sawdust bread was scarcely a problem. He needed time to unravel the events, the new discovery, and the conclusion. *Sleep on it. Things might be clearer tomorrow.*

The fog rolled in from the sea thick as spit, pressing the sunrise into obliteration. The men queued up for yet another countdown. Repeatedly, the guards tried to reach the same number, until finally, they matched. Andy stood with the POWs in their khaki undershirts, mindful that at least the warmth of summer had not succumbed to an early fall.

"Holy cow!" Bulldog said, followed by a self-deprecating laugh when the guards released the men. "Let's go grab some bacon and eggs. Scrambled."

"Dream on!" Tex said, just as Commandant Scherer passed the group. He bowed down and said to the commandant, "Guten Morgen, *Good Morning.*"

"Your German is getting better," the commandant replied and then mimicked Bulldog's laugh.

Andy chuckled at the early morning scoffing. "This place is not for wimps, gentlemen. Let's get some chow."

Andy, Bulldog, Tex, Pops, and Johnny made their way to the mess hall. The Brits dillydallied as if avoiding their roommates.

After leaving the mess hall, Andy went straight to the library to comb over law books in search of answers. This was his number one priority. Lest he forget, he alone was the reason Brad became a POW.

He dropped his pencil next to the book to battle the demons shouting inside of him once more, "You failed Brad and Marta. You failed…" His insides erupted in spasms. He jumped up and rammed his fist into the wall. "Settle down," he told himself, rubbing his injured hand.

Andy quickly glanced around for early morning visitors. He was lucky. He paced the floor until serenity trickled back into his being—calmness he hadn't felt since March. It was as if someone had whispered *I forgive you.* It was *Godlike.*

He plopped down and tackled the books once again. Brad would be his next stop.

Andy arrived at the solitary confinement building, and the guard unlocked the bolted door. Andy entered Brad's cell. The room was long and narrow with no hint of daylight—only a smidgeon of light seeped through the edges of the door, until the guard flipped the switch from outside the cell, which lit a single bulb screwed into an overhead receptacle. A solid wooden bunk, no mattress, and a bucket for a latrine furnished the cell essentials. Brad stopped his pacing and rushed over to Andy, his knuckles clinched so tight they turned white.

"Where have you been? Do you have any idea what it's like locked up in this hole with no windows and not a soul to talk to? How would you like to be in my place? Huh?"

"Lt. Graham! Calm down! Listen. I've a lot of questions to ask, and you've gotta give me accurate answers. You understand?" Andy rested his right hand on Brad's left shoulder.

"Yes sir." Brad moved over to the bunk where Andy had placed his books and note pad. He dropped his body on one end, head in hands hiding his eyes.

Andy reached across the papers and pulled Brad's hands away from his face. "All is not lost, fella." The tenderness shown to Brad even surprised Andy.

Brad jumped up and kicked the end of the bunk.

Andy followed, placed his arm around Brad's shoulder and led him back to the end of the bunk. "Brad. I'm here to help. Now let's get to work."

"What do you know? You're not a lawyer. Besides. I'm here because of you!" Brad's eyes narrowed with contempt.

Andy's hand stretched out again, grabbed Brad's chin, and fixed his eyes on Brad's. Andy's mouth tightened into a stubborn line. "That has caused a living hell for me, buster, and now I intend to give everything I can possibly muster in your defense." With that, he tapped Brad's chin and then withdrew his hand. He morphed his own face into a slow, appraising glance.

Brad raised his head up and back, peering down his nose. "You really think you can save me?"

"I can't promise you anything except my best effort. Come on, let's get to work." Andy pulled open his composition book. "Did you leave the barracks the night of the murder?"

"No. I slept straight through, not waking until the sound of the commotion outside the barracks." He shifted on his bunk and stared saucer-eyed at Andy.

"All right. Let's go deeper. You have a record of creating conflict with Simon. Why?"

"I just don't like Jews."

"Can't be that simple."

"Sure can. What do you know? You never hated anyone, except possibly me." Brad turned his head away, facing the drab, aged walls.

"That's not the point. Why do you hate all Jews?" Andy stuck to his point, jotting down questions and answers as he went along.

"Why? I never thought about it. Um…" Brad caught his hand and cracked each knuckle.

Andy waited patiently.

"I a…it might be…a Jew ran down my mom when she crossed the road. He never even looked!" Brad's voice grew shrill. "I was ten. The son-of-a-bitch got away with it—said she didn't look before crossing. I watched it all. She was crossing the road to help me carry a heavy croaker sack of corn. He ran right over her. Didn't even attempt to stop." He buried his face in his hands.

"Where was your dad?"

"In the house. Drunk."

"Do you have sisters or brothers?"

"A brother. Ten years older. He got me into college."

"Who was the fellow that ran your mother down?"

"I told you. A Jew."

"No. I want to know more about him. How old, did he work, what else?"

"He was the teenage son of a local tailor shop owner."

"What happened to your dad after your mother died?"

"He's serving a jail term for bursting into their shop and shooting at the kid's parents. He was so drunk he didn't hit either of them. They sent him to jail. After he got out, he robbed a grocery store. He needed money for booze. The police caught him and threw him back in jail. He'll be there forever. They might as well keep him—he's no good. Just like me."

"I wouldn't say that."

"I was angry as hell about Mom's death. After Dad was arrested, I grew to hate everyone. Within a month, I had lost my mother, my father, and then there was only my brother and me."

"Did you hate the kid enough to kill him?"

"Yes. But I would never wish that on anyone. No. You're asking me if I could have killed him. No. Never. You believe me, don't you?" Brad stood, placed his hands on his hips, and paced once again.

Andy remained on the bunk. "Yes, I do. Now for the good news. Simon didn't die from the twine around his neck."

"What?" Brad reeled in astonishment and blinked in surprise.

"Yes. Listen to me. Simon didn't die from strangulation. He died from a severe blow to the back of the head at the base of the brain stem."

"But who…how…Do you know who did it?" Brad's mood became buoyant.

"No. Don't have a clue. But I'm working on it. We've less than ten days before the trial." Andy ran his hand through his hair, gathered his papers, and walked over to Brad.

"Buck up! I'm with you, Brad. See you later." Andy rapped on the door for the guard to let him out. He turned, "Oh. Sorry about your mom."

"Thanks, Captain."


The next morning Andy rested on his bunk, debating whether to get up and start another day. He marked another "X" on the calendar.

A news runner, sent from Col. Brawley's barracks, burst through the door with information announced over the makeshift BBC radio.

"News from home! President Roosevelt is running for reelection against Thomas E. Dewey. This'll be his fourth term if he wins. Reports say the president is in the lead." The runner turned and ran out of the barracks.

The news from home brightened Andy's days. He slipped his shoes on and wandered over to the window beyond his bunk, rested his hands on the windowsill, and absorbed the sea of color tinting the clouds with yellows, oranges, and brilliant reds from the sun's rays.

After experiencing days of misty dreary gloom, Andy stared into the rising sun, when a hawk soared high in the sky. *My hawk? Is this an omen of good things to come?* He stood back and slid his hand down into his pocket. The buckeye. He fondled it several times.

For three days, Andy interviewed all but two of the men in his barracks. Jack and Gino remained. He arranged to talk with Jack after breakfast and then Gino later in the day. Both had avoided him like he had a dreaded disease. Undaunted, he was determined to wrap up the interviews.

Later that morning, Andy and Bulldog were eating breakfast in the packed mess hall when loud shouts in German came from the cooking area.

"How do you expect me to keep the fire going if I can't get inside the stove? Who's got the iron lifter?" The cook shouted angrily at his helpers, shaking his hand from an apparent burn.

Andy tensed. "Bulldog, did he say 'iron lifter?'" He stretched his neck as far as possible to get a glimpse of the stove.

"Beats me. You know I don't speak no German."

"Our stove in the barracks has a removable iron top plate for dropping in briquettes and for stoking the fire." Thinking aloud, Andy massaged his temples.

"Andy, what ya getting at?" Bulldog had a deep burrow in his forehead.

"The iron lifter has a hook on the end that fits into the metal plate. And the iron rod is curved near the end. That's it!" Andy jumped from his seat and raced from the building.

"Hey…" Bulldog shouted after him.

Andy ignored the call. He sensed Bulldog's piercing eyes followed him as he fled the mess hall. He had one thing in mind. *Could this be the break? But wait a minute; I always fed the briquettes from the front. The spiral aluminum handle was permanently attached to the stove door. Gotta check it out.*

He bounded up the steps into the barracks and headed straight for the stove. Stopping in front of it, he snapped his right fingers, pulling his hand into his chest. "Drat it!" He gritted his teeth and whirled around face to face with Gino.

"Gino," he said in alarm. "Didn't you go to the mess hall?"

"I'm not hungry, sir." Gino turned his face away from Andy as he spoke. He locked his hands together.

"Gino. Are you trying to tell me something? What do you know?" Andy caught Gino's shoulder, as he attempted to move away.

"N…n…no. I don't know nothing. Please. Leave me alone." His eyes transfixed with fright.

"Lieutenant. You need to talk to me. Now!" Andy moved into Gino's breathing space.

"Sir. I don't know nothing." His facial muscles twitched nervously. He turned and rushed out of the building. Had he been a larger man, he would have knocked Bulldog over when the two collided at the entrance.

"Andy. What's going on?" Bulldog rushed over to the stove where Andy stood.

"I thought I had a grasp on something to help Brad." He clinched his fists in an abrupt shake.

"What did that have to do with the iron lifter?" By then he was in Andy's face.

"I can't discuss it now. Where's Jack?"

"He's still in the mess hall. Why?"

"I haven't interviewed him yet. Think I'll go over there." Andy walked past Bulldog and headed for the mess hall. He saw his shadow crisp and clear from an early warm sun.

Lt. Jack Newton stepped out of the mess hall as Andy arrived.

"Lt. Newton, let's go to the library. I need to ask you a few questions." He caught Jack firmly by the arm and led him to the library.

"Why me?" Jack slowed his pace, resisting Andy's force.

"I need answers." Andy bit his lower lip while he held a firm grip on Jack.

# Chapter Thirty

"Betty Jane, help me remove all this clutter from the parlor. Today's my quilting party. And when you get home from music lessons, we could use your nimble fingers."

"Maybe I'll have time to help you set up the loom before I leave." Betty Jane wore her pink poodle shirt, white bobby socks, and black and white saddle shoes. "Do you think this angora sweater is too tight, Mom?" She didn't wait for her mother to respond. "It was really nice of Mrs. Martin to pass it down to me, though it is a little snug."

"You look adorable, honey. The pink matches your skirt perfectly."

"You know, Mom, I need some new shoes—now. Water is already seeping through."

Jane picked up her knitting she'd been working on the night before and strode over to her daughter placing an arm around her waist. "I know sweetheart. But we'll have to wait until Andy's next check comes in. Since Dad's stroke, he hasn't been able to do as much work. I'm grateful that the Martin's have helped us as much as they could. You do understand, don't you?"

Betty Jane hugged her mom, careful to dodge the knitting needles sticking out of her apron, "You know I do. Mr. Brown said I could work a couple of hours at the soda fountain after school and before my music lessons to help out. Would that be okay?"

"You know how your dad feels about his women working outside the home…"

The kitchen door opened and John Walters entered. "What's that I hear about working?"

"Oh, John. Betty Jane wants to work a couple of hours at Brown's Drug Store soda fountain. She wants to buy a pair of shoes."

"Now Jane, you know how I feel about that."

Betty Jane rushed up to him with a hug. "Daddy. This would mean so much to me. Please?"

"Baby. You know I'd give you the moon if I could." His voice grew rough. "No child in my house will have an outside job while going to school."

"But Daddy…"

"There'll be no more discussion, ya hear?" He didn't wait for an answer before leaving the room.

Betty Jane scampered from the kitchen.

Jane stared after her daughter knowing the hurt she felt. She feared John was beginning to treat his daughter as he did Andy—especially since she found some independence. Jane stormed after John following him into the bedroom. She placed her hand around her throat as if to halt the redness creeping up.

"Now John Walters, here you go again. You stubborn 'ole fool! What is wrong with you? Your daughter wants to help financially and you can't bend an inch because of your pride. What kind of pride is it when she has to wear shoes with holes in them. Huh? Tell me!"

"What do you mean? Holes in her shoes."

She got his attention that time. "Yes, holes in her shoes! Baby needs a pair of shoes and this baby wants to earn the money to buy them. I can make her clothes but I can't make her shoes."

"Calm down, little lady. I didn't know about the shoes." He sat on the bed, head bent down shaking it back and forth. "I don't know what we're going to do. I'm still not up to my old self. Don't have my left arm strength back yet."

"Then let her work at the soda fountain for a spell. She can handle it and she'll love contributing to the family."

"I'll think about it." He laid back on the bed hands clasped behind his head.

Jane leaned over and kissed him gently on his cheek. "Thank you. That's more like the man I love." She left the room to prepare for the quilting party.

Later John meandered into the parlor where he helped assemble the quilting loom. Betty Jane joined them.

Giggling, Jane said, "My, my, this looks like a four post bed big enough for six families if only it had a mattress." She spread out the partially finished quilt as John and Betty Ann each caught a side of the frame, slipped the quilt edges between wooden blocks using washers, wing nuts, and bolts to stretch and tighten the quilt around the frame.

"Come in, Sarah and you too, Suzie and Emily." Jane enjoyed Sarah's contagious laugh; no matter how serious the discussion, she made everyone smile. It was not a loud laugh, but a lady-like laugh that seemed strange coming from a tiny wisp of a woman. Suzie, the youngest, fit the perfect tomboy image—mischievous, rambunctious, and an absolute angel when trouble happened. Emily sweet and calm. Jane looked forward to Sarah's girls harmonizing beautiful songs under the quilt.

"Hello. Are we late? Oh, I hope not." Madge, behind Sarah and the girls, rushed up the steps with six-year-old Adrian—her curly hair framed a perfectly round little face—a carbon copy of her mother.

Jane had closed the door when a few minutes later Peggy and little Nancy burst inside. "It's beginning to rain. How dreadful. What will the children do today?"

"Now don't you fret over a little rain. We'll have plenty for them to do. May I take your coats? How's your husband, Peggy?"

"I haven't heard from him in a while. Ever since the 30th division of the National Guard was called up, I've scarcely heard a word from Thomas. I miss him and need his help around the farm."

"Peggy, we understand how badly the military needs officers to train our young sons. Your husband is a Major, isn't he?" Jane put her arms around Peggy's shoulder.

Before Peggy could answer, Doris arrived with eight-year-old Elizabeth. "Well, hey, Doris. Y'all arrived at the same time. Come in out of the rain." She stood back as stocky Doris slid past. Elizabeth mirrored her mother's chubbiness. Jane patted Doris on the back. Noise from the walkway captured Jane's attention.

"Hey, Barbara and Rachel. Come in. Oh, here comes Millie. Good. Everyone's here. We can get an early start. Rachel, we're glad to have you today. Y'all get taller every time I see you. Your mother needs to set an encyclopedia on your head to keep you from growing so tall. There's dolls, crayons, scissors and boxes under the quilt to play with."

Jane held the door, "Why, Millie. How are you?" She helped her up the steps. "You never age a bit. I hope I look as good as you do if I ever reach your age—what is it? Ah…76?

"You always were the kindest of the lot. You can add a lot of years to that and you know it. I'm doing well, thank you." Millie clung to Jane's arm. She was the only great-grandmother in the group and had the sharpest tongue. A gold comb stuck out of the gray hair bun pulled tight from her face.

Jane watched the ladies take the usual seats around the huge wooden frame that filled the living room. Sections of scrap fabric had already been sewn together and laid over cotton batting which was basted and held secure on solid bottom fabric.

"Since our last meeting," Millie said, "I'd forgotten, which I do regularly now-a-days, the beautiful navy blue fabric on the bottom. Where on earth did you get this fabric and during war time?"

As in every session Jane held up her finger to pray. "Children, pray with us. Dear Heavenly Father, please guide our fingers with every stitch as we honor you for your greatness and the wonderful creation of our world and life for which to live on this earth. Help us to care for this land and the freedoms you have bestowed upon us and which you placed in our care to protect and honor and to use in your greatness and teachings. With every stitch, let each one honor the dead, the injured, and the living—our men and boys—as we create this master piece. We pray for our President that he might lead us into a safe world and the freedom we all cherish. May we bless each of the children with us today, their mothers and fathers whether here or away. Bless them and keep them safe in your arms. Amen.'

"Amen" All the women replied.

"Now, let's do something different today. See this thing in my hand? It's a buckeye—traditionally known as a good-luck piece. I gave one to Andy before he left for basic. I'm going to pass one around and I want each of you to rub it several times." Jane heard the oh's and ah's from doubters. "I know, you think I've lost my marbles, right?"

"Not yet, but you're getting close," teased Madge. "By the way, answer Millie's question. Where did you get that beautiful navy blue fabric for the quilt backing?"

"I bought it years ago and found it in the bottom of my hope chest before we started the quilt. Couldn't find this quality of material today. The military needs it all for uniforms, underwear, etc."

"Okay. But what about the buckeye? I'm curious," Madge continued to tout Jane.

"Yes. After the buckeye has made the rounds at least two times, been rubbed by all participants, the next time you receive the buckeye, share your biggest worry. Once you know that we are praying for you, trust that He will take care of our boys and answer our prayers." She rubbed the buckeye with each hand and passed it to the first person on her left—Madge.

It traveled around the quilting form two times and ended up with Madge once again. She began. "None of us live in the 'got rocks' (wealthy) section of Fayetteville. We're mostly sharecropper wives or children of sharecroppers. Understand I'm not complaining—I'm grateful for everything God has provided for my family and me. Our son, Benny, is being sent overseas next month and I'm scared to death—frightened beyond reason. I know he wants to do his part and Joe wants him to do the same. But not me. Is that so bad? Am I unpatriotic when I don't want to sacrifice my first-born? He's going regardless of what I want, but I can't bear it." She rubbed the buckeye unconsciously.

Silence prevailed—even underneath the quilt. The children did not move. Jane realized it must be because they understood Madge's heartfelt anguish.

"Madge, you are not alone. Never alone. We've all been through this and even if we haven't said it, we've all felt it. We'll all be praying for Benny—rest assured." Jane gazed at the other women and each nodded their heads.

Madge passed the buckeye to Peggy who repeated her worry about her husband Thomas—not hearing from him—if he's all right or laying up in a hospital. "I've got nobody to mend fences, milk the cows, get the hay up. I'm slap worn out. If it weren't for the quilting party, I'd be home crying my eyes out." She sucked air and pointed under the quilt mouthing 'Nancy'.

"My twelve-year-old twins, James and Robert, can come over every day after school and help for a couple hours each day. Bill can double up on their chores. We'll help as long as you need us." Sarah reached over and hugged Peggy.

Teary-eyed, Peggy said, "God bless you!"

Sarah's daughter, Suzie, crawled from under the quilt and handed Peggy a large silver ball. "I been collecting gum wrappers but think you need it more than me."

"Suzie, you don't need to do this. It took a lot of time to make a ball of tinfoil this big. Besides you need to turn this in as soon as you can." Peggy wrapped her arms around her and kissed her forehead. "You are so sweet."

"You can go play now, Suzie. Thank you." Sarah helped her back under the tomb like quilt.

"I can't believe how quiet the children are today. Seen and not heard? Hummmm." Jane walked into the kitchen and came back with a tray of cookies and milk. *This'll wake them up, or do we want that?* She giggled to herself.

Peggy rubbed the buckeye, kissed it, and passed it on to Sarah.

"I don't need this to remind me to pray, but it will remind me that I'm not the only one with troublesome worries and I will pray for of each of you. My boys are not old enough to go to war and my husband is 4F. Good or bad, he is here and we'll gladly help any of you that needs an extra boot up. Bill tried to join up but was turned down because he has one leg shorter than the other due to polio. That's why he works for the railroad—whatever they need him to do.

"Seriously, I feel blessed and if we can help in any way, we'll be happy to." Sarah held the buckeye up, "I want one of these." She passed it on to Doris.

"I'm happy for you, Sarah. May God always bless you and your family. Our family is not at a happy place. Our son has been missing in action for four months. We think he is in one of the bad Army POW camps in Germany. Not being an officer, we are frightened for him. Linda, Tommy's wife, is beside herself. With a one-year-old and another on the way, our hands are full taking care of her. The worry has caused numerous trips to the hospital. If that baby arrives on time, there will be only one year and thirteen days between the two babies. We roll bandages for the Red Cross on her better days. My Edward is out at the Boeing plant in Seattle attaching metal sheets of the outer covering to the fuselage sections for new B-17Gs (Flying Fortress) bombers. He's out there surrounded by Rosie the Riveters and a few 4F men. Once in a while he'll catch a military plane back to Fort Bragg. If it wasn't for his diabetes, he'd be off fighting."

"I don't know who is the luckiest, Rosie the Riveter or Edward. Surrounded with all those women. Wow!" Madge chuckled as she turned to Sarah.

"Madge, you hush up. You don't know my Edward."

"I was just teasing, Sarah. No need to jump on me. I shouldn't have said that. I'm sorry."

"I'm just too edgy now about everything…"

Jane interrupted, "It's all right girls, now let's continue."

After rubbing the buckeye a few more times, she passed it on to Barbara. "Lawsey me, I wanna cry listening to y'all. I got me own troubles, but when I hear yours, I got none. My Henry and me lost our son during Pearl Harbor. He was on the USS Tennessee—he was a gunner. I want a buckeye too. Every time I think of it, I'll pray for each of you and ask God to bless all of you. Now that it's made the rounds, guess you're last, Jane."

"Yes, you all shall leave with a buckeye. Keep it in your pocket at all times and rub it often to remind you of all our boys fighting around the world and pray for them and their families back home. We received a letter from the Adjutant General that Andy is believed to be a POW and probably in Stalag Luft I which is a POW camp for officers. Better treatment—so they say.

Jane continued, "Have you ever seen so many women pitch in and do the jobs of their men? Sewing parachutes, uniforms, riveting, running trains, you name it—they're doing it. What with baking for the Fayetteville Tavern and taking care of John, I've no time for the rest. So, let's get down to this fun part—quilting!"

A little later, beautiful singing filtered up through the quilt. Suzie and Emily were harmonizing as they always did, only more meaningful than ever, "The Old Rugged Cross."

Jane scanned the quilting frame. Not a dry eye.

Through blurry eyes, Jane noticed John standing near the kitchen door listening. He pulled out his handkerchief.

# Chapter Thirty-one

In the library, Andy stopped pacing and motioned Jack to take a seat at the rectangular wooden table. He propped his foot on the bench opposite Jack. Sparse bookshelves lined the walls.

"Did you see anything unusual the night Simon was murdered?"

"No. I slept through the night."

"No strange sounds or any movements?"

"I said I slept through the night." Indignation resounded in Jack's words and his face flushed.

"Who do you think killed Simon?" Andy, now sitting opposite Jack, probed him vigorously.

"That bloke, Lt. Graham. I say, he'd be the one!"

Andy suspected hostility from Jack and kept pumping him to keep the interrogation going for an hour until Jack jumped up and stormed toward the door shouting, "You've lost your bloody marbles, old chap! Think you're a clever dick, eh?"

Jack burst out the door, and Andy stretched his feet on the length of the bench. A satisfactory smile crossed his face. A few minutes later, he gathered his papers and was about to leave the library when the drone of bombers high above echoed down to earth. Air-raid sirens sang in harmony, announcing their arrival.

POWs poured from the barracks, filling the yards shouting and waving frantically. Guards rushed into the area, shouting, "Verboten, (forbidden) go back in the barracks." They used the butts of their rifles freely, encouraging the men to move inside, but the minute the guards went after others, the men rushed outside again. Angry guards shot their guns in the air to drive the men inside.

Andy watched from the library door. A new American P-51 fighter plane was in hot pursuit of a German FW 190 fighter. The two planes raced across the sky—the P-51 streaming shots at the fighter—missed. A Bf 109F joined the foray, chased the P-51, and pumped a 20mm cannon toward it. The P-51 abruptly turned upward, and the 20mm cannon hit the first German fighter. It exploded over the camp.

The P-51 looped over, came in behind the second fighter, and extinguished it with the first round of shots. A large piece of flaming metal fell over Stalag Luft I. The POWs filled the yards. Cheers echoed throughout the prison while men scampered for shelter.

Andy watched in horror as the ball of fire crashed into the interrogation building—where Simon's body rested. He made a beeline straight toward the building but realized the gates were locked. He shouted at the guards to unlock the gate. No response. He shook the gates. All he could do was watch the flames shoot up the back of the building.

Guards formed a human chain with buckets of water and eventually doused the flames. Heinrich rushed over to the gate and let Andy pass through.

He dashed into the building. Smoke had barely filtered into the room. A large wooden box lay before him; he raised the lid. Satisfied, he lowered the top.

"It wouldn't hurt to sprinkle Benzin (gasoline) on the building, Captain." Commandant Scherer stood behind Andy. "Are you ready for your trial Saturday?"

"There may not be a trial, sir."

"What do you say?"

"There may not be a trial."

"How so?"

"You'll see before long."

"Ah hah."

"I think I know who murdered Simon."

"Who?"

"Ja…you'll know soon enough." Andy slipped on his knit cap and left the building. The smell of wet ashes irritated his nose.

Bulldog was waiting on the other side of the gate. "Was the body all right?" He stepped back as Andy passed through the gate.

"Yeah. Very little smoke." He continued on to the barracks, and Bulldog tagged along.

"You must have talked with Jack. He looked like one pissed-off Brit with a cow chip on his shoulder."

"Keep an eye on him, Bulldog. Can't discuss it now. You seen Gino? I need to talk with him."

"Think he went back to the barracks after the air battle."

"Thanks." They had arrived in front of the barracks.

"There he is, Andy. Look." Bulldog pointed beyond the left of the entrance. "He's leaning against the barracks."

Gino inhaled a drag from his cigarette.

"Bulldog, I think he knows something but is afraid to talk. I'll be in shortly."

Gino tilted his head back and blew "Os" as cigarette smoke curled high above.

"Lieutenant." Andy called.

Gino spun around like a startled deer, his face etched in fear, his body rigid. He pitched his cigarette and stomped it. "Si, sir." He reverted momentarily to his native Italian.

"You know something, don't you?"

"Addio" (Good-bye). He brushed past Andy and dashed into the barracks attempting to postpone further discussion.

"Gino. You're gonna have to talk to me sooner or later," Andy shouted after him. Gino never looked back.

Andy decided to go back to the library where he could concentrate. On the way, he passed a group playing baseball.

"Hey, Andy. How 'bout joining us? We need a pitcher," Tex called. He crouched down to catch another pitch and lunged for a wild ball.

"Sorry fellas. Catch ya later."

In the library, he spread his papers over the rectangular table and opened a "whodunit" book" by Agatha Christie, *The Body in the Library*, published in 1942. Flipping through the pages looking for motives, he picked up his pencil to make a list of possible motives:

Prejudice
Loyalty (family, crew)
Competition
Blackmail
Disclosure
Cover-up

He then wrote a list of possible suspects. Only two names. The first name that surfaced was Gino. But why, he wondered?

Gino
Brad

Obviously something about the actions of the slicked-back, dark-haired half-Italian appeared suspicious. Andy indulged himself, going over every recent visual of Gino—something spooking him— jumpy with darting eyes. Visible goose bumps on his arms in warm weather when Andy approached him.

*This guy's frightened. He knows something. No doubt about it. But how do I get it out of him?*

He searched back over his list of motives.

Prejudice: Brad.
Loyalty, family or crew.
Simon - a Jew—no relatives.
Simon - gets along well with fellow officers.
Gino - avoids Jack lately.
Gino – avoids Brad recently.
    Competition: Not obvious.
    Blackmail: By whom?
    Disclosure: Blackmail connection? Possible.
    Cover-up: Why and what?

Andy stayed in the library until just before supper, going over the list, probing for answers. POWs came and went, picking up books, returning books, and some actually sat near him in search of a quiet place to read.

He left the library with a heavy air of urgency. He knew his days were running out, and he needed to move swiftly.

The next day after the usual lineup and countdown, the POWs broke for the mess hall. All but Gino.

Late summer storms had rolled through the camp during the night saturating the sand, and each footstep was like squeezing water from a dishrag. Even the wood on the buildings had a wet smell. Mourning Doves sang hollow mournful coah-coos.

Andy watched Gino slip back into the barracks. He followed him into the center hall between the two rooms, careful not to create noise. He stood back and peeked from behind the partially open door, studying Gino's movements.

Gino climbed over to the opposite side of Jack's bunk to the section that extended beyond the brick behind the heat stove. Some of the bricks protruded, while others were almost recessed. He tested each brick pulling on them. So far none moved. Even from the distance, Andy could see Gino's hands trembling. He quickly slipped back as Gino shot a glance toward the door.

Gino continued his probe until an adjacent board popped out as he loosened a brick next to it.

Andy guessed from a distance that the board was approximately four inches wide and twelve inches long. He decided to make an entrance.

"What you got there, Gino?" Andy bounded over to Jack's bunk.

Gino shot upright hitting his head on the bunk above. "What're you doing here?"

"Look, Gino. I know you're hiding something. You've gotta talk to me, fella."

Gino slid down on the bunk, throwing up his hands in resignation. "No Dio (God)."

"Gino. Look at me. English! Do you understand?" Andy caught Gino's shoulders and forced him to look directly at him.

"Si…yes sir."

"Tell me what's going on."

"Can you protect me, sir?" He raised his eyes searching Andy's face.

"Protect? Are you in danger?"

"Once they find out what I know, I will be."

"We'll go to Col. Brawley. He'll get you protection. Talk to me, Gino."

"The night Simon was killed, I heard him get up. His bunk was over mine. He had an urgent call to the latrine and slipped out. He didn't want to use the bucket. Soon as he sneaked out through the hole in the disconnected lavatory, Jack followed him. After about twenty minutes, Jack returned. He fumbled around on the wall of his bunk until something moved. I heard a clunk and then he shoved something back. I couldn't see what he actually did.

"I waited for Simon to come back, but eventually I fell asleep. Jack didn't know Simon and I were amici (friends). We talked. Simon became friends with one of the guards, Friedrich Hockenheim. He thought that by making friends of the guards, they would be unlikely to discover his Jewish background."

"Simon told you that?"

"Si. Remember how many times the guards caught us tunneling while attempting to escape? And how the colonel's radio disappeared after he got another radio put together? Simon discovered that Friedrich was Jack's cousin. Jack was ratting on the POWs."

"Are you sure about that?" Andy listened in amazement as Gino spilled out everything.

"Si, Captain. Jack found out that Simon made this discovery and feared he would blab to save his own skin. So, Jack threatened to expose Simon to the commandant—that he was a Jew.

"Jack used Simon to get him food supplies and necessities that the other POWs couldn't get. Simon worked in the Red Cross distribution area, and he bribed the guards with cigarettes and stuff to look the other way when he separated the supplies. He loaded Jack with the good canned foods and medicines. Notice Jack has not lost weight like the rest of us."

"But he eats with the other POWs, especially your group."

"Does he actually eat or does he play with his food?"

"I never really noticed."

"Jack is the Germans' main informer. He exposes every attempt the POWs make to escape. Simon became more difficult for Jack to control. He told me. He worried that Jack would turn him in, no matter what. He knew that Jack could have a guard kill him simply by telling them he was a Jew. But Jack was concerned that Simon would spill the beans and implicate him as a camp spy. He knew if the POWs found out, he would be doomed."

"It's like he planned this."

"Si, when Simon got up, I heard Jack remove something behind his bunk and then follow him. The moon was so bright that night it lit the room even through the tiniest cracks in the shutters. I could see he carried something in his hand." Gino's body shuddered as if a horrible thought had run through his mind.

Andy turned when he heard Bulldog come through the door.

"Bulldog, get Col. Brawley. Ask him to summon the commandant." He turned back to Gino, "Don't you move. We'll wait until the colonel gets here."

Andy tried to digest everything Gino set forth. He pulled a note pad from his pants pocket and retrieved his pencil from his shirt pocket. Next, he listed the timeline of events as explained by Gino.

Within minutes Col. Brawley arrived. Andy quickly briefed him just before the commandant arrived with two guards, Heinrich and Friedrich.

The colonel informed the commandant who ordered his guard, Heinrich, to search the wall area.

"Up." Heinrich signaled Gino to get off the bunk. Heinrich knelt on the bunk, leaned over to the wall, and reached his hand down the cavity. The first thing brought up resembled a black metal piece of iron. It had a curve near the end and a V-shaped hook similar to a crowbar at the end of the iron.

The commandant reached for the iron.

Andy stepped in front of the commandant. "Sir, I must warn you. It is possible this is the murder weapon. The iron must be checked for hair and blood. I need it for evidence."

Commandant Scherer looked at Andy and then Col. Brawley. "Ja, I understand. This bunk belongs to…"

"Me, sir. This is my bunk. What's going on here?" Lt. Jack Newton had entered the room, his face pale for a warm day.

Without hesitation, Andy began his questioning. "Lt. Newton, where did you get this iron?"

Jack walked over to his bunk and eyed the iron. "That's not mine. We don't need one of those for our stove."

Andy glanced at the colonel. "Col. Brawley, I need to talk with the mess hall workers. Right away!"

"I suggest you hustle over before they close the mess hall, Captain. I'll stay here. Perhaps the commandant would be good enough to go with you." The colonel flashed a gleeful grin at the commandant and twisted his mustache on one side.

"Lead the way, Commandant Scherer." Andy swung his arm wide as if showing him the way.

"Friedrich Hockenheim, come!" Commandant Scherer ordered.

"No!" Andy blocked Friedrich's movement. "Bitte. I have my reasons. How about Heinrich?"

Puzzled, the commandant hooked his hands behind his back, hesitated for several minutes, but agreed to Andy's request. "Jawohl. Come."

Andy and Heinrich fell into place behind the commandant. "Take care of that iron, Col. Brawley, sir," Andy requested just before leaving the barracks.

A short time later, they entered the mess hall, and made their way to the cooking area where cleanup was in progress.

"Sir," Andy said, "Can you or Heinrich interpret for me? I want to speak with the cook that asked for the 'iron lift' yesterday."

Heinrich requested the cook to step forward.

"Ja," he said, coughing nervously.

"Können Sie bitte langsam sprechen? (Will you speak slowly, please?) English?" Andy struggled with his German but evidently the cook understood.

"Ja." He held up his hand, spread his forefinger and thumb a half-inch apart indicating a little English.

"Yesterday you were looking for the iron lid lifter, right?"

"Ja."

"Did you find it?"

"Nein. Worker let someone use it days ago. Not come back. Had to use front loader."

"Who loaned it out?"

"Rudy."

"Is he here?"

"Ja." The cook pointed to a worker and motioned him to come over.

"English?" Andy asked.

"Nein." The worker shoved his hands in his pockets and twisted from side to side.

"Who picked up the iron lift and when?" Andy turned to Heinrich to ask the question. Heinrich faced the worker and repeated it in German.

"The British officer," he replied in German. "Friedrich Hockenheim's family."

Commandant Scherer moved in closer and asked in German for the worker to repeat his statement.

"The British officer. Friedrich Hockenheim's family.

"Friedrich's family? Nein, nein," the Commandant replied.

"Ja, ja," the worker said emphatically nodding his head up and down.

Andy said, "Lt. Jack Newton?"

"Ja," the worker answered.

Andy looked at the commandant and Heinrich, "Shall we go?" He walked closer to the cook and worker, "Danke schön! Auf Wiedersehen!" Andy stopped long enough to write their names in his note pad: Hamlin Wagner and Rudy Vogel.

"Commandant Scherer, we need to talk with Col. Brawley." Andy led the way from the building.

"Ja." The commandant moved ahead of Andy, gesturing with a follow-me motion. His shiny black boots slapped the ground with each step, demanding attention. His breath expelled in loud "harrumphs." "Heinrich, guard Lt. Newton."

Andy reached the barracks and opened the door to his section. "Col. Brawley, we need to see you. Bulldog, fetch Lt. Chandler."

The three men went straight to the commandant's office, and a few minutes later, Lt. Chandler, the temporary doctor, arrived. The four men sat down.

Andy traced his entire findings from the murder back to motive; Lt. Chandler issued a report on the cause of death of Lt. Simon; the location of the murder weapon (the iron lifter) found hidden in the wall behind Lt. Newton's bunk; witnesses stating the lieutenant borrowed the iron lifter from the mess hall kitchen before the murder and never returned it.

"Number one – Lt. Newton was an informant."

"Number two – Lt. Newton acquired Red Cross supplies that should have gone to all the men."

"Number three – Lt. Newton was blackmailing Simon, threatening to tell he was a Jew."

"Number four – Lt. Newton is Friedrich Hockenheim's cousin."

"Lt. Newton planted the twine under Lt. Graham's jacket. Everyone knew he hated Simon. A perfect motive for murder—or so Lt. Newton thought."

Andy's tone was raspy as he detailed each item. He had everyone's attention. His voice cleared and revealed a level of confidence unknown to him. He was simple but definite. On his game.

Commandant Scherer and Col. Brawley stood spellbound as Andy handed them papers documenting the information he set forth.

Col. Brawley rose from his seat, "Well done, Captain. This apparently has cleared Lt. Graham. How can we be sure that Lt. Newton committed the murder?"

"Lt. Newton's scam was crumbling beneath him. He borrowed the iron lid lifter; we found it hidden behind his bunk; Gino saw him carry something long in his hand when the lieutenant followed Simon. Had I not overheard the cook yelling for the iron lid lifter yesterday, I could not have fathomed the type of weapon used. No one would have known to question the cook." Andy paused between each fact, allowing his audience to digest his words. He sat rigid in a wooden chair; his eyes bounced from one man to the other like watching a tennis game.

"Captain," the commandant said, "Lt. Graham shall be released immediately, and Lt. Newton will be held for the murder of Lt. Simon. Will you defend Lt. Newton?"

"No, no. No! I would be too prejudiced and not a proper defender, Commandant." Andy wiped his brow, hopeful of the commandant's acceptance of his reply.

"Too bad for the lieutenant. Very well, you may go. 'Scoot' is that how they say it?"

"You got it, Commandant." Col. Brawley turned to leave with Andy—Lt. Chandler close on their heels.

Andy stopped abruptly when an afterthought popped in his head. "Oh, Commandant. I want to deliver the message to Lt. Graham."

"Ja. The guard will escort you." The commandant puffed out his chest with self-importance.

Andy smiled. Once outside the building he jumped up and kicked his heels together sparking a feeling of being airborne. "Whooooeeeee!"

"Seems I've heard that sound before, Captain." The colonel's sunken jowls bulged slightly when he laughed at Andy.

"You're kidding, sir. Did you really hear me holler when you said you were sending me to pilot training school? Did you?"

"'Deed I did, son. Was I wrong?" He placed his arm affectionately around Andy's shoulder.

Andy chuckled and wrapped his arm under the colonel's arm. "You know me pretty well, sir." Soon he broke away and rushed over to Brad's cell. A guard stood at the entrance.

"Here to see Lt. Graham."

The guard unlocked the outer door, and led Andy to the cell, unlocking the door. Andy shuffled from one foot to the other, face beaming. He was ready to go, ready to free Brad.

The cell door opened, and Andy spilled in. Brad jumped up from the bunk.

"What's happening?"

Andy rushed over and hugged him.

Brad didn't return the hug. "What!"

"Buck up, ole buddy, you're free!"

"You're joshing me."

"No. I'm serious." Andy caught Brad by the shoulders and shook him. "Fella, you're free. Soon as they pick up Jack, they'll move you out."

Brad knocked Andy's arms from his shoulders and hugged him. "I don't believe this. I thought I'd never see daylight again."

Andy pushed back and looked into Brad's eyes. "Where's your trust?"

"Andy, I don't know what to say. I've been such an idiot."

Brad glanced away, and Andy could have sworn he saw moisture in Brad's eyes.

Heinrich bounded through the main door with Lt. Jack Newton in tow. He hesitated at Brad's open cell door. Jack spat at them before Heinrich moved him beyond their sight.

Andy heard a cell door shut and lock. Footsteps returned to Brad's cell, and Heinrich crossed the threshold. He caught Brad's arm and said in German, "Free to go, Lt. Graham."

Brad, just stood there cracking his knuckles like he couldn't believe it. "What'd he say?" Brad asked. The whites of his eyes showed.

Heinrich displayed a quirky smile and repeated in broken English, "Free to go."

Brad rushed from the cell and darted through the main entrance. He jumped down the steps, stretched his arms out, and twisted around in circles.

Andy propped on the door watching him, and a sense of joy washed over him. He knew he'd done good. He'd helped a friend. Yes, his friend. Andy felt a certain satisfaction of payback for causing Brad's capture in the first place. Still tortured by the death of Marta and her baby, his defense of Brad somewhat eased his pain. But the guilt, he knew, would never leave him—never. He slipped his right hand into his pocket, rubbed the buckeye.

He wondered how he could live with the scars that would remain with him forever. *How will it affect my life with Rose? With our children after we marry? How do I face my dad? I've surely let him down. Or will he understand? What would he have done?*

# Chapter Thirty-two

After Brad's release, the two men made a pact. Andy locked eyes with Brad's. "You'll follow all the camp rules until liberation, right?"

"Yes sir!" Brad replied with a salute and a click of his heels.

Brad continued to honor the agreement with Andy, and so far, had weathered scorn and ridicule from other POWs.

At first Bulldog resumed his taunting of Brad until one day Bulldog caught sight of Andy glaring at him.

Andy felt the veins in his neck pulse, and heat rose to his face. "Back off, Bulldog!"

"Yes sir!" Bulldog spun around and walked away.

Col. Brawley suggested a reassignment of the British officers to a different barracks within the same compound. But Andy had earlier captured the respect of the remaining four British men, Randy, Art, Roy, and Gino, and the last officers assigned to their room.

Earlier, the commandant moved all Jewish POWs into barracks next to the ammunition storage area. Andy believed that they segregated them and chose that particular building so if the American P-51s attacked close to the POW camp and struck the ammunitions dump, it would blow up the Jews as well. The Germans desperately wanted to be rid of the Jewish population in the camp. A couple of Jews disappeared each month.

October rolled in unlike the fall festival of colors in Andy's hometown. No sugar maple trees to turn a brilliant red against the green, long needle pines. No leaves to fall in the POW camp. Sand. Lots of sand.

Football was the game, and Andy kept his throwing arm in good shape and regularly performed strenuous exercises to stay fit.

Late in the afternoon following a rough football game, Andy jogged to the library and spread books across one end of a table, honing in on his law study. He was so engrossed in his work, he didn't hear Bulldog rush in until he flopped two letters on the table in front of Andy.

"What's this?" Andy asked looking up at Bulldog instead of the envelopes.

"Letters, sir!" Bulldog spread the two letters patting each.

Andy reeled with intoxication at the thought of words from Rose and home. He picked up the letters and kissed each, then looked up at Bulldog, "You get mail?"

"Naw. Looks like it's finally beginning to come through. Jeanie, the Red Cross lady, said sometimes it takes four to nine months to begin receiving mail. Well, it's been at least nine months. I'll get some soon. Go ahead and read yours. I'm outta here."

"Thanks, Bulldog. Your turn next." Andy watched him leave with no giddy-up in his step. He understood just how Bulldog felt— word from home was like a breath of fresh air.

Andy's hands shook as he opened the letter from Rose first. It was postmarked April. Seven months ago.

*Dear Andy,*
*It's only April, and I don't know if you are dead or alive. Something inside keeps telling me you are alive, and*

*I pray every day that you'll come back to me. I long to feel your arms around me and sink into your warm embrace. The times we spent together in England—those last few weeks—your burning eyes searching deep into my soul. I miss you terribly and want you with me. Never fear, my darling, I'll be waiting for your return. Forever if I must.*

*A little distraction came along in January—someone I fell deeply in love with. Don't worry, my love. Not as much as I love you. Remember the little two-year-old? I don't think I told you much about her. I was so upset.*

*All the nurses fell in love with her—she's a beautiful little angel. She has light brown curly hair and large brown eyes, almost black.*

*Oh, Andy, you'd fall in love with her too. To make a long story short, she grew extremely attached to me as well, but I knew I had to locate her parents. So I found the soldier that brought her in, and he drove me to the area.*

*Her name is Lizzy, short for Elizabeth, the name of her mother's sister. Lizzy's parents were killed in a bombing. Her Aunt Elizabeth and her baby are the only family she has left. They live in one of only a couple of houses spared from bombs. No running water. Intolerable living conditions. No place for a baby or young child.*

*Lt. Col. Lawing warned me that I was becoming too fond of Lizzy. He told me I shouldn't visit her once she went to live with Elizabeth. I didn't listen. I knew better but couldn't stay away. It's like she was a part of me, and there was no way I could abandon her. Years ago I dreamt of a child—like Lizzy. Just like I dreamt of you, only I didn't realize I already knew you.*

*It's as if I have no resistance when it comes to Lizzy or you. Every week I take food and supplies to Elizabeth. Lt. Col. Lawing is truly upset with me, but I can't let them starve. I could never forgive myself. Even if I have to stay here forever, I'll take care of them.*

*If you get this letter, please know that I love you and miss you. Hurry back, Andy. You've just got to be all right. I want you back in my life.*

> *All my love,*
> *Rose*

Andy read the letter over three times before he folded it and shoved it back into the envelope. He held the letter to his chest for several minutes as if inhaling the love within. After a bit, he placed the letter on the table and picked up the other one, slowly ripping it open as if savoring the moment. This one postmarked May.

*Dear Andy,*

*You can't imagine the relief and joy in our hearts that you are alive. We received a postcard from someone in Connecticut with your message. We love you, son and can't wait for you to come home.*

*Dad has been busy planting and tending the new tobacco. He seems extremely tired lately, but I think he's just been so worried about you. Thanks to God, you made it safely to the ground. Did the entire crew bail out? Are they all right? Were they captured as well?*

*So many questions. There'll be plenty of time for those when you get home. Maybe the Red Cross will have more news soon.*

*How are they treating you? We hope and pray they take care of you boys.*

*Betty Jane is working hard on her music. Her voice is like an angel. Can't wait for you to get home and hear her sing.*

*This is my third letter since we received word that you were a POW in Germany. The first two came back. We'll try to send a package in a day or two and hope it gets to you.*

*We hope and pray you'll be home soon.*

> *We love you, son,*
> *Mom*

Andy reread this letter as well. His throat constricted, and his body racked with convulsive grief. He placed his arms on the table and lowered his head. Minutes passed when he subconsciously sensed someone's eyes resting on him. He raised his head and turned to see Pops smiling at him.

He placed his hand on Andy's shoulder. "It's all right, Andy. It's good to let it go."

"I didn't hear you come in." Andy slipped the letters into his pants pocket and closed the books on the table. Then slid his chair back and returned the books to their proper slots on the shelves.

"I came in and saw you engrossed in something. Decided it best not to bother you." Pops picked up the last book on the table and carried it over to Andy.

"I was reading my first mail in nine months."

"Two days ago I got a letter from my wife. I know how you feel."

"Thanks, Pops." Andy glanced past Pops through a window at one of the barracks silhouetted against the dove gray edge of the evening. "I'll see you later."

He left the library and returned to his barracks. Brad, Tex, Bulldog, and Johnny sat around the table engaged in a game of Hearts. They barely glanced his way. He decided to go straight to his bunk.

Flat on his back, he pulled out Rose's letter. Flashes of loneliness stabbed at his heart. A cold shiver spread over his body, and he reached down for his blanket. The image of her face appeared on the bottom of the overhead bunk, and he slowly allowed the vision to engulf him as he dropped off to sleep. *She loves me....*

Winter arrived early with a vengeance. Its icy wind cut into the faces of all who ventured outdoors. Andy's hands chafed and his lips cracked so deep a dime could slip into the painful splits.

Andy burst into the barracks. "Hey fellas. Get a load of this. The guards cut the October and November Red Cross packets to two per month. BBC radio reports German trains traveling north were blown up by American bombers."

"Yeah. Remember when we talked 'bout sex and food. Food and sex. Now all we talk 'bout is food." Bulldog rubbed his belly. His crop of dark hair had grown wild and unruly.

"The trains carrying the Red Cross supplies probably weren't marked. Bet the Germans confiscated the salvageable food for their own people," Andy said.

Pops backed up to the stove and said, "Why rush to the mess hall? They've already split the packets between two men."

"We'll need to parcel out the food and make it last as long as possible. It's gonna get worse yet." Andy lowered his head after he spoke.

The walk to the mess hall became less urgent. Deprivation of food kept the POWs weak and orderly, making the guards' jobs easier.

Andy remembered when they first arrived at Stalag Luft I, each received about 1800 calories per day, and then after a few months, it went down to 1200 calories per day. By October, he noticed most men resembled shadows of their original selves with only 800 calories, not enough for a grown man to maintain his weight and health.

"After I get home, I'm gonna have three plates. One piled high of fried chicken, the second one a mound of mashed taters with a valley in the middle filled with gravy, and the third one a stack of hot biscuits. Fellows, that's mighty fine eating." Bulldog smiled and clasped his hands behind his head.

Andy joined in the conversation. "No more black bread made with sawdust. But I bet even the black bread would be welcomed now."

Tex added, "Don't mention black bread. It makes my mouth water. Can't believe I'm saying that. What are we to do with no food? The war's not close to being over much less us being rescued."

Before Andy could answer, Brad jumped in. "What do you think he can do about it? You think he can produce a magic wand and suddenly food appears?"

Not wanting to answer Tex's question, Andy tried something different. "Let's play a game of make believe. Shut your eyes and hold out your hand, palms up." He grabbed a pencil and touched each man's hand. "Pretend your hand is full of food." He creased his forehead and his voice grew serious. "Before you open your eyes, say a prayer and ask God to make it true as soon as possible. Keep praying every day and believe in your heart that he will answer all of our prayers soon."

"How do you know that?" Bulldog was more serious than Andy had ever seen him.

"Look at us. You, Pops, Tex, Brad, and me. We're still alive. We'll get out of here, you'll see."

"Some of us don't think God or anybody gives a damn." Brad sat on the edge of Andy's bunk.

"Yeah, who does care? We're stuck here and must rely on our enemy for food. They don't give a crap. Their bellies are not flat like ours. Bet they haven't missed a meal." Tex rammed his fist into his bunk.

"Settle down, fellas." Andy recognized the anxiety in each man's voice. "We've a while to go but it won't get here any sooner by getting all worked up. Jesus, y'all could start a riot. Listen to y'all. Remember, God first. We are the greatest military in the world. Liberation will come!"

The barracks grew still. Brad went back to his bunk and Andy said his own prayer.

November brought snow followed by more snow every few days. In early December food rations picked up for a while, and the starvation of the POWs slowed significantly. But only for a short time.

A runner from Col. Brawley's barracks barged into the room with news. "The BBC announced the Germans are strategically withdrawing!"

"Yeah boy!" Bulldog jumped up shaking his right fist in the air.

"Hot doggies!" Tex shouted.

"Push 'em back, push 'em back!" Andy joined the men and spun around in jubilation.

Days later, news came of the Germans launching an offense in the Ardennes in Belgium creating ups and downs for Andy and the men. Daily missions flew overhead. POWs raced out of their barracks to wave encouragement until the Germans became so angered they fired directly at the men forcing them inside.

Christmas Eve found Andy on his bunk wrapped in blankets like the other men, striving to keep warm. Bulldog had moved down to Andy's bunk several weeks ago to share body heat—they all doubled up. New POWs poured into the camp; additional men moved into Barracks #2.

The same skimpy food supply, then serving sixteen, was now split between twenty-four POWs.

Andy's entire body had succumbed to the tides of weariness and hopelessness shared by other POWs. His thoughts turned to his family, and their last Christmas together only two years ago—seemed like an eternity. Aunts, uncles, cousins, and his mom, dad, and sister gathered around the Christmas tree singing carols. Betty Jane played the piano and led the singing.

Andy's body shook from freezing temperatures inside as well as out. Vivid pictures raced through his mind as he clung to the memories of Rose and his family while consoling himself beyond his present tortured existence. His paramount survival dominated his thoughts shoving Marta and her baby deep into a crevice in his brain. The calendar went unmarked when glacial cold set in early in December, and movement away from the bunks became less desirable.

The Red Cross managed to get additional packages through for Stalag Luft I, providing them with a nice Christmas dinner. Bulldog attempted to drum up merriment with Christmas carols, but Andy knew the men were not physically or emotionally up to it. There could be only one celebration—the liberation of all POWs.

"Come on fellas! Let's sing!" Bulldog stood up and pushed on with "Joy to the World..." He moved his right hand as if leading a choir.

Andy laughed aloud for the first time in months at the sight of Bulldog: knit cap pulled down over his eyebrows, his left hand clutching a blanket draped around his shoulders. His stature, a shadow of earlier days, emerged strangely while his large head showed no visible neck.

"Now I know where you got that nickname. You resemble a bulldog more and more every day," Andy said.

The edgy men broke into laughter, easing some of the built-up tensions due to cramped quarters and inability to go outdoors except for lineups, mess hall, and latrines. The bitter cold kept the men from blowing off steam by playing sports.

Andy heard a loud commotion in the barracks' hallway followed by Heinrich flinging open their door. Even the guards had displayed grumpiness over the last few months. But not this time. A mile-wide smile spread across Heinrich's face as he carried a box under his arm.

The men ditched their coverings and rushed over. He spit out words that even the worst interpreter could understand. Andy replied behind him, "Merry Christmas."

Heinrich placed the box on the table in front of Andy who shot a surprised glance at Heinrich and then opened the box. "Look fellas! Coals! Coals!" He couldn't believe his own excitement over such a simple gift for an extraordinary time.

For the first night in months, the room was warmer than the outside temperature. Andy considered it a Merry Christmas after all.

February 1945 the following bulletin arrived from Col. Brawley with woeful news:

1. Menu: German Soup (no potatoes) – no bread
2. No lights and water – Lights will now be turned off for the duration. Water will be shut off without warning. Keep an ample supply on hand.
3. Red Cross food will run out this weekend.
4. Any persons desirous of helping to dig a well, report to Group Maintenance officer at 1100 hours today.

5. German authorities have informed us that the coal ration will be cut another 20% effective immediately. They can guarantee no more coal.

6. German Memorandum, Feb. 24: "Any Prisoner of War found outside his barracks or looking out the windows during an air raid will be fired upon without warning."

7. Personnel who received bones from the Mess Hall for purposes of making soup, will return same immediately—for re-issue—they've already been cooked twice.

(This information from http://www.merkki.com)

After reading the note, Andy realized that cutting the power to the barracks would render the colonel's prize possession useless—the radio Johnny put together for him.

Back in the barracks, Andy asked, "Johnny, what can we do about the colonel's radio? We need to move it and get a power supply somehow. Any suggestions?"

"The library is the closest building to German Headquarters. Bet we could bribe Heinrich to run a wire. He always needs cigarettes."

"Go for it, fella. We can hide the radio behind the books. Let's make sure the right people know which books."

"Yes sir, Captain." After confiscating numerous cigarettes, Johnny hurried off to the library.

A few hours later, he returned. "Done, sir. The colonel's all set." Johnny handed Andy a piece of paper with the location written on it.

"Good job, Johnny." Andy left the room to give the colonel the location of the radio.

By the end of the week Andy received another letter from home dated December 10, 1944, two months late.

*Dear Son,*

*You don't know how happy we were to receive your last letter. I assume you never received the packages sent so far. Maybe they'll arrive soon. We mailed a birthday package several months ago. Don't know if you received it.*

*I hate to bring you bad news from home while you're suffering so much yourself. Dad had a stroke while working in the tobacco fields last fall. He spent three weeks in the hospital. While there, he underwent extensive exercises in an effort to regain use of his left arm and leg. His speech returned early on, but the leg and arm were a slow go. I can tell you all of this since he has recovered miraculously.*

*Son, I don't know what we would have done if you didn't send money home. It stopped when they thought you were "killed in action" but picked up again when they discovered you were a POW. We know Mr. Martin would not evict us, but he needed help. Though Dad is in pretty good shape, Ralph brought in young boys to get ready before winter sets in. It helped Dad a lot.*

*Thank goodness Betty Jane started driving in August. Can you believe she's old enough for that? You children grew up much too fast. Her music is going well, and we think she'll get a scholarship for college. Heaven knows we couldn't afford to pay for it. She practices every spare minute and continues to bring home straight A's.*

*Son, I think about the day we drove you to college, your first long time away from home. I didn't want to cry and embarrass you in front of your roommate. It was so hard to hold back the tears. You thought I acted strange, but this was the real reason. Keeping my emotions in check has always been hard for me when it's about my family.*

*Dad and I are so proud of you. I know he was terribly hard with his demands while you were growing up. He was determined that you would not end up like him. We thought that we taught you a bunch, but we've learned so much from you as we watched you grow to the fine young man you are today. The confidence you have in your beliefs, the goals you have set for yourself, and your ambitions make us extremely proud of you.*

*We pray for you every day, Andy, and we want you back home with us. We miss you. Take good care of yourself.*

> *Your loving,*
> *Mom*

Andy wiped his sleeve across his eyes, folded the letter, and returned it to its jacket. He struggled to control the leaking dam.

His birthday had come and gone. So far no packages from home. For two years there was no celebration—though the war had taken its toll and aged him considerably. Andy told Bulldog, "Stalag Luft I is no place for honoring birthdays."

# Chapter Thirty-three

Word spread around the North Compound in late February that overnight the Jewish barracks turned up empty. BBC information stated that American forces had bombed Dresden and killed thousands of people—a brutal blow to the Reich. Andy surmised that the increase of Jewish extermination resulted in retaliation—Jews from all countries.

Andy traipsed across the snow to the colonel's barracks to check on his health and find out what he knew about the Jews. He discovered that Col. Brawley had sent a letter of protest to the Red Cross about the Germans violating the Geneva Convention.

"I can't believe they'd incinerate all those men. All because they're Jews!" Col. Brawley said.

"Though we didn't know of the incineration back then, Colonel, I'm glad we joined up to stop this evil man." Andy sat across the scarred table from the frail man wrapped in blankets.

A sudden contempt flashed in the colonel's hollowed eyes. "I never received a response!"

"We might know that would happen, sir, ever since they moved them to the barracks next to the ammunitions supply."

The colonel had become a father figure to Andy. He knew the colonel's health had deteriorated even more. The yellow hue of the colonel's skin had deepened, and he rarely stood—comfortable enough around Andy not to attempt it.

"Hitler's running scared now, though he refuses to admit any possibility of defeat. No telling what he'll do—even to us. Weak as we are, we must stay alert and protect ourselves. There's got to be over 9,000 men in this camp. If our lives become threatened, we'll be forced to try to overthrow them."

"A lot of men will be killed."

"Yes, but we'll all die if Hitler decides to eradicate us. They'll kill us off by starvation if we don't get some food in here. I've ordered guards on the garbage cans. Some men are terribly sick from eating from those cans."

"Sir, I'm amazed the guards haven't located your last radio. You're getting good information."

"Only because you've managed to protect the radio with much needed supplies to a couple of guards—not many, I might add. Cigarettes mostly. If it weren't for lineup every morning and night, the guards would never come out in this dastardly weather."

"Well, sir, I'll see you later." Andy left the colonel's barracks in time to see the sun reflect a rainbow off the glistening snow. "Yep. God's promise," Andy said aloud, after smiling at the sight of the rainbow in midwinter. He reached down into his pocket and rubbed the buckeye. Hope returned for a fleeting moment.

When he entered his room, a letter lay on his bunk. He grabbed it up and tore open the end. It was from Rose, postmarked September 1944.

*My Love,*

*I sense in your letters how tense and uneasy you are. I wish I could save you from all the suffering you're going through, but I know I can't. Don't give up hope. Even though things are rough now, we still have each other.*

351

*That's all I need to know—that you love me and I love you. Remember, when this ugly war is over, we'll be together again.*

*I miss your smile and how tenderly you look at me when we're together. My life is so empty without your arms around me. I never had an unhappy moment when we were together. I hate all the time wasted growing up next to each other. Please hurry back to me.*

*My darling, I have wonderful news, but I don't know how you will accept it. Elizabeth wants me to take Lizzy home with me to the States. Can you believe it? She is my second love, Andy, and I know you'll love her too.*

*My next free day, I shall search for a new home for them. Elizabeth must have help.*

*I pray that one day soon, we all can be together. When you asked me to marry you in your last letter, I was thrilled. More than anything I want to be Mrs. Andrew Walters. But I don't know how you feel about bringing Lizzy back with us. I await your decision, my love.*

> *Always loving you,*
> *Rose (and Lizzy)*

Andy let the letter drift down onto his chest. In spite of the noisy card game, and the musty smell of the room, he remained on his bunk tossing the letter over and over in his mind as if it were urgent to make a momentous decision right then. *What can I do now? I'm trapped. We're all trapped here for God knows how long. And Anna. How could I have been so weak and gullible? Neither of us knew we'd get out of this alive. But that's no excuse. Rose, I'm so sorry. You must never know. How about Marta and her baby? Okay! Okay! Pile on! Why not! Everything since Feb. 24th will not stop playing with my brain.*

Sunk in the squalors of gloom, the tortured realization of the inability to control his own destiny, the suffering of the POWs, the unknown and lack of a secure future overwhelmed him. Something he had fought for almost a year now.

Still prone on his bunk, he balled his right hand into a fist, clamped his thumb around his forefinger, and pounded his forehead.

*Stop! Stop! You idiot! I can't believe I'm so out of control now. My insides are rubbing against each other. My stomach's so empty. I don't know if any of us will make it out of here. Look at the guards. How come they are not losing weight?*

He opened his eyes and there stood Pops—someone he could trust—someone who knew him better than anyone—someone who would understand. Andy sat up, and the letter slipped from his chest to the bare wooden floor.

"You all right, Andy?" Pops' reached down and picked up the letter and handed it to Andy.

"Yeah. Just a bad day." He took the letter and slipped it back into the envelope. Andy noticed Pops' sunken cheeks and his belt pulled snug with the end dangling at least six inches down the front of his pants.

"Bad news?" Concern filled Pops' face.

"Not really. Like everyone else, don't know how much longer I can stand being locked up. I want my life back." He looked down at the envelope, avoiding Pops' eyes.

"I know, Andy. But it's not like you to give up."

Andy shook his head as if to clear it, "I'm okay, Pops. Just give me a few minutes. I'll not let you down." He stood, placed his arm around Pops' shoulder and managed his famous smile. "We'll get back home, Pops. We'll get out of here. Just you wait and see."

Pops slapped Andy's back and moved on.

Andy sat down and pulled out his note pad.

*Dear Rose,*
  *Got your letter about Lizzy…*

Before continuing, Andy pondered about Lizzy. *An instant family. Hummm. I want Rose all to myself when I get back. Just the two of us. Yes, I want a family, but not right away.* He stroked his chin. A vision flashed before his eyes of his flight over Birmingham and Coventry, England, showing the destruction the Luftwaffe heaped upon so many innocent families. Devastated families, children without homes—without parents. *I wonder. Knowing Rose, this little girl must be extra special and needs lots of love. Gotta think about this.*

*     *     *

Easter came early in '45—April 1st. The Catholic Church service, the only service, drew most of the North Compound—same as Christmas.

A few days later, around 0400, Andy awoke to the sound of a siren loud enough to shake everyone out of their bunks. He rushed to the nearby window.

"Crap. The shutters are closed tight!" He raced into the hall and to the exterior door—a direct view of the kitchen and mess hall. Flames leapt high from the building lighting the night for the first time in months.

Andy shouted to the men, "Hurry! Something's on fire. I can see through the cracks. Bring every container you can find." He and several POWs jammed against the exterior door and forced it open.

POWs scampered in total chaos. Andy hustled over to the gates where a guard dumped a stack of buckets at the entrance. He shoved one into each extended hand.

"Turn the water on," he shouted to the guards. To the men he ordered, "Find any spigot you can. Make haste!" Andy ran with two buckets, turned the spigot full open. It sputtered and belched air until a flow of water filled each bucket. He started a human chain passing the containers from one man to the other until the closest man threw it on the fire. No matter how many chains and how many buckets of water poured on the fire, it was all in vain. The entire building turned to ashes in a matter of minutes.

Andy watched as the remaining embers smoldered. Exhausted from the exertion and the weakened condition of his body, he pulled his shirt up from under his jacket and rubbed it across his face smearing the soot.

Bulldog stepped over to him. "Just what we needed. Damn! Now where's our food gonna come from?"

"I don't know, but I doubt this was an accident. Why aren't the POW cooks losing weight like us? What the hell's going on?"

"I wondered 'bout that too. Reckon we'll find who set the fire?" White streaks of perspiration dribbled down through the black soot on Bulldog's face.

"Naw, the Germans don't give a crap. Let's go back to…"

"I'm so weak I can hardly stand. How 'bout you?"

"Yep, same here. Nothing we can do now. Before you know it, we'll be lining up again." Andy trudged back to the barracks with Bulldog trailing behind. Daylight was in full swing. No food that day.

The guards took pity on the men and skipped the lineup count.

At 1500, Col. Brawley sent word to the entire compound for the head officers to gather in the library. A special request came for Andy to accompany the colonel.

He dashed over to the colonel's barracks just in time to catch the colonel's arm and help him down the steps. Andy did not understand how the man had the strength to stand much less walk.

"Sir. I tell ya, you need to be in the compound hospital. At least you'd get food there."

"I'll have no more than my men do!"

Andy, the colonel, and two of the colonel's aides arrived at the library. The building bulged with brass.

The colonel rested for a few moments before standing to address the group.

"The Germans are retreating, and some are marching their prisoners east. American forces are rapidly advancing into Germany. We've got them on the run. Russians are getting closer. Some of our men are too weak to march." He stopped to rest and catch his breath, then continued. "We'll rise up and fight the guards if they attempt to force us to march. The strongest of us will lead the fight—maybe one hundred men. Select them carefully, gentlemen, because they'll be unarmed against the guards. The least strong are the backup.

"I'm meeting with the commandant in the morning to discuss the situation. Many men are physically unable to walk as far as two feet.

"Food supplies are critical—lost in the fire—what little there was. Thank God we lost those soup bones. I don't believe I could partake of another bowl of soup."

The men roared with laughter, giving the colonel time to catch his breath.

The colonel paused, leaned heavily on his cane and then continued, "Our days are about to turn into pandemonium. It's important that all orders are obeyed. The Russians will be knocking on our door before long, and we don't want to fall under their command. Order your men not to tangle with them. They're a lowly lot, Mongolians probably, a ragtag army of soldiers. In closing, be prepared for anything. Good luck, and I'll see you on the other side of the fence."

Andy and the other officers stood and cheered. "Don't know how he's still standing," he said to the man next to him.

The colonel turned to leave and Andy caught up to him, taking hold of his arm. They crept back to the colonel's barracks and just before reaching the steps, the colonel's knees gave way. Andy reached under the colonel's back and one of his aides grabbed the other side. They lifted him up the steps, into his room and onto his bunk.

"You gotta go to the compound hospital, sir." Andy spread the blanket over him.

"I'll be fine, son."

Andy realized more than ever how strong the bond had formed between the two men. He had come to love and respect the colonel like a father. The colonel's eyes shut, and Andy's thoughts once again focused on his own dad as he returned to his barracks. In spite of their differences, his father loved him and desired nothing more than success for him. *Well, Dad, it's taken a war for me to excel, but I have arrived. Everything you wanted—better yet, everything I wanted. I will get out of here!*

Back at his barracks, Andy gathered the men together from each room, bringing them up to date on the latest events. Speculation ran rampant. The frailest of men got a second wind. Others danced around in the tight quarters.

"Whoa! We're not free yet!" Andy cautioned.

With no electricity, the gray of the evening set in, but the darkness couldn't curb their joy as they fumbled their way back to their rooms.

A few days later, Andy rushed back from the colonel's barracks. He gathered all the men in Barracks #2 for an announcement. They lined the hallway, shifting from one foot to another.

"I have grave news. President Roosevelt died today. April 12, 1945." Gasps rose from the group. "Cut black socks for armbands to mourn his death." Andy slipped an armband over his jacket sleeve.

"But the guards will know the colonel has a radio, won't they?" Bulldog asked.

"By the time the word spreads to 9,000 men, they'll have no idea where the information came from." Andy stared into the anxious faces of the men.

Tex broke the silence. "What about the war?"

"The secretary of war, and chairman of the Joint Chiefs of Staff, are running everything. Always have. No need to worry. Gen. Eisenhower's still in control. I do have other news. Good news. The BBC reported that Hitler has continued to pull back, and there is a possibility of a surrender before long." Andy had a difficult time believing that this evil tyrant would admit defeat. *Impossible.*

Andy and long-faced men set about cutting armbands. The 32$^{nd}$ president's four terms stretched almost a lifetime—the only president Andy and most of these men had ever known.

"After Roosevelt's death, there ain't much to rejoice about Hitler," Johnny added. "They sworn in Truman yet?" He rubbed the stubble on his lower face.

"Yes. Right after they pronounced Roosevelt dead. Pops? Want to say a word of prayer?"

When the prayer was over, the men went back to their rooms, where silence ruled the balance of the day.

On the morning of May 1, Andy got up from a restless night's sleep. He slipped outside the unlocked barracks to greet the sunrise. Thought it strange—no lock—eerie. Quiet. Like the birds were still asleep. He turned toward the tower next to his barracks. Empty. He swung around to the corner tower. Empty. He raced to all the towers in North 1 Compound. Empty, empty, empty!

He rushed back inside his barracks, jumping, yelling, raising both fists, "They're gone! Get up! Get up! They're gone!"

Doors flung open and men poured out of every unit. The word echoed from compound to compound. Nine thousand men filled the yards of the three compounds. The shouting roared to a deafening crescendo. A dry eye wasn't found. POWs climbed into the towers while others tore down gates.

Andy, Bulldog, Brad, Pops, Tex, and Johnny fled to the commandant's headquarters.

"Bulldog, grab the radio," Andy ordered.

Bulldog rushed to the library and returned to headquarters, scarcely losing a step. "Got the short wave radio," Bulldog said, with it bundled under his arm.

"Where's the power switch?" Andy asked while searching the wall.

"I'll check behind this door," Pops said as he entered a back room. Opened Red Cross packets piled to the ceiling. "Hey Andy. They didn't eat all of the packets."

Andy had followed him into the room. He stepped over discarded gloves, toboggans, and sweaters during a search for food. "That's why the commandant and his guards never lost weight."

He shoved a stack of boxes aside and found the panel housing the power switches. After turning them all on, nothing happened. No power into the compounds, only German headquarters and the line run to the library. Andy left the building and headed to Col. Brawley's barracks.

He could see the colonel sitting on the steps too weak to walk. "Sir, I've ordered all the food supplies released, what little is left. There's gonna be a lot of sick men gorging themselves. We gotta find more food somewhere."

The colonel turned to Andy, "I've sent two contact parties to hook up with the Russian's advance troops. We estimate they're as close as four kilometers. Keep your men in the compound. It's not safe out there."

"Yes sir." Andy saluted and left the colonel on the steps. He arrived back at his barracks in time to join the men devouring food supplies allotted to them.

Bulldog set an open can of Spam in front of Andy, who reached in with his fingers and tore the Spam apart. His hunger pains had grown fierce, but he ignored them during the celebration. He bit down on the Spam, and his teeth moved. His gums had softened due to the lack of proper foods. But that didn't stop him. He chewed the meat slowly savoring every bite.

By nighttime, the men were exhausted and nauseated from celebration and overeating. Many of them turned in at dark. Unarmed POWs stood guard in the watchtowers.

In the middle of the night, shouts came over the loudspeaker— liberation by the Russians. The BBC announced rescue was imminent. Cheers drowned out the loudspeaker as the men jumped up and down, hugging each other, singing and shouting.

"The Russians are coming!" Andy shouted, overwhelmed by waves of pride and gratitude. He glanced toward the men in front of him, his view obstructed by the wash of his own tears. His skin grew clammy as spurts of adrenalin shot through his veins. He bit his lip to keep his body from erupting with euphoria.

Once the national anthem finished playing, Andy wrapped his arms around his buddies and began singing, "Pack up your troubles in your old kit-bag and smile, smile, smile…"

A newsflash came over the short-wave radio through the loudspeaker. "The Germans report that Hitler has committed suicide."

Mayhem commenced drowning out the news. Andy slammed his fist into an open hand, muscles tensed, knowing that the evil dictator could no longer murder and maim innocent victims. And best of all, Hitler had committed the most cowardly act of all. Suicide. *There is justice after all!*

Later, Andy noticed a stretcher being carried into Barracks #1. He hurried to the colonel's room in time to see Lt. Browser (the compound doctor) lean over the stretcher.

"Is he all right?" Andy removed his hat.

"He's in a bad way, Captain. He needs medical care right away but won't leave until the last sick man has been removed from camp. He's a stubborn man. He'll not make it 'til then."

Andy leaned down over the stretcher. "Colonel, can I do anything for you?"

The colonel opened his jaundiced eyes, caught Andy's hand and said, "You've been like a son to me, Andy. Thank you." His eyes slipped shut and his head fell to the side.

Lt. Browser ordered the stretcher to the floor. He knelt over the colonel, checked the pulse in his neck, and shook his head. "He put up a good fight, Captain. I'm sorry. His liver just plum gave out."

The celebration continued until "The Star Spangled Banner" rang through Stalag Luft I loudspeaker. The men jumped to attention. Andy's heart felt like it swelled three times its size.

Moments later he knelt on the floor beside the stretcher and persisted in holding the colonel's hand until Lt. Browser pried it loose. Andy sat down on the floor, his chin buried in his chest while his body rocked from the emotional upheaval.

Lt. Browser stroked Andy's shoulder. A few minutes later he and another officer picked up the stretcher and carried the colonel away.

Andy looked up as the colonel slowly disappeared from sight. His mentor. His friend. A gnawing ache arose in his stomach. He thought of his own father. *I've got to get home and put these sixteen months behind me. See Dad. Make things right.*

# Chapter Thirty-four

Liberation and death. All in the same day. Andy had watched the colonel struggle to hang on until his men were free. He had fought the battle to keep his men in the compound until the Russians arrived. No marching into the unknown. His men came first. *A true hero.*

Men lined up outside their barracks, stood at attention, and saluted as they loaded the wooden box onto the wagon that carried their colonel away. A POW raced to lower the American flag at half-staff—the same flag so nobly raised in exhilaration earlier in the day after discovering the Germans had fled.

Uncertainty engulfed the entire compound. Questions raced through Andy's head with no immediate answers. Who would lead? What do you do with 9,000 men? When can they leave the prison? What about the Russians? *Play the waiting game—again.*

Back in the barracks, Andy paced the floor waiting for the scouting party to return after linking up with the Russians. They would inform the Russians of the POW camp location and eliminate possible shelling on their allies.

He decided to go to the commandant's headquarters for an update on the BBC radio. His step quickened when he caught sight of a hawk gliding gracefully through the sky. Its wings dipped and rose with each gust of wind—it soared like a proud eagle, swooping low, and rising higher and higher. Andy reached in his pocket and wrapped his hand around the buckeye. *I'm gonna fly again.* Andy jumped up and clicked his heels, shouting, "Whooooeeeee!"

The lieutenant manning the radio shook his head when Andy entered the building. "Our men are advancing, Captain. Storms of war are entering Barth. No official information. Nothing specific yet."

"Thanks, Lieutenant. Keep me posted."

"Yes sir."

Andy retreated toward his barracks with battle night sounds echoing in his ears. Against the pearl gray backdrop of the evening, he glimpsed a figure entering the gate of the North 1 Compound. The man sported a dark beard, unusual for an officer, but the closer he got, the redder the beard appeared. He finally came within clear view.

"Maj. Zimmer." Andy saluted. "That was quite a haul from North 3 Compound." He noted two lieutenants trailed a short distance behind. "Didn't recognize you at first with the beard."

The major returned his salute. "At ease, Captain. Our razor blades totally wore out." He chuckled as he stroked his beard.

"I'll be in charge through the duration," he continued. "Fill me in on what you know."

Andy proceeded to bring him up to date. "Russians approaching from the east—Americans and British from the west.

A distant BOOM sharply stole their attention. The fury of the ensuing battle lit up the eastern sky. Both men swung around in the direction of the noise. Heavy artillery rocked the earth with multiple blasts. Andy assumed the Russians engaged in one skirmish after another plowing their way to Stalag Luft I. A welcome conflict—a long yearning about to end for Andy and the POWs. He restrained from expressing his jubilance in the presence of the major.

The major flashed a brilliant smile. "Go ahead, Captain. Shout as loud as you want. I'm with you!" The major began shouting at the top of his lungs.

"Whooooeeeee! Bulldog, Pops, Tex, Johnny, Brad! Get out here. The Russians are coming!" Andy was ecstatic. He cupped his hands around his mouth. "Drag your butts out here!"

He tried to swallow the lump stuck in his throat. *Nobody can possibly understand the sheer euphoria of liberated men after imprisonment—many for years—me, sixteen months.*

"I'm sorry, sir. I'm not believing this. It's too much. Losing the colonel. Freedom. All within twenty-four hours." Andy reeled in delirious intoxication.

Maj. Zimmer shook his head. "I've only been here six months, the starvation period. Oh, God! For some decent food, a warm room, and soft bed. How long was the colonel here?"

"I think about eighteen months. I understand he became sick shortly after his arrival. He simply wouldn't allow himself to give up. What a man!"

"Obviously."

The men poured from the barracks, filling the grounds as the news spread. No more lineup and countdowns. Dizzy with glee, they cheered the Russians on.

"Come on Joe," they shouted referencing the Russian leader, Joseph Stalin, commander of the Soviet military.

The scouting party sent to link up with the Russians pushed through the gate and approached Andy and the major.

After salutes, a gap-toothed, long-legged skin-and-bone officer handed the major a piece of paper.

The major unfolded the paper and attempted to read the message. "Hell, this thing's in Russian. How the devil am I supposed to read it? Got a Russian interpreter?"

The same lieutenant who delivered the paper spoke up. "That would be me, sir. Lt. Sparks here."

He studied the paper, his eyes brightened. "It says the Russians will arrive at 2200 hours!"

The crowd around him exploded. Andy and Maj. Zimmer joined in.

Andy watched even the weakest engage in the celebration. "Look-a-here." *They got a second wind.* After clapping his hands for the weak, he hugged some, danced with the ones that could, and shouted and yelled with all of them.

"We're going home!" One of the men barked.

"You betcha!" Andy observed many moist eyes.

The men partied well into the night until the Russians arrived.

On their way to Stalag Luft I, the Russians killed local cattle and hauled them to the starving men. It didn't take Andy's men long to dress a head of cattle and prepare a feast for shrunken stomachs. The POWs tore down all the fences and used the wood for heat and cook stoves. The blustery arctic air off the Baltic Sea blew in like a nor'easter, even in early May.

By dark, some of the men in other barracks slipped out of the compound in search of female companionship. Some never returned; others reported rapes and murders of the locals by the ruthless, undisciplined Russians.

Andy kept watch over his men during the first night of real freedom. The next morning, the sun climbed above the horizon in all its brilliance, electrifying the sky as if in celebration of their freedom.

"Okay fellas. Round up the men in the barracks. Outside at 0800."

Andy rushed out the barracks' door. The men piled out of the building and circled around their captain.

He spoke, "You are ordered to stay on the compound until we secure transportation out of here. Maj. Zimmer reported two men killed last night in skirmishes with the Russians over women. We've paid the price, tolerated the burden, survived the hardship, supported each other, defied our enemy, and lived to tell the tale. We've all endured the life as a POW; now don't cut it short after liberation. These Russians are hard as nails. They don't care about you or me.

Don't rock their boat, and you'll survive. We've gotta get back to civilization. Right?

"I've no idea how they're gonna move 9,000 men. I've been told that some of us may have to march to the closest airfield. The sick will be transported by Russian trucks. They'll be flown out first. B-17s, B-24s, and other planes will fly the rest of us to Camp Lucky Strike, Le Havre, France. From there we'll take whatever means they have to get us home. I urge you not to mess up now. Stay safe. I'm as anxious to get home as you are. Okay?"

The meeting ended and the men scattered to wait. And wait. And wait.

The Russians continued to bring confiscated food from the locals. Two weeks later, the Russians vacated the camp, after transporting the sick from Stalag Luft 1. That left the balance of the original 9,000 men to fend for themselves.

Andy met with Maj. Zimmer to discuss their prospects. "We can't stay here forever. We've got to go on foot or else we'll die of starvation, sir."

"That's it. Get on the loudspeaker and order the men to spread the word. Pack up and get ready to leave."

At daylight the next morning, thousands of men walked out of Stalag Luft 1 heading for the advancing American troops. Andy and the men from Barracks #2 traveled together as much as possible. Shoe soles thin and worn out, shoe tacks cutting into bloody feet, but they trudged on.

Near Barth, Maj. Zimmer spotted U.S. military trucks traveling their way. "Trucks, men, trucks!"

The men shouted and waved their hands frantically to attract their attention.

"Line up, men. You're on your way home!" Andy said.

As many men as possible crammed into each truck. Andy's group, Maj. Zimmer, and the balance of men unable to hitch a ride continued marching until they came upon the airport outside of Barth destroyed by the American bombers. A makeshift airfield had been constructed, where B-17s took off and landed.

Andy's crew gathered around one of the older green B-17s.

"Good gosh almighty," Bulldog spewed out after climbing into the plane. "Didn't know how lucky we was with our new silver B-17."

"You damn straight. This baby's been patched up and brought back from the dead. Guess we can't be choosy. Let's just hope it gets us there."

Andy and his men piled in sitting on plywood inserted over the bomb drop area.

"Capt'n? What happens if the plane shifts and the wood slides." Bulldog wiggled his butt as if securing his seat.

"With your weight gain, ole buddy, you're our anchor." Tex dusted his cowboy hat on his pants.

"Watch it, buster. This ain't lard. It's all muscle. Want to feel?" Bulldog flexed his biceps.

"Listen, fellows. We're going home." Andy held his breath as each engine caught on and rocked the ship with vibrations. The warm-up process began.

Once safe altitude without oxygen masks had been attained, the plane's port and starboard sides dipped up and down.

"What the hell...?" Andy rushed to the cockpit. "What's happening?"

"Dunno. It's leveling off a little now. We needed all the planes we could find to fly the 9,000 POW'S's out of Germany. You a pilot? Make a guess."


"Well, my guess would be something's gone wrong with the gyro that senses deviation about the yaw, or vertical axis of the airplane. Feels all right now. Let's wait and see."

"How about staying up here till we get to Camp Lucky Strike. I'm new to this plane, sir."

"Sure thing." Andy sighed inwardly.

The flight continued on to Camp Lucky Strike without further incidents much to Andy's relief.

After arriving at Camp Lucky Strike, Le Harve, France, the military refused to release the POWs until they had physical exams and fattened up before returning home. Andy, Bulldog, Brad, Tex, and Pops were assigned to the same tent. More waiting.

As soon as Andy could get to an available phone, he called Rose. "Hello, Rose?"

"Andy! It's so good to hear from you." She jabbered with a million questions.

"Rose," he interrupted. "I know I asked you by mail, but I want to hear your answer. Will…will you marry me?" First time he could ever remember stuttering.

"Oh, Andy. Of course I will."

"You will? Yeoooooow!" He finally calmed enough to continue the conversation. "How about soon as we get home? It doesn't need to be a big wedding. When we get home, we can go out to Pope Field, and they'll help make all the arrangements for a military wedding. What do you think?"

"Yes. That'll be wonderful. I've missed you so much."

"I can't wait to see you—to hold you, Rosie. I've missed you, too. Well, gotta go. Lots of fellas waiting to use the phone. Remember the invisible drawing on the table of a family—our family? It's coming true soon as I get home."

"That drawing never left me, Andy. I love you."

"Love you more. See ya soon. Bye."

Frustration set in, and Andy and his men grew more impatient by the day. *Okay! I've gained five pounds. Let us go home! I'm ready to leave this Gateway to America.* He hid his anxiety from his men until one day a man wearing a pilot's uniform popped through the door.

"Who wants to ride a B-17 back to England?"

\*   \*   \*

Andy settled in for the night, once more playing the waiting game, wondering when the B-17 would arrive. His mind shifted into overdrive. *It's like the waiting before takeoff, the weight of responsibility on your shoulders, the protection of your crew, lending an ear to their struggles and no one to listen to your own inner demons. You relive the previous near misses, the fear that jabbed at your heart, even now, when all of it's behind you. Your brain keeps reminding you, so you won't slip into the young, happy-go-lucky fella you once were some thirty short months ago. The Plexiglas windshield with holes here and there flashes before you. You see the spider webs of frozen blood and guts on your windshield and an eyeball that looks back at you—the loss of its owner, a friend. The picture of Marta and her baby surfaces, digging deeper into your heart and consciousness. Your baptism by fire starts all over. You only thought you had put it aside.*

Andy woke up with a start. *Liesel's brother Dietrich—dead, no family now—blind. Marta and her baby—dead. Gotta write Rose.* He grabbed his flashlight and a pad and pencil.

*My dearest Rose,*

*My heart aches to be near you, to hold you in my arms, to sit with you in front of a crackling fire. Instead I'm writing this note to you in the wee hours. I gaze around this tent, unable to close out the deep breathing, snoring, and wheezing that vibrates in my ears. These men sleeping on bunks around me counted the hours last night before going home. I realize the enormity of what they've gone through— all of us. Bulldog's cheerful attempt to lift my despair fell on deaf ears. The cold truth and darkness are overwhelming.*

*My anguished thoughts have inventoried the missing— the ones who will never go home—the loved ones who will never see them again—the children who will grow up without fathers. The guilt of Marta and her baby's death has haunted me until I can't bear it another minute. Dietrich's death—if not for me, he would still be alive and his sister Liesel, blind Liesel, would not be left alone. I cannot share the details with you yet, but when I return you'll understand. The torment continues to chisel away at any possibility of future happiness. At this point I can't think of anything until I find a way to live with myself—rid myself of the intolerable guilt, the crippling guilt, the horrible visions. I am no good for you now, but I will find a way to work through the horrors of war, the suffering of good people, the loss of friends.*

*Please be patient. I promise you, I shall return. I have never lost sight of the drawing on the English pub's table outside of Snetterton Airfield. Our future. Our love united. Our love forever.*

*When you receive this letter, I'll be on the way to find Liesel. We have thirty days to report to Snetterton and with so many trying to get to their camps first, it will be easier to hitch a plane ride when we get back.*

*Liesel has no one. No one at all. She risked her life while helping me escape after our plane crashed over Steyr, Austria. I owe her this. Perhaps this will ease my conscience and I can get on with my life—become that lawyer I studied for before this God-awful war.*

*Rose, my lovely Rose. You are my goal, my heart, my love. I will return. We have the rest of our lives. Please wait for me.*

> *My love forever,*
> *Andy*

He jumped up, folded the letter, shoved it in his shirt pocket, rushed over to Brad, and plopped down on the edge of his bunk. "Brad! Wake up. Remember Liesel?"

"What?"

"Liesel."

"What about Liesel?"

"Remember her?"

"Sure. How could I forget? What's up?"

"Let's go find her and bring her back to the States. She has no family now. We owe her that."

"Are you telling me we're not going home yet?"

"You got it, buddy."

Brad rubbed the sand from his eyes. "When?"

"Now. We're already packed and ready to leave. Let's hit it."

Andy quietly returned to his bunk, gathered his things, and both men eased out of the tent.

As Andy and Brad scurried through Camp Lucky Strike, on a new journey, this time to Austria, Andy forced himself to think of Rose. He smiled inside. *She took a piece of my heart, and little by little, she stole it all. Her face is the last thing I see at night and the first thing before opening my eyes in the morning. She's the reason I'll make it back home.*

His racing thoughts returned to a phone call made when he arrived at Camp Lucky Strike…Rose. Her every word lingered, etched in his memory. He loved her, loved her more than any man could love a woman, loved her more than life itself. He wished he was on that plane—headed to England. But this was his war. It had brought him to a new country, a new love, new friends, and a new baptism.

Now with that baptism, he had something to do—something to make his future better—something to make things right, something to ease his conscience—return a favor—Liesel.

## THE END

# Inspiration to Write *The Liberators*

While interviewing an elderly cousin for my genealogy book, his bravery as a bombardier and prisoner of war in WWII impressed me so much that I began researching WWII history. It became an addiction. I could not let it go. These fictional stories based on historical events flew through my fingertips into the computer as I propelled my protagonist on a journey to England, France, Germany, and Austria. The story not only changed my protagonist's life, it changed mine as well.

While performing an extensive research on WWII, I grew to understand that longing, uncertainty and loss was the norm for WWII. Emptiness and dread of the uncontrollable consumed each man. Fear reigned throughout the air fields. No one acknowledged it—for if spoken, it became true. I had to write their story.

# Historical Events

*The Liberators'* plot is woven around three historical WWII events:

Schweinfurt I – August 1943

Schweinfurt II – October 14, 1943

Big Week (also referred to as Operation Argument) –
    February 20 - 25, 1944

The length of missions varied from 25 to 50 depending on the location where the men flew out of. In Italy, it was 50 missions most of the time.

## Fictionalization

Certainly we know that the 8th Army Air Force did not fly out of Italy to Steyr, Austria. It was the 15th Army Air Force.

We also are aware that the B-17G model did not roll off the production line until after August 1943.

### *The Liberators* (specifics)

My novel, *The Liberators*, tells the story of three major missions to destroy ball bearing plants, the first mission, August 17, 1943, Schweinfurt, Germany, the second "Black Thursday," October 14, 1943, Schweinfurt again, and the third mission "Operation Big Week" Steyr, Austria, February 24, 1944. The first two missions tragically took its toll on the USAAF losing 600 plus men during EACH mission—1200 men within two months.

The length of missions varied from 25 to 50 depending on where the men flew out of. In Italy, it was 50 missions most of the time.

### Time Period

*The Liberators* takes place during WWII from December 1942 through June 1945.

### Locations

The plot begins in Fayetteville, North Carolina, on to Medford Air Field, Indiana, McMillian Air Base, Texas, progresses on to Ludlow Air Field, Denver, Colorado, overseas to Snetterton Air Field, England, transferred to Foggia, Italy, shot down over Steyr, Austria, Stalag Luft 1 (Officer Prison Camp) near Barth, Germany, and lastly Le Harve, France (Camp Lucky Strike).

## Comparison

Two good comparisons are *CATCH 22*, and *MEMPHIS BELL. The Liberators* show real fear not shown prior to *MEMPHIS BELL*, how the families coped back home, the fast action in *PEARL HARBOR*, and the love of a Red Cross Nurse who's story becomes complicated by  a two-year old orphan girl.

Jerri Gibson McCloud

Made in the USA
San Bernardino, CA
12 July 2013